The Purcell Papers

COMPLETE IN ONE VOLUME

JOSEPH SHERIDAN LE FANU,

Author of 'Uncle Silas

With a Memoir by ALFRED PERCEVAL GRAVES

Serenity
Publishers, LLC

ROCKVILLE, MARYLAND
2011

ISBN: 978-1-60450-879-6

Published by Serenity Publishers
An Arc Manor Company
P. O. Box 10339
Rockville, MD 20849-0339
www.SerenityPublishers.com

Printed in the United States of America/United Kingdom

Contents

VOLUME ONE

Memoir
of
Joseph Sheridan Le Fanu

A NOBLE Huguenot family, owning considerable property in Normandy, the Le Fanus of Caen, were, upon the revocation of the Edict of Nantes, deprived of their ancestral estates of Mandeville, Sequeville, and Cresseron; but, owing to their possessing influential relatives at the court of Louis the Fourteenth, were allowed to quit their country for England, unmolested, with their personal property. We meet with John Le Fanu de Sequeville and Charles Le Fanu de Cresseron, as cavalry officers in William the Third's army; Charles being so distinguished a member of the King's staff that he was presented with William's portrait from his master's own hand. He afterwards served as a major of dragoons under Marlborough.

At the beginning of the eighteenth century, William Le Fanu was the sole survivor of his family. He married Henrietta Raboteau de Puggibaut, the last of another great and noble Huguenot family, whose escape from France, as a child, by the aid of a Roman Catholic uncle in high position at the French court, was effected after adventures of the most romantic danger.

Joseph Le Fanu, the eldest of the sons of this marriage who left issue, held the office of Clerk of the Coast in Ireland. He married for the second time Alicia, daughter of Thomas Sheridan and sister of Richard Brinsley Sheridan; his brother, Captain Henry Le Fanu, of Leamington, being united to the only other sister of the great wit and orator.

Dean Thomas Philip Le Fanu, the eldest son of Joseph Le Fanu, became by his wife Emma, daughter of Dr. Dobbin, F.T.C.D., the father of Joseph Sheridan Le Fanu, the subject of this memoir, whose name is so familiar to English and American readers as one of the greatest masters of the weird and the terrible amongst our modern novelists.

Born in Dublin on the 28th of August, 1814, he did not begin to speak until he was more than two years of age; but when he had once started, the boy showed an unusual aptitude in acquiring fresh words, and using them correctly.

The first evidence of literary taste which he gave was in his sixth year, when he made several little sketches with explanatory remarks written beneath them, after the manner of Du Maurier's, or Charles Keene's humorous illustrations in 'Punch.'

One of these, preserved long afterwards by his mother, represented a balloon in mid-air, and two aeronauts, who had occupied it, falling headlong to earth, the disaster being explained by these words: 'See the effects of trying to go to Heaven.'

As a mere child, he was a remarkably good actor, both in tragic and comic pieces, and was hardly twelve years old when he began to write verses of singular spirit for one so young. At fourteen, he produced a long Irish poem, which he never permitted anyone but his mother and brother to read. To that brother, Mr. William Le Fanu, Commissioner of Public Works, Ireland, to whom, as the suggester of Sheridan Le Fanu's 'Phaudrig Croohore' and 'Shamus O'Brien,' Irish ballad literature owes a delightful debt, and whose richly humorous and passionately pathetic powers as a raconteur of these poems have only doubled that obligation in the hearts of those who have been happy enough to be his hearers—to Mr. William Le Fanu we are indebted for the following extracts from the first of his works, which the boy-author seems to have set any store by:

'Muse of Green Erin, break thine icy slumbers!
    Strike once again thy wreathed lyre!
Burst forth once more and wake thy tuneful numbers!
    Kindle again thy long-extinguished fire!

'Why should I bid thee, Muse of Erin, waken?
    Why should I bid thee strike thy harp once more?
Better to leave thee silent and forsaken
    Than wake thee but thy glories to deplore.

'How could I bid thee tell of Tara's Towers,
    Where once thy sceptred Princes sate in state—
Where rose thy music, at the festive hours,
    Through the proud halls where listening thousands sate?

'Fallen are thy fair palaces, thy country's glory,
    Thy tuneful bards were banished or were slain,
Some rest in glory on their deathbeds gory,
    And some have lived to feel a foeman's chain.

'Yet for the sake of thy unhappy nation,
    Yet for the sake of Freedom's spirit fled,
Let thy wild harpstrings, thrilled with indignation,
    Peal a deep requiem o'er thy sons that bled.

'O yes! like the last breath of evening sighing,
　　Sweep thy cold hand the silent strings along,
Flash like the lamp beside the hero dying,
　　Then hushed for ever be thy plaintive song.'

To Mr. William Le Fanu we are further indebted for the accompany-ing specimens of his brother's serious and humorous powers in verse, writ-ten when he was quite a lad, as valentines to a Miss **G. K.**:

'Life were too long for me to bear
　　If banished from thy view;
Life were too short, a thousand year,
　　If life were passed with you.

'Wise men have said "Man's lot on earth
　　Is grief and melancholy,"
But where thou art, there joyous mirth
　　Proves all their wisdom folly.

'If fate withhold thy love from me,
　　All else in vain were given;
Heaven were imperfect wanting thee,
　　And with thee earth were heaven.'

A few days after, he sent the following sequel:

'My dear good Madam,
You can't think how very sad I'm.
I sent you, or I mistake myself foully,
A very excellent imitation of the poet Cowley,
Containing three very fair stanzas,
Which number Longinus, a very critical man, says,
And Aristotle, who was a critic ten times more caustic,
To a nicety fits a valentine or an acrostic.
And yet for all my pains to this moving epistle,
I have got no answer, so I suppose I may go whistle.
Perhaps you'd have preferred that like an old monk I had pattered on
In the style and after the manner of the unfortunate Chatterton;
Or that, unlike my reverend daddy's son,
I had attempted the classicalities of the dull, though immortal Addison.
I can't endure this silence another week;
What shall I do in order to make you speak?
　　Shall I give you a trope
　　In the manner of Pope,
Or hammer my brains like an old smith
To get out something like Goldsmith?

Or shall I aspire on
To tune my poetic lyre on
The same key touched by Byron,
And laying my hand its wire on,
With its music your soul set fire on
By themes you ne'er could tire on?
      Or say,
      I pray,
      Would a lay
      Like Gay
      Be more in your way?
   I leave it to you,
   Which am I to do?
   It plain on the surface is
   That any metamorphosis,
   To affect your study
   You may work on my soul or body.
Your frown or your smile makes me Savage or Gay
   In action, as well as in song;
And if 'tis decreed I at length become Gray,
   Express but the word and I'm Young;
And if in the Church I should ever aspire
   With friars and abbots to cope,
By a nod, if you please, you can make me a Prior—
   By a word you render me Pope.
If you'd eat, I'm a Crab; if you'd cut, I'm your Steel,
   As sharp as you'd get from the cutler;
I'm your Cotton whene'er you're in want of a reel,
   And your livery carry, as Butler.
     I'll ever rest your debtor
     If you'll answer my first letter;
     Or must, alas, eternity
     Witness your taciturnity?
     Speak—and oh! speak quickly
     Or else I shall grow sickly,
       And pine,
       And whine,
And grow yellow and brown
   As e'er was mahogany,
And lie me down
   And die in agony.

P.S.—*You'll allow I have the gift*
     To write like the immortal Swift.'

But besides the poetical powers with which he was endowed, in common with the great Brinsley, Lady Dufferin, and the Hon. Mrs. Norton, young Sheridan Le Fanu also possessed an irresistible humour and oratorical gift that, as a student of Old Trinity, made him a formidable rival of the best of the young debaters of his time at the 'College Historical,' not a few of whom have since reached the highest eminence at the Irish Bar, after having long enlivened and charmed St. Stephen's by their wit and oratory.

Amongst his compeers he was remarkable for his sudden fiery eloquence of attack, and ready and rapid powers of repartee when on his defence. But Le Fanu, whose understanding was elevated by a deep love of the classics, in which he took university honours, and further heightened by an admirable knowledge of our own great authors, was not to be tempted away by oratory from literature, his first and, as it proved, his last love.

Very soon after leaving college, and just when he was called to the Bar, about the year 1838, he bought the 'Warder,' a Dublin newspaper, of which he was editor, and took what many of his best friends and admirers, looking to his high prospects as a barrister, regarded at the time as a fatal step in his career to fame.

Just before this period, Le Fanu had taken to writing humorous Irish stories, afterwards published in the 'Dublin University Magazine,' such as the 'Quare Gander,' 'Jim Sulivan's Adventure,' 'The Ghost and the Bonesetter,' etc.

These stories his brother William Le Fanu was in the habit of repeating for his friends' amusement, and about the year 1837, when he was about twenty-three years of age, Joseph Le Fanu said to him that he thought an Irish story in verse would tell well, and that if he would choose him a subject suitable for recitation, he would write him one. 'Write me an Irish "Young Lochinvar,"' said his brother; and in a few days he handed him 'Phaudrig Croohore'—Anglice, 'Patrick Crohore.'

Of course this poem has the disadvantage not only of being written after 'Young Lochinvar,' but also that of having been directly inspired by it; and yet, although wanting in the rare and graceful finish of the original, the Irish copy has, we feel, so much fire and feeling that it at least tempts us to regret that Scott's poem was not written in that heart-stirring Northern dialect without which the noblest of our British ballads would lose half their spirit. Indeed, we may safely say that some of Le Fanu's lines are finer than any in 'Young Lochinvar,' simply because they seem to speak straight from a people's heart, not to be the mere echoes of medieval romance.

'Phaudrig Croohore' did not appear in print in the 'Dublin University Magazine' till 1844, twelve years after its composition, when it was included amongst the Purcell Papers.

To return to the year 1837. Mr. William Le Fanu, the suggester of this ballad, who was from home at the time, now received daily instalments of the second and more remarkable of his brother's Irish poems—'Shamus O'Brien' (James O'Brien)—learning them by heart as they reached him, and, fortunately, never forgetting them, for his brother Joseph kept no copy of the ballad, and he had himself to write it out from memory ten years after, when the poem appeared in the 'University Magazine.'

Few will deny that this poem contains passages most faithfully, if fearfully, picturesque, and that it is characterised throughout by a profound pathos, and an abundant though at times a too grotesquely incongruous humour. Can we wonder, then, at the immense popularity with which Samuel Lover recited it in the United States? For to Lover's admiration of the poem, and his addition of it to his entertainment, 'Shamus O'Brien' owes its introduction into America, where it is now so popular. Lover added some lines of his own to the poem, made Shamus emigrate to the States, and set up a public-house. These added lines appeared in most of the published versions of the poem. But they are indifferent as verse, and certainly injure the dramatic effect of the poem.

'Shamus O'Brien' is so generally attributed to Lover (indeed we remember seeing it advertised for recitation on the occasion of a benefit at a leading London theatre as 'by Samuel Lover') that it is a satisfaction to be able to reproduce the following letter upon the subject from Lover to William le Fanu:

Astor House,
New York, U.S. America.
Sept. 30, 1846.

MY DEAR LE FANU,

In reading over your brother's poem while I crossed the Atlantic, I became more and more impressed with its great beauty and dramatic effect—so much so that I determined to test its effect in public, and have done so here, on my first appearance, with the greatest success. Now I have no doubt there will be great praises of the poem, and people will suppose, most likely, that the composition is mine, and as you know (I take for granted) that I would not wish to wear a borrowed feather, I should be glad to give your brother's name as the author, should he not object to have it known; but as his writings are often of so different a tone, I would not speak without permission to do so. It is true that in my programme my name is attached to other pieces, and no name appended to the recitation; so far, you will see, I have done all I could to avoid "appropriating," the spirit of which I might have caught here, with Irish aptitude;

but I would like to have the means of telling all whom it may concern the name of the author, to whose head and heart it does so much honour. Pray, my dear Le Fanu, inquire, and answer me here by next packet, or as soon as convenient. My success here has been quite triumphant.

Yours very truly,
SAMUEL LOVER.

We have heard it said (though without having inquired into the truth of the tradition) that 'Shamus O'Brien' was the result of a match at pseudo-national ballad writing made between Le Fanu and several of the most brilliant of his young literary confreres at **T. C. D.** But however this may be, Le Fanu undoubtedly was no young Irelander; indeed he did the stoutest service as a press writer in the Conservative interest, and was no doubt provoked as well as amused at the unexpected popularity to which his poem attained amongst the Irish Nationalists. And here it should be remembered that the ballad was written some eleven years before the outbreak of '48, and at a time when a '98 subject might fairly have been regarded as legitimate literary property amongst the most loyal.

We left Le Fanu as editor of the 'Warder.' He afterwards purchased the 'Dublin Evening Packet,' and much later the half-proprietorship of the 'Dublin Evening Mail.' Eleven or twelve years ago he also became the owner and editor of the 'Dublin University Magazine,' in which his later as well as earlier Irish Stories appeared. He sold it about a year before his death in 1873, having previously parted with the 'Warder' and his share in the 'Evening Mail.'

He had previously published in the 'Dublin University Magazine' a number of charming lyrics, generally anonymously, and it is to be feared that all clue to the identification of most of these is lost, except that of internal evidence.

The following poem, undoubtedly his, should make general our regret at being unable to fix with certainty upon its fellows:

'One wild and distant bugle sound
  Breathed o'er Killarney's magic shore
Will shed sweet floating echoes round
  When that which made them is no more.

'So slumber in the human heart
  Wild echoes, that will sweetly thrill
The words of kindness when the voice
  That uttered them for aye is still.

'Oh! memory, though thy records tell
  Full many a tale of grief and sorrow,

Of mad excess, of hope decayed,
  Of dark and cheerless melancholy;
'Still, memory, to me thou art*
  The dearest of the gifts of mind,
For all the joys that touch my heart
  Are joys that I have left behind.

Le Fanu's literary life may be divided into three distinct periods. During the first of these, and till his thirtieth year, he was an Irish ballad, song, and story writer, his first published story being the 'Adventures of Sir Robert Ardagh,' which appeared in the 'Dublin University Magazine' of 1838.

In 1844 he was united to Miss Susan Bennett, the beautiful daughter of the late George Bennett, Q.C. From this time until her decease, in 1858, he devoted his energies almost entirely to press work, making, however, his first essays in novel writing during that period. The 'Cock and Anchor,' a chronicle of old Dublin city, his first and, in the opinion of competent critics, one of the best of his novels, seeing the light about the year 1850. This work, it is to be feared, is out of print, though there is now a cheap edition of 'Torlogh O'Brien,' its immediate successor. The comparative want of success of these novels seems to have deterred Le Fanu from using his pen, except as a press writer, until 1863, when the 'House by the Churchyard' was published, and was soon followed by 'Uncle Silas' and his five other well-known novels.

We have considered Le Fanu as a ballad writer and poet. As a press writer he is still most honourably remembered for his learning and brilliancy, and the power and point of his sarcasm, which long made the 'Dublin Evening Mail' one of the most formidable of Irish press critics; but let us now pass to the consideration of him in the capacity of a novelist, and in particular as the author of 'Uncle Silas.'

There are evidences in 'Shamus O'Brien,' and even in 'Phaudrig Croohore,' of a power over the mysterious, the grotesque, and the horrible, which so singularly distinguish him as a writer of prose fiction.

'Uncle Silas,' the fairest as well as most familiar instance of this enthralling spell over his readers, is too well known a story to tell in detail. But how intensely and painfully distinct is the opening description of the silent, inflexible Austin Ruthyn of Knowl, and his shy, sweet daughter Maude, the one so resolutely confident in his brother's honour, the other so romantically and yet anxiously interested in her uncle—the sudden arrival of Dr. Bryerly, the strange Swedenborgian, followed by the equally unexpected apparition of Madame de la Rougiere, Austin Ruthyn's painful death, and the reading of his strange will consigning poor Maude to the protection of her unknown Uncle Silas—her cousin, good, bright devoted Monica Knollys, and her dreadful distrust of Silas—Bartram Haugh and its uncanny occupants, and foremost amongst them Uncle Silas.

This is his portrait:

'A face like marble, with a fearful monumental look, and for an old man, singularly vivid, strange eyes, the singularity of which rather grew upon me as I looked; for his eyebrows were still black, though his hair descended from his temples in long locks of the purest silver and fine as silk, nearly to his shoulders.

'He rose, tall and slight, a little stooped, all in black, with an ample black velvet tunic, which was rather a gown than a coat. . . .

'I know I can't convey in words an idea of this apparition, drawn, as it seemed, in black and white, venerable, bloodless, fiery-eyed, with its singular look of power, and an expression so bewildering—was it derision, or anguish, or cruelty, or patience?

'The wild eyes of this strange old man were fixed on me as he rose; an habitual contraction, which in certain lights took the character of a scowl, did not relax as he advanced towards me with a thin-lipped smile.'

Old Dicken and his daughter Beauty, old L'Amour and Dudley Ruthyn, now enter upon the scene, each a fresh shadow to deepen its already sombre hue, while the gloom gathers in spite of the glimpse of sunshine shot through it by the visit to Elverston. Dudley's brutal encounter with Captain Oakley, and vile persecution of poor Maude till his love marriage comes to light, lead us on to the ghastly catastrophe, the hideous conspiracy of Silas and his son against the life of the innocent girl.

It is interesting to know that the germ of Uncle Silas first appeared in the 'Dublin University Magazine' of 1837 or 1838, as the short tale, entitled, 'A Passage from the Secret History of an Irish Countess,' which is printed in this collection of Stories. It next was published as 'The Murdered Cousin' in a collection of Christmas stories, and finally developed into the three-volume novel we have just noticed.

There are about Le Fanu's narratives touches of nature which reconcile us to their always remarkable and often supernatural incidents. His characters are well conceived and distinctly drawn, and strong soliloquy and easy dialogue spring unaffectedly from their lips. He is a close observer of Nature, and reproduces her wilder effects of storm and gloom with singular vividness; while he is equally at home in his descriptions of still life, some of which remind us of the faithfully minute detail of old Dutch pictures.

Mr. Wilkie Collins, amongst our living novelists, best compares with Le Fanu. Both of these writers are remarkable for the ingenious mystery with which they develop their plots, and for the absorbing, if often over-sensational, nature of their incidents; but whilst Mr. Collins excites and fascinates our attention by an intense power of realism which carries us with unreasoning haste from cover to cover of his works, Le Fanu is an idealist, full of high imagination, and an artist who devotes deep attention to the most delicate detail in his portraiture of men and women, and his descriptions of the outdoor and indoor worlds—a writer, therefore, through whose pages it would be often an indignity to hasten. And this more leisurely, and certainly more classical, conduct of his stories makes us remember them more fully and faithfully than those of the author of the 'Woman in White.' Mr. Collins is generally dramatic, and sometimes stagy, in his effects. Le Fanu, while less careful to arrange his plots, so as to admit of their being readily adapted for the stage, often surprises us by scenes of so much greater tragic intensity that we cannot but lament that he did not, as Mr. Collins has done, attempt the drama, and so furnish another ground of comparison with his fellow-countryman, Maturin (also, if we mistake not, of French origin), whom, in his writings, Le Fanu far more closely resembles than Mr. Collins, as a master of the darker and stronger emotions of human character. But, to institute a broader ground of comparison between Le Fanu and Mr. Collins, whilst the idiosyncrasies of the former's characters, however immaterial those characters may be, seem always to suggest the minutest detail of his story, the latter would appear to consider plot as the prime, character as a subsidiary element in the art of novel writing.

Those who possessed the rare privilege of Le Fanu's friendship, and only they, can form any idea of the true character of the man; for after the death of his wife, to whom he was most deeply devoted, he quite forsook general society, in which his fine features, distinguished bearing, and charm of conversation marked him out as the beau-ideal of an Irish wit and scholar of the old school.

From this society he vanished so entirely that Dublin, always ready with a nickname, dubbed him 'The Invisible Prince;' and indeed he was for long almost invisible, except to his family and most familiar friends, unless at odd hours of the evening, when he might occasionally be seen stealing, like the ghost of his former self, between his newspaper office and his home in Merrion Square; sometimes, too, he was to be encountered in an old out-of-the-way bookshop poring over some rare black letter Astrology or Demonology.

To one of these old bookshops he was at one time a pretty frequent visitor, and the bookseller relates how he used to come in and ask with his peculiarly pleasant voice and smile, 'Any more ghost stories for me, Mr.—?' and how, on a fresh one being handed to him, he would seldom leave the shop until he had looked it through. This taste for the supernatural seems to have grown upon him after his wife's death, and influenced him so deeply that, had he not been possessed of a deal of shrewd common sense, there might have been danger of his embracing some of the visionary doctrines in which he was so learned. But no! even Spiritualism, to which not a few of his brother novelists succumbed, whilst affording congenial material for our artist of the superhuman to work upon, did not escape his severest satire.

Shortly after completing his last novel, strange to say, bearing the title 'Willing to Die,' Le Fanu breathed his last at his home No. 18, Merrion Square South, at the age of fifty-nine.

'He was a man,' writes the author of a brief memoir of him in the 'Dublin University Magazine,' 'who thought deeply, especially on religious subjects. To those who knew him he was very dear; they admired him for his learning, his sparkling wit, and pleasant conversation, and loved him for his manly virtues, for his noble and generous qualities, his gentleness, and his loving, affectionate nature.' And all who knew the man must feel how deeply deserved are these simple words of sincere regard for Joseph Sheridan Le Fanu.

Le Fanu's novels are accessible to all; but his Purcell Papers are now for the first time collected and published, by the permission of his eldest son (the late Mr. Philip Le Fanu), and very much owing to the friendly and active assistance of his brother, Mr. William Le Fanu.

The Purcell Papers

The Ghost and the Bone Setter

IN LOOKING over the papers of my late valued and respected friend, Francis Purcell, who for nearly fifty years discharged the arduous duties of a parish priest in the south of Ireland, I met with the following document. It is one of many such; for he was a curious and industrious collector of old local traditions—a commodity in which the quarter where he resided mightily abounded. The collection and arrangement of such legends was, as long as I can remember him, his hobby; but I had never learned that his love of the marvellous and whimsical had carried him so far as to prompt him to commit the results of his inquiries to writing, until, in the character of residuary legatee, his will put me in possession of all his manuscript papers. To such as may think the composing of such productions as these inconsistent with the character and habits of a country priest, it is necessary to observe, that there did exist a race of priests—those of the old school, a race now nearly extinct—whose education abroad tended to produce in them tastes more literary than have yet been evinced by the alumni of Maynooth.

It is perhaps necessary to add that the superstition illustrated by the following story, namely, that the corpse last buried is obliged, during his juniority of interment, to supply his brother tenants of the churchyard in which he lies, with fresh water to allay the burning thirst of purgatory, is prevalent throughout the south of Ireland.

The writer can vouch for a case in which a respectable and wealthy farmer, on the borders of Tipperary, in tenderness to the corns of his departed helpmate, enclosed in her coffin two pair of brogues, a light and a heavy, the one for dry, the other for sloppy weather; seeking thus to mitigate the fatigues of her inevitable perambulations in procuring water and administering it to the thirsty souls of purgatory. Fierce and desperate conflicts have ensued in the case of two funeral parties approaching the same churchyard together, each endeavouring to secure to his own dead priority of sepulture, and a consequent immunity from the tax levied upon the pedestrian powers of the last-comer. An instance not long since occurred, in which one of two such parties, through fear of losing to their deceased friend this inestimable advantage, made their way to the churchyard by a short cut, and, in violation of one of their strongest prejudices, actually threw the coffin over the wall, lest time should be lost in making their entrance through the gate. Innumerable instances of the same kind might be quoted, all tending to show how strongly among the peasantry of the south this superstition is entertained. However, I shall not detain the reader further by any prefatory remarks, but shall proceed to lay before him the following:

EXTRACT FROM THE MS. PAPERS OF
THE LATE REV. FRANCIS PURCELL, OF DRUMCOOLAGH.

I tell the following particulars, as nearly as I can recollect them, in the words of the narrator. It may be necessary to observe that he was what is termed a well-spoken man, having for a considerable time instructed the ingenious youth of his native parish in such of the liberal arts and sciences as he found it convenient to profess—a circumstance which may account for the occurrence of several big words in the course of this narrative, more distinguished for euphonious effect than for correctness of application. I proceed then, without further preface, to lay before you the wonderful adventures of Terry Neil.

'Why, thin, 'tis a quare story, an' as thrue as you're sittin' there; and I'd make bould to say there isn't a boy in the seven parishes could tell it better nor crickther than myself, for 'twas my father himself it happened to, an' many's the time I heerd it out iv his own mouth; an' I can say, an' I'm proud av that same, my father's word was as incredible as any squire's oath in the counthry; and so signs an' if a poor man got into any unlucky throuble, he was the boy id go into the court an' prove; but that doesn't signify—he was as honest and as sober a man, barrin' he was a little bit too partial to the glass, as you'd find in a day's walk; an' there wasn't the likes of him in the counthry round for nate labourin' an' baan diggin'; and he was mighty handy entirely for carpenther's work, and men din' ould spudethrees, an' the likes i' that. An' so he tuk up with bone-settin', as was most nathural, for none of them could come up to him in mendin' the leg iv a stool or a table; an' sure, there never was a bone-setter got so much custom-man an' child, young an' ould—there never was such breakin' and mendin' of bones known in the memory of man. Well, Terry Neil—for that was my father's name—began to feel his heart growin' light, and his purse heavy; an' he took a bit iv a farm in Squire Phelim's ground, just undher the ould castle, an' a pleasant little spot it was; an' day an' mornin' poor crathurs not able to put a foot to the ground, with broken arms and broken legs, id be comin' ramblin' in from all quarters to have their bones spliced up. Well, yer honour, all this was as well as well could be; but it was customary when Sir Phelim id go anywhere out iv the country, for some iv the tinants to sit up to watch in the ould castle, just for a kind of compliment to the ould family—an' a mighty unplisant compliment it was for the tinants, for there wasn't a man of them but knew there was something quare about the ould castle. The neighbours had it, that the squire's ould grandfather, as good a gintlenlan—God be with him—as I heer'd, as ever stood in shoe-leather, used to keep walkin' about in the middle iv the night, ever sinst he bursted a blood vessel pullin' out a cork out iv a bottle, as you or I might be doin', and will too, plase God—but that doesn't signify. So, as I was sayin', the ould squire used to come down out of the frame, where his picthur was hung up, and to break the bottles and glasses—God be marciful to us all—an' dthrink all he could come at—an' small blame to him for that same; and then if any of the family id be comin' in, he id be up again in his place, looking as quite an' as innocent as if he didn't know anything about it—the mischievous ould chap

'Well, your honour, as I was sayin', one time the family up at the castle was stayin' in Dublin for a week or two; and so, as usual, some of the tinants had to sit up in the castle, and the third night it kem to my father's turn. "Oh, tare an' ouns!" says he unto himself, "an' must I sit up all night, and that ould vagabone of a sperit, glory be to God," says he, "serenadin' through the house, an' doin' all sorts iv mischief?" However, there was no gettin' aff, and so he put a bould face on it, an' he went up at nightfall with a bottle of pottieen, and another of holy wather.

'It was rainin' smart enough, an' the evenin' was darksome and gloomy, when my father got in; and what with the rain he got, and the holy wather he sprinkled on himself, it wasn't long till he had to swally a cup iv the pottieen, to keep the cowld out iv his heart. It was the ould steward, Lawrence Connor, that opened the door—and he an' my father wor always very great. So when he seen who it was, an' my father tould him how it was his turn to watch in the castle, he offered to sit up along with him; and you may be sure my father wasn't sorry for that same. So says Larry:

"'We'll have a bit iv fire in the parlour," says he.

"'An' why not in the hall?" says my father, for he knew that the squire's picthur was hung in the parlour.

"'No fire can be lit in the hall," says Lawrence, "for there's an ould jackdaw's nest in the chimney."

"'Oh thin," says my father, "let us stop in the kitchen, for it's very un-proper for the likes iv me to be sittin' in the parlour," says he.

"'Oh, Terry, that can't be," says Lawrence; "if we keep up the ould custom at all, we may as well keep it up properly," says he.

"'Divil sweep the ould custom!" says my father—to himself, do ye mind, for he didn't like to let Lawrence see that he was more afeard himself.

"'Oh, very well," says he. "I'm agreeable, Lawrence," says he; and so down they both wint to the kitchen, until the fire id be lit in the parlour—an' that same wasn't long doin'.

'Well, your honour, they soon wint up again, an' sat down mighty comfortable by the parlour fire, and they beginned to talk, an' to smoke, an' to dhrink a small taste iv the pottieen; and, moreover, they had a good rousin' fire o' bogwood and turf, to warm their shins over.

'Well, sir, as I was sayin' they kep' convarsin' and smokin' together most agreeable, until Lawrence beginn'd to get sleepy, as was but nathural for him, for he was an ould sarvint man, and was used to a great dale iv sleep.

"'Sure it's impossible," says my father, "it's gettin' sleepy you are?"

"'Oh, divil a taste," says Larry; "I'm only shuttin' my eyes," says he, "to keep out the parfume o' the tibacky smoke, that's makin' them wather," says he. "So don't you mind other people's business," says he, stiff enough, for he had a mighty high stomach av his own (rest his sowl), "and go on," says he, "with your story, for I'm listenin'," says he, shuttin' down his eyes.

'Well, when my father seen spakin' was no use, he went on with his story. By the same token, it was the story of Jim Sooolivan and his ould goat he was tellin'—an' a plisant story it is—an' there was so much divar-sion in it, that it was enough to waken a dormouse, let alone to pervint a Christian goin' asleep. But, faix, the way my father tould it, I believe there never was the likes heerd sinst nor before, for he bawled out every word av it, as if the life was fairly lavin' him, thrying to keep ould Larry awake; but, faix, it was no use, for the hoorsness came an him, an' before he kem to the end of his story Larry O'Connor beginned to snore like a bagpipes.

"'Oh, blur an' agres," says my father, "isn't this a hard case," says he, "that ould villain, lettin' on to be my friend, and to go asleep this way, an' us both in the very room with a sperit," says he. "The crass o' Christ about us!" says he; and with that he was goin' to shake Lawrence to waken him, but he just remimbered if he roused him, that he'd surely go off to his bed, an' lave him complately alone, an' that id be by far worse.

"'Oh thin," says my father, "I'll not disturb the poor boy. It id be neither friendly nor good-nathured," says he, "to tormint him while he is asleep," says he; "only I wish I was the same way, myself," says he.

'An' with that he beginned to walk up an' down, an' sayin' his prayers, until he worked himself into a sweat, savin' your presence. But it was all no good; so he dthrunk about a pint of sperits, to compose his mind.

"'Oh," says he, "I wish to the Lord I was as asy in my mind as Larry there. Maybe," says he, "if I thried I could go asleep;" an' with that he pulled a big arm-chair close beside Lawrence, an' settled himself in it as well as he could.

'But there was one quare thing I forgot to tell you. He couldn't help, in spite av himself, lookin' now an' thin at the picthur, an' he immediately obsarved that the eyes av it was follyin' him about, an' starin' at him, an' winkin' at him, wher-iver he wint. "Oh," says he, when he seen that, "it's a poor chance I have," says he; "an' bad luck was with me the day I kem into this unforthunate place," says he. "But any way there's no use in bein' freckened now," says he; "for if I am to die, I may as well parspire undaunted," says he.

'Well, your honour, he thried to keep himself quite an' asy, an' he thought two or three times he might have wint asleep, but for the way the storm was groanin' and creakin' through the great heavy branches outside, an' whistlin' through the ould chimleys iv the castle. Well, afther one great roarin' blast iv the wind, you'd think the walls iv the castle was just goin' to fall, quite an' clane, with the shakin' iv it. All av a suddint the storm stopt, as silent an' as quite as if it was a July evenin'. Well, your honour, it wasn't stopped blowin' for three minnites, before he thought he hard a sort iv a noise over the chimley-piece; an' with that my father just opened his eyes the smallest taste in life, an' sure enough he seen the ould squire gettin' out iv the picthur, for all the world as if he was throwin' aff his ridin' coat, until he stept out clane an' complate, out av the chimley-piece, an' thrun himself down an the floor. Well, the slieveen ould chap—an' my father thought it was the dirtiest turn iv all—before he beginned to do anything out iv the way, he stopped for a while to listen wor they both asleep; an' as soon as he thought all was quite, he put out his hand and tuk hould iv the whisky bottle, an dhrank at laste a pint iv it. Well, your honour, when he tuk his turn out iv it, he settled it back mighty cute entirely, in the very same spot it was in before. An' he beginned to walk up an' down the room, lookin' as sober an' as solid as if he never done the likes at all. An' whinever he went apast my father, he thought he felt a great scent of brimstone, an' it was that that freckened him entirely; for he knew it was brimstone that was burned in hell, savin' your presence. At any rate, he often heerd it from

Father Murphy, an' he had a right to know what belonged to it—he's dead since, God rest him. Well, your honour, my father was asy enough until the sperit kem past him; so close, God be marciful to us all, that the smell iv the sulphur tuk the breath clane out iv him; an' with that he tuk such a fit iv coughin', that it al-a-most shuk him out iv the chair he was sittin' in.

"'Ho, ho!" says the squire, stoppin' short about two steps aff, and turnin' round facin' my father, "is it you that's in it?—an' how's all with you, Terry Neil?"

"'At your honour's sarvice," says my father (as well as the fright id let him, for he was more dead than alive), "an' it's proud I am to see your honour to-night," says he.

"'Terence," says the squire, "you're a respectable man" (an' it was thrue for him), "an industhrious, sober man, an' an example of inebriety to the whole parish," says he.

"'Thank your honour," says my father, gettin' courage, "you were always a civil spoken gintleman, God rest your honour."

"'*Rest* my honour?" says the sperit (fairly gettin' red in the face with the madness), "Rest my honour?" says he. "Why, you ignorant spalpeen," says he, "you mane, niggarly ignoramush," says he, "where did you lave your manners?" says he. "If I *am* dead, it's no fault iv mine," says he; "an' it's not to be thrun in my teeth at every hand's turn, by the likes iv you," says he, stampin' his foot an the flure, that you'd think the boords id smash undther him.

"'Oh," says my father, "I'm only a foolish, ignorant poor man," says he.

"'You're nothing else," says the squire: "but any way," says he, "it's not to be listenin' to your gosther, nor convarsin' with the likes iv you, that I came *up*—down I mane," says he—(an' as little as the mistake was, my father tuk notice iv it). "Listen to me now, Terence Neil," says he: "I was always a good masther to Pathrick Neil, your grandfather," says he.

"' 'Tis thrue for your honour," says my father.

"'And, moreover, I think I was always a sober, riglar gintleman," says the squire.

"'That's your name, sure enough," says my father (though it was a big lie for him, but he could not help it).

"'Well," says the sperit, "although I was as sober as most men—at laste as most gintlemin," says he; "an' though I was at different pariods a most extempory Christian, and most charitable and inhuman to the poor," says he; "for all that I'm not as asy where I am now," says he, "as I had a right to expect," says he.

"'An' more's the pity," says my father. "Maybe your honour id wish to have a word with Father Murphy?"

"'Hould your tongue, you misherable bliggard," says the squire; "it's not iv my sowl I'm thinkin'—an' I wondther you'd have the impitence to talk to a gintleman consarnin' his sowl; and when I want *that* fixed," says he, slappin' his thigh, "I'll go to them that knows what belongs to the likes," says he. "It's not my sowl," says he, sittin' down opossite my father; "it's not my sowl that's annoyin' me most—I'm unasy on my right leg," says he, "that I bruk at Glenvarloch cover the day I killed black Barney."

'My father found out afther, it was a favourite horse that fell undher him, afther leapin' the big fence that runs along by the glin.

"'I hope," says my father, "your honour's not unasy about the killin' iv him?"

"'Hould your tongue, ye fool," said the squire, "an' I'll tell you why I'm unasy on my leg," says he. "In the place, where I spend most iv my time," says he, "except the little leisure I have for lookin' about me here," says he, "I have to walk a great dale more than I was ever used to," says he, "and by far more than is good for me either," says he; "for I must tell you," says he, "the people where I am is ancommonly fond iv cowld wather, for there is nothin' betther to be had; an', moreover, the weather is hotter than is altogether plisant," says he; "and I'm appinted," says he, "to assist in carryin' the wather, an' gets a mighty poor share iv it myself," says he, "an' a mighty throublesome, wearin' job it is, I can tell you," says he; "for they're all iv them surprisinly dthry, an' dthrinks it as fast as my legs can carry it," says he; "but what kills me intirely," says he, "is the wakeness in my leg," says he, "an' I want you to give it a pull or two to bring it to shape," says he, "and that's the long an' the short iv it," says he.

"'Oh, plase your honour," says my father (for he didn't like to handle the sperit at all), "I wouldn't have the impidence to do the likes to your honour," says he; "it's only to poor crathurs like myself I'd do it to," says he.

"'None iv your blarney," says the squire. "Here's my leg," says he, cockin' it up to him—"pull it for the bare life," says he; an "'if you don't, by the immortial powers I'll not lave a bone in your carcish I'll not powdher," says he.

'When my father heerd that, he seen there was no use in purtendin', so he tuk hould iv the leg, an' he kep' pullin' an' pullin', till the sweat, God bless us, beginned to pour down his face.

"'Pull, you divil!" says the squire.

"'At your sarvice, your honour," says my father.

"'Pull harder," says the squire.

'My father pulled like the divil.

"'I'll take a little sup," says the squire, rachin' over his hand to the bottle, "to keep up my courage," says he, lettin' an to be very wake in himself

25

intirely. But, as cute as he was, he was out here, for he tuk the wrong one. "Here's to your good health, Terence," says he; "an' now pull like the very divil." An' with that he lifted the bottle of holy wather, but it was hardly to his mouth, whin he let a screech out, you'd think the room id fairly split with it, an' made one chuck that sent the leg clane aff his body in my father's hands. Down wint the squire over the table, an' bang wint my father half-way across the room on his back, upon the flure. Whin he kem to himself the cheerful mornin' sun was shinin' through the windy shutthers, an' he was lying flat an his back, with the leg iv one of the great ould chairs pulled clane out iv the socket an' tight in his hand, pintin' up to the ceilin', an' ould Larry fast asleep, an' snorin' as loud as ever. My father wint that mornin' to Father Murphy, an' from that to the day of his death, he never neglected confission nor mass, an' what he tould was betther believed that he spake av it but seldom. An', as for the squire, that is the sperit, whether it was that he did not like his liquor, or by rason iv the loss iv his leg, he was never known to walk agin.'

The Fortunes of Sir Robert Ardagh

BEING A SECOND EXTRACT FROM THE PAPERS OF THE LATE FATHER PURCELL.

'The earth hath bubbles as the water hath—
And these are of them.'

IN THE south of Ireland, and on the borders of the county of Limerick, there lies a district of two or three miles in length, which is rendered interesting by the fact that it is one of the very few spots throughout this country, in which some vestiges of aboriginal forest still remain. It has little or none of the lordly character of the American forest, for the axe has felled its oldest and its grandest trees; but in the close wood which survives, live all the wild and pleasing peculiarities of nature: its complete irregularity, its vistas, in whose perspective the quiet cattle are peacefully browsing; its refreshing glades, where the grey rocks arise from amid the nodding fern; the silvery shafts of the old birch trees; the knotted trunks of the hoary oak, the grotesque but graceful branches which never shed their honours under the tyrant pruning-hook; the soft green sward; the chequered light and shade; the wild luxuriant weeds; the lichen and the moss—all, all are beautiful alike in the green freshness of spring, or in the sadness and sere of autumn. Their beauty is of that kind which makes the heart full with joy—appealing to the affections with a power which belongs to nature only. This wood runs up, from below the base, to the ridge of a long line of irregular hills, having perhaps, in primitive times, formed but the skirting of some mighty forest which occupied the level below.

But now, alas! whither have we drifted? whither has the tide of civilisation borne us? It has passed over a land unprepared for it—it has left nakedness behind it; we have lost our forests, but our marauders remain; we have destroyed all that is picturesque, while we have retained everything that is revolting in barbarism. Through the midst of this woodland there runs a deep gully or glen, where the stillness of the scene is broken in upon by the brawling of a mountain-stream, which, however, in the winter season, swells into a rapid and formidable torrent.

There is one point at which the glen becomes extremely deep and narrow; the sides descend to the depth of some hundred feet, and are so steep as to be nearly perpendicular. The wild trees which have taken root in the crannies and chasms of the rock have so intersected and entangled, that one can with difficulty catch a glimpse of the stream, which wheels, flashes, and foams below, as if exulting in the surrounding silence and solitude.

This spot was not unwisely chosen, as a point of no ordinary strength, for the erection of a massive square tower or keep, one side of which rises as if in continuation of the precipitous cliff on which it is based. Originally, the only mode of ingress was by a narrow portal in the very wall which overtopped the precipice, opening upon a ledge of rock which afforded a precarious pathway, cautiously intersected, however, by a deep trench cut with great labour in the living rock; so that, in its original state, and before the introduction of artillery into the art of war, this tower might have been pronounced, and that not presumptuously, almost impregnable.

The progress of improvement and the increasing security of the times had, however, tempted its successive proprietors, if not to adorn, at least to enlarge their premises, and at about the middle of the last century, when the castle was last inhabited, the original square tower formed but a small part of the edifice.

The castle, and a wide tract of the sur-rounding country, had from time immemorial belonged to a family which, for distinctness, we shall call by the name of Ardagh; and owing to the associations which, in Ireland, almost always attach to scenes which have long witnessed alike the exercise of stern feudal authority, and of that savage hospitality which distinguished the good old times, this building has become the subject and the scene of many wild and extraordinary traditions. One of them I have been enabled, by a personal acquaintance with an eye-witness of the events, to trace to its origin; and yet it is hard to say whether the events which I am about to record appear more strange or improbable as seen through the distorting medium of tradition, or in the appalling dimness of uncertainty which surrounds the reality.

Tradition says that, sometime in the last century, Sir Robert Ardagh, a young man, and the last heir of that family, went abroad and served in foreign armies; and that, having acquired considerable honour and emolument, he settled at Castle Ardagh, the building we have just now attempted to describe. He was what the country people call a *dark* man; that is, he was considered morose, reserved, and ill-tempered; and, as it was supposed from the utter solitude of his life, was upon no terms of cordiality with the other members of his family.

The only occasion upon which he broke through the solitary monotony of his life was during the continuance of the racing season, and immediately subsequent to it; at which time he was to be seen among the busiest upon the course, betting deeply and unhesitatingly, and invariably with success. Sir Robert was, however, too well known as a man of honour, and of too high a family, to be suspected of any unfair dealing. He was, moreover, a soldier, and a man of an intrepid as well as of a haughty character; and no one cared to hazard a surmise, the consequences of which would be felt most probably by its originator only.

Gossip, however, was not silent; it was remarked that Sir Robert never appeared at the race-ground, which was the only place of public resort which he frequented, except in company with a certain strange-looking person, who was never seen elsewhere, or under other circumstances. It was remarked, too, that this man, whose relation to Sir Robert was never distinctly ascertained, was the only person to whom he seemed to speak unnecessarily; it was observed that while with the country gentry he exchanged no further communication than what was unavoidable in arranging his sporting transactions, with this person he would converse earnestly and frequently. Tradition asserts that, to enhance the curiosity which this unaccountable and exclusive preference excited, the stranger possessed some striking and unpleasant peculiarities of person and of garb—she does not say, however, what these were—but they, in conjunction with Sir Robert's secluded habits and extraordinary run of luck—a success which was supposed to result from the suggestions and immediate advice of the unknown—were sufficient to warrant report in pronouncing that there was something *queer* in the wind, and in surmising that Sir Robert was playing a fearful and a hazardous game, and that, in short, his strange companion was little better than the devil himself

Years, however, rolled quietly away, and nothing novel occurred in the arrangements of Castle Ardagh, excepting that Sir Robert parted with his odd companion, but as nobody could tell whence he came, so nobody could say whither he had gone. Sir Robert's habits, however, underwent no consequent change; he continued regularly to frequent the race meetings, without mixing at all in the convivialities of the gentry, and immediately afterwards to relapse into the secluded monotony of his ordinary life.

It was said that he had accumulated vast sums of money—and, as his bets were always successful, and always large, such must have been the case. He did not suffer the acquisition of wealth, however, to influence his hospitality or his housekeeping—he neither purchased land, nor extended his establishment; and his mode of enjoying his money must have been altogether that of the miser—consisting merely in the pleasure of touching and telling his gold, and in the consciousness of wealth.

Sir Robert's temper, so far from improving, became more than ever gloomy and morose. He sometimes carried the indulgence of his evil dispositions to such a height that it bordered upon insanity. During these paroxysms he would neither eat, drink, nor sleep. On such occasions he insisted on perfect privacy, even from the intrusion of his most trusted servants; his voice was frequently heard, sometimes in earnest supplication, sometime as if in loud and angry altercation with some unknown visitant; sometimes he would, for hours together, walk to and fro throughout the long oak wainscoted apartment, which he generally occupied, with wild gesticulations and agitated pace, in the manner of one who has been roused to a state of unnatural excitement by some sudden and appalling intimation.

These paroxysms of apparent lunacy were so frightful, that during their continuance even his oldest and most-faithful domestics dared not approach him; consequently, his hours of agony were never intruded upon, and the mysterious causes of his sufferings appeared likely to remain hidden for ever.

On one occasion a fit of this kind continued for an unusual time, the ordinary term of their duration—about two days—had been long past, and the old servant who generally waited upon Sir Robert after these visitations, having in vain listened for the well-known tinkle of his master's hand-bell, began to feel extremely anxious; he feared that his master might have died from sheer exhaustion, or perhaps put an end to his own existence during his miserable depression. These fears at length became so strong, that having in vain urged some of his brother servants to accompany him, he determined to go up alone, and himself see whether any accident had befallen Sir Robert.

He traversed the several passages which conducted from the new to the more ancient parts of the mansion, and having arrived in the old hall of the castle, the utter silence of the hour, for it was very late in the night, the idea of the nature of the enterprise in which he was engaging himself, a sensation of remoteness from anything like human companionship, but, more than all, the vivid but undefined anticipation of something horrible, came upon him with such oppressive weight that he hesitated as to whether he should proceed. Real uneasiness, however, respecting the fate of his master, for whom he felt that kind of attachment which the force of habitual intercourse not unfrequently engenders respecting objects not in themselves amiable, and also a latent unwillingness to expose his weakness to the ridicule of his fellow-servants, combined to overcome his reluctance; and he had just placed his foot upon the first step of the staircase which conducted to his master's chamber, when his attention was arrested by a low but distinct knocking at the hall-door. Not, perhaps, very sorry at finding thus an excuse even for deferring his intended expedition, he placed the candle upon a stone block which lay in the hall, and approached the door, uncertain whether his ears had not deceived him. This doubt was justified by the circumstance that the hall entrance had been for nearly fifty years disused as a mode of ingress to the castle. The situation of this gate also, which we have endeavoured to describe, opening upon a narrow ledge of rock which overhangs a perilous cliff, rendered it at all times, but particularly at night, a dangerous entrance. This shelving platform of rock, which formed the only avenue to the door, was divided, as I have already stated, by a broad chasm, the planks across which had long disappeared by decay or otherwise, so that it seemed at least highly im-probable that any man could have found his way across the passage in safety to the door, more particularly on a night like that, of singular darkness. The old man, therefore, listened attentively, to ascertain whether the first application should be followed by another. He had not long to wait; the same low but singularly distinct knocking was repeated; so low that it seemed as if the applicant had employed no harder or heavier instrument than his hand, and yet, despite the immense thickness of the door, with such strength that the sound was distinctly audible.

The knock was repeated a third time, without any increase of loudness; and the old man, obeying an impulse for which to his dying hour he could never account, proceeded to remove, one by one, the three great oaken bars which secured the door. Time and damp had effectually corroded the iron chambers of the lock, so that it afforded little resistance. With some effort, as he believed, assisted from without, the old servant succeeded in opening the door; and a low, square-built figure, apparently that of a man wrapped in a large black cloak, entered the hall. The servant could not see much of this visitant with any distinctness; his dress appeared foreign, the skirt of his ample cloak was thrown over one shoulder; he wore a large felt hat, with a very heavy leaf, from under which escaped what appeared to be a mass of long sooty-black hair; his feet were cased in heavy riding-boots. Such were the few particulars which the servant had time and light to observe. The stranger desired him to let his master know instantly that a friend had come, by appointment, to settle some business with him. The servant hesitated, but a slight motion on the part of his visitor, as if to possess himself of the candle, determined him; so, taking it in his hand, he ascended the castle stairs, leaving his guest in the hall.

On reaching the apartment which opened upon the oak-chamber he was surprised to observe the door of that room partly open, and the room itself lit up. He paused, but there was no sound; he looked in, and saw Sir Robert, his head and the upper part of his body reclining on a table, upon which burned a lamp; his arms were stretched forward on either side, and perfectly motionless; it appeared that, having been sitting at the table, he had thus sunk forward, either dead or in a swoon. There was no sound of breathing; all was silent, except the sharp ticking of a watch, which lay beside the lamp. The servant coughed twice or thrice, but with no effect; his fears now almost amounted to certainty, and he was approaching the table on which his master partly lay, to satisfy himself of his death, when Sir Robert slowly raised his head, and throwing himself back in his chair, fixed his eyes in a ghastly and uncertain gaze upon his attendant. At length he said, slowly and painfully, as if he dreaded the answer:

'In God's name, what are you?"

'Sir,' said the servant, 'a strange gentleman wants to see you below.'

At this intimation Sir Robert, starting on his feet and tossing his arms wildly upwards, uttered a shriek of such appalling and despairing terror that it was almost too fearful for human endurance; and long after the sound had ceased it seemed to the terrified imagination of the old servant to roll through the deserted passages in bursts of unnatural laughter. After a few moments Sir Robert said:

'Can't you send him away? Why does he come so soon? O God! O God! let him leave me for an hour; a little time. I can't see him now; try to get him away. You see I can't go down now; I have not strength. O God! O God! let him come back in an hour; it is not long to wait. He cannot lose anything by it; nothing, nothing, nothing. Tell him that; say anything to him.'

The servant went down. In his own words, he did not feel the stairs under him till he got to the hall. The figure stood exactly as he had left it. He delivered his master's message as coherently as he could. The stranger replied in a careless tone:

'If Sir Robert will not come down to me, I must go up to him.'

The man returned, and to his surprise he found his master much more composed in manner. He listened to the message, and though the cold perspiration rose in drops upon his forehead faster than he could wipe it away, his manner had lost the dreadful agitation which had marked it before. He rose feebly, and casting a last look of agony behind him, passed from the room to the lobby, where he signed to his attendant not to follow him. The man moved as far as the head of the staircase, from whence he had a tolerably distinct view of the hall, which was imperfectly lighted by the candle he had left there.

He saw his master reel, rather than walk down the stairs, clinging all the way to the banisters. He walked on, as if about to sink every moment from weakness. The figure advanced as if to meet him, and in passing struck down the light. The servant could see no more; but there was a sound of struggling, renewed at intervals with silent but fearful energy. It was evident, however, that the parties were approaching the door, for he heard the solid oak sound twice or thrice, as the feet of the combatants, in shuffling hither and thither over the floor, struck upon it. After a slight pause he heard the door thrown open with such violence that the leaf seemed to strike the side-wall of the hall, for it was so dark without that this could only be surmised by the sound. The struggle was renewed with an agony and intenseness of energy that betrayed itself in deep-drawn gasps. One desperate effort, which terminated in the breaking of some part of the door, producing a sound as if the door-post was wrenched from its position, was followed by another wrestle, evidently upon the narrow ledge which ran outside the door, overtopping the precipice. This proved to be the final struggle, for it was followed by a crashing sound as if some heavy body had fallen over, and was rushing down the precipice, through the light boughs that crossed near the top. All then became still as the grave, except when the moan of the night wind sighed up the wooded glen.

The old servant had not nerve to return through the hall, and to him the darkness seemed all but endless; but morning at length came, and with it the disclosure of the events of the night. Near the door, upon the ground, lay Sir Robert's sword-belt, which had given way in the scuffle. A huge splinter from the massive door-post had been wrenched off by an almost superhuman effort—one which nothing but the gripe of a despairing man could have severed—and on the rock outside were left the marks of the slipping and sliding of feet.

At the foot of the precipice, not immediately under the castle, but dragged some way up the glen, were found the remains of Sir Robert, with hardly a vestige of a limb or feature left distinguishable. The right hand, however, was uninjured, and in its fingers were clutched, with the fixedness of death, a long lock of coarse sooty hair—the only direct circumstantial evidence of the presence of a second person. So says tradition.

This story, as I have mentioned, was current among the dealers in such lore; but the original facts are so dissimilar in all but the name of the principal person mentioned and his mode of life, and the fact that his death was accompanied with circumstances of extraordinary mystery, that the two narratives are totally irreconcilable (even allowing the utmost for the exaggerating influence of tradition), except by supposing report to have combined and blended together the fabulous histories of several distinct bearers of the family name. However this may be, I shall lay before the reader a distinct recital of the events from which the foregoing tradition arose. With respect to these there can be no mistake; they are authenticated as fully as anything can be by human testimony; and I state them principally upon the evidence of a lady who herself bore a prominent part in the strange events which she related, and which I now record as being among the few well-attested tales of the marvellous which it has been my fate to hear. I shall, as far as I am able, arrange in one combined narrative the evidence of several distinct persons who were eye-witnesses of what they related, and with the truth of whose testimony I am solemnly and deeply impressed.

Sir Robert Ardagh, as we choose to call him, was the heir and representative of the family whose name he bore; but owing to the prodigality of his father, the estates descended to him in a very impaired condition. Urged by the restless spirit of youth, or more probably by a feeling of pride which could not submit to witness, in the paternal mansion, what he considered a humiliating alteration in the style and hospitality which up to that time had distinguished his family, Sir Robert left Ireland and went abroad. How he occupied himself, or what countries he visited during his absence, was never known, nor did he afterwards make any allusion or encourage any inquiries touching his foreign sojourn. He left Ireland in the year 1742, being then just of age, and was not heard of until the year 1760—about eighteen years afterwards—at which time he returned. His personal appearance was, as might have been expected, very greatly altered, more altered, indeed, than the time of his absence might have warranted one in supposing likely. But to counterbalance the unfavourable change which time had wrought in his form and features, he had acquired all the advantages of polish of manner and refinement of taste which foreign travel is sup-posed to bestow. But what was truly surprising was that it soon became evident that Sir Robert was very wealthy—wealthy to an extraordinary and unaccountable degree; and this fact was made manifest, not only by his expensive style of living, but by his proceeding to dis-embarrass his property, and to purchase extensive estates in addition. Moreover, there could be nothing deceptive in these appearances, for he paid ready money for everything, from the most important purchase to the most trifling.

Sir Robert was a remarkably agreeable man, and possessing the combined advantages of birth and property, he was, as a matter of course, gladly received into the highest society which the metropolis then commanded. It was thus that he became acquainted with the two beautiful Miss F—ds, then among the brightest ornaments of the highest circle of Dublin fashion. Their family was in more than one direction allied to nobility; and Lady D—, their elder sister by many years, and sometime married to a once well-known nobleman, was now their protectress. These considerations, beside the fact that the young ladies were what is usually termed heiresses, though not to a very great amount, secured to them a high position in the best society which Ireland then produced. The two young ladies differed strongly, alike in appearance and in character. The elder of the two, Emily, was generally considered the handsomer—for her beauty was of that impressive kind which never failed to strike even at the first glance, possessing as it did all the advantages of a fine person and a commanding carriage. The beauty of her features strikingly assorted in character with that of her figure and deportment. Her hair was raven-black and richly luxuriant, beautifully contrasting with the perfect whiteness of her forehead—her finely pencilled brows were black as the ringlets that clustered near them—and her blue eyes, full, lustrous, and animated, possessed all the power and brilliancy of brown ones, with more than their softness and variety of expression. She was not, however, merely the tragedy queen. When she smiled, and that was not seldom, the dimpling of cheek and chin, the laughing display of the small and beautiful teeth—but, more than all, the roguish archness of her deep, bright eye, showed that nature had not neglected in her the lighter and the softer characteristics of woman.

Her younger sister Mary was, as I believe not unfrequently occurs in the case of sisters, quite in the opposite style of beauty. She was light-haired, had more colour, had nearly equal grace, with much more liveliness of manner. Her eyes were of that dark grey which poets so much admire—full of expression and vivacity. She was altogether a very beautiful and animated girl—though as unlike her sister as the presence of those two qualities would permit her to be. Their dissimilarity did not stop here—it was deeper than mere appearance—the character of their minds differed almost as strikingly as did their complexion. The fair-haired beauty had a large proportion of that softness and pliability of temper which physiognomists assign as the characteristics of such complexions. She was much more the creature of impulse than of feeling, and consequently more the victim of extrinsic circumstances than was her sister. Emily, on the contrary, possessed considerable firmness and decision. She was less excitable, but when excited her feelings were more intense and enduring. She wanted much of the gaiety, but with it the volatility of her younger sister. Her opinions were adopted, and her friendships formed more reflectively, and her affections seemed to move, as it were, more slowly, but more determinedly. This firmness of character did not amount to anything masculine, and did not at all impair the feminine grace of her manners.

Sir Robert Ardagh was for a long time apparently equally attentive to the two sisters, and many were the conjectures and the surmises as to which would be the lady of his choice. At length, however, these doubts were determined; he proposed for and was accepted by the dark beauty, Emily F—d.

The bridals were celebrated in a manner becoming the wealth and connections of the parties; and Sir Robert and Lady Ardagh left Dublin to pass the honeymoon at the family mansion, Castle Ardagh, which had lately been fitted up in a style bordering upon magnificent. Whether in compliance with the wishes of his lady, or owing to some whim of his own, his habits were henceforward strikingly altered; and from having moved among the gayest if not the most profligate of the votaries of fashion, he suddenly settled down into a quiet, domestic, country gentleman, and seldom, if ever, visited the capital, and then his sojourns were as brief as the nature of his business would permit.

Lady Ardagh, however, did not suffer from this change further than in being secluded from general society; for Sir Robert's wealth, and the hospitality which he had established in the family mansion, commanded that of such of his lady's friends and relatives as had leisure or inclination to visit the castle; and as their style of living was very handsome, and its internal resources of amusement considerable, few invitations from Sir Robert or his lady were neglected.

Many years passed quietly away, during which Sir Robert's and Lady Ardagh's hopes of issue were several times disappointed. In the lapse of all this time there occurred but one event worth recording. Sir Robert had brought with him from abroad a valet, who sometimes professed himself

35

to be French, at others Italian, and at others again German. He spoke all these languages with equal fluency, and seemed to take a kind of pleasure in puzzling the sagacity and balking the curiosity of such of the visitors at the castle as at any time happened to enter into conversation with him, or who, struck by his singularities, became inquisitive respecting his country and origin. Sir Robert called him by the French name, *Jacque*, and among the lower orders he was familiarly known by the title of 'Jack, the devil,' an appellation which originated in a supposed malignity of disposition and a real reluctance to mix in the society of those who were believed to be his equals. This morose reserve, coupled with the mystery which enveloped all about him, rendered him an object of suspicion and inquiry to his fellow-servants, amongst whom it was whispered that this man in secret governed the actions of Sir Robert with a despotic dictation, and that, as if to indemnify himself for his public and apparent servitude and self-denial, he in private exacted a degree of respectful homage from his so-called master, totally inconsistent with the relation generally supposed to exist between them.

This man's personal appearance was, to say the least of it, extremely odd; he was low in stature; and this defect was enhanced by a distortion of the spine, so considerable as almost to amount to a hunch; his features, too, had all that sharpness and sickliness of hue which generally accompany deformity; he wore his hair, which was black as soot, in heavy neglected ringlets about his shoulders, and always without powder—a peculiarity in those days. There was something unpleasant, too, in the circumstance that he never raised his eyes to meet those of another; this fact was often cited as a proof of his being something not quite right, and said to result not from the timidity which is supposed in most cases to induce this habit, but from a consciousness that his eye possessed a power which, if exhibited, would betray a supernatural origin. Once, and once only, had he violated this sinister observance: it was on the occasion of Sir Robert's hopes having been most bitterly disappointed; his lady, after a severe and dangerous confinement, gave birth to a dead child. Immediately after the intelligence had been made known, a servant, having upon some business passed outside the gate of the castle-yard, was met by Jacque, who, contrary to his wont, accosted him, observing, 'So, after all the pother, the son and heir is still-born.' This remark was accompanied by a chuckling laugh, the only approach to merriment which he was ever known to exhibit. The servant, who was really disappointed, having hoped for holiday times, feasting and debauchery with impunity during the rejoicings which would have accompanied a christening, turned tartly upon the little valet, telling him that he should let Sir Robert know how he had received the tidings which should have filled any faithful servant with sorrow; and having once broken the ice, he was proceeding with increasing fluency, when his harangue was cut short and his temerity punished, by the little man raising his head and treating him to a scowl so fearful, half-demoniac, half-insane, that it haunted his imagination in nightmares and nervous tremors for months after.

To this man Lady Ardagh had, at first sight, conceived an antipathy amounting to horror, a mixture of loathing and dread so very powerful that she had made it a particular and urgent request to Sir Robert, that he would dismiss him, offering herself, from that property which Sir Robert had by the marriage settlements left at her own disposal, to provide handsomely for him, provided only she might be relieved from the continual anxiety and discomfort which the fear of encountering him induced.

Sir Robert, however, would not hear of it; the request seemed at first to agitate and distress him; but when still urged in defiance of his peremptory refusal, he burst into a violent fit of fury; he spoke darkly of great sacrifices which he had made, and threatened that if the request were at any time renewed he would leave both her and the country for ever. This was, however, a solitary instance of violence; his general conduct towards Lady Ardagh, though at no time uxorious, was certainly kind and respectful, and he was more than repaid in the fervent attachment which she bore him in return.

Some short time after this strange interview between Sir Robert and Lady Ardagh; one night after the family had retired to bed, and when everything had been quiet for some time, the bell of Sir Robert's dressing-room rang suddenly and violently; the ringing was repeated again and again at still shorter intervals, and with increasing violence, as if the person who pulled the bell was agitated by the presence of some terrifying and imminent danger. A servant named Donovan was the first to answer it; he threw on his clothes, and hurried to the room.

Sir Robert had selected for his private room an apartment remote from the bed-chambers of the castle, most of which lay in the more modern parts of the mansion, and secured at its entrance by a double door. As the servant opened the first of these, Sir Robert's bell again sounded with a longer and louder peal; the inner door resisted his efforts to open it; but after a few violent struggles, not having been perfectly secured, or owing to the inadequacy of the bolt itself, it gave way, and the servant rushed into the apartment, advancing several paces before he could recover himself. As he entered, he heard Sir Robert's voice exclaiming loudly—'Wait without, do not come in yet;' but the prohibition came too late. Near a low truckle-bed, upon which Sir Robert sometimes slept, for he was a whimsical man, in a large armchair, sat, or rather lounged, the form of the valet Jacque, his arms folded, and his heels stretched forward on the floor, so as fully to exhibit his misshapen legs, his head thrown back, and his eyes fixed upon his master with a look of indescribable defiance and derision, while, as if to add to the strange insolence of his attitude and expression, he had placed upon his head the black cloth cap which it was his habit to wear.

Sir Robert was standing before him, at the distance of several yards, in a posture expressive of despair, terror, and what might be called an agony of humility. He waved his hand twice or thrice, as if to dismiss the servant, who, however, remained fixed on the spot where he had first stood; and then, as if forgetting everything but the agony within him, he pressed his clenched hands on his cold damp brow, and dashed away the heavy drops that gathered chill and thickly there.

Jacque broke the silence.

'Donovan,' said he, 'shake up that drone and drunkard, Carlton; tell him that his master directs that the travelling carriage shall be at the door within half-an-hour.'

The servant paused, as if in doubt as to what he should do; but his scruples were resolved by Sir Robert's saying hurriedly, 'Go—go, do what-ever he directs; his commands are mine; tell Carlton the same.'

The servant hurried to obey, and in about half-an-hour the carriage was at the door, and Jacque, having directed the coachman to drive to B—n, a small town at about the distance of twelve miles—the nearest point, however, at which post-horses could be obtained—stepped into the vehicle, which accordingly quitted the castle immediately.

Although it was a fine moonlight night, the carriage made its way but very slowly, and after the lapse of two hours the travellers had arrived at a point about eight miles from the castle, at which the road strikes through a desolate and heathy flat, sloping up distantly at either side into bleak undulatory hills, in whose monotonous sweep the imagination beholds the heaving of some dark sluggish sea, arrested in its first commotion by some preternatural power. It is a gloomy and divested spot; there is neither tree nor habitation near it; its monotony is unbroken, except by here and there the grey front of a rock peering above the heath, and the effect is rendered yet more dreary and spectral by the exaggerated and misty shadows which the moon casts along the sloping sides of the hills.

When they had gained about the centre of this tract, Carlton, the coachman, was surprised to see a figure standing at some distance in ad-vance, immediately beside the road, and still more so when, on coming up, he observed that it was no other than Jacque whom he believed to be at that moment quietly seated in the carriage; the coachman drew up, and nodding to him, the little valet exclaimed:

'Carlton, I have got the start of you; the roads are heavy, so I shall even take care of myself the rest of the way. Do you make your way back as best you can, and I shall follow my own nose.'

So saying, he chucked a purse into the lap of the coachman, and turning off at a right angle with the road, he began to move rapidly away in the direction of the dark ridge that lowered in the distance.

The servant watched him until he was lost in the shadowy haze of night; and neither he nor any of the inmates of the castle saw Jacque again. His disappearance, as might have been expected, did not cause any regret among the servants and dependants at the castle; and Lady Ardagh did not attempt to conceal her delight; but with Sir Robert matters were different, for two or three days subsequent to this event he confined himself to his room, and when he did return to his ordinary occupations, it was with a gloomy indifference, which showed that he did so more from habit than from any interest he felt in them. He appeared from that moment unaccountably and strikingly changed, and thenceforward walked through life as a thing from which he could derive neither profit nor pleasure. His temper, however, so far from growing wayward or morose, became, though gloomy, very—almost unnaturally—placid and cold; but his spirits totally failed, and he grew silent and abstracted.

These sombre habits of mind, as might have been anticipated, very materially affected the gay house-keeping of the castle; and the dark and melancholy spirit of its master seemed to have communicated itself to the very domestics, almost to the very walls of the mansion.

Several years rolled on in this way, and the sounds of mirth and wassail had long been strangers to the castle, when Sir Robert requested his lady, to her great astonishment, to invite some twenty or thirty of their friends to spend the Christmas, which was fast approaching, at the castle. Lady Ardagh gladly complied, and her sister Mary, who still continued unmarried, and Lady D—were of course included in the invitations. Lady Ardagh had requested her sisters to set forward as early as possible, in order that she might enjoy a little of their society before the arrival of the other guests; and in compliance with this request they left Dublin almost immediately upon receiving the invitation, a little more than a week before the arrival of the festival which was to be the period at which the whole party were to muster.

For expedition's sake it was arranged that they should post, while Lady D—'s groom was to follow with her horses, she taking with herself her own maid and one male servant. They left the city when the day was considerably spent, and consequently made but three stages in the first day; upon the second, at about eight in the evening, they had reached the town of K—k, distant about fifteen miles from Castle Ardagh. Here, owing to Miss F—d's great fatigue, she having been for a considerable time in a very delicate state of health, it was determined to put up for the night. They, accord-ingly, took possession of the best sitting-room which the inn commanded, and Lady D—remained in it to direct and urge the preparations for some refreshment, which the fatigues of the day had rendered necessary, while her younger sister retired to her bed-chamber to rest there for a little time, as the parlour commanded no such luxury as a sofa.

Miss F—d was, as I have already stated, at this time in very delicate health; and upon this occasion the exhaustion of fatigue, and the dreary badness of the weather, combined to depress her spirits. Lady D—had not been left long to herself, when the door communicating with the passage was abruptly opened, and her sister Mary entered in a state of great agitation; she sat down pale and trembling upon one of the chairs, and it was not until a copious flood of tears had relieved her, that she became sufficiently calm to relate the cause of her excitement and distress. It was simply this. Almost immediately upon lying down upon the bed she sank into a feverish and unrefreshing slumber; images of all grotesque shapes and startling colours flitted before her sleeping fancy with all the rapidity and variety of the changes in a kaleidoscope. At length, as she described it, a mist seemed to interpose itself between her sight and the ever-shifting scenery which sported before her imagination, and out of this cloudy shadow gradually emerged a figure whose back seemed turned towards the sleeper; it was that of a lady, who, in perfect silence, was expressing as far as pantomimic gesture could, by wringing her hands, and throwing her head from side to side, in the manner of one who is exhausted by the over indulgence, by the very sickness and impatience of grief; the extremity of misery. For a long time she sought in vain to catch a glimpse of the face of the apparition, who thus seemed to stir and live before her. But at length the figure seemed to move with an air of authority, as if about to give directions to some inferior, and in doing so, it turned its head so as to display, with a ghastly distinctness, the features of Lady Ardagh, pale as death, with her dark hair all dishevelled, and her eyes dim and sunken with weeping. The revulsion of feeling which Miss F—d experienced at this disclosure—for up to that point she had contemplated the appearance rather with a sense of curiosity and of interest, than of anything deeper—was so horrible, that the shock awoke her perfectly. She sat up in the bed, and looked fearfully around the room, which was imperfectly lighted by a single candle burning dimly, as if she almost expected to see the reality of her dreadful vision lurking in some corner of the chamber. Her fears were, however, verified, though not in the way she expected; yet in a manner sufficiently horrible—

for she had hardly time to breathe and to collect her thoughts, when she heard, or thought she heard, the voice of her sister, Lady Ardagh, sometimes sobbing violently, and sometimes almost shrieking as if in terror, and calling upon her and Lady D—, with the most imploring earnestness of despair, for God's sake to lose no time in coming to her. All this was so horribly distinct, that it seemed as if the mourner was standing within a few yards of the spot where Miss F—d lay. She sprang from the bed, and leaving the candle in the room behind her, she made her way in the dark through the passage, the voice still following her, until as she arrived at the door of the sitting-room it seemed to die away in low sobbing.

As soon as Miss F—d was tolerably recovered, she declared her determination to proceed directly, and without further loss of time, to Castle Ardagh. It was not without much difficulty that Lady D—at length prevailed upon her to consent to remain where they then were, until morning should arrive, when it was to be expected that the young lady would be much refreshed by at least remaining quiet for the night, even though sleep were out of the question. Lady D—was convinced, from the nervous and feverish symptoms which her sister exhibited, that she had already done too much, and was more than ever satisfied of the necessity of prosecuting the journey no further upon that day. After some time she persuaded her sister to return to her room, where she remained with her until she had gone to bed, and appeared comparatively composed. Lady D—then returned to the parlour, and not finding herself sleepy, she remained sitting by the fire. Her solitude was a second time broken in upon, by the entrance of her sister, who now appeared, if possible, more agitated than before. She said that Lady D—had not long left the room, when she was roused by a repetition of the same wailing and lamentations, accom-panied by the wildest and most agonized supplications that no time should be lost in coming to Castle Ardagh, and all in her sister's voice, and uttered at the same proximity as before. This time the voice had followed her to the very door of the sitting-room, and until she closed it, seemed to pour forth its cries and sobs at the very threshold.

Miss F—d now most positively declared that nothing should prevent her proceeding instantly to the castle, adding that if Lady D—would not accompany her, she would go on by herself. Superstitious feelings are at all times more or less contagious, and the last century afforded a soil much more congenial to their growth than the present. Lady D—was so far affected by her sister's terrors, that she became, at least, uneasy; and seeing that her sister was immovably determined upon setting forward immediately, she consented to accompany her forthwith. After a slight delay, fresh horses were procured, and the two ladies and their attendants renewed their journey, with strong injunctions to the driver to quicken their rate of travelling as much as possible, and promises of reward in case of his doing so.

Roads were then in much worse condition throughout the south, even than they now are; and the fifteen miles which modern posting would have passed in little more than an hour and a half, were not completed even with every possible exertion in twice the time. Miss F—d had been nervously restless during the journey. Her head had been constantly out of the carriage window; and as they ap-proached the entrance to the castle demesne, which lay about a mile from the building, her anxiety began to communicate itself to her sister. The postillion had just dismounted, and was endeavouring to open the gate—at that time a necessary trouble; for in the middle of the last century porter's lodges were not common in the south of Ireland, and locks and keys almost unknown. He had just suc-ceeded in rolling back the heavy oaken gate so as to admit the vehicle, when a mounted servant rode rapidly down the avenue, and drawing up at the carriage, asked of the postillion who the party were; and on hearing, he rode round to the carriage window and handed in a note, which Lady D—received. By the assistance of one of the coach-lamps they succeeded in deciphering it. It was scrawled in great agitation, and ran thus:

MY DEAR SISTER—MY DEAR SISTERS BOTH,

In God's name lose no time, I am frightened and miserable; I cannot explain all till you come. I am too much terrified to write coherently; but understand me—hasten—do not waste a minute. I am afraid you will come too late.

E. A.

The servant could tell nothing more than that the castle was in great confusion, and that Lady Ardagh had been crying bitterly all the night. Sir Robert was perfectly well. Altogether at a loss as to the cause of Lady Ardagh's great distress, they urged their way up the steep and broken av-enue which wound through the crowding trees, whose wild and grotesque branches, now left stripped and naked by the blasts of winter, stretched drearily across the road. As the carriage drew up in the area before the door, the anxiety of the ladies almost amounted to agony; and scarcely waiting for the assistance of their attendant, they sprang to the ground, and in an instant stood at the castle door. From within were distinctly audible the sounds of lamentation and weeping, and the suppressed hum of voices as if of those endeavouring to soothe the mourner. The door was speedily opened, and when the ladies entered, the first object which met their view was their sister, Lady Ardagh, sitting on a form in the hall, weeping and wringing her hands in deep agony. Beside her stood two old, withered crones, who were each endeavouring in their own way to administer consolation, without even knowing or caring what the subject of her grief might be.

Immediately on Lady Ardagh's seeing her sisters, she started up, fell on their necks, and kissed them again and again without speaking, and then taking them each by a hand, still weeping bitterly, she led them into a small room adjoining the hall, in which burned a light, and, having closed the door, she sat down between them. After thanking them for the haste they had made, she proceeded to tell them, in words incoherent from agitation, that Sir Robert had in private, and in the most solemn manner, told her that he should die upon that night, and that he had occupied himself during the evening in giving minute directions respecting the arrangements of his funeral. Lady D—here suggested the possibility of his labouring under the hallucinations of a fever; but to this Lady Ardagh quickly replied:

'Oh! no, no! Would to God I could think it. Oh! no, no! Wait till you have seen him. There is a frightful calmness about all he says and does; and his directions are all so clear, and his mind so perfectly collected, it is impossible, quite impossible.' And she wept yet more bitterly.

At that moment Sir Robert's voice was heard in issuing some directions, as he came downstairs; and Lady Ardagh exclaimed, hurriedly:

'Go now and see him yourself. He is in the hall.'

Lady D—accordingly went out into the hall, where Sir Robert met her; and, saluting her with kind politeness, he said, after a pause:

'You are come upon a melancholy mission—the house is in great confusion, and some of its inmates in considerable grief.' He took her hand, and looking fixedly in her face, continued: 'I shall not live to see to-morrow's sun shine.'

'You are ill, sir, I have no doubt,' replied she; 'but I am very certain we shall see you much better to-morrow, and still better the day following.'

'I am *not* ill, sister,' replied he. 'Feel my temples, they are cool; lay your finger to my pulse, its throb is slow and temperate. I never was more perfectly in health, and yet do I know that ere three hours be past, I shall be no more.'

'Sir, sir,' said she, a good deal startled, but wishing to conceal the impression which the calm solemnity of his manner had, in her own despite, made upon her, 'Sir, you should not jest; you should not even speak lightly upon such subjects. You trifle with what is sacred—you are sporting with the best affections of your wife—'

'Stay, my good lady,' said he; 'if when this clock shall strike the hour of three, I shall be anything but a helpless clod, then upbraid me. Pray return now to your sister. Lady Ardagh is, indeed, much to be pitied; but what is past cannot now be helped. I have now a few papers to arrange, and some to destroy. I shall see you and Lady Ardagh before my death; try to compose her—her sufferings distress me much; but what is past cannot now be mended.'

Thus saying, he went upstairs, and Lady D—returned to the room where her sisters were sitting.

'Well,' exclaimed Lady Ardagh, as she re-entered, 'is it not so?—do you still doubt?—do you think there is any hope?"

Lady D—was silent.

'Oh! none, none, none,' continued she; 'I see, I see you are convinced.' And she wrung her hands in bitter agony.

'My dear sister,' said Lady D—, 'there is, no doubt, something strange in all that has appeared in this matter; but still I cannot but hope that there may be something deceptive in all the apparent calmness of Sir Robert. I still must believe that some latent fever has affected his mind, or that, owing to the state of nervous depression into which he has been sinking, some trivial occurrence has been converted, in his disordered imagination, into an augury foreboding his immediate dissolution.'

In such suggestions, unsatisfactory even to those who originated them, and doubly so to her whom they were intended to comfort, more than two hours passed; and Lady D—was beginning to hope that the fated term might elapse without the occurrence of any tragical event, when Sir Robert entered the room. On coming in, he placed his finger with a warning gesture upon his lips, as if to enjoin silence; and then having successively pressed the hands of his two sisters-in-law, he stooped sadly over the fainting form of his lady, and twice pressed her cold, pale forehead, with his lips, and then passed silently out of the room.

Lady D—, starting up, followed to the door, and saw him take a candle in the hall, and walk deliberately up the stairs. Stimulated by a feeling of horrible curiosity, she continued to follow him at a distance. She saw him enter his own private room, and heard him close and lock the door after him. Continuing to follow him as far as she could, she placed herself at the door of the chamber, as noiselessly as possible, where after a little time she was joined by her two sisters, Lady Ardagh and Miss F—d. In breathless silence they listened to what should pass within. They distinctly heard Sir Robert pacing up and down the room for some time; and then, after a pause, a sound as if some one had thrown himself heavily upon the bed. At this moment Lady D—, forgetting that the door had been secured within, turned the handle for the purpose of entering; when some one from the inside, close to the door, said, 'Hush! hush!' The same lady, now much alarmed, knocked violently at the door; there was no answer. She knocked again more vio-lently, with no further success. Lady Ardagh, now uttering a piercing shriek, sank in a swoon upon the floor. Three or four servants, alarmed by the noise, now hurried upstairs, and Lady Ardagh was carried apparently lifeless to her own chamber. They then, after having knocked long and loudly in vain, applied themselves to forcing an entrance into Sir Robert's room. After resisting some violent efforts, the door at length gave way, and all entered the room nearly together. There was a single candle burning upon a table at the far end of the apartment; and stretched upon the bed lay Sir Robert Ardagh. He was a corpse—the eyes were open—no convulsion had passed over the features, or distorted the limbs—it seemed as if the soul had sped from the body without a struggle to remain there. On touching the body it was found to be cold as clay—all lingering of the vital heat had left it. They closed the ghastly eyes of the corpse, and leaving it to the care of those who seem to consider it a privilege of their age and sex to gloat over the revolting spectacle of death in all its stages, they returned to Lady Ardagh, now a widow. The party assembled at the castle, but the atmosphere was tainted with death. Grief there was not much, but awe and panic were expressed in every face. The guests talked in whispers, and the servants walked on tiptoe, as if afraid of the very noise of their own footsteps.

The funeral was conducted almost with splendour. The body, having been conveyed, in compliance with Sir Robert's last directions, to Dublin, was there laid within the ancient walls of St. Audoen's Church—where I have read the epitaph, telling the age and titles of the departed dust. Neither painted escutcheon, nor marble slab, have served to rescue from oblivion the story of the dead, whose very name will ere long moulder from their tracery

'Et sunt sua fata sepulchris.'[1]

The events which I have recorded are not imaginary. They are *facts*; and there lives one whose authority none would venture to question, who could vindicate the accuracy of every statement which I have set down, and that, too, with all the circumstantiality of an eye-witness.[2]

---

1   This prophecy has since been realised; for the aisle in which Sir Robert's remains were laid has been suffered to fall completely to decay; and the tomb which marked his grave, and other monuments more curious, form now one indistinguishable mass of rubbish.

2   This paper, from a memorandum, I find to have been written in 1803. The lady to whom allusion is made, I believe to be Miss Mary F—d. She never married, and survived both her sisters, living to a very advanced age.

The Last Heir of Castle Connor

BEING A THIRD EXTRACT FROM THE LEGACY OF THE LATE FRANCIS PURCELL, P. P. OF DRUMCOOLAGH.

THERE IS something in the decay of ancient grandeur to interest even the most unconcerned spectator—the evidences of greatness, of power, and of pride that survive the wreck of time, proving, in mournful contrast with present desolation and decay, what *was* in other days, appeal, with a resistless power, to the sympathies of our nature. And when, as we gaze on the scion of some ruined family, the first impulse of nature that bids us regard his fate with interest and respect is justified by the recollection of great exertions and self-devotion and sacrifices in the cause of a lost country and of a despised religion—sacrifices and efforts made with all the motives of faithfulness and of honour, and terminating in ruin—in such a case respect becomes veneration, and the interest we feel amounts almost to a passion.

It is this feeling which has thrown the magic veil of romance over every roofless castle and ruined turret throughout our country; it is this feeling that, so long as a tower remains above the level of the soil, so long as one scion of a prostrate and impoverished family survives, will never suffer Ireland to yield to the stranger more than the 'mouth honour' which fear compels.[3] I who have conversed viva voce et propria persona with those whose recollections could run back so far as the times previous to the confiscations which followed the Revolution of 1688—whose memory could repeople halls long roofless and desolate, and point out the places where greatness once had been, may feel all this more strongly, and with a more vivid interest, than can those whose sympathies are awakened by the feebler influence of what may be called the *Picturesque* effects of ruin and decay.

There do, indeed, still exist some fragments of the ancient Catholic families of Ireland; but, alas! what *very* fragments! They linger like the remnants of her aboriginal forests, reft indeed of their strength and greatness, but proud even in decay. Every winter thins their ranks, and strews the ground with the wreck of their loftiest branches; they are at best but

---

3   This passage serves (mirabile dictu) to corroborate a statement of Mr. O'Connell's, which occurs in his evidence given before the House of Commons, wherein he affirms that the principles of the Irish priesthood 'are democratic, and were those of Jacobinism.'—See digest of the evidence upon the state of Ireland, given before the House of Commons.

tolerated in the land which gave them birth—objects of curiosity, perhaps of pity, to one class, but of veneration to another.

The O'Connors, of Castle Connor, were an ancient Irish family. The name recurs frequently in our history, and is generally to be found in a prominent place whenever periods of tumult or of peril called forth the courage and the enterprise of this country. After the accession of William III., the storm of confiscation which swept over the land made woeful havoc in their broad domains. Some fragments of property, however, did remain to them, and with it the building which had for ages formed the family residence.

About the year 17—, my uncle, a Catholic priest, became acquainted with the inmates of Castle Connor, and after a time introduced me, then a lad of about fifteen, full of spirits, and little dreaming that a profession so grave as his should ever become mine.

The family at that time consisted of but two members, a widow lady and her only son, a young man aged about eighteen. In our early days the progress from acquaintance to intimacy, and from intimacy to friendship is proverbially rapid; and young O'Connor and I became, in less than a month, close and confidential companions—an intercourse which ripened gradually into an attachment ardent, deep, and devoted—such as I believe young hearts only are capable of forming.

He had been left early fatherless, and the representative and heir of his family. His mother's affection for him was intense in proportion as there existed no other object to divide it—indeed—such love as that she bore him I have never seen elsewhere. Her love was better bestowed than that of mothers generally is, for young O'Connor, not without some of the faults, had certainly many of the most engaging qualities of youth. He had all the frankness and gaiety which attract, and the generosity of heart which confirms friendship; indeed, I never saw a person so universally popular; his very faults seemed to recommend him; he was wild, extravagant, thoughtless, and fearlessly adventurous—defects of character which, among the peasantry of Ireland, are honoured as virtues. The combination of these qualities, and the position which O'Connor occupied as representative of an ancient Irish Catholic family—a peculiarly interesting one to me, one of the old faith—endeared him to me so much that I have never felt the pangs of parting more keenly than when it became necessary, for the finishing of his education, that he should go abroad.

Three years had passed away before I saw him again. During the interval, however, I had frequently heard from him, so that absence had not abated the warmth of our attachment. Who could tell of the rejoicings that marked the evening of his return? The horses were removed from the chaise at the distance of a mile from the castle, while it and its contents were borne rapidly onward almost by the pressure of the multitude, like a log upon a torrent. Bonfires blared far and near—bagpipes roared and fiddles squeaked; and, amid the thundering shouts of thousands, the carriage drew up before the castle.

In an instant young O'Connor was upon the ground, crying, 'Thank you, boys—thank you, boys;' while a thousand hands were stretched out from all sides to grasp even a finger of his. Still, amid shouts of 'God bless your honour—long may you reign!' and 'Make room there, boys! clear the road for the masther!' he reached the threshold of the castle, where stood his mother weeping for joy.

Oh! who could describe that embrace, or the enthusiasm with which it was witnessed? 'God bless him to you, my lady—glory to ye both!' and 'Oh, but he is a fine young gentleman, God bless him!' resounded on all sides, while hats flew up in volleys that darkened the moon; and when at length, amid the broad delighted grins of the thronging domestics, whose sense of decorum precluded any more boisterous evidence of joy, they reached the parlour, then giving way to the fulness of her joy the widowed mother kissed and blessed him and wept in turn. Well might any parent be proud to claim as son the handsome stripling who now represented the Castle Connor family; but to her his beauty had a peculiar charm, for it bore a striking resemblance to that of her husband, the last O'Connor.

I know not whether partiality blinded me, or that I did no more than justice to my friend in believing that I had never seen so handsome a young man. I am inclined to think the latter. He was rather tall, very slightly and elegantly made; his face was oval, and his features decidedly Spanish in cast and complexion, but with far more vivacity of expression than generally belongs to the beauty of that nation. The extreme delicacy of his features and the varied animation of his countenance made him appear even younger than his years—an illusion which the total absence of everything studied in his manners seemed to confirm. Time had wrought no small change in me, alike in mind and spirits; but in the case of O'Connor it seemed to have lost its power to alter. His gaiety was undamped, his generosity unchilled; and though the space which had intervened between our parting and reunion was but brief, yet at the period of life at which we were, even a shorter interval than that of three years has frequently served to form or DEform a character.

Weeks had passed away since the return of O'Connor, and scarce a day had elapsed without my seeing him, when the neighbourhood was thrown into an unusual state of excitement by the announcement of a race-ball to be celebrated at the assembly-room of the town of T—, distant scarcely two miles from Castle Connor.

Young O'Connor, as I had expected, determined at once to attend it; and having directed in vain all the powers of his rhetoric to persuade his mother to accompany him, he turned the whole battery of his logic upon me, who, at that time, felt a reluctance stronger than that of mere apathy to mixing in any of these scenes of noisy pleasure for which for many reasons I felt myself unfitted. He was so urgent and persevering, however, that I could not refuse; and I found myself reluctantly obliged to make up my mind to attend him upon the important night to the spacious but ill-finished building, which the fashion and beauty of the county were pleased to term an assembly-room.

When we entered the apartment, we found a select few, surrounded by a crowd of spectators, busily performing a minuet, with all the congees and flourishes which belonged to that courtly dance; and my companion, infected by the contagion of example, was soon, as I had anticipated, waving his chapeau bras, and gracefully bowing before one of the prettiest girls in the room. I had neither skill nor spirits to qualify me to follow his example; and as the fulness of the room rendered it easy to do so without its appearing singular, I determined to be merely a spectator of the scene which surrounded me, without taking an active part in its amusements.

The room was indeed very much crowded, so that its various groups, formed as design or accident had thrown the parties together, afforded no small fund of entertainment to the contemplative observer. There were the dancers, all gaiety and good-humour; a little further off were the tables at which sat the card-players, some plying their vocation with deep and silent anxiety—for in those days gaming often ran very high in such places—and others disputing with all the vociferous pertinacity of undisguised ill-temper. There, again, were the sallow, blue-nosed, grey-eyed dealers in whispered scandal; and, in short, there is scarcely a group or combination to be met with in the court of kings which might not have found a humble parallel in the assembly-room of T—.

I was allowed to indulge in undisturbed contemplation, for I suppose I was not known to more than five or six in the room. I thus had leisure not only to observe the different classes into which the company had divided itself, but to amuse myself by speculating as to the rank and character of many of the individual actors in the drama.

Among many who have long since passed from my memory, one person for some time engaged my attention, and that person, for many reasons, I shall not soon forget. He was a tall, square-shouldered man, who stood in a careless attitude, leaning with his back to the wall; he seemed to have secluded himself from the busy multitudes which moved noisily and gaily around him, and nobody seemed to observe or to converse with him.

He was fashionably dressed, but perhaps rather extravagantly; his face was full and heavy, expressive of sullenness and stupidity, and marked with the lines of strong vulgarity; his age might be somewhere between forty and fifty. Such as I have endeavoured to describe him, he remained motionless, his arms doggedly folded across his broad chest, and turning his sullen eyes from corner to corner of the room, as if eager to detect some object on which to vent his ill-humour.

It is strange, and yet it is true, that one sometimes finds even in the most commonplace countenance an undefinable something, which fascinates the attention, and forces it to recur again and again, while it is impossible to tell whether the peculiarity which thus attracts us lies in feature or in expression. or in both combined, and why it is that our observation should be engrossed by an object which, when analysed, seems to possess no claim to interest or even to notice. This unaccountable feeling I have often experienced, and I believe I am not singular. but never in so remarkable a degree as upon this occasion. My friend O'Connor, having disposed of his fair partner, was crossing the room for the purpose of joining me, in doing which I was surprised to see him exchange a familiar, almost a cordial, greeting with the object of my curiosity. I say I was surprised, for independent of his very questionable appearance, it struck me as strange that though so constantly associated with O'Connor, and, as I thought, personally acquainted with all his intimates, I had never before even seen this individual. I did not fail immediately to ask him who this gentleman was. I thought he seemed slightly embarrassed, but after a moment's pause he laughingly said that his friend over the way was too mysterious a personage to have his name announced in so giddy a scene as the present; but that on the morrow he would furnish me with all the information which I could desire. There was, I thought, in his affected jocularity a real awkwardness which appeared to me unaccountable, and consequently increased my curiosity; its gratification, however, I was obliged to defer. At length, wearied with witnessing amusements in which I could not sympathise, I left the room, and did not see O'Connor until late in the next day.

I had ridden down towards the castle for the purpose of visiting the O'Connors, and had nearly reached the avenue leading to the mansion, when I met my friend. He was also mounted; and having answered my inquiries respecting his mother, he easily persuaded me to accompany him in his ramble. We had chatted as usual for some time, when, after a pause, O'Connor said:

'By the way, Purcell, you expressed some curiosity respecting the tall, handsome fellow to whom I spoke last night.'

'I certainly did question you about a *tall* gentleman, but was not aware of his claims to beauty,' replied I.

'Well, that is as it may be,' said he; 'the ladies think him handsome, and their opinion upon that score is more valuable than yours or mine. Do you know,' he continued, 'I sometimes feel half sorry that I ever made the fellow's acquaintance: he is quite a marked man here, and they tell stories of him that are anything but reputable, though I am sure without foundation. I think I know enough about him to warrant me in saying so.'

'May I ask his name?' inquired I.

'Oh! did not I tell you his name?' rejoined he. 'You should have heard that first; he and his name are equally well known. You will recognise the individual at once when I tell you that his name is—Fitzgerald.'

'Fitzgerald!' I repeated. 'Fitzgerald!—can it be Fitzgerald the duellist?'

'Upon my word you have hit it,' replied he, laughing; 'but you have accompanied the discovery with a look of horror more tragic than appropriate. He is not the monster you take him for—he has a good deal of old Irish pride; his temper is hasty, and he has been unfortunately thrown in the way of men who have not made allowance for these things. I am convinced that in every case in which Fitzgerald has fought, if the truth could be discovered, he would be found to have acted throughout upon the defensive. No man is mad enough to risk his own life, except when the doing so is an alternative to submitting tamely to what he considers an insult. I am certain that no man ever engaged in a duel under the consciousness that he had acted an intentionally aggressive part.'

'When did you make his acquaintance?' said I.

'About two years ago,' he replied. 'I met him in France, and you know when one is abroad it is an ungracious task to reject the advances of one's countryman, otherwise I think I should have avoided his society—less upon my own account than because I am sure the acquaintance would be a source of continual though groundless uneasiness to my mother. I know, therefore, that you will not unnecessarily mention its existence to her.'

I gave him the desired assurance, and added:

'May I ask you. O'Connor, if, indeed, it be a fair question, whether this Fitzgerald at any time attempted to engage you in anything like gaming?'

This question was suggested by my having frequently heard Fitzgerald mentioned as a noted gambler, and sometimes even as a blackleg. O'Connor seemed, I thought, slightly embarrassed. He answered:

'No, no—I cannot say that he ever attempted anything of the kind. I certainly have played with him, but never lost to any serious amount; nor can I recollect that he ever solicited me—indeed he knows that I have a strong objection to deep play. *You* must be aware that my finances could not bear much pruning down. I never lost more to him at a sitting than about five pounds, which you know is nothing. No, you wrong him if you imagine that he attached himself to me merely for the sake of such contemptible winnings as those which a broken-down Irish gentleman could afford him. Come, Purcell, you are too hard upon him—you judge only by report; you must see him, and decide for yourself.—Suppose we call upon him now; he is at the inn, in the High Street, not a mile off.'

I declined the proposal drily.

'Your caution is too easily alarmed,' said he. 'I do not wish you to make this man your bosom friend: I merely desire that you should see and speak to him, and if you form any acquaintance with him, it must be of that slight nature which can be dropped or continued at pleasure.'

From the time that O'Connor had announced the fact that his friend was no other than the notorious Fitzgerald, a foreboding of something calamitous had come upon me, and it now occurred to me that if any unpleasantness were to be feared as likely to result to O'Connor from their connection, I might find my attempts to extricate him much facilitated by my being acquainted, however slightly, with Fitzgerald. I know not whether the idea was reasonable—it was certainly natural; and I told O'Connor that upon second thoughts I would ride down with him to the town, and wait upon Mr. Fitzgerald.

We found him at home; and chatted with him for a considerable time. To my surprise his manners were perfectly those of a gentleman, and his conversation, if not peculiarly engaging, was certainly amusing. The politeness of his demeanour, and the easy fluency with which he told his stories and his anecdotes, many of them curious, and all more or less entertaining, accounted to my mind at once for the facility with which he had improved his acquaintance with O'Connor; and when he pressed upon us an invitation to sup with him that night, I had almost joined O'Connor in accepting it. I determined, however, against doing so, for I had no wish to be on terms of familiarity with Mr. Fitzgerald; and I knew that one evening spent together as he proposed would go further towards establishing an intimacy between us than fifty morning visits could do. When I arose to depart, it was with feelings almost favourable to Fitzgerald; indeed I was more than half ashamed to acknowledge to my companion how complete a revolution in my opinion respecting his friend half an hour's conversation with him had wrought. His appearance certainly *was* against him; but then, under the influence of his manner, one lost sight of much of its ungainliness, and of nearly all its vulgarity; and, on the whole, I felt convinced that report had done him grievous wrong, inasmuch as anybody, by an observance of the common courtesies of society, might easily avoid coming into personal collision with a gentleman so studiously polite as Fitzgerald. At parting, O'Connor requested me to call upon him the next day, as he intended to make trial of the merits of a pair of greyhounds, which he had thoughts of purchasing; adding, that if he could escape in anything like tolerable time from Fitzgerald's supper-party, he would take the field soon after ten on the next morning. At the appointed hour, or perhaps a little later, I dismounted at Castle Connor; and, on entering the hall, I observed a gentleman issuing from O'Connor's private room. I recognised him, as he approached, as a Mr. M'Donough, and, being but slightly acquainted with him, was about to pass him with a bow, when he stopped me. There was something in his manner which struck me as odd; he seemed a good deal flurried if not agitated, and said, in a hurried tone:

'This is a very foolish business, Mr. Purcell. You have some influence with my friend O'Connor; I hope you can induce him to adopt some more moderate line of conduct than that he has decided upon. If you will allow me, I will return for a moment with you, and talk over the matter again with O'Connor.'

As M'Donough uttered these words, I felt that sudden sinking of the heart which accompanies the immediate anticipation of something dreaded and dreadful. I was instantly convinced that O'Connor had quarrelled with Fitzgerald, and I knew that if such were the case, nothing short of a miracle could extricate him from the consequences. I signed to M'Donough to lead the way, and we entered the little study together. O'Connor was standing with his back to the fire; on the table lay the breakfast-things in the disorder in which a hurried meal had left them; and on another smaller table, placed near the hearth, lay pen, ink, and paper. As soon as O'Connor saw me, he came forward and shook me cordially by the hand.

'My dear Purcell,' said he, 'you are the very man I wanted. I have got into an ugly scrape, and I trust to my friends to get me out of it.'

'You have had no dispute with that man—that Fitzgerald, I hope,' said I, giving utterance to the conjecture whose truth I most dreaded.

'Faith, I cannot say exactly what passed between us,' said he, 'inasmuch as I was at the time nearly half seas over; but of this much I am certain, that we exchanged angry words last night. I lost my temper most confoundedly; but, as well as I can recollect, he appeared perfectly cool and collected. What he said was, therefore, deliberately said, and on that account must be resented.'

'My dear O'Connor, are you mad?' I exclaimed. 'Why will you seek to drive to a deadly issue a few hasty words, uttered under the influence of wine, and forgotten almost as soon as uttered? A quarrel with Fitzgerald it is twenty chances to one would terminate fatally to you.'

'It is exactly because Fitzgerald *is* such an accomplished shot,' said he, 'that I become liable to the most injurious and intolerable suspicions if I submit to anything from him which could be construed into an affront; and for that reason Fitzgerald is the very last man to whom I would concede an inch in a case of honour.'

'I do not require you to make any, the slightest sacrifice of what you term your honour,' I replied; 'but if you have actually written a challenge to Fitzgerald, as I suspect you have done, I conjure you to reconsider the matter before you despatch it. From all that I have heard you say, Fitzgerald has more to complain of in the altercation which has taken place than you. You owe it to your only surviving parent not to thrust yourself thus wantonly upon—I will say it, the most appalling danger. Nobody, my dear O'Connor, can have a doubt of your courage; and if at any time, which God forbid, you shall be called upon thus to risk your life, you should have it in your power to enter the field under the consciousness that you have acted throughout temperately and like a man, and not, as I fear you now would do, having rashly and most causelessly endangered your own life and that of your friend.'

'I believe, Purcell, your are right,' said he. 'I believe *I have* viewed the matter in too decided a light; my note, I think, scarcely allows him an honourable alternative, and that is certainly going a step too far—further than I intended. Mr. M'Donough, I'll thank you to hand me the note.'

He broke the seal, and, casting his eye hastily over it, he continued:

'It is, indeed, a monument of folly. I am very glad, Purcell, you happened to come in, otherwise it would have reached its destination by this time.'

He threw it into the fire; and, after a moment's pause, resumed:

'You must not mistake me, however. I am perfectly satisfied as to the propriety, nay, the necessity, of communicating with Fitzgerald. The difficulty is in what tone I should address him. I cannot say that the man directly affronted me—I cannot recollect any one expression which I could lay hold upon as offensive—but his language was ambiguous, and admitted frequently of the most insulting construction, and his manner throughout was insupportably domineering. I know it impressed me with the idea that he presumed upon his reputation as a *Dead shot*, and that would be utterly unendurable'

'I would now recommend, as I have already done,' said M'Donough, 'that if you write to Fitzgerald, it should be in such a strain as to leave him at perfect liberty, without a compromise of honour, in a friendly way, to satisfy your doubts as to his conduct.'

I seconded the proposal warmly, and O'Connor, in a few minutes, finished a note, which he desired us to read. It was to this effect:

O'Connor, of Castle Connor, feeling that some expressions employed by Mr. Fitzgerald upon last night, admitted of a construction offensive to him, and injurious to his character, requests to know whether Mr. Fitzgerald intended to convey such a meaning.

CASTLE CONNOR, *Thursday morning.*

This note was consigned to the care of Mr. M'Donough, who forthwith departed to execute his mission. The sound of his horse's hoofs, as he rode rapidly away, struck heavily at my heart; but I found some satisfaction in the reflection that M'Donough appeared as averse from extreme measures as I was myself, for I well knew, with respect to the final result of the affair, that as much depended upon the tone adopted by the *Second*, as upon the nature of the written communication.

I have seldom passed a more anxious hour than that which intervened between the departure and the return of that gentleman. Every instant I imagined I heard the tramp of a horse approaching, and every time that a door opened I fancied it was to give entrance to the eagerly expected courier. At length I did hear the hollow and rapid tread of a horse's hoof upon the avenue. It approached—it stopped—a hurried step traversed the hall—the room door opened, and M'Donough entered.

'You have made great haste,' said O'Connor; 'did you find him at home?'

'I did,' replied M'Donough, 'and made the greater haste as Fitzgerald did not let me know the contents of his reply.'

At the same time he handed a note to O'Connor, who instantly broke the seal. The words were as follow:

Mr. Fitzgerald regrets that anything which has fallen from him should have appeared to Mr. O'Connor to be intended to convey a reflection upon his honour (none such having been meant), and begs leave to disavow any wish to quarrel unnecessarily with Mr. O'Connor.

T—INN, *Thursday morning.*

I cannot describe how much I felt relieved on reading the above communication. I took O'Connor's hand and pressed it warmly, but my emotions were deeper and stronger than I cared to show, for I was convinced that he had escaped a most imminent danger. Nobody whose notions upon the subject are derived from the duelling of modern times, in which matters are conducted without any very sanguinary determination upon either side, and with equal want of skill and coolness by both parties, can form a just estimate of the danger incurred by one who ventured to encounter a duellist of the old school. Perfect coolness in the field, and a steadiness and accuracy (which to the unpractised appeared almost miraculous) in the use of the pistol, formed the characteristics of this class; and in addition to this there generally existed a kind of professional pride, which prompted the duellist, in default of any more malignant feeling, from motives of mere vanity, to seek the life of his antagonist. Fitzgerald's career had been a remarkably successful one, and I knew that out of thirteen duels which he had fought in Ireland, in nine cases he had *killed* his man. In those days one never heard of the parties leaving the field, as not unfrequently now occurs, without blood having been spilt; and the odds were, of course, in all cases tremendously against a young and unpractised man, when matched with an experienced antagonist. My impression respecting the magnitude of the danger which my friend had incurred was therefore by no means unwarranted.

I now questioned O'Connor more accurately respecting the circumstances of his quarrel with Fitzgerald. It arose from some dispute respecting the application of a rule of piquet, at which game they had been playing, each interpreting it favourably to himself, and O'Connor, having lost considerably, was in no mood to conduct an argument with temper— an altercation ensued, and that of rather a pungent nature, and the result was that he left Fitzgerald's room rather abruptly, determined to demand an explanation in the most peremptory tone. For this purpose he had sent for M'Donough, and had commissioned him to deliver the note, which my arrival had fortunately intercepted.

As it was now past noon, O'Connor made me promise to remain with him to dinner; and we sat down a party of three, all in high spirits at the termination of our anxieties. It is necessary to mention, for the purpose of accounting for what follows, that Mrs. O'Connor, or, as she was more euphoniously styled, the lady of Castle Connor, was precluded by ill-health from taking her place at the dinner-table, and, indeed, seldom left her room before four o'clock.[4] We were sitting after dinner sipping our claret, and talking, and laughing, and enjoying ourselves exceedingly, when a servant, stepping into the room, informed his master that a gentleman wanted to speak with him.

'Request him, with my compliments, to walk in,' said O'Connor; and in a few moments a gentleman entered the room.

His appearance was anything but prepossessing. He was a little above the middle size, spare, and raw-boned; his face very red, his features sharp and bluish, and his age might be about sixty. His attire savoured a good deal of the *Shabby-Genteel*; his clothes, which had much of tarnished and faded pretension about them, did not fit him, and had not improbably fluttered in the stalls of Plunket Street. We had risen on his entrance, and

---

4   It is scarcely necessary to remind the reader, that at the period spoken of, the impor-
     tant hour of dinner occurred very nearly at noon.

O'Connor had twice requested of him to take a chair at the table, without his hearing, or at least noticing, the invitation; while with a slow pace, and with an air of mingled importance and effrontery, he advanced into the centre of the apartment, and regarding our small party with a supercilious air, he said:

'I take the liberty of introducing myself—I am Captain M'Creagh, formerly of the—infantry. My business here is with a Mr. O'Connor, and the sooner it is despatched the better.'

'I am the gentleman you name,' said O'Connor; 'and as you appear impatient, we had better proceed to your commission without delay.'

'Then, Mr. O'Connor, you will please to read that note,' said the captain, placing a sealed paper in his hand.

O'Connor read it through, and then observed:

'This is very extraordinary indeed. This note appears to me perfectly unaccountable.'

'You are very young, Mr. O'Connor,' said the captain, with vulgar familiarity; 'but, without much experience in these matters, I think you might have anticipated something like this. You know the old saying, "Second thoughts are best;" and so they are like to prove, by G—!'

'You will have no objection, Captain M'Creagh, on the part of your friend, to my reading this note to these gentlemen; they are both confidential friends of mine, and one of them has already acted for me in this business.'

'I can have no objection,' replied the captain, 'to your doing what you please with your own. I have nothing more to do with that note once I put it safe into your hand; and when that is once done, it is all one to me, if you read it to half the world—that's *your* concern, and no affair of mine.'

O'Connor then read the following:

Mr. Fitzgerald begs leave to state, that upon re-perusing Mr. O'Connor's communication of this morning carefully, with an experienced friend, he is forced to consider himself as challenged. His friend, Captain M'Creagh, has been empowered by him to make all the necessary arrangements.

T—INN, *Thursday*.

I can hardly describe the astonishment with which I heard this note. I turned to the captain, and said:

'Surely, sir, there is some mistake in all this?'

'Not the slightest, I'll assure you, sir.' said he, coolly; 'the case is a very clear one, and I think my friend has pretty well made up his mind upon it. May I request your answer?' he continued, turning to O'Connor; 'time is precious, you know.'

O'Connor expressed his willingness to comply with the suggestion, and in a few minutes had folded and directed the following rejoinder:

> Mr. O'Connor having received a satisfactory explanation from Mr. Fitzgerald, of the language used by that gentleman, feels that there no longer exists any grounds for misunderstanding, and wishes further to state, that the note of which Mr. Fitzgerald speaks was not intended as a challenge.

With this note the captain departed; and as we did not doubt that the message which he had delivered had been suggested by some unintentional misconstruction of O'Connor's first billet, we felt assured that the conclusion of his last note would set the matter at rest. In this belief, however, we were mistaken; before we had left the table, and in an incredibly short time, the captain returned. He entered the room with a countenance evidently tasked to avoid expressing the satisfaction which a consciousness of the nature of his mission had conferred; but in spite of all his efforts to look gravely unconcerned, there was a twinkle in the small grey eye, and an almost imperceptible motion in the corner of the mouth, which sufficiently betrayed his internal glee, as he placed a note in the hand of O'Connor. As the young man cast his eye over it, he coloured deeply, and turning to M'Donough, he said:

> 'You will have the goodness to make all the necessary arrangements for a meeting. Something has occurred to render one between me and Mr. Fitzgerald inevitable. Understand me literally, when I say that it is now totally impossible that this affair should be amicably arranged. You will have the goodness, M'Donough, to let me know as soon as all the particulars are arranged. Purcell,' he continued, 'will you have the kindness to accompany me?' and having bowed to M'Creagh, we left the room.

As I closed the door after me, I heard the captain laugh, and thought I could distinguish the words—'By—I knew Fitzgerald would bring him to his way of thinking before he stopped.'

I followed O'Connor into his study, and on entering, the door being closed, he showed me the communication which had determined him upon hostilities. Its language was grossly impertinent, and it concluded by actually threatening to '*post*' him, in case he further attempted 'to be *off*.' I cannot describe the agony of indignation in which O'Connor writhed under this insult. He said repeatedly that 'he was a degraded and dishohoured man,' that 'he was dragged into the field,' that 'there was ignominy in the very thought that such a letter should have been directed to him.' It was in vain that I reasoned against this impression; the conviction that he had been disgraced had taken possession of his mind. He said again and again that nothing but his *death* could remove the stain which his indecision had cast upon the name of his family. I hurried to the hall, on hearing M'Donough and the captain passing, and reached the door just in time to hear the latter say, as he mounted his horse:

'All the rest can be arranged on the spot; and so farewell, Mr. M'Donough—we'll meet at Philippi, you know;' and with this classical allusion, which was accompanied with a grin and a bow, and probably served many such occasions, the captain took his departure.

M'Donough briefly stated the few particulars which had been arranged. The parties were to meet at the stand-house, in the race-ground, which lay at about an equal distance between Castle Connor and the town of T—. The hour appointed was half-past five on the next morning, at which time the twilight would be sufficiently advanced to afford a distinct view; and the weapons to be employed were *pistols*—M'Creagh having claimed, on the part of his friend, all the advantages of the *challenged* party, and having, consequently, insisted upon the choice of *'tools,'* as he expressed himself; and it was further stipulated that the utmost secrecy should be observed, as Fitzgerald would incur great risk from the violence of the peasantry, in case the affair took wind. These conditions were, of course, agreed upon by O'Connor, and M'Donough left the castle, having appointed four o'clock upon the next morning as the hour of his return, by which time it would be his business to provide everything necessary for the meeting. On his departure, O'Connor requested me to remain with him upon that evening, saying that 'he could not bear to be alone with his mother.' It was to me a most painful request, but at the same time one which I could not think of refusing. I felt, however, that the difficulty at least of the task which I had to perform would be in some measure mitigated by the arrival of two relations of O'Connor upon that evening.

'It is very fortunate,' said O'Connor, whose thoughts had been running upon the same subject, 'that the O'Gradys will be with us to-night; their gaiety and good-humour will relieve us from a heavy task. I trust that nothing may occur to prevent their coming.' Fervently concurring in the same wish, I accompanied O'Connor into the parlour, there to await the arrival of his mother.

God grant that I may never spend such another evening! The O'Gradys *did* come, but their high and noisy spirits, so far from relieving me, did but give additional gloom to the despondency, I might say the despair, which filled my heart with misery—the terrible forebodings which I could not for an instant silence, turned their laughter into discord, and seemed to mock the smiles and jests of the unconscious party. When I turned my eyes upon the mother, I thought I never had seen her look so proudly and so lovingly upon her son before—it cut me to the heart—oh, how cruelly I was deceiving her! I was a hundred times on the very point of start-ing up, and, at all hazards, declaring to her how matters were; but other feelings subdued my better emotions. Oh, what monsters are we made of by the fashions of the world! how are our kindlier and nobler feelings warped or destroyed by their baleful influences! I felt that it would not be *honourable*, that it would not be *etiquette*, to betray O'Connor's secret. I sacrificed a higher and a nobler duty than I have since been called upon to perform, to the dastardly fear of bearing the unmerited censure of a world from which I was about to retire. O Fashion! thou gaudy idol, whose feet are red with the blood of human sacrifice, would I had always felt towards thee as I now do!

O'Connor was not dejected; on the contrary, he joined with loud and lively alacrity in the hilarity of the little party; but I could see in the flush of his cheek, and in the unusual brightness of his eye, all the excitement of fever—he was making an effort almost beyond his strength, but he suc-ceeded—and when his mother rose to leave the room, it was with the im-pression that her son was the gayest and most light-hearted of the company. Twice or thrice she had risen with the intention of retiring, but O'Connor, with an eagerness which I alone could understand, had persuaded her to remain until the usual hour of her departure had long passed; and when at length she arose, declaring that she could not possibly stay longer, I alone could comprehend the desolate change which passed over his manner; and when I saw them part, it was with the sickening conviction that those two beings, so dear to one another, so loved, so cherished, should meet no more.

O'Connor briefly informed his cousins of the position in which he was placed, requesting them at the same time to accompany him to the field, and this having been settled, we separated, each to his own apart-ment. I had wished to sit up with O'Connor, who had matters to arrange sufficient to employ him until the hour appointed for M'Donough's visit; but he would not hear of it, and I was forced, though sorely against my will, to leave him without a companion. I went to my room, and, in a state of excitement which I cannot describe, I paced for hours up and down its narrow precincts. I could not—who could?—analyse the strange, con-tradictory, torturing feelings which, while I recoiled in shrinking horror from the scene which the morning was to bring, yet forced me to wish the intervening time annihilated; each hour that the clock told seemed to vibrate and tinkle through every nerve; my agitation was dreadful; fancy conjured up the forms of those who filled my thoughts with more than the vividness of reality; things seemed to glide through the dusky shadows of the room. I saw the dreaded form of Fitzgerald—I heard the hated laugh of the captain—and again the features of O'Connor would appear before me, with ghastly distinctness, pale and writhed in death, the gouts of gore clotted in the mouth, and the eye-balls glared and staring. Scared with the visions which seemed to throng with unceasing rapidity and vividness, I threw open the window and looked out upon the quiet scene around. I turned my eyes in the direction of the town; a heavy cloud was lowering darkly about it, and I, in impious frenzy, prayed to God that it might burst in avenging fires upon the murderous wretch who lay beneath. At length, sick and giddy with excess of excitement, I threw myself upon the bed without removing my clothes, and endeavoured to compose myself so far as to remain quiet until the hour for our assembling should arrive.

A few minutes before four o'clock I stole noiselessly downstairs, and made my way to the small study already mentioned. A candle was burning within; and, when I opened the door, O'Connor was reading a book, which, on seeing me, he hastily closed, colouring slightly as he did so. We exchanged a cordial but mournful greeting; and after a slight pause he said, laying his hand upon the volume which he had shut a moment before:

'Purcell, I feel perfectly calm, though I cannot say that I have much hope as to the issue of this morning's rencounter. I shall avoid half the danger. If I must fall, I am determined I shall not go down to the grave with his blood upon my hands. I have resolved not to fire at Fitzgerald—that is, to fire in such a direction as to assure myself against hitting him. Do not say a word of this to the O'Gradys. Your doing so would only produce fruitless altercation; they could not understand my motives. I feel convinced that I shall not leave the field alive. If I must die to-day, I shall avoid an awful aggravation of wretchedness. Purcell,' he continued, after a little space, 'I was so weak as to feel almost ashamed of the manner in which I was occupied as you entered the room. Yes, I—I who will be, before this evening, a cold and lifeless clod, was ashamed to have spent my last moment of reflection in prayer. God pardon me! God pardon me!' he repeated.

I took his hand and pressed it, but I could not speak. I sought for words of comfort, but they would not come. To have uttered one cheering sentence I must have contradicted every impression of my own mind. I felt too much awed to attempt it. Shortly afterwards, M'Donough arrived. No wretched patient ever underwent a more thrilling revulsion at the first sight of the case of surgical instruments under which he had to suffer, than did I upon beholding a certain oblong flat mahogany box, bound with brass, and of about two feet in length, laid upon the table in the hall. O'Connor, thanking him for his punctuality, requested him to come into his study for a moment, when, with a melancholy collectedness, he proceeded to make arrangements for our witnessing his will. The document was a brief one, and the whole matter was just arranged, when the two O'Gradys crept softly into the room.

'So! last will and testament,' said the elder. 'Why, you have a very *blue* notion of these matters. I tell you, you need not be uneasy. I remember very well, when young Ryan of Ballykealey met M'Neil the duellist, bets ran twenty to one against him. I stole away from school, and had a peep at the fun as well as the best of them. They fired together. Ryan received the ball through the collar of his coat, and M'Neil in the temple; he spun like a top: it was a most unexpected thing, and disappointed his friends damnably. It was admitted, however, to have been very pretty shooting upon both sides. To be sure,' he continued, pointing to the will, 'you are in the right to keep upon the safe side of fortune; but then, there is no occasion to be altogether so devilish down in the mouth as you appear to be.'

'You will allow,' said O'Connor, 'that the chances are heavily against me.'

'Why, let me see,' he replied, 'not so hollow a thin,, either. Let me see, we'll say about four to one against you; you may chance to throw doublets like him I told you of, and then what becomes of the odds I'd like to know? But let things go as they will, I'll give and take four to one, in pounds and tens of pounds. There, M'Donough, there's a *get* for you; b—t me, if it is not. Poh! the fellow is stolen away,' he continued, observing that the object of his proposal had left the room; 'but d—it, Purcell, you are fond of a *soft thing*, too, in a quiet way—I'm sure you are—so curse me if I do not make you the same offer-is it a go?'

I was too much disgusted to make any reply, but I believe my looks expressed my feelings sufficiently, for in a moment he said:

'Well, I see there is nothing to be done, so we may as well be stirring. M'Donough, myself, and my brother will saddle the horses in a jiffy, while you and Purcell settle anything which remains to be arranged.'

So saying, he left the room with as much alacrity as if it were to prepare for a fox-hunt. Selfish, heartless fool! I have often since heard him spoken of as *a cursed good-natured dog* and a D—*good fellow*; but such eulogies as these are not calculated to mitigate the abhorrence with which his conduct upon that morning inspired me.

The chill mists of night were still hovering on the landscape as our party left the castle. It was a raw, comfortless morning—a kind of drizzling fog hung heavily over the scene, dimming the light of the sun, which had now risen, into a pale and even a grey glimmer. As the appointed hour was fast approaching, it was proposed that we should enter the race-ground at a point close to the stand-house—a measure which would save us a ride of nearly two miles, over a broken road; at which distance there was an open entrance into the race-ground. Here, accordingly, we dismounted, and leaving our horses in the care of a country fellow who happened to be stirring at that early hour, we proceeded up a narrow lane, over a side wall of which we were to climb into the open ground where stood the now deserted building, under which the meeting was to take place. Our progress was intercepted by the unexpected appearance of an old woman, who, in the scarlet cloak which is the picturesque characteristic of the female peasantry of the south, was moving slowly down the avenue to meet us, uttering that peculiarly wild and piteous lamentation well known by the name of 'the Irish cry,' accompanied throughout by all the customary gesticulation of passionate grief. This rencounter was more awkward than we had at first anticipated; for, upon a nearer approach, the person proved to be no other than an old attached dependent of the family, and who had her-self nursed O'Connor. She quickened her pace as we advanced almost to a run; and, throwing her arms round O'Connor's neck, she poured forth such a torrent of lamentation, reproach, and endearment, as showed that she was aware of the nature of our purpose, whence and by what means I knew not. It was in vain that he sought to satisfy her by evasion, and gently to extricate himself from her embrace. She knelt upon the ground, and clasped her arms round his legs, uttering all the while such touching supplications, such cutting and passionate expressions of woe, as went to my very heart.

At length, with much difficulty, we passed this most painful interruption; and, crossing the boundary wall, were placed beyond her reach. The O'Gradys damned her for a troublesome hag, and passed on with O'Connor, but I remained behind for a moment. The poor woman looked hopelessly at the high wall which separated her from him she had loved from infancy, and to be with whom at that minute she would have given worlds, she took her seat upon a solitary stone under the opposite wall, and there, in a low, subdued key, she continued to utter her sorrow in words so desolate, yet expressing such a tenderness of devotion as wrung my heart.

'My poor woman,' I said, laying my hand gently upon her shoulder, 'you will make yourself ill; the morning is very cold, and your cloak is but a thin defence against the damp and chill. Pray return home and take this; it may be useful to you.'

So saying, I dropped a purse, with what money I had about me, into her lap, but it lay there unheeded; she did not hear me.

'Oh I my child, my child, my darlin',' she sobbed, 'are you gone from me? are you gone from me? Ah, mavourneen, mavourneen, you'll never come back alive to me again. The crathur that slept on my bosom—the lovin' crathur that I was so proud of—they'll kill him, they'll kill him. Oh, voh! voh!'

The affecting tone, the feeling, the abandonment with which all this was uttered, none can conceive who have not heard the lamentations of the Irish peasantry. It brought tears to my eyes. I saw that no consolation of mine could soothe her grief, so I turned and departed; but as I rapidly traversed the level sward which separated me from my companions, now considerably in advance, I could still hear the wailings of the solitary mourner.

As we approached the stand-house, it was evident that our antagonists had already arrived. Our path lay by the side of a high fence constructed of loose stones, and on turning a sharp angle at its extremity, we found ourselves close to the appointed spot, and within a few yards of a crowd of persons, some mounted and some on foot, evidently awaiting our arrival. The affair had unaccountably taken wind, as the number of the expectants clearly showed; but for this there was now no remedy.

As our little party advanced we were met and saluted by several acquaintances, whom curiosity, if no deeper feeling, had brought to the place. Fitzgerald and the Captain had arrived, and having dismounted, were standing upon the sod. The former, as we approached, bowed slightly and sullenly—while the latter, evidently in high good humour, made his most courteous obeisance. No time was to be lost; and the two seconds immediately withdrew to a slight distance, for the purpose of completing the last minute arrangements. It was a brief but horrible interval—each returned to his principal to communicate the result, which was soon caught up and repeated from mouth to mouth throughout the crowd. I felt a strange and insurmountable reluctance to hear the sickening particulars detailed; and as I stood irresolute at some distance from the principal parties, a top-booted squireen, with a hunting whip in his hand, bustling up to a companion of his, exclaimed:

"Not fire together!—did you ever hear the like? If Fitzgerald gets the first shot all is over. M'Donough sold the pass, by—, and that is the long and the short of it.'

The parties now moved down a little to a small level space, suited to the purpose; and the captain, addressing M'Donough, said:

'Mr. M'Donough, you'll now have the goodness to toss for choice of ground; as the light comes from the east the line must of course run north and south. Will you be so obliging as to toss up a crown-piece, while I call?'

A coin was instantly chucked into the air. The captain cried, 'Harp.' The *head* was uppermost, and M'Donough immediately made choice of the southern point at which to place his friend—a position which it will be easily seen had the advantage of turning his back upon the light—no trifling superiority of location. The captain turned with a kind of laugh, and said:

'By—, sir, you are as cunning as a dead pig; but you forgot one thing. My friend is a left-handed gunner, though never a bit the worse for that; so you see there is no odds as far as the choice of light goes.'

He then proceeded to measure nine paces in a direction running north and south, and the principals took their ground.

'I must be troublesome to you once again, Mr. M'Donough. One toss more, and everything is complete. We must settle who is to have the *first slap.*'

A piece of money was again thrown into the air; again the captain lost the toss and M'Donough proceeded to load the pistols. I happened to stand near Fitzgerald, and I overheard the captain, with a chuckle, say something to him in which the word 'cravat' was repeated. It instantly occurred to me that the captain's attention was directed to a bright-coloured muffler which O'Connor wore round his neck, and which would afford his antagonist a distinct and favourable mark. I instantly urged him to remove it, and at length, with difficulty, succeeded. He seemed perfectly careless as to any precaution. Everything was now ready; the pistol was placed in O'Connor's hand, and he only awaited the word from the captain.

M'Creagh then said:

'Mr. M'Donough, is your principal ready?'

M'Donough replied in the affirmative; and, after a slight pause, the captain, as had been arranged, uttered the words:

'Ready—fire.'

O'Connor fired, but so wide of the mark that some one in the crowd exclaimed:

'Fired in the air.'

'Who says he fired in the air?' thundered Fitzgerald. 'By—he lies, whoever he is.' There was a silence. 'But even if he was fool enough to fire in the air, it is not in *his* power to put an end to the quarrel by *that*. D—my soul, if I am come here to be played with like a child, and by the Almighty—you shall hear more of this, each and everyone of you, before I'm satisfied.'

A kind of low murmur, or rather groan, was now raised, and a slight motion was observable in the crowd, as if to intercept Fitzgerald's passage to his horse. M'Creagh, drawing the horse close to the spot where Fitzgerald stood, threatened, with the most awful imprecations, 'to blow the brains out of the first man who should dare to press on them.'

O'Connor now interfered, requesting the crowd to forbear, and some degree of order was restored. He then said, 'that in firing as he did, he had no intention whatever of waiving his right of firing upon Fitzgerald, and of depriving that gentleman of his right of prosecuting the affair to the utmost—that if any person present imagined that he intended to fire in the air, he begged to set him right; since, so far from seeking to exort an unwilling reconciliation, he was determined that no power on earth should induce him to concede one inch of ground to Mr. Fitzgerald.'

This announcement was received with a shout by the crowd, who now resumed their places at either side of the plot of ground which had been measured. The principals took their places once more, and M'Creagh proceeded, with the nicest and most anxious care, to load the pistols; and this task being accomplished, Fitzgerald whispered something in the Captain's ear, who instantly drew his friend's horse so as to place him within a step of his rider, and then tightened the girths. This accomplished, Fitzgerald proceeded deliberately to remove his coat, which he threw across his horse in front of the saddle; and then, with the assistance of M'Creagh, he rolled the shirt sleeve up to the shoulder, so as to leave the whole of his muscular arm perfectly naked. A cry of 'Coward, coward! butcher, butcher!' arose from the crowd. Fitzgerald paused.

'Do you object, Mr. M'Donough? and upon what grounds, if you please?' said he.

'Certainly he does not,' replied O'Connor; and, turning to M'Donough, he added, 'pray let there be no unnecessary delay.'

'There is no objection, then,' said Fitzgerald.

'I object,' said the younger of the O'Gradys, 'if nobody else will.'

' And who the devil are you, that *dares* to object?' shouted Fitzgerald; 'and what d—d presumption prompts you to *dare* to wag your tongue here?'

'I am Mr. O'Grady, of Castle Blake,' replied the young man, now much enraged; 'and by—, you shall answer for your language to me.'

'Shall I, by—? Shall I?' cried he, with a laugh of brutal scorn; 'the more the merrier, d—n the doubt of it—so now hold your tongue, for I promise you you shall have business enough of your own to think about, and that before long.'

There was an appalling ferocity in his tone and manner which no words could convey. He seemed transformed; he was actually like a man possessed. Was it possible, I thought, that I beheld the courteous gentleman, the gay, good-humoured retailer of amusing anecdote with whom, scarce two days ago, I had laughed and chatted, in the blasphemous and murderous ruffian who glared and stormed before me!

O'Connor interposed, and requested that time should not be unnecessarily lost.

'You have not got a second coat on?' inquired the Captain. 'I beg pardon, but my duty to my friend requires that I should ascertain the point.'

O'Connor replied in the negative. The Captain expressed himself as satisfied, adding, in what he meant to be a complimentary strain, 'that he knew Mr. O'Connor would scorn to employ padding or any unfair mode of protection.'

There was now a breathless silence. O'Connor stood perfectly motionless; and, excepting the death-like paleness of his features, he exhibited no sign of agitation. His eye was steady—his lip did not tremble—his attitude was calm. The Captain, having re-examined the priming of the pistols, placed one of them in the hand of Fitzgerald.—M'Donough inquired whether the parties were prepared, and having been answered in the affirmative, he proceeded to give the word, 'Ready.' Fitzgerald raised his hand, but almost instantly lowered it again. The crowd had pressed too much forward as it appeared, and his eye had been unsteadied by the flapping of the skirt of a frieze riding-coat worn by one of the spectators.

'In the name of my principal,' said the Captain, 'I must and do insist upon these gentlemen moving back a little. We ask but little; fair play, and no favour.'

The crowd moved as requested. M'Donough repeated his former question, and was answered as before. There was a breathless silence. Fitzgerald fixed his eye upon O'Connor. The appointed signal, 'Ready, fire!' was given. There was a pause while one might slowly reckon three—Fitzgerald fired—and O'Connor fell helplessly upon the ground.

'There is no time to be lost,' said M'Creagrh; 'for, by—, you have done for him.'

So saying, he threw himself upon his horse, and was instantly followed at a hard gallop by Fitzgerald.

'Cold-blooded murder, if ever murder was committed,' said O'Grady. 'He shall hang for it; d—n me, but he shall.'

A hopeless attempt was made to overtake the fugitives; but they were better mounted than any of their pursuers, and escaped with ease. Curses and actual yells of execration followed their course; and as, in crossing the brow of a neighbouring hill, they turned round in the saddle to observe if they were pursued, every gesture which could express fury and defiance was exhausted by the enraged and defeated multitude.

'Clear the way, boys,' said young O'Grady, who with me was kneeling beside O'Connor, while we supported him in our arms; 'do not press so close, and be d—d; can't you let the fresh air to him; don't you see he's dying?'

On opening his waistcoat we easily detected the wound: it was a little below the chest—a small blue mark, from which oozed a single heavy drop of blood.

'He is bleeding but little—that is a comfort at all events,' said one of the gentlemen who surrounded the wounded man.

Another suggested the expediency of his being removed homeward with as little delay as possible, and recommended, for this purpose, that a door should be removed from its hinges, and the patient, laid upon this, should be conveyed from the field. Upon this rude bier my poor friend was carried from that fatal ground towards Castle Connor. I walked close by his side, and observed every motion of his. He seldom opened his eyes, and was perfectly still, excepting a nervous *working* of the fingers, and a slight, almost imperceptible twitching of the features, which took place, however, only at intervals. The first word he uttered was spoken as we approached the entrance of the castle itself, when he said; repeatedly, 'The back way, the back way.' He feared lest his mother should meet him abruptly and without preparation; but although this fear was groundless, since she never left her room until late in the day, yet it was thought advisable, and, indeed, necessary, to caution all the servants most strongly against breathing a hint to their mistress of the events which had befallen.

Two or three gentlemen had ridden from the field one after another, promising that they should overtake our party before it reached the castle, bringing with them medical aid from one quarter or another; and we determined that Mrs. O'Connor should not know anything of the occurrence until the opinion of some professional man should have determined the extent of the injury which her son had sustained—a course of conduct which would at least have the effect of relieving her from the horrors of suspense. When O'Connor found himself in his own room, and laid upon his own bed, he appeared much revived—so much so, that I could not help admitting a strong hope that all might yet be well.

'After all, Purcell,' said he, with a melancholy smile, and speaking with evident difficulty, 'I believe I have got off with a trifling wound. I am sure it cannot be fatal I feel so little pain—almost none.'

I cautioned him against fatiguing himself by endeavouring to speak; and he remained quiet for a little time. At length he said:

'Purcell, I trust this lesson shall not have been given in vain. God has been very merciful to me; I feel—I have an internal confidence that I am not wounded mortally. Had I been fatally wounded—had I been killed upon the spot, only think on it'—and he closed his eyes as if the very thought made him dizzy—'struck down into the grave, unprepared as I am, in the very blossom of my sins, without a moment of repentance or of reflection; I must have been lost—lost for ever and ever.'

I prevailed upon him, with some difficulty, to abstain from such agitating reflections, and at length induced him to court such repose as his condition admitted of, by remaining perfectly silent, and as much as possible without motion.

O'Connor and I only were in the room; he had lain for some time in tolerable quiet, when I thought I distinguished the bustle attendant upon the arrival of some one at the castle, and went eagerly to the window, believing, or at least hoping, that the sounds might announce the approach of the medical man, whom we all longed most impatiently to see.

My conjecture was right; I had the satisfaction of seeing him dismount and prepare to enter the castle, when my observations were interrupted, and my attention was attracted by a smothered, gurgling sound proceeding from the bed in which lay the wounded man. I instantly turned round, and in doing so the spectacle which met my eyes was sufficiently shocking.

I had left O'Connor lying in the bed, supported by pillows, perfectly calm, and with his eyes closed: he was now lying nearly in the same position, his eyes open and almost starting from their sockets, with every feature pale and distorted as death, and vomiting blood in quantities that were frightful. I rushed to the door and called for assistance; the paroxysm, though violent, was brief, and O'Connor sank into a swoon so deep and death-like, that I feared he should waken no more.

The surgeon, a little, fussy man, but I believe with some skill to justify his pretensions, now entered the room, carry-ing his case of instruments, and followed by servants bearing basins and water and bandages of linen. He relieved our doubts by instantly assuring us that 'the patient' was still living; and at the same time professed his determination to take advantage of the muscular relaxation which the faint had induced to examine the wound—adding that a patient was more easily 'handled' when in a swoon than under other circumstances.

After examining the wound in front where the ball had entered, he passed his hand round beneath the shoulder, and after a little pause he shook his head, observing that he feared very much that one of the vertebrae was fatally injured, but that he could not say decidedly until his patient should revive a little. 'Though his language was very technical, and consequently to me nearly unintelligible, I could perceive plainly by his manner that he considered the case as almost hopeless.

O'Connor gradually gave some signs of returning animation, and at length was so far restored as to be enabled to speak. After some few general questions as to how he felt affected, etc., etc., the surgeon, placing his hand upon his leg and pressing it slightly, asked him if he felt any pressure upon the limb? O'Connor answered in the negative—he pressed harder, and repeated the question; still the answer was the same, till at length, by repeated experiments, he ascertained that all that part of the body which lay behind the wound was paralysed, proving that the spine must have received some fatal injury.

'Well, doctor,' said O'Connor, after the examination of the wound was over; 'well, I shall do, shan't I?'

The physician was silent for a moment, and then, as if with an effort, he replied:

'Indeed, my dear sir, it would not be honest to flatter you with much hope.'

'Eh?' said O'Connor with more alacrity than I had seen him exhibit since the morning; 'surely I did not hear you aright; I spoke of my recovery—surely there is no doubt; there can be none—speak frankly, doctor, for God's sake—am I dying?'

The surgeon was evidently no stoic, and his manner had extinguished in me every hope, even before he had uttered a word in reply.

'You are—you are indeed dying. There is no hope; I should but deceive you if I held out any.'

As the surgeon uttered these terrible words, the hands which O'Connor had stretched towards him while awaiting his reply fell powerless by his side; his head sank forward; it seemed as if horror and despair had unstrung every nerve and sinew; he appeared to collapse and shrink together as a plant might under the influence of a withering spell.

It has often been my fate, since then, to visit the chambers of death and of suffering; I have witnessed fearful agonies of body and of soul; the mysterious shudderings of the departing spirit, and the heart-rending desolation of the survivors; the severing of the tenderest ties, the piteous yearnings of unavailing love—of all these things the sad duties of my profession have made me a witness. But, generally speaking, I have observed in such scenes some thing to mitigate, if not the sorrows, at least the terrors, of death; the dying man seldom seems to feel the reality of his situation; a dull consciousness of approaching dissolution, a dim anticipation of unconsciousness and insensibility, are the feelings which most nearly border upon an appreciation of his state; the film of death seems to have overspread the mind's eye, objects lose their distinctness, and float cloudily before it, and the apathy and apparent indifference with which men recognise the sure advances of immediate death, rob that awful hour of much of its terrors, and the death-bed of its otherwise inevitable agonies.

This is a merciful dispensation; but the rule has its exceptions—its terrible exceptions. When a man is brought in an instant, by some sudden accident, to the very verge of the fathomless pit of death, with all his recollections awake, and his perceptions keenly and vividly alive, without previous illness to subdue the tone of the mind as to dull its apprehensions—then, and then only, the death-bed is truly terrible.

Oh, what a contrast did O'Connor afford as he lay in all the abject helplessness of undisguised terror upon his death-bed, to the proud composure with which he had taken the field that morning. I had always before thought of death as of a quiet sleep stealing gradually upon exhausted nature, made welcome by suffering, or, at least, softened by resignation; I had never before stood by the side of one upon whom the hand of death had been thus suddenly laid; I had never seen the tyrant arrayed in his terror till then. Never before or since have I seen horror so intensely depicted. It seemed actually as if O'Connor's mind had been unsettled by the shock; the few words he uttered were marked with all the incoherence of distraction; but it was not words that marked his despair most strongly, the appalling and heart-sickening groans that came from the terror-stricken and dying man must haunt me while I live; the expression, too, of hopeless, imploring agony with which he turned his eyes from object to object, I can never forget. At length, appearing suddenly to recollect himself, he said, with startling alertness, but in a voice so altered that I scarce could recognise the tones:

'Purcell, Purcell, go and tell my poor mother; she must know all, and then, quick, quick, quick, call your uncle, bring him here; I must have a chance.' He made a violent but fruitless effort to rise, and after a slight pause continued, with deep and urgent solemnity: 'Doctor, how long shall I live? Don't flatter me. Compliments at a death-bed are out of place; doctor, for God's sake, as you would not have my soul perish with my body, do not mock a dying man; have I an hour to live?'

'Certainly,' replied the surgeon; 'if you will but endeavour to keep yourself tranquil; otherwise I cannot answer for a moment.'

'Well, doctor,' said the patient, 'I will obey you; now, Purcell, my first and dearest friend, will you inform my poor mother of—of what you see, and return with your uncle; I know you will.'

I took the dear fellow's hand and kissed it, it was the only answer I could give, and left the room. I asked the first female servant I chanced to meet, if her mistress were yet up, and was answered in the affirmative. Without giving myself time to hesitate, I requested her to lead me to her lady's room, which she accordingly did; she entered first, I supposed to announce my name, and I followed closely; the poor mother said something, and held out her hands to welcome me; I strove for words; I could not speak, but nature found expression; I threw myself at her feet and covered her hands with kisses and tears. My manner was enough; with a quickness almost preternatural she understood it all; she simply said the words: 'O'Connor is killed;' she uttered no more.

How I left the room I know not; I rode madly to my uncle's residence, and brought him back with me—all the rest is a blank. I remember standing by O'Connor's bedside, and kissing the cold pallid forehead again and again; I remember the pale serenity of the beautiful features; I remember that I looked upon the dead face of my friend, and I remember no more.

For many months I lay writhing and raving in the frenzy of brain fever; a hundred times I stood tottering at the brink of death, and long after my restoration to bodily health was assured, it appeared doubtful whether I should ever be restored to reason. But God dealt very mercifully with me; His mighty hand rescued me from death and from madness when one or other appeared inevitable. As soon as I was permitted pen and ink, I wrote to the bereaved mother in a tone bordering upon frenzy. I accused myself of having made her childless; I called myself a murderer; I believed myself accursed; I could not find terms strong enough to express my abhorrence of my own conduct. But, oh! what an answer I received, so mild, so sweet, from the desolate, childless mother! its words spoke all that is beautiful in Christianity—it was forgiveness—it was resignation. I am convinced that to that letter, operating as it did upon a mind already predisposed, is owing my final determination to devote myself to that profession in which, for more than half a century, I have been a humble minister.

Years roll away, and we count them not as they pass, but their influence is not the less certain that it is silent; the deepest wounds are gradually healed, the keenest griefs are mitigated, and we, in character, feelings, tastes, and pursuits, become such altered beings, that but for some few indelible marks which past events must leave behind them, which time may soften, but can never efface; our very identity would be dubious. Who has not felt all this at one time or other? Who has not mournfully felt it? This trite, but natural train of reflection filled my mind as I approached the domain of Castle Connor some ten years after the occurrence of the events above narrated. Everything looked the same as when I had left it; the old trees stood as graceful and as grand as ever; no plough had violated the soft green sward; no utilitarian hand had constrained the wanderings of the clear and sportive stream, or disturbed the lichen-covered rocks through which it gushed, or the wild coppice that over-shadowed its sequestered nooks—but the eye that looked upon these things was altered, and memory was busy with other days, shrouding in sadness every beauty that met my sight.

As I approached the castle my emotions became so acutely painful that I had almost returned the way I came, without accomplishing the purpose for which I had gone thus far; and nothing but the conviction that my having been in the neighbourhood of Castle Connor without visiting its desolate mistress would render me justly liable to the severest censure, could overcome my reluctance to encountering the heavy task which was before me. I recognised the old servant who opened the door, but he did not know me. I was completely changed; suffering of body and mind had altered me in feature and in bearing, as much as in character. I asked the man whether his mistress ever saw visitors. He answered:

'But seldom; perhaps, however, if she knew that an old friend wished to see her for a few minutes, she would gratify him so far.'

At the same time I placed my card in his hand, and requested him to deliver it to his mistress. He returned in a few moments, saying that his lady would be happy to see me in the parlour, and I accordingly followed him to the door, which he opened. I entered the room, and was in a moment at the side of my early friend and benefactress. I was too much agitated to speak; I could only hold the hands which she gave me, while, spite of every effort, the tears flowed fast and bitterly.

'It was kind, very, very kind of you to come to see me,' she said, with far more composure than I could have commanded; 'I see it is very painful to you.'

I endeavoured to compose myself, and for a little time we remained silent; she was the first to speak:

'You will be surprised, Mr. Purcell, when you observe the calmness with which I can speak of him who was dearest to me, who is gone; but my thoughts are always with him, and the recollections of his love'—her voice faltered a little—'and the hope of meeting him hereafter enables me to bear existence.'

I said I know not what; something about resignation, I believe.

'I hope I am resigned; God made me more: so,' she said. 'Oh, Mr. Purcell, I have often thought I loved my lost child *too* well. It was natural—he was my only child—he was—' She could not proceed for a few moments: 'It was very natural that I should love him as I did; but it may have been sinful; I have often thought so. I doated upon him—I idolised him—I thought too little of other holier affections; and God may have taken him from me, only to teach me, by this severe lesson, that I owed to heaven a larger share of my heart than to anything earthly. I cannot think of him now without more solemn feelings than if he were with me. There is something holy in our thoughts of the dead; I feel it so.' After a pause, she continued—'Mr. Purcell, do you remember his features well? they were very beautiful.' I assured her that I did. 'Then you can tell me if you think this a faithful likeness.' She took from a drawer a case in which lay a miniature. I took it reverently from her hands; it was indeed very like—touchingly like. I told her so; and she seemed gratified.

As the evening was wearing fast, and I had far to go, I hastened to terminate my visit, as I had intended, by placing in her hand a letter from her son to me, written during his sojourn upon the Continent. I requested her to keep it; it was one in which he spoke much of her, and in terms of the tenderest affection. As she read its contents the heavy tears gathered in her eyes, and fell, one by one, upon the page; she wiped them away, but they still flowed fast and silently. It was in vain that she tried to read it; her eyes were filled with tears: so she folded the letter, and placed it in her bosom. I rose to depart, and she also rose.

'I will not ask you to delay your departure,' said she; 'your visit here must have been a painful one to you. I cannot find words to thank you for the letter as I would wish, or for all your kindness. It has given me a pleasure greater than I thought could have fallen to the lot of a creature so very desolate as I am; may God bless you for it!' And thus we parted; I never saw Castle Connor or its solitary inmate more.

The Drunkard's Dream

BEING A FOURTH EXTRACT FROM THE LEGACY OF
THE LATE F. PURCELL, P. P. OF DRUMCOOLAGH.

'All this **HE** *told with some confusion and*
Dismay, the usual consequence of dreams
Of the unpleasant kind, with none at hand
To expound their vain and visionary gleams,
I've known some odd ones which seemed really planned
Prophetically, as that which one deems
"A strange coincidence," to use a phrase
By which such things are settled nowadays.'

BYRON.

DREAMS! What age, or what country of the world, has not and acknowledged the mystery of their origin and end? I have thought not a little upon the subject, seeing it is one which has been often forced upon my attention, and sometimes strangely enough; and yet I have never arrived at anything which at all appeared a satisfactory conclusion. It does appear that a mental phenomenon so extraordinary cannot be wholly without its use. We know, indeed, that in the olden times it has been made the organ of communication between the Deity and His creatures; and when, as I have seen, a dream produces upon a mind, to all appearance hopelessly reprobate and depraved, an effect so powerful and so lasting as to break down the inveterate habits, and to reform the life of an abandoned sinner, we see in the result, in the reformation of morals which appeared incorrigible, in the reclamation of a human soul which seemed to be irre-trievably lost, something more than could be produced by a mere chimera of the slumbering fancy, something more than could arise from the capricious images of a terrified imagination; but once presented, we behold in all these things, and in their tremendous and mysterious results, the operation of the hand of God. And while Reason rejects as absurd the superstition which will read a prophecy in every dream, she may, without violence to herself, recognise, even in the wildest and most incongruous of the wanderings of a slumbering intellect, the evidences and the fragments of a language which may be spoken, which has been spoken, to terrify, to warn, and to command. We have reason to believe too, by the promptness of action which in the age of the prophets followed all intimations of this kind, and by the strength of conviction and strange permanence of the effects resulting from certain dreams in latter times, which effects we ourselves may have witnessed, that when this medium of communication has been employed by the Deity, the evidences of His presence have been unequivocal. My thoughts were directed to this subject, in a manner to leave a lasting impression upon my mind, by the events which I shall now relate, the statement of which, however extraordinary, is nevertheless accurately correct.

About the year 17—, having been appointed to the living of C—h, I rented a small house in the town, which bears the same name: one morning in the month of November, I was awakened before my usual time by my servant, who bustled into my bedroom for the purpose of announcing a sick call. As the Catholic Church holds her last rites to be totally indispensable to the safety of the departing sinner, no conscientious clergyman can afford a moment's unnecessary delay, and in little more than five minutes I stood ready cloaked and booted for the road, in the small front parlour, in which the messenger, who was to act as my guide, awaited my coming. I found a poor little girl crying piteously near the door, and after some slight difficulty I ascertained that her father was either dead or just dying.

'And what may be your father's name, my poor child?' said I. She held down her head, as if ashamed. I repeated the question, and the wretched little creature burst into floods of tears still more bitter than she had shed before. At length, almost provoked by conduct which appeared to me so unreasonable, I began to lose patience, spite of the pity which I could not help feeling towards her, and I said rather harshly:

'If you will not tell me the name of the person to whom you would lead me, your silence can arise from no good motive, and I might be justified in refusing to go with you at all.'

'Oh, don't say that—don't say that!' cried she. 'Oh, sir, it was that I was afeard of when I would not tell you—I was afeard, when you heard his name, you would not come with me; but it is no use hidin' it now—it's Pat Connell, the carpenter, your honour.'

She looked in my face with the most earnest anxiety, as if her very existence depended upon what she should read there; but I relieved her at once. The name, indeed, was most unpleasantly familiar to me; but, however fruitless my visits and advice might have been at another time, the present was too fearful an occasion to suffer my doubts of their utility or my reluctance to re-attempting what appeared a hopeless task to weigh even against the lightest chance that a consciousness of his imminent danger might produce in him a more docile and tractable disposition. Accordingly I told the child to lead the way, and followed her in silence. She hurried rapidly through the long narrow street which forms the great thoroughfare of the town. The darkness of the hour, rendered still deeper by the close approach of the old-fashioned houses, which lowered in tall obscurity on either side of the way; the damp, dreary chill which renders the advance of morning peculiarly cheerless, combined with the object of my walk, to visit the death-bed of a presumptuous sinner, to endeavour, almost against my own conviction, to infuse a hope into the heart of a dying reprobate—a drunkard but too probably perishing under the consequences of some mad fit of intoxication; all these circumstances united served to enhance the gloom and solemnity of my feelings, as I silently followed my little guide, who with quick steps traversed the uneven pavement of the main street. After a walk of about five minutes she turned off into a narrow lane, of that obscure and comfortless class which is to be found in almost all small old-fashioned towns, chill, without ventilation, reeking with all manner of offensive effluviae, and lined by dingy, smoky, sickly and pent-up buildings, frequently not only in a wretched but in a dangerous condition.

'Your father has changed his abode since I last visited him, and, I am afraid, much for the worse,' said I.

'Indeed he has, sir; but we must not complain,' replied she. 'We have to thank God that we have lodging and food, though it's poor enough, it is, your honour.'

Poor child! thought I, how many an older head might learn wisdom from thee—how many a luxurious philosopher, who is skilled to preach but not to suffer, might not thy patient words put to the blush! The manner and language of this child were alike above her years and station; and, indeed, in all cases in which the cares and sorrows of life have anticipated their usual date, and have fallen, as they sometimes do, with melancholy prematurity to the lot of childhood, I have observed the result to have proved uniformly the same. A young mind, to which joy and indulgence have been strangers, and to which suffering and self-denial have been familiarised from the first, acquires a solidity and an elevation which no other discipline could have bestowed, and which, in the present case, communicated a striking but mournful peculiarity to the manners, even to the voice, of the child. We paused before a narrow, crazy door, which she opened by means of a latch, and we forthwith began to ascend the steep and broken stairs which led upwards to the sick man's room.

As we mounted flight after flight towards the garret-floor, I heard more and more distinctly the hurried talking of many voices. I could also distinguish the low sobbing of a female. On arriving upon the uppermost lobby these sounds became fully audible.

'This way, your honour,' said my little conductress; at the same time, pushing open a door of patched and half-rotten plank, she admitted me into the squalid chamber of death and misery. But one candle, held in the fingers of a scared and haggard-looking child, was burning in the room, and that so dim that all was twilight or darkness except within its immediate influence. The general obscurity, however, served to throw into prominent and startling relief the death-bed and its occupant. The light was nearly approximated to, and fell with horrible clearness upon, the blue and swollen features of the drunkard. I did not think it possible that a human countenance could look so terrific. The lips were black and drawn apart; the teeth were firmly set; the eyes a little unclosed, and nothing but the whites appearing. Every feature was fixed and livid, and the whole face wore a ghastly and rigid expression of despairing terror such as I never saw equalled. His hands were crossed upon his breast, and firmly clenched; while, as if to add to the corpse-like effect of the whole, some white cloths, dipped in water, were wound about the forehead and temples.

As soon as I could remove my eyes from this horrible spectacle, I observed my friend Dr. D—, one of the most humane of a humane profession, standing by the bedside. He had been attempting, but unsuccessfully, to bleed the patient, and had now applied his finger to the pulse.

'Is there any hope?' I inquired in a whisper.

A shake of the head was the reply. There was a pause while he continued to hold the wrist; but he waited in vain for the throb of life—it was not there: and when he let go the hand, it fell stiffly back into its former position upon the other.

'The man is dead,' said the physician, as he turned from the bed where the terrible figure lay.

Dead! thought I, scarcely venturing to look upon the tremendous and revolting spectacle. Dead! without an hour for repentance, even a moment for reflection; dead I without the rites which even the best should have. Is there a hope for him? The glaring eyeball, the grinning mouth, the distorted brow—that unutterable look in which a painter would have sought to embody the fixed despair of the nethermost hell. These were my answer.

The poor wife sat at a little distance, crying as if her heart would break—the younger children clustered round the bed, looking with wondering curiosity upon the form of death never seen before.

When the first tumult of uncontrollable sorrow had passed away, availing myself of the solemnity and impressiveness of the scene, I desired the heart-stricken family to accompany me in prayer, and all knelt down while I solemnly and fervently repeated some of those prayers which appeared most applicable to the occasion. I employed myself thus in a manner which, I trusted, was not unprofitable, at least to the living, for about ten minutes; and having accomplished my task, I was the first to arise.

I looked upon the poor, sobbing, helpless creatures who knelt so humbly around me, and my heart bled for them. With a natural transition I turned my eyes from them to the bed in which the body lay; and, great God! what was the revulsion, the horror which I experienced on seeing the corpse-like terrific thing seated half upright before me; the white cloths which had been wound about the head had now partly slipped from their position, and were hanging in grotesque festoons about the face and shoulders, while the distorted eyes leered from amid them—

'A sight to dream of, not to tell.'

I stood actually riveted to the spot. The figure nodded its head and lifted its arm, I thought, with a menacing gesture. A thousand confused and horrible thoughts at once rushed upon my mind. I had often read that the body of a presumptuous sinner, who, during life, had been the willing creature of every satanic impulse, after the human tenant had deserted it, had been known to become the horrible sport of demoniac possession.

I was roused from the stupefaction of terror in which I stood, by the piercing scream of the mother, who now, for the first time, perceived the change which had taken place. She rushed towards the bed, but stunned by the shock, and overcome by the conflict of violent emotions, before she reached it she fell prostrate upon the floor.

I am perfectly convinced that had I not been startled from the torpidity of horror in which I was bound by some powerful and arousing stimulant, I should have gazed upon this unearthly apparition until I had fairly lost my senses. As it was, however, the spell was broken—superstition gave way to reason: the man whom all believed to have been actually dead was living!

Dr. D—was instantly standing by the bedside, and upon examination he found that a sudden and copious flow of blood had taken place from the wound which the lancet had left; and this, no doubt, had effected his sudden and almost preternatural restoration to an existence from which all thought he had been for ever removed. The man was still speechless, but he seemed to understand the physician when he forbid his repeating the painful and fruitless attempts which he made to articulate, and he at once resigned himself quietly into his hands.

I left the patient with leeches upon his temples, and bleeding freely, apparently with little of the drowsiness which accompanies apoplexy; indeed, Dr. D—told me that he had never before witnessed a seizure which seemed to combine the symptoms of so many kinds, and yet which belonged to none of the recognised classes; it certainly was not apoplexy, catalepsy, nor delirium tremens, and yet it seemed, in some degree, to partake of the properties of all. It was strange, but stranger things are coming.

During two or three days Dr. D—would not allow his patient to converse in a manner which could excite or exhaust him, with anyone; he suffered him merely as briefly as possible to express his immediate wants. And it was not until the fourth day after my early visit, the particulars of which I have just detailed, that it was thought expedient that I should see him, and then only because it appeared that his extreme importunity and impatience to meet me were likely to retard his recovery more than the mere exhaustion attendant upon a short conversation could possibly do; perhaps, too, my friend entertained some hope that if by holy confession his patient's bosom were eased of the perilous stuff which no doubt oppressed it, his recovery would be more assured and rapid. It was then, as I have said, upon the fourth day after my first professional call, that I found myself once more in the dreary chamber of want and sickness.

The man was in bed, and appeared low and restless. On my entering the room he raised himself in the bed, and muttered, twice or thrice:

'Thank God! thank God!'

I signed to those of his family who stood by to leave the room, and took a chair beside the bed. So soon as we were alone, he said, rather doggedly:

'There's no use in telling me of the sinfulness of bad ways—I know it all. I know where they lead to—I seen everything about it with my own eyesight, as plain as I see you.' He rolled himself in the bed, as if to hide his face in the clothes; and then suddenly raising himself, he exclaimed with startling vehemence: 'Look, sir! there is no use in mincing the matter: I'm blasted with the fires of hell; I have been in hell. What do you think of that? In hell—I'm lost for ever—I have not a chance. I am damned already—damned—damned!'

The end of this sentence he actually shouted. His vehemence was perfectly terrific; he threw himself back, and laughed, and sobbed hysterically. I poured some water into a tea-cup, and gave it to him. After he had swallowed it, I told him if he had anything to communicate, to do so as briefly as he could, and in a manner as little agitating to himself as possible; threatening at the same time, though I had no intention of doing so, to leave him at once, in case he again gave way to such passionate excitement.

'It's only foolishness,' he continued, 'for me to try to thank you for coming to such a villain as myself at all. It's no use for me to wish good to you, or to bless you; for such as me has no blessings to give.'

I told him that I had but done my duty, and urged him to proceed to the matter which weighed upon his mind. He then spoke nearly as follows:

'I came in drunk on Friday night last, and got to my bed here; I don't remember how. Sometime in the night it seemed to me I wakened, and feeling unasy in myself, I got up out of the bed. I wanted the fresh air; but I would not make a noise to open the window, for fear I'd waken the crathurs. It was very dark and throublesome to find the door; but at last I did get it, and I groped my way out, and went down as asy as I could. I felt quite sober, and I counted the steps one after another, as I was going down, that I might not stumble at the bottom.

'When I came to the first landing-place—God be about us always!—the floor of it sunk under me, and I went down—down—down, till the senses almost left me. I do not know how long I was falling, but it seemed to me a great while. When I came rightly to myself at last, I was sitting near the top of a great table; and I could not see the end of it, if it had any, it was so far off. And there was men beyond reckoning, sitting down all along by it, at each side, as far as I could see at all. I did not know at first was it in the open air; but there was a close smothering feel in it that was not natural. And there was a kind of light that my eyesight never saw before, red and unsteady; and I did not see for a long time where it was coming from, until I looked straight up, and then I seen that it came from great balls of blood-coloured fire that were rolling high over head with a sort of rushing, trembling sound, and I perceived that they shone on the ribs of a great roof of rock that was arched overhead instead of the sky. When I seen this, scarce knowing what I did, I got up, and I said, "I have no right to be here; I must go." And the man that was sitting at my left hand only smiled, and said, "Sit down again; you can *never* leave this place." And his voice was weaker than any child's voice I ever heerd; and when he was done speaking he smiled again.

'Then I spoke out very loud and bold, and I said, "In the name of God, let me out of this bad place." And there was a great man that I did not see before, sitting at the end of the table that I was near; and he was taller than twelve men, and his face was very proud and terrible to look at. And he stood up and stretched out his hand before him; and when he stood up, all that was there, great and small, bowed down with a sighing sound, and a dread came on my heart, and he looked at me, and I could not speak. I felt I was his own, to do what he liked with, for I knew at once who he was; and he said, "If you promise to return, you may depart for a season;" and the voice he spoke with was terrible and mournful, and the echoes of it went rolling and swelling down the endless cave, and mixing with the trembling of the fire overhead; so that when he sat down there was a sound after him, all through the place, like the roaring of a furnace, and I said, with all the strength I had, "I promise to come back—in God's name let me go!"

'And with that I lost the sight and the hearing of all that was there, and when my senses came to me again, I was sitting in the bed with the blood all over me, and you and the rest praying around the room.'

Here he paused and wiped away the chill drops of horror which hung upon his forehead.

I remained silent for some moments. The vision which he had just described struck my imagination not a little, for this was long before Vathek and the 'Hall of Eblis' had delighted the world; and the description which he gave had, as I received it, all the attractions of novelty beside the impressiveness which always belongs to the narration of an *eye-witness*, whether in the body or in the spirit, of the scenes which he describes. There was something, too, in the stern horror with which the man related these things, and in the incongruity of his description, with the vulgarly received notions of the great place of punishment, and of its presiding spirit, which struck my mind with awe, almost with fear. At length he said, with an expression of horrible, imploring earnestness, which I shall never forget—'Well, sir, is there any hope; is there any chance at all? or, is my soul pledged and promised away for ever? is it gone out of my power? must I go back to the place?'

In answering him, I had no easy task to perform; for however clear might be my internal conviction of the groundlessness of his tears, and however strong my scepticism respecting the reality of what he had described, I nevertheless felt that his impression to the contrary, and his humility and terror resulting from it, might be made available as no mean engines in the work of his conversion from prodigacy, and of his restoration to decent habits, and to religious feeling.

I therefore told him that he was to regard his dream rather in the light of a warning than in that of a prophecy; that our salvation depended not upon the word or deed of a moment, but upon the habits of a life; that, in fine, if he at once discarded his idle companions and evil habits, and firmly adhered to a sober, industrious, and religious course of life, the powers of darkness might claim his soul in vain, for that there were higher and firmer pledges than human tongue could utter, which promised salvation to him who should repent and lead a new life.

I left him much comforted, and with a promise to return upon the next day. I did so, and found him much more cheerful and without any remains of the dogged sullenness which I suppose had arisen from his despair. His promises of amendment were given in that tone of deliberate earnestness, which belongs to deep and solemn determination; and it was with no small delight that I observed, after repeated visits, that his good resolutions, so far from failing, did but gather strength by time; and when I saw that man shake off the idle and debauched companions, whose society had for years formed alike his amusement and his ruin, and revive his long discarded habits of industry and sobriety, I said within myself, there is something more in all this than the operation of an idle dream.

One day, sometime after his perfect restoration to health, I was surprised on ascending the stairs, for the purpose of visiting this man, to find him busily employed in nailing down some planks upon the landing-place, through which, at the commencement of his mysterious vision, it seemed to him that he had sunk. I perceived at once that he was strengthening the floor with a view to securing himself against such a catastrophe, and could scarcely forbear a smile as I bid 'God bless his work.'

He perceived my thoughts, I suppose, for he immediately said:

'I can never pass over that floor without trembling. I'd leave this house if I could, but I can't find another lodging in the town so cheap, and I'll not take a better till I've paid off all my debts, please God; but I could not be asy in my mind till I made it as safe as I could. You'll hardly believe me, your honour, that while I'm working, maybe a mile away, my heart is in a flutter the whole way back, with the bare thoughts of the two little steps I have to walk upon this bit of a floor. So it's no wonder, sir, I'd thry to make it sound and firm with any idle timber I have.'

I applauded his resolution to pay off his debts, and the steadiness with which he perused his plans of conscientious economy, and passed on.

Many months elapsed, and still there appeared no alteration in his resolutions of amendment. He was a good workman, and with his better habits he recovered his former extensive and profitable employment. Everything seemed to promise comfort and respectability. I have little more to add, and that shall be told quickly. I had one evening met Pat Connell, as he returned from his work, and as usual, after a mutual, and on his side respectful salutation, I spoke a few words of encouragement and approval. I left him industrious, active, healthy—when next I saw him, not three days after, he was a corpse.

The circumstances which marked the event of his death were somewhat strange—I might say fearful. The unfortunate man had accidentally met an early friend just returned, after a long absence, and in a moment of excitement, forgetting everything in the warmth of his joy, he yielded to his urgent invitation to accompany him into a public-house, which lay close by the spot where the encounter had taken place. Connell, however, previously to entering the room, had announced his determination to take nothing more than the strictest temperance would warrant.

But oh! who can describe the inveterate tenacity with which a drunkard's habits cling to him through life? He may repent—he may reform—he may look with actual abhorrence upon his past profligacy; but amid all this reformation and compunction, who can tell the moment in which the base and ruinous propensity may not recur, triumphing over resolution, remorse, shame, everything, and prostrating its victim once more in all that is destructive and revolting in that fatal vice?

The wretched man left the place in a state of utter intoxication. He was brought home nearly insensible. and placed in his bed, where he lay in the deep calm lethargy of drunkenness. The younger part of the family retired to rest much after their usual hour; but the poor wife remained up sitting by the fire, too much grieved and shocked at the occur-rence of what she had so little expected, to settle to rest; fatigue, however, at length overcame her, and she sank gradually into an uneasy slumber. She could not tell how long she had remained in this state, when she awakened, and immediately on opening her eyes, she perceived by the faint red light of the smouldering turf embers, two persons, one of whom she recognised as her husband, noiselessly gliding out of the room.

'Pat, darling, where are you going?' said she. There was no answer—the door closed after them; but in a moment she was startled and terrified by a loud and heavy crash, as if some ponderous body had been hurled down the stair. Much alarmed, she started up, and going to the head of the staircase, she called repeatedly upon her husband, but in vain. She returned to the room, and with the assistance of her daughter, whom I had occasion to mention before, she succeeded in finding and lighting a candle, with which she hurried again to the head of the staircase.

At the bottom lay what seemed to be a bundle of clothes, heaped together, motionless, lifeless—it was her husband. In going down the stair, for what purpose can never now be known, he had fallen helplessly and violently to the bottom, and coming head foremost, the spine at the neck had been dislocated by the shock, and instant death must have ensued. The body lay upon that landing-place to which his dream had referred. It is scarcely worth endeavouring to clear up a single point in a narrative where all is mystery; yet I could not help suspecting that the second figure which had been seen in the room by Connell's wife on the night of his death, might have been no other than his own shadow. I suggested this solution of the difficulty; but she told me that the unknown person had been considerably in advance of the other, and on reaching the door, had turned back as if to communicate something to his companion. It was then a mystery.

Was the dream verified?—whither had the disembodied spirit sped?—who can say? We know not. But I left the house of death that day in a state of horror which I could not describe. It seemed to me that I was scarce awake. I heard and saw everything as if under the spell of a night-mare. The coincidence was terrible.

VOLUME TWO

Passage in the
Secret History of an Irish Countess.

BEING A FIFTH EXTRACT FROM THE LEGACY OF
THE LATE FRANCIS PURCELL, P.P. OF DRUMCOOLAGH.

THE FOLLOWING paper is written in a female hand, and was no doubt communicated to my much-regretted friend by the lady whose early history it serves to illustrate, the Countess D—. She is no more—she long since died, a childless and a widowed wife, and, as her letter sadly predicts, none survive to whom the publication of this narrative can prove 'injurious, or even painful.' Strange! two powerful and wealthy families, that in which she was born, and that into which she had married, have ceased to be—they are utterly extinct.

To those who know anything of the history of Irish families, as they were less than a century ago, the facts which immediately follow will at once suggest *the names* of the principal actors; and to others their publication would be useless—to us, possibly, if not probably, injurious. I have, therefore, altered such of the names as might, if stated, get us into difficulty; others, belonging to minor characters in the strange story, I have left untouched.

My dear friend,—You have asked me to furnish you with a detail of the strange events which marked my early history, and I have, without hesitation, applied myself to the task, knowing that, while I live, a kind consideration for my feelings will prevent your giving publicity to the statement; and conscious that, when I am no more, there will not survive one to whom the narrative can prove injurious, or even painful.

My mother died when I was quite an infant, and of her I have no recollection, even the faintest. By her death, my education and habits were left solely to the guidance of my surviving parent; and, as far as a stern attention to my religious instruction, and an active anxiety evinced by his procuring for me the best masters to perfect me in those accomplishments which my station and wealth might seem to require, could avail, he amply discharged the task.

My father was what is called an oddity, and his treatment of me, though uniformly kind, flowed less from affection and tenderness than from a sense of obligation and duty. Indeed, I seldom even spoke to him except at meal-times, and then his manner was silent and abrupt; his leisure hours, which were many, were passed either in his study or in solitary walks; in short, he seemed to take no further interest in my happiness or improvement than a conscientious regard to the discharge of his own duty would seem to claim.

Shortly before my birth a circumstance had occurred which had contributed much to form and to confirm my father's secluded habits—it was the fact that a suspicion of *murder* had fallen upon his younger brother, though not sufficiently definite to lead to an indictment, yet strong enough to ruin him in public opinion.

This disgraceful and dreadful doubt cast upon the family name, my father felt deeply and bitterly, and not the less so that he himself was thoroughly convinced of his brother's innocence. The sincerity and strength of this impression he shortly afterwards proved in a manner which produced the dark events which follow. Before, however, I enter upon the statement of them, I ought to relate the circumstances which had awakened the suspicion; inasmuch as they are in themselves somewhat curious, and, in their effects, most intimately connected with my after-history.

My uncle, Sir Arthur T—n, was a gay and extravagant man, and, among other vices, was ruinously addicted to gaming; this unfortunate propensity, even after his fortune had suffered so severely as to render inevitable a reduction in his expenses by no means inconsiderable, nevertheless continued to actuate him, nearly to the exclusion of all other pursuits; he was, however, a proud, or rather a vain man, and could not bear to make the diminution of his income a matter of gratulation and triumph to those with whom he had hitherto competed, and the consequence was, that he frequented no longer the expensive haunts of dissipation, and retired from the gay world, leaving his coterie to discover his reasons as best they might.

He did not, however, forego his favourite vice, for, though he could not worship his great divinity in the costly temples where it was formerly his wont to take his stand, yet he found it very possible to bring about him a sufficient number of the votaries of chance to answer all his ends. The consequence was, that Carrickleigh, which was the name of my uncle's residence, was never without one or more of such visitors as I have described.

It happened that upon one occasion he was visited by one Hugh Tisdall, a gentleman of loose habits, but of considerable wealth, and who had, in early youth, travelled with my uncle upon the Con-tinent; the period of his visit was winter, and, consequently, the house was nearly deserted excepting by its regular inmates; it was therefore highly acceptable, particularly as my uncle was aware that his visitor's tastes accorded exactly with his own.

Both parties seemed determined to avail themselves of their suitability during the brief stay which Mr. Tisdall had promised; the consequence was, that they shut themselves up in Sir Arthur's private room for nearly all the day and the greater part of the night, during the space of nearly a week, at the end of which the servant having one morning, as usual, knocked at Mr. Tisdall's bed-room door repeatedly, received no answer, and, upon attempting to enter, found that it was locked; this appeared suspicious, and, the inmates of the house having been alarmed, the door was forced open, and, on proceeding to the bed, they found the body of its occupant perfectly lifeless, and hanging half-way out, the head downwards, and near the floor. One deep wound had been inflicted upon the temple, apparently with some blunt instrument which had penetrated the brain; and another blow, less effective, probably the first aimed, had grazed the head, removing some of the scalp, but leaving the skull untouched. The door had been double-locked upon the *inside*, in evidence of which the key still lay where it had been placed in the lock.

The window, though not secured on the interior, was closed—a circumstance not a little puzzling, as it afforded the only other mode of escape from the room; it looked out, too, upon a kind of courtyard, round which the old buildings stood, formerly accessible by a narrow doorway and passage lying in the oldest side of the quadrangle, but which had since been built up, so as to preclude all ingress or egress; the room was also upon the second story, and the height of the window considerable. Near the bed were found a pair of razors belonging to the murdered man, one of them upon the ground, and both of them open. The weapon which had inflicted the mortal wound was not to be found in the room, nor were any footsteps or other traces of the murderer discoverable.

At the suggestion of Sir Arthur himself, a coroner was instantly summoned to attend, and an inquest was held; nothing, however, in any degree conclusive was elicited; the walls, ceiling, and floor of the room were carefully examined, in order to ascertain whether they contained a trap-door or other concealed mode of entrance—but no such thing appeared.

Such was the minuteness of investigation employed, that, although the grate had contained a large fire during the night, they proceeded to examine even the very chimney, in order to discover whether escape by it were possible; but this attempt, too, was fruitless, for the chimney, built in the old fashion, rose in a perfectly perpendicular line from the hearth to a height of nearly fourteen feet above the roof, affording in its interior scarcely the possibility of ascent, the flue being smoothly plastered, and sloping towards the top like an inverted funnel, promising, too, even if the summit were attained, owing to its great height, but a precarious descent upon the sharp and steep-ridged roof; the ashes, too, which lay in the grate, and the soot, as far as it could be seen, were undisturbed, a circumstance almost conclusive of the question.

Sir Arthur was of course examined; his evidence was given with clearness and unreserve, which seemed calculated to silence all suspicion. He stated that, up to the day and night immediately preceding the catastrophe, he had lost to a heavy amount, but that, at their last sitting, he had not only won back his original loss, but upwards of four thousand pounds in addition; in evidence of which he produced an acknowledgment of debt to that amount in the handwriting of the deceased, and bearing the date of the fatal night. He had mentioned the circumstance to his lady, and in presence of some of the domestics; which statement was supported by *their* respective evidence.

One of the jury shrewdly observed, that the circumstance of Mr. Tisdall's having sustained so heavy a loss might have suggested to some ill-minded persons accidentally hearing it, the plan of robbing him, after having murdered him in such a manner as might make it appear that he had committed suicide; a supposition which was strongly supported by the razors having been found thus displaced, and removed from their case. Two persons had probably been engaged in the attempt, one watching by the sleeping man, and ready to strike him in case of his awakening suddenly, while the other was procuring the razors and employed in inflicting the fatal gash, so as to make it appear to have been the act of the murdered man himself. It was said that while the juror was making this suggestion Sir Arthur changed colour.

Nothing, however, like legal evidence appeared against him, and the consequence was that the verdict was found against a person or persons unknown; and for some time the matter was suffered to rest, until, after about five months, my father received a letter from a person signing himself Andrew Collis, and representing himself to be the cousin of the deceased. This letter stated that Sir Arthur was likely to incur not merely suspicion, but personal risk, unless he could account for certain circumstances connected with the recent murder, and contained a copy of a letter written by the deceased, and bearing date, the day of the week, and of the month, upon the night of which the deed of blood had been perpetrated. Tisdall's note ran as follows:

DEAR COLLIS,

I have had sharp work with Sir Arthur; he tried some of his stale tricks, but soon found that I was Yorkshire too: it would not do—you understand me. We went to the work like good ones, head, heart and soul; and, in fact, since I came here, I have lost no time. I am rather fagged, but I am sure to be well paid for my hardship; I never want sleep so long as I can have the music of a dice-box, and wherewithal to pay the piper. As I told you, he tried some of his queer turns, but I foiled him like a man, and, in return, gave him more than he could relish of the genuine *dead knowledge*.

In short, I have plucked the old baronet as never baronet was plucked before; I have scarce left him the stump of a quill; I have got promissory notes in his hand to the amount of—if you like round numbers, say, thirty thousand pounds, safely deposited in my portable strong-box, alias double-clasped pocket-book. I leave this ruinous old rat-hole early on to-morrow, for two reasons—first, I do not want to play with Sir Arthur deeper than I think his security, that is, his money, or his money's worth, would warrant; and, secondly, because I am safer a hundred miles from Sir Arthur than in the house with him. Look you, my worthy, I tell you this between ourselves—I may be wrong, but, by G—, I am as sure as that I am now living, that Sir A—attempted to poison me last night; so much for old friendship on both sides.

When I won the last stake, a heavy one enough, my friend leant his forehead upon his hands, and you'll laugh when I tell you that his head literally smoked like a hot dumpling. I do not know whether his agitation was produced by the plan which he had against me, or by his having lost so heavily—though it must be allowed that he had reason to be a little funked, whichever way his thoughts went; but he pulled the bell, and ordered two bottles of champagne. While the fellow was bringing them he drew out a promissory note to the full amount, which he signed, and, as the man came in with the bottles and glasses, he desired him to be off; he filled out a glass for me, and, while he thought my eyes were off, for I was putting up his note at the time, he dropped something slyly into it, no doubt to sweeten it; but I saw it all, and, when he handed it to me, I said, with an emphasis which he might or might not understand:

"There is some sediment in this; I'll not drink it."

"Is there?" said he, and at the same time snatched it from my hand and threw it into the fire. What do you think of that? have I not a tender chicken to manage? Win or lose, I will not play beyond five thousand to-night, and to-morrow sees me safe out of the reach of Sir Arthur's champagne. So, all things considered, I think you must allow that you are not the last who have found a knowing boy in

Yours to command,
HUGH TISDALL.

Of the authenticity of this document I never heard my father express a doubt; and I am satisfied that, owing to his strong conviction in favour of his brother, he would not have admitted it without sufficient inquiry, inasmuch as it tended to confirm the suspicions which already existed to his prejudice.

Now, the only point in this letter which made strongly against my uncle, was the mention of the 'double-clasped pocket-book' as the receptacle of the papers likely to involve him, for this pocket-book was not forthcoming, nor anywhere to be found, nor had any papers referring to his gaming transactions been found upon the dead man. However, whatever might have been the original intention of this Collis, neither my uncle nor my father ever heard more of him; but he published the letter in Faulkner's newspaper, which was shortly afterwards made the vehicle of a much more mysterious attack. The passage in that periodical to which I allude, occurred about four years afterwards, and while the fatal occurrence was still fresh in public recollection. It commenced by a rambling preface, stating that 'a *certain person* whom *certain* persons thought to be dead, was not so, but living, and in full possession of his memory, and moreover ready and able to make *great* delinquents tremble.' It then went on to describe the murder, without, however, mentioning names; and in doing so, it entered into minute and circumstantial particulars of which none but an *eye-witness* could have been possessed, and by implications almost too unequivocal to be regarded in the light of insinuation, to involve the '*titled gambler*' in the guilt of the transaction.

My father at once urged Sir Arthur to proceed against the paper in an action of libel; but he would not hear of it, nor consent to my father's taking any legal steps whatever in the matter. My father, however, wrote in a threatening tone to Faulkner, demanding a surrender of the author of the obnoxious article. The answer to this application is still in my possession, and is penned in an apologetic tone: it states that the manuscript had been handed in, paid for, and inserted as an advertisement, without sufficient inquiry, or any knowledge as to whom it referred.

No step, however, was taken to clear my uncle's character in the judgment of the public; and as he immediately sold a small property, the application of the proceeds of which was known to none, he was said to have disposed of it to enable himself to buy off the threatened information. However the truth might have been, it is certain that no charges respecting the mysterious murder were afterwards publicly made against my uncle, and, as far as external disturbances were concerned, he enjoyed henceforward perfect security and quiet.

A deep and lasting impression, however, had been made upon the public mind, and Sir Arthur T—n was no longer visited or noticed by the gentry and aristocracy of the county, whose attention and courtesies he had hitherto received. He accordingly affected to despise these enjoyments which he could not procure, and shunned even that society which he might have commanded.

This is all that I need recapitulate of my uncle's history, and I now recur to my own. Although my father had never, within my recollection, visited, or been visited by, my uncle, each being of sedentary, procrastinating, and secluded habits, and their respective residences being very far apart—the one lying in the county of Galway, the other in that of Cork—he was strongly attached to his brother, and evinced his affection by an active correspondence, and by deeply and proudly resenting that neglect which had marked Sir Arthur as unfit to mix in society.

When I was about eighteen years of age, my father, whose health had been gradually declining, died, leaving me in heart wretched and desolate, and, owing to his previous seclusion, with few acquaintances, and almost no friends.

The provisions of his will were curious, and when I had sufficiently come to myself to listen to or comprehend them, surprised me not a little: all his vast property was left to me, and to the heirs of my body, for ever; and, in default of such heirs, it was to go after my death to my uncle, Sir Arthur, without any entail.

At the same time, the will appointed him my guardian, desiring that I might be received within his house, and reside with his family, and under his care, during the term of my minority; and in consideration of the increased expense consequent upon such an arrangement, a handsome annuity was allotted to him during the term of my proposed residence.

The object of this last provision I at once understood: my father desired, by making it the direct, apparent interest of Sir Arthur that I should die without issue, while at the same time he placed me wholly in his power, to prove to the world how great and unshaken was his confidence in his brother's innocence and honour, and also to afford him an opportunity of showing that this mark of confidence was not unworthily bestowed.

It was a strange, perhaps an idle scheme; but as I had been always brought up in the habit of considering my uncle as a deeply-injured man, and had been taught, almost as a part of my religion, to regard him as the very soul of honour, I felt no further uneasiness respecting the arrangement than that likely to result to a timid girl, of secluded habits, from the immediate prospect of taking up her abode for the first time in her life among total strangers. Previous to leaving my home, which I felt I should do with a heavy heart, I re-ceived a most tender and affectionate letter from my uncle, calculated, if anything could do so, to remove the bitterness of parting from scenes familiar and dear from my earliest childhood, and in some degree to reconcile me to the measure.

It was during a fine autumn that I approached the old domain of Carrickleigh. I shall not soon forget the impression of sadness and of gloom which all that I saw produced upon my mind; the sunbeams were falling with a rich and melancholy tint upon the fine old trees, which stood in lordly groups, casting their long, sweeping shadows over rock and sward. There was an air of neglect and decay about the spot, which amounted almost to desolation; the symptoms of this increased in number as we approached the building itself, near which the ground had been originally more artificially and carefully cultivated than elsewhere, and whose neglect consequently more immediately and strikingly betrayed itself.

As we proceeded, the road wound near the beds of what had been formally two fish-ponds, which were now nothing more than stagnant swamps, overgrown with rank weeds, and here and there encroached upon by the straggling underwood; the avenue itself was much broken, and in many places the stones were almost concealed by grass and nettles; the loose stone walls which had here and there intersected the broad park were, in many places, broken down, so as no longer to answer their original purpose as fences; piers were now and then to be seen, but the gates were gone; and, to add to the general air of dilapidation, some huge trunks were lying scattered through the venerable old trees, either the work of the winter storms, or perhaps the victims of some extensive but desultory scheme of denudation, which the projector had not capital or perseverance to carry into full effect.

After the carriage had travelled a mile of this avenue, we reached the summit of rather an abrupt eminence, one of the many which added to the picturesqueness, if not to the convenience of this rude passage. From the top of this ridge the grey walls of Carrickleigh were visible, rising at a small distance in front, and darkened by the hoary wood which crowded around them. It was a quadrangular building of considerable extent, and the front which lay towards us, and in which the great entrance was placed, bore unequivocal marks of antiquity; the time-worn, solemn aspect of the old building, the ruinous and deserted appearance of the whole place, and the associations which connected it with a dark page in the history of my family, combined to depress spirits already predisposed for the reception of sombre and dejecting impressions.

When the carriage drew up in the grass-grown court yard before the hall-door, two lazy-looking men, whose appearance well accorded with that of the place which they tenanted, alarmed by the obstreperous barking of a great chained dog, ran out from some half-ruinous out-houses, and took charge of the horses; the hall-door stood open, and I entered a gloomy and imperfectly lighted apartment, and found no one within. However, I had not long to wait in this awkward predicament, for before my luggage had been deposited in the house, indeed, before I had well removed my cloak and other wraps, so as to enable me to look around, a young girl ran lightly into the hall, and kissing me heartily, and somewhat boisterously, exclaimed:

'My dear cousin, my dear Margaret—I am so delighted—so out of breath. We did not expect you till ten o'clock; my father is somewhere about the place, he must be close at hand. James—Corney—run out and tell your master—my brother is seldom at home, at least at any reasonable hour—you must be so tired—so fatigued—let me show you to your room—see that Lady Margaret's luggage is all brought up—you must lie down and rest yourself—Deborah, bring some coffee—up these stairs; we are so delighted to see you—you cannot think how lonely I have been—how steep these stairs are, are not they? I am so glad you are come—I could hardly bring myself to believe that you were really coming—how good of you, dear Lady Margaret.'

There was real good-nature and delight in my cousin's greeting, and a kind of constitutional confidence of manner which placed me at once at ease, and made me feel immediately upon terms of intimacy with her. The room into which she ushered me, although partaking in the general air of decay which pervaded the mansion and all about it, had nevertheless been fitted up with evident attention to comfort, and even with some dingy attempt at luxury; but what pleased me most was that it opened, by a second door, upon a lobby which communicated with my fair cousin's apartment; a circumstance which divested the room, in my eyes, of the air of solitude and sadness which would otherwise have characterised it, to a degree almost painful to one so dejected in spirits as I was.

After such arrangements as I found necessary were completed, we both went down to the parlour, a large wainscoted room, hung round with grim old portraits, and, as I was not sorry to see, containing in its ample grate a large and cheerful fire. Here my cousin had leisure to talk more at her ease; and from her I learned something of the manners and the habits of the two remaining members of her family, whom I had not yet seen.

On my arrival I had known nothing of the family among whom I was come to reside, except that it consisted of three individuals, my uncle, and his son and daughter, Lady T—n having been long dead. In addition to this very scanty stock of information, I shortly learned from my communicative companion that my uncle was, as I had suspected, completely retired in his habits, and besides that, having been so far back as she could well recollect, always rather strict, as reformed rakes frequently become, he had latterly been growing more gloomily and sternly religious than heretofore.

Her account of her brother was far less favourable, though she did not say anything directly to his disadvantage. From all that I could gather from her, I was led to suppose that he was a specimen of the idle, coarse-mannered, profligate, low-minded 'squirearchy'—a result which might naturally have flowed from the circum-stance of his being, as it were, outlawed from society, and driven for companionship to grades below his own—enjoying, too, the dangerous prerogative of spending much money.

However, you may easily suppose that I found nothing in my cousin's communication fully to bear me out in so very decided a conclusion.

I awaited the arrival of my uncle, which was every moment to be expected, with feelings half of alarm, half of curiosity—a sensation which I have often since experienced, though to a less degree, when upon the point of standing for the first time in the presence of one of whom I have long been in the habit of hearing or thinking with interest.

It was, therefore, with some little perturbation that I heard, first a slight bustle at the outer door, then a slow step traverse the hall, and finally witnessed the door open, and my uncle enter the room. He was a striking-looking man; from peculiarities both of person and of garb, the whole effect of his appearance amounted to extreme singularity. He was tall, and when young his figure must have been strikingly elegant; as it was, however, its effect was marred by a very decided stoop. His dress was of a sober colour, and in fashion anterior to anything which I could remember. It was, however, handsome, and by no means carelessly put on; but what completed the singularity of his appearance was his uncut, white hair, which hung in long, but not at all neglected curls, even so far as his shoulders, and which combined with his regularly classic features, and fine dark eyes, to bestow upon him an air of venerable dignity and pride, which I have never seen equalled elsewhere. I rose as he entered, and met him about the middle of the room; he kissed my cheek and both my hands, saying:

'You are most welcome, dear child, as welcome as the command of this poor place and all that it contains can make you. I am most rejoiced to see you—truly rejoiced. I trust that you are not much fatigued—pray be seated again.' He led me to my chair, and continued: 'I am glad to perceive you have made acquaintance with Emily already; I see, in your being thus brought together, the foundation of a lasting friendship. You are both innocent, and both young. God bless you—God bless you, and make you all that I could wish.'

He raised his eyes, and remained for a few moments silent, as if in secret prayer. I felt that it was impossible that this man, with feelings so quick, so warm, so tender, could be the wretch that public opinion had represented him to be. I was more than ever convinced of his innocence.

His manner was, or appeared to me, most fascinating; there was a mingled kindness and courtesy in it which seemed to speak benevolence itself. It was a manner which I felt cold art could never have taught; it owed most of its charm to its appearing to emanate directly from the heart; it must be a genuine index of the owner's mind. So I thought.

My uncle having given me fully to understand that I was most welcome, and might command whatever was his own, pressed me to take some refreshment; and on my refusing, he observed that previously to bidding me good-night, he had one duty further to perform, one in whose observance he was convinced I would cheerfully acquiesce.

He then proceeded to read a chapter from the Bible; after which he took his leave with the same affectionate kindness with which he had greeted me, having repeated his desire that I should consider everything in his house as altogether at my disposal. It is needless to say that I was much pleased with my uncle—it was impossible to avoid being so; and I could not help saying to myself, if such a man as this is not safe from the assaults of slander, who is? I felt much happier than I had done since my father's death, and enjoyed that night the first refreshing sleep which had visited me since that event.

My curiosity respecting my male cousin did not long remain unsatisfied—he appeared the next day at dinner. His manners, though not so coarse as I had expected, were exceedingly disagreeable; there was an assurance and a forwardness for which I was not prepared; there was less of the vulgarity of manner, and almost more of that of the mind, than I had anticipated. I felt quite uncomfortable in his presence; there was just that confidence in his look and tone which would read encouragement even in mere toleration; and I felt more disgusted and annoyed at the coarse and extravagant compliments which he was pleased from time to time to pay me, than perhaps the extent of the atrocity might fully have warranted. It was, however, one consolation that he did not often appear, being much engrossed by pursuits about which I neither knew nor cared anything; but when he did appear, his attentions, either with a view to his amusement or to some more serious advantage, were so obviously and perseveringly directed to me, that young and inexperienced as I was, even I could not be ignorant of his preference. I felt more provoked by this odious persecution than I can express, and discouraged him with so much vigour, that I employed even rudeness to convince him that his assiduities were unwelcome; but all in vain.

This had gone on for nearly a twelve-month, to my infinite annoyance, when one day as I was sitting at some needle-work with my companion Emily, as was my habit, in the parlour, the door opened, and my cousin Edward entered the room. There was something, I thought, odd in his manner—a kind of struggle between shame and impudence—a kind of flurry and ambiguity which made him appear, if possible, more than ordinarily disagreeable.

'Your servant, ladies,' he said, seating himself at the same time; 'sorry to spoil your tête-à-tête, but never mind, I'll only take Emily's place for a minute or two; and then we part for a while, fair cousin. Emily, my father wants you in the corner turret. No shilly-shally; he's in a hurry.' She hesitated. 'Be off—tramp, march!' he exclaimed, in a tone which the poor girl dared not disobey.

She left the room, and Edward followed her to the door. He stood there for a minute or two, as if reflecting what he should say, perhaps satisfying himself that no one was within hearing in the hall.

At length he turned about, having closed the door, as if carelessly, with his foot; and advancing slowly, as if in deep thought, he took his seat at the side of the table opposite to mine.

There was a brief interval of silence, after which he said:

'I imagine that you have a shrewd suspicion of the object of my early visit; but I suppose I must go into particulars. Must I?'

'I have no conception,' I replied, 'what your object may be.'

'Well, well,' said he, becoming more at his ease as he proceeded, 'it may be told in a few words. You know that it is totally impossible—quite out of the question—that an offhand young fellow like me, and a good-looking girl like yourself, could meet continually, as you and I have done, without an attachment—a liking growing up on one side or other; in short, I think I have let you know as plain as if I spoke it, that I have been in love with you almost from the first time I saw you.'

He paused; but I was too much horrified to speak. He interpreted my silence favourably.

'I can tell you,' he continued, 'I'm reckoned rather hard to please, and very hard to *hit*. I can't say when I was taken with a girl before; so you see fortune reserved me—'

Here the odious wretch wound his arm round my waist. The action at once restored me to utterance, and with the most indignant vehemence I released myself from his hold, and at the same time said:

'I have not been insensible, sir, of your most disagreeable attentions—they have long been a source of much annoyance to me; and you must be aware that I have marked my disapprobation—my disgust—as unequivocally as I possibly could, without actual indelicacy.'

I paused, almost out of breath from the rapidity with which I had spoken; and without giving him time to renew the conversation, I hastily quitted the room, leaving him in a paroxysm of rage and mortification. As I ascended the stairs, I heard him open the parlour-door with violence, and take two or three rapid strides in the direction in which I was moving. I was now much frightened, and ran the whole way until I reached my room; and having locked the door, I listened breathlessly, but heard no sound. This relieved me for the present; but so much had I been overcome by the agitation and annoyance attendant upon the scene which I had just gone through, that when my cousin Emily knocked at my door, I was weeping in strong hysterics.

You will readily conceive my distress, when you reflect upon my strong dislike to my cousin Edward, combined with my youth and extreme inexperience. Any proposal of such a nature must have agitated me; but that it should have come from the man whom of all others I most loathed and abhorred, and to whom I had, as clearly as manner could do it, expressed the state of my feelings, was almost too overwhelming to be borne. It was a calamity, too, in which I could not claim the sym-pathy of my cousin Emily, which had always been extended to me in my minor grievances. Still I hoped that it might not be unattended with good; for I thought that one inevitable and most welcome consequence would result from this painful eclaircissment, in the discontinuance of my cousin's odious persecution.

When I arose next morning, it was with the fervent hope that I might never again behold the face, or even hear the name, of my cousin Edward; but such a consummation, though devoutly to be wished, was hardly likely to occur. The painful impressions of yesterday were too vivid to be at once erased; and I could not help feeling some dim foreboding of coming annoyance and evil.

To expect on my cousin's part anything like delicacy or consideration for me, was out of the question. I saw that he had set his heart upon my property, and that he was not likely easily to forego such an acquisition—possessing what might have been considered opportunities and facilities almost to compel my compliance.

I now keenly felt the unreasonableness of my father's conduct in placing me to reside with a family of all whose members, with one exception, he was wholly ignorant, and I bitterly felt the helplessness of my situation. I determined, however, in case of my cousin's persevering in his addresses, to lay all the particulars before my uncle, although he had never in kindness or intimacy gone a step beyond our first interview, and to throw myself upon his hospitality and his sense of honour for protection against a repetition of such scenes.

My cousin's conduct may appear to have been an inadequate cause for such serious uneasiness; but my alarm was caused neither by his acts nor words, but entirely by his manner, which was strange and even intimidating to excess. At the beginning of the yesterday's interview there was a sort of bullying swagger in his air, which towards the end gave place to the brutal vehemence of an undisguised ruffian—a transition which had tempted me into a belief that he might seek even forcibly to extort from me a consent to his wishes, or by means still more horrible, of which I scarcely dared to trust myself to think, to possess himself of my property.

I was early next day summoned to attend my uncle in his private room, which lay in a corner turret of the old building; and thither I accordingly went, wondering all the way what this unusual measure might prelude. When I entered the room, he did not rise in his usual courteous way to greet me, but simply pointed to a chair opposite to his own. This boded nothing agreeable. I sat down, however, silently waiting until he should open the conversation.

'Lady Margaret,' at length he said, in a tone of greater sternness than I thought him capable of using, 'I have hitherto spoken to you as a friend, but I have not forgotten that I am also your guardian, and that my authority as such gives me a right to control your conduct. I shall put a question to you, and I expect and will demand a plain, direct answer. Have I rightly been informed that you have con-temptuously rejected the suit and hand of my son Edward?'

I stammered forth with a good deal of trepidation:

'I believe—that is, I have, sir, rejected my cousin's proposals; and my coldness and discouragement might have convinced him that I had determined to do so.'

'Madam,' replied he, with suppressed, but, as it appeared to me, intense anger, 'I have lived long enough to know that *coldness* and discouragement, and such terms, form the common cant of a worthless coquette. You know to the full, as well as I, that *coldness and discouragement* may be so exhibited as to convince their object that he is neither distasteful or indifferent to the person who wears this manner. You know, too, none better, that an affected neglect, when skilfully managed, is amongst the most formidable of the engines which artful beauty can employ. I tell you, madam, that having, without one word spoken in discouragement, permitted my son's most marked attentions for a twelvemonth or more, you have no right to dismiss him with no further explanation than demurely telling him that you had always looked coldly upon him; and neither your wealth nor your *ladyship*' (there was an emphasis of scorn on the word, which would have become Sir Giles Overreach himself) 'can warrant you in treating with contempt the affectionate regard of an honest heart.'

I was too much shocked at this undisguised attempt to bully me into an acquiescence in the interested and unprincipled plan for their own aggrandisement, which I now perceived my uncle and his son to have deliberately entered into, at once to find strength or collectedness to frame an answer to what he had said. At length I replied, with some firmness:

'In all that you have just now said, sir, you have grossly misstated my conduct and motives. Your information must have been most incorrect as far as it regards my conduct towards my cousin; my manner towards him could have conveyed nothing but dislike; and if anything could have added to the strong aversion which I have long felt towards him, it would be his attempting thus to trick and frighten me into a marriage which he knows to be revolting to me, and which is sought by him only as a means for securing to himself whatever property is mine.'

As I said this, I fixed my eyes upon those of my uncle, but he was too old in the world's ways to falter beneath the gaze of more searching eyes than mine; he simply said:

'Are you acquainted with the provisions of your father's will?'

I answered in the affirmative; and he continued:

'Then you must be aware that if my son Edward were—which God forbid—the unprincipled, reckless man you pretend to think him'—(here he spoke very slowly, as if he intended that every word which escaped him should be registered in my memory, while at the same time the expression of his countenance underwent a gradual but horrible change, and the eyes which he fixed upon me became so darkly vivid, that I almost lost sight of everything else)—'if he were what you have described him, think you, girl, he could find no briefer means than wedding contracts to gain his ends? 'twas but to gripe your slender neck until the breath had stopped, and lands, and lakes, and all were his.'

I stood staring at him for many minutes after he had ceased to speak, fascinated by the terrible serpent-like gaze, until he continued with a welcome change of countenance:

'I will not speak again to you upon this—topic until one month has passed. You shall have time to consider the relative advantages of the two courses which are open to you. I should be sorry to hurry you to a decision. I am satisfied with having stated my feelings upon the subject, and pointed out to you the path of duty. Remember this day month—not one word sooner.'

He then rose, and I left the room, much agitated and exhausted.

This interview, all the circumstances attending it, but most particularly the formidable expression of my uncle's countenance while he talked, though hypothetically, of murder, combined to arouse all my worst suspicions of him. I dreaded to look upon the face that had so recently worn the appalling livery of guilt and malignity. I regarded it with the mingled fear and loathing with which one looks upon an object which has tortured them in a nightmare.

In a few days after the interview, the particulars of which I have just related, I found a note upon my toilet-table, and on opening it I read as follows:

MY DEAR LADY MARGARET,

You will be perhaps surprised to see a strange face in your room to-day. I have dismissed your Irish maid, and secured a French one to wait upon you—a step rendered necessary by my proposing shortly to visit the Continent, with all my family.

Your faithful guardian,
ARTHUR T——N.

On inquiry, I found that my faithful attendant was actually gone, and far on her way to the town of Galway; and in her stead there appeared a tall, raw-boned, ill-looking, elderly Frenchwoman, whose sullen and presuming manners seemed to imply that her vocation had never before been that of a lady's-maid. I could not help regarding her as a creature of my uncle's, and therefore to be dreaded, even had she been in no other way suspicious.

Days and weeks passed away without any, even a momentary doubt upon my part, as to the course to be pursued by me. The allotted period had at length elapsed; the day arrived on which I was to communicate my decision to my uncle. Although my resolution had never for a moment wavered, I could not shake of the dread of the approaching colloquy; and my heart sunk within me as I heard the expected summons.

I had not seen my cousin Edward since the occurrence of the grand eclaircissment; he must have studiously avoided me—I suppose from policy, it could not have been from delicacy. I was prepared for a terrific burst of fury from my uncle, as soon as I should make known my determination; and I not unreasonably feared that some act of violence or of intimidation would next be resorted to.

Filled with these dreary forebodings, I fearfully opened the study door, and the next minute I stood in my uncle's presence. He received me with a politeness which I dreaded, as arguing a favourable anticipation respecting the answer which I was to give; and after some slight delay, he began by saying:

'It will be a relief to both of us, I believe, to bring this conversation as soon as possible to an issue. You will excuse me, then, my dear niece, for speaking with an abruptness which, under other circumstances, would be unpardonable. You have, I am certain, given the subject of our last interview fair and serious con-sideration; and I trust that you are now prepared with candour to lay your answer before me. A few words will suffice—we perfectly understand one another.'

He paused, and I, though feeling that I stood upon a mine which might in an instant explode, nevertheless answered with perfect composure:

'I must now, sir, make the same reply which I did upon the last occasion, and I reiterate the declaration which I then made, that I never can nor will, while life and reason remain, consent to a union with my cousin Edward.'

This announcement wrought no apparent change in Sir Arthur, except that he became deadly, almost lividly pale. He seemed lost in dark thought for a minute, and then with a slight effort said:

'You have answered me honestly and directly; and you say your resolution is unchangeable. Well, would it had been otherwise—would it had been otherwise—but be it as it is—I am satisfied.'

He gave me his hand—it was cold and damp as death; under an assumed calmness, it was evident that he was fearfully agitated. He continued to hold my hand with an almost painful pressure, while, as if unconsciously, seeming to forget my presence, he muttered:

'Strange, strange, strange, indeed! fatuity, helpless fatuity!' there was here a long pause. 'Madness *indeed* to strain a cable that is rotten to the very heart—it must break—and then—all goes.'

There was again a pause of some minutes, after which, suddenly changing his voice and manner to one of wakeful alacrity, he exclaimed:

'Margaret, my son Edward shall plague you no more. He leaves this country on to-morrow for France—he shall speak no more upon this subject—never, never more—whatever events depended upon your answer must now take their own course; but, as for this fruitless proposal, it has been tried enough; it can be repeated no more.'

At these words he coldly suffered my hand to drop, as if to express his total abandonment of all his projected schemes of alliance; and certainly the action, with the accompanying words, produced upon my mind a more solemn and depressing effect than I believed possible to have been caused by the course which I had determined to pursue; it struck upon my heart with an awe and heaviness which *will* accompany the accomplishment of an important and irrevocable act, even though no doubt or scruple remains to make it possible that the agent should wish it undone.

'Well,' said my uncle, after a little time, 'we now cease to speak upon this topic, never to resume it again. Remember you shall have no farther uneasiness from Edward; he leaves Ireland for France on to-morrow; this will be a relief to you. May I depend upon your *honour* that no word touching the subject of this interview shall ever escape you?'

I gave him the desired assurance; he said:

'It is well—I am satisfied—we have nothing more, I believe, to say upon either side, and my presence must be a restraint upon you, I shall therefore bid you farewell.'

I then left the apartment, scarcely knowing what to think of the strange interview which had just taken place.

On the next day my uncle took occasion to tell me that Edward had actually sailed, if his intention had not been interfered with by adverse circumstances; and two days subsequently he actually produced a letter from his son, written, as it said, *on board*, and despatched while the ship was getting under weigh. This was a great satisfaction to me, and as being likely to prove so, it was no doubt communicated to me by Sir Arthur.

During all this trying period, I had found infinite consolation in the society and sympathy of my dear cousin Emily. I never in after-life formed a friendship so close, so fervent, and upon which, in all its progress, I could look back with feelings of such unalloyed pleasure, upon whose termination I must ever dwell with so deep, yet so unembittered regret. In cheerful converse with her I soon recovered my spirits considerably, and passed my time agreeably enough, although still in the strictest seclusion.

Matters went on sufficiently smooth, although I could not help sometimes feeling a momentary, but horrible uncertainty respecting my uncle's character; which was not altogether unwarranted by the circumstances of the two trying interviews whose particulars I have just detailed. The unpleasant impression which these conferences were calculated to leave upon my mind, was fast wearing away, when there occurred a circumstance, slight indeed in itself, but calculated irresistibly to awaken all my worst suspicions, and to overwhelm me again with anxiety and terror.

I had one day left the house with my cousin Emily, in order to take a ramble of considerable length, for the purpose of sketching some favourite views, and we had walked about half a mile when I perceived that we had forgotten our drawing materials, the absence of which would have defeated the object of our walk. Laughing at our own thoughtlessness, we returned to the house, and leaving Emily without, I ran upstairs to procure the drawing-books and pencils, which lay in my bedroom.

As I ran up the stairs I was met by the tall, ill-looking Frenchwoman, evidently a good deal flurried.

'Que veut, madame?' said she, with a more decided effort to be polite than I had ever known her make before.

'No, no—no matter,' said I, hastily running by her in the direction of my room.

'Madame,' cried she, in a high key, 'restez ici, s'il vous plait; votre chambre n'est pas faite—your room is not ready for your reception yet.'

I continued to move on without heeding her. She was some way behind me, and feeling that she could not otherwise prevent my entrance, for I was now upon the very lobby, she made a desperate attempt to seize hold of my person: she succeeded in grasping the end of my shawl, which she drew from my shoulders; but slipping at the same time upon the polished oak floor, she fell at full length upon the boards.

A little frightened as well as angry at the rudeness of this strange woman, I hastily pushed open the door of my room, at which I now stood, in order to escape from her; but great was my amazement on entering to find the apartment preoccupied.

The window was open, and beside it stood two male figures; they appeared to be examining the fastenings of the casement, and their backs were turned towards the door. One of them was my uncle; they both turned on my entrance, as if startled. The stranger was booted and cloaked, and wore a heavy broad-leafed hat over his brows. He turned but for a moment, and averted his face; but I had seen enough to convince me that he was no other than my cousin Edward. My uncle had some iron instrument in his hand, which he hastily concealed behind his back; and coming towards me, said something as if in an explanatory tone; but I was too much shocked and confounded to understand what it might be. He said something about '*repairs*—window—frames—cold, and safety.'

I did not wait, however, to ask or to receive explanations, but hastily left the room. As I went down the stairs I thought I heard the voice of the Frenchwoman in all the shrill volubility of excuse, which was met, however, by suppressed but vehement imprecations, or what seemed to me to be such, in which the voice of my cousin Edward distinctly mingled.

I joined my cousin Emily quite out of breath. I need not say that my head was too full of other things to think much of drawing for that day. I imparted to her frankly the cause of my alarms, but at the same time as gently as I could; and with tears she promised vigilance, and devotion, and love. I never had reason for a moment to repent the unreserved confidence which I then reposed in her. She was no less surprised than I at the unexpected appearance of Edward, whose departure for France neither of us had for a moment doubted, but which was now proved by his actual presence to be nothing more than an imposture, practised, I feared, for no good end.

The situation in which I had found my uncle had removed completely all my doubts as to his designs. I magnified suspicions into certainties, and dreaded night after night that I should be murdered in my bed. The nervousness produced by sleepless nights and days of anxious fears increased the horrors of my situation to such a degree, that I at length wrote a letter to a Mr. Jefferies, an old and faithful friend of my father's, and perfectly acquainted with all his affairs, praying him, for God's sake, to relieve me from my present terrible situation, and communicating without reserve the nature and grounds of my suspicions.

This letter I kept sealed and directed for two or three days always about my person, for discovery would have been ruinous, in expectation of an opportunity which might be safely trusted, whereby to have it placed in the post-office. As neither Emily nor I were permitted to pass beyond the precincts of the demesne itself, which was surrounded by high walls formed of dry stone, the difficulty of procuring such an opportunity was greatly enhanced.

At this time Emily had a short conver-sation with her father, which she reported to me instantly.

After some indifferent matter, he had asked her whether she and I were upon good terms, and whether I was unreserved in my disposition. She answered in the affirmative; and he then inquired whether I had been much surprised to find him in my chamber on the other day. She answered that I had been both surprised and amused.

'And what did she think of George Wilson's appearance?'

'Who?' inquired she.

'Oh, the architect,' he answered, 'who is to contract for the repairs of the house; he is accounted a handsome fellow.'

'She could not see his face,' said Emily, 'and she was in such a hurry to escape that she scarcely noticed him.'

Sir Arthur appeared satisfied, and the conversation ended.

This slight conversation, repeated accurately to me by Emily, had the effect of confirming, if indeed anything was required to do so, all that I had before believed as to Edward's actual presence; and I naturally became, if possible, more anxious than ever to despatch the letter to Mr. Jefferies. An opportunity at length occurred.

As Emily and I were walking one day near the gate of the demesne, a lad from the village happened to be passing down the avenue from the house; the spot was secluded, and as this person was not connected by service with those whose observation I dreaded, I committed the letter to his keeping, with strict injunctions that he should put it without delay into the receiver of the town post-office; at the same time I added a suitable gratuity, and the man having made many protestations of punctuality, was soon out of sight.

He was hardly gone when I began to doubt my discretion in having trusted this person; but I had no better or safer means of despatching the letter, and I was not warranted in suspecting him of such wanton dishonesty as an inclination to tamper with it; but I could not be quite satisfied of its safety until I had received an answer, which could not arrive for a few days. Before I did, however, an event occurred which a little surprised me.

I was sitting in my bedroom early in the day, reading by myself, when I heard a knock at the door.

'Come in,' said I; and my uncle entered the room.

'Will you excuse me?' said he. 'I sought you in the parlour, and thence I have come here. I desired to say a word with you. I trust that you have hitherto found my conduct to you such as that of a guardian towards his ward should be.'

I dared not withhold my consent.

'And,' he continued, 'I trust that you have not found me harsh or unjust, and that you have perceived, my dear niece, that I have sought to make this poor place as agreeable to you as may be.'

I assented again; and he put his hand in his pocket, whence he drew a folded paper, and dashing it upon the table with startling emphasis, he said:

'Did you write that letter?'

The sudden and tearful alteration of his voice, manner, and face, but, more than all, the unexpected production of my letter to Mr. Jefferies, which I at once recognised, so confounded and terrified me, that I felt almost choking.

I could not utter a word.

'Did you write that letter?' he repeated with slow and intense emphasis.' You did, liar and hypocrite! You dared to write this foul and infamous libel; but it shall be your last. Men will universally believe you mad, if I choose to call for an inquiry. I can make you appear so. The suspicions expressed in this letter are the hallucinations and alarms of moping lunacy. I have defeated your first attempt, madam; and by the holy God, if ever you make another, chains, straw, darkness, and the keeper's whip shall be your lasting portion!'

With these astounding words he left the room, leaving me almost fainting.

I was now almost reduced to despair; my last cast had failed; I had no course left but that of eloping secretly from the castle, and placing myself under the protection of the nearest magistrate. I felt if this were not done, and speedily, that I should be *murdered*.

No one, from mere description, can have an idea of the unmitigated horror of my situation—a helpless, weak, inexperienced girl, placed under the power and wholly at the mercy of evil men, and feeling that she had it not in her power to escape for a moment from the malignant influences under which she was probably fated to fall; and with a consciousness that if violence, if murder were designed, her dying shriek would be lost in void space; no human being would be near to aid her, no human interposition could deliver her.

I had seen Edward but once during his visit, and as I did not meet with him again, I began to think that he must have taken his departure— a conviction which was to a certain degree satisfactory, as I regarded his absence as indicating the removal of immediate danger.

Emily also arrived circuitously at the same conclusion, and not without good grounds, for she managed indirectly to learn that Edward's black horse had actually been for a day and part of a night in the castle stables, just at the time of her brother's supposed visit. The horse had gone, and, as she argued, the rider must have departed with it.

This point being so far settled, I felt a little less uncomfortable: when being one day alone in my bedroom, I happened to look out from the window, and, to my un-utterable horror, I beheld, peering through an op- posite casement, my cousin Edward's face. Had I seen the evil one himself in bodily shape, I could not have experienced a more sickening revulsion.

I was too much appalled to move at once from the window, but I did so soon enough to avoid his eye. He was looking fixedly into the narrow quadrangle upon which the window opened. I shrank back unperceived, to pass the rest of the day in terror and despair. I went to my room early that night, but I was too miserable to sleep.

At about twelve o'clock, feeling very nervous, I determined to call my cousin Emily, who slept, you will remember, in the next room, which com- municated with mine by a second door. By this private entrance I found my way into her chamber, and without difficulty persuaded her to return to my room and sleep with me. We accordingly lay down together, she undressed, and I with my clothes on, for I was every moment walking up and down the room, and felt too nervous and miserable to think of rest or comfort.

Emily was soon fast asleep, and I lay awake, fervently longing for the first pale gleam of morning, reckoning every stroke of the old clock with an impatience which made every hour appear like six.

It must have been about one o'clock when I thought I heard a slight noise at the partition-door between Emily's room and mine, as if caused by somebody's turning the key in the lock. I held my breath, and the same sound was repeated at the second door of my room—that which opened upon the lobby—the sound was here distinctly caused by the revolution of the bolt in the lock, and it was followed by a slight pressure upon the door itself, as if to ascertain the security of the lock.

The person, whoever it might be, was probably satisfied, for I heard the old boards of the lobby creak and strain, as if under the weight of somebody moving cautiously over them. My sense of hearing became unnaturally, almost painfully acute. I suppose the imagination added distinctness to sounds vague in themselves. I thought that I could actually hear the breathing of the person who was slowly returning down the lobby. At the head of the staircase there appeared to occur a pause; and I could distinctly hear two or three sentences hastily whispered; the steps then descended the stairs with apparently less caution. I now ventured to walk quickly and lightly to the lobby-door, and attempted to open it; it was indeed fast locked upon the outside, as was also the other.

I now felt that the dreadful hour was come; but one desperate expedient remained—it was to awaken Emily, and by our united strength to attempt to force the partition-door, which was slighter than the other, and through this to pass to the lower part of the house, whence it might be possible to escape to the grounds, and forth to the village.

I returned to the bedside and shook Emily, but in vain. Nothing that I could do availed to produce from her more than a few incoherent words—it was a death-like sleep. She had certainly drank of some narcotic, as had I probably also, spite of all the caution with which I had examined everything presented to us to eat or drink.

I now attempted, with as little noise as possible, to force first one door, then the other—but all in vain. I believe no strength could have effected my object, for both doors opened inwards. I therefore collected whatever movables I could carry thither, and piled them against the doors, so as to assist me in whatever attempts I should make to resist the entrance of those without. I then returned to the bed and endeavoured again, but fruitlessly, to awaken my cousin. It was not sleep, it was torpor, lethargy, death. I knelt down and prayed with an agony of earnestness; and then seating myself upon the bed, I awaited my fate with a kind of terrible tranquillity.

I heard a faint clanking sound from the narrow court which I have already mentioned, as if caused by the scraping of some iron instrument against stones or rubbish. I at first determined not to disturb the calmness which I now felt, by uselessly watching the proceedings of those who sought my life; but as the sounds continued, the horrible curiosity which I felt overcame every other emotion, and I determined, at all hazards, to gratify it. I therefore crawled upon my knees to the window, so as to let the smallest portion of my head appear above the sill.

The moon was shining with an uncertain radiance upon the antique grey buildings, and obliquely upon the narrow court beneath, one side of which was therefore clearly illuminated, while the other was lost in obscurity, the sharp outlines of the old gables, with their nodding clusters of ivy, being at first alone visible.

Whoever or whatever occasioned the noise which had excited my curiosity, was concealed under the shadow of the dark side of the quadrangle. I placed my hand over my eyes to shade them from the moonlight, which was so bright as to be almost dazzling, and, peering into the darkness, I first dimly, but afterwards gradually, almost with full distinctness, beheld the form of a man engaged in digging what appeared to be a rude hole close under the wall. Some implements, probably a shovel and pickaxe, lay beside him, and to these he every now and then applied himself as the nature of the ground required. He pursued his task rapidly, and with as little noise as possible.

'So,' thought I, as, shovelful after shovel-ful, the dislodged rubbish mounted into a heap, 'they are digging the grave in which, before two hours pass, I must lie, a cold, mangled corpse. I am *theirs*—I cannot escape.'

I felt as if my reason was leaving me. I started to my feet, and in mere despair I applied myself again to each of the two doors alternately. I strained every nerve and sinew, but I might as well have attempted, with my single strength, to force the building itself from its foundation. I threw myself madly upon the ground, and clasped my hands over my eyes as if to shut out the horrible images which crowded upon me.

The paroxysm passed away. I prayed once more, with the bitter, agonised fervour of one who feels that the hour of death is present and inevitable. When I arose, I went once more to the window and looked out, just in time to see a shadowy figure glide stealthily along the wall. The task was finished. The catastrophe of the tragedy must soon be accomplished.

I determined now to defend my life to the last; and that I might be able to do so with some effect, I searched the room for something which might serve as a weapon; but either through accident, or from an anticipation of such a possibility, everything which might have been made available for such a purpose had been carefully removed. I must then die tamely and without an effort to defend myself.

A thought suddenly struck me—might it not be possible to escape through the door, which the assassin must open in order to enter the room? I resolved to make the attempt. I felt assured that the door through which ingress to the room would be effected, was that which opened upon the lobby. It was the more direct way, besides being, for obvious reasons, less liable to interruption than the other. I resolved, then, to place myself behind a projection of the wall, whose shadow would serve fully to conceal me, and when the door should be opened, and before they should have discovered the identity of the occupant of the bed, to creep noiselessly from the room, and then to trust to Providence for escape.

In order to facilitate this scheme, I removed all the lumber which I had heaped against the door; and I had nearly completed my arrangements, when I perceived the room suddenly darkened by the close approach of some shadowy object to the window. On turning my eyes in that direction, I observed at the top of the casement, as if suspended from above, first the feet, then the legs, then the body, and at length the whole figure of a man present himself. It was Edward T——n.

He appeared to be guiding his descent so as to bring his feet upon the centre of the stone block which occupied the lower part of the window; and, having secured his footing upon this, he kneeled down and began to gaze into the room. As the moon was gleaming into the chamber, and the bed-curtains were drawn, he was able to distinguish the bed itself and its contents. He appeared satisfied with his scrutiny, for he looked up and made a sign with his hand, upon which the rope by which his descent had been effected was slackened from above, and he proceeded to disengage it from his waist; this accom-plished, he applied his hands to the window-frame, which must have been ingeniously contrived for the purpose, for, with apparently no resistance, the whole frame, containing casement and all, slipped from its position in the wall, and was by him lowered into the room.

The cold night wind waved the bed-curtains, and he paused for a moment—all was still again—and he stepped in upon the floor of the room. He held in his hand what appeared to be a steel instrument, shaped something like a hammer, but larger and sharper at the extremities. This he held rather behind him, while, with three long, tip-toe strides, he brought himself to the bedside.

I felt that the discovery must now be made, and held my breath in momentary expectation of the execration in which he would vent his surprise and disappointment. I closed my eyes—there was a pause, but it was a short one. I heard two dull blows, given in rapid succession: a quivering sigh, and the long-drawn, heavy breathing of the sleeper was for ever suspended. I unclosed my eyes, and saw the murderer fling the quilt across the head of his victim: he then, with the instrument of death still in his hand, proceeded to the lobby-door, upon which he tapped sharply twice or thrice. A quick step was then heard approaching, and a voice whispered something from without. Edward answered, with a kind of chuckle, 'Her ladyship is past complaining; unlock the door, in the devil's name, unless you're afraid to come in, and help me to lift the body out of the window.'

The key was turned in the lock—the door opened—and my uncle entered the room.

I have told you already that I had placed myself under the shade of a projection of the wall, close to the door. I had instinctively shrunk down, cowering towards the ground on the entrance of Edward through the window. When my uncle entered the room he and his son both stood so very close to me that his hand was every moment upon the point of touching my face. I held my breath, and remained motionless as death.

'You had no interruption from the next room?' said my uncle.

'No,' was the brief reply.

'Secure the jewels, Ned; the French harpy must not lay her claws upon them. You're a steady hand, by G—! not much blood—eh?'

'Not twenty drops,' replied his son, 'and those on the quilt.'

'I'm glad it's over,' whispered my uncle again. 'We must lift the—the *thing* through the window, and lay the rubbish over it.'

They then turned to the bedside, and, winding the bed-clothes round the body, carried it between them slowly to the window, and, exchanging a few brief words with some one below, they shoved it over the window-sill, and I heard it fall heavily on the ground underneath.

'I'll take the jewels,' said my uncle; 'there are two caskets in the lower drawer.'

He proceeded, with an accuracy which, had I been more at ease, would have furnished me with matter of astonishment, to lay his hand upon the very spot where my jewels lay; and having possessed himself of them, he called to his son:

'Is the rope made fast above?'

'I'm not a fool—to be sure it is,' replied he.

They then lowered themselves from the window. I now rose lightly and cautiously, scarcely daring to breathe, from my place of concealment, and was creeping towards the door, when I heard my cousin's voice, in a sharp whisper, exclaim: 'Scramble up again! G—d d—n you, you've forgot to lock the room-door!' and I perceived, by the straining of the rope which hung from above, that the mandate was instantly obeyed.

Not a second was to be lost. I passed through the door, which was only closed, and moved as rapidly as I could, consistently with stillness, along the lobby. Before I had gone many yards, I heard the door through which I had just passed double-locked on the inside. I glided down the stairs in terror, lest, at every corner, I should meet the murderer or one of his accomplices.

I reached the hall, and listened for a moment to ascertain whether all was silent around; no sound was audible. The parlour windows opened on the park, and through one of them I might, I thought, easily effect my escape. Accordingly, I hastily entered; but, to my consternation, a candle was burning in the room, and by its light I saw a figure seated at the dinner-table, upon which lay glasses, bottles, and the other accompaniments of a drinking-party. Two or three chairs were placed about the table irregularly, as if hastily abandoned by their occupants.

A single glance satisfied me that the figure was that of my French attendant. She was fast asleep, having probably drank deeply. There was something malignant and ghastly in the calmness of this bad woman's features, dimly illuminated as they were by the flickering blaze of the candle. A knife lay upon the table, and the terrible thought struck me—'Should I kill this sleeping accomplice in the guilt of the murderer, and thus secure my retreat?'

Nothing could be easier—it was but to draw the blade across her throat—the work of a second. An instant's pause, however, corrected me. 'No,' thought I, 'the God who has conducted me thus far through the valley of the shadow of death, will not abandon me now. I will fall into their hands, or I will escape hence, but it shall be free from the stain of blood. His will be done.'

I felt a confidence arising from this reflection, an assurance of protection which I cannot describe. There was no other means of escape, so I advanced, with a firm step and collected mind, to the window. I noiselessly withdrew the bars and unclosed the shutters—I pushed open the casement, and, without waiting to look behind me, I ran with my utmost speed, scarcely feeling the ground under me, down the avenue, taking care to keep upon the grass which bordered it.

I did not for a moment slack my speed, and I had now gained the centre point between the park-gate and the mansion-house. Here the avenue made a wider circuit, and in order to avoid delay, I directed my way across the smooth sward round which the pathway wound, intending, at the opposite side of the flat, at a point which I distinguished by a group of old birch-trees, to enter again upon the beaten track, which was from thence tolerably direct to the gate.

I had, with my utmost speed, got about half way across this broad flat, when the rapid treading of a horse's hoofs struck upon my ear. My heart swelled in my bosom as though I would smother. The clattering of galloping hoofs approached—I was pursued—they were now upon the sward on which I was running—there was not a bush or a bramble to shelter me—and, as if to render escape altogether desperate, the moon, which had hitherto been obscured, at this moment shone forth with a broad clear light, which made every object distinctly visible.

The sounds were now close behind me. I felt my knees bending under me, with the sensation which torments one in dreams. I reeled—I stumbled—I fell—and at the same instant the cause of my alarm wheeled past me at full gallop. It was one of the young fillies which pastured loose about the park, whose frolics had thus all but maddened me with terror. I scrambled to my feet, and rushed on with weak but rapid steps, my sportive companion still galloping round and round me with many a frisk and fling, until, at length, more dead than alive, I reached the avenue-gate and crossed the stile, I scarce knew how.

I ran through the village, in which all was silent as the grave, until my progress was arrested by the hoarse voice of a sentinel, who cried: 'Who goes there?' I felt that I was now safe. I turned in the direction of the voice, and fell fainting at the soldier's feet. When I came to myself; I was sitting in a miserable hovel, surrounded by strange faces, all bespeaking curiosity and compassion.

Many soldiers were in it also: indeed, as I afterwards found, it was employed as a guard-room by a detachment of troops quartered for that night in the town. In a few words I informed their officer of the circumstances which had occurred, describing also the appearance of the persons engaged in the murder; and he, without loss of time, proceeded to the mansion-house of Carrickleigh, taking with him a party of his men. But the villains had discovered their mistake, and had effected their escape before the arrival of the military.

The Frenchwoman was, however, arrested in the neighbourhood upon the next day. She was tried and condemned upon the ensuing assizes; and previous to her execution, confessed that *'she had a hand in making hugh tisdal's bed.'* She had been a housekeeper in the castle at the time, and a kind of chère amie of my uncle's. She was, in reality, able to speak English like a native, but had exclusively used the French language, I suppose to facilitate her disguise. She died the same hardened wretch which she had lived, confessing her crimes only, as she alleged, that her doing so might involve Sir Arthur T—n, the great author of her guilt and misery, and whom she now regarded with unmitigated detestation.

With the particulars of Sir Arthur's and his son's escape, as far as they are known, you are acquainted. You are also in possession of their after fate—the terrible, the tremendous retribution which, after long delays of many years, finally overtook and crushed them. Wonderful and inscrutable are the dealings of God with His creatures.

Deep and fervent as must always be my gratitude to heaven for my deliverance, effected by a chain of providential occurrences, the failing of a single link of which must have ensured my destruction, I was long before I could look back upon it with other feelings than those of bitterness, almost of agony.

The only being that had ever really loved me, my nearest and dearest friend, ever ready to sympathise, to counsel, and to assist—the gayest, the gentlest, the warmest heart—the only creature on earth that cared for me—*her* life had been the price of my deliverance; and I then uttered the wish, which no event of my long and sorrowful life has taught me to recall, that she had been spared, and that, in her stead, I were mouldering in the grave, forgotten and at rest.

The Bridal of Carrigvarah

BEING A SIXTH EXTRACT FROM THE LEGACY OF THE LATE FRANCIS PURCELL, P. P. OF DRUMCOOLAGH.

IN A sequestered district of the county of Limerick, there stood my early life, some forty years ago, one of those strong stone buildings, half castle, half farm-house, which are not unfrequent in the South of Ireland, and whose solid masonry and massive construction seem to prove at once the insecurity and the caution of the Cromwellite settlers who erected them. At the time of which I speak, this building was tenanted by an elderly man, whose starch and puritanic mien and manners might have become the morose preaching parliamentarian captain, who had raised the house and ruled the household more than a hundred years before; but this man, though Protestant by descent as by name, was not so in religion; he was a strict, and in outward observances, an exemplary Catholic; his father had returned in early youth to the true faith, and died in the bosom of the church.

Martin Heathcote was, at the time of which I speak, a widower, but his house-keeping was not on that account altogether solitary, for he had a daughter, whose age was now sufficiently advanced to warrant her father in imposing upon her the grave duties of domestic superintendence.

This little establishment was perfectly isolated, and very little intruded upon by acts of neighbourhood; for the rank of its occupants was of that equivocal kind which precludes all familiar association with those of a decidedly inferior rank, while it is not sufficient to entitle its possessors to the society of established gentility, among whom the nearest residents were the O'Maras of Carrigvarah, whose mansion-house, constructed out of the ruins of an old abbey, whose towers and cloisters had been levelled by the shot of Cromwell's artillery, stood not half a mile lower upon the river banks.

Colonel O'Mara, the possessor of the estates, was then in a declining state of health, and absent with his lady from the country, leaving at the castle, his son young O'Mara, and a kind of humble companion, named Edward Dwyer, who, if report belied him not, had done in his early days some *peculiar services* for the Colonel, who had been a gay man—perhaps worse—but enough of recapitulation.

It was in the autumn of the year 17—that the events which led to the catastrophe which I have to detail occurred. I shall run through the said recital as briefly as clearness will permit, and leave you to moralise, if such be your mood, upon the story of real life, which I even now trace at this distant period not without emotion.

It was upon a beautiful autumn evening, at that glad period of the season when the harvest yields its abundance, that two figures were seen sauntering along the banks of the winding river, which I described as bounding the farm occupied by Heathcote; they had been, as the rods and landing-nets which they listlessly carried went to show, plying the gentle, but in this case not altogether solitary craft of the fisherman. One of those persons was a tall and singularly handsome young man, whose dark hair and complexion might almost have belonged to a Spaniard, as might also the proud but melancholy expression which gave to his countenance a character which contrasts sadly, but not uninterestingly, with extreme youth; his air, as he spoke with his companion, was marked by that careless familiarity which denotes a conscious superiority of one kind or other, or which may be construed into a species of contempt; his comrade afforded to him in every respect a striking contrast. He was rather low in stature—a defect which was enhanced by a broad and square-built figure—his face was sallow, and his features had that prominence and sharpness which frequently accompany personal deformity—a remarkably wide mouth, with teeth white as the fangs of a wolf, and a pair of quick, dark eyes, whose effect was heightened by the shadow of a heavy black brow, gave to his face a power of expression, particularly when sarcastic or malignant emotions were to be exhibited, which features regularly handsome could scarcely have possessed.

'Well, sir,' said the latter personage, 'I have lived in hall and abbey, town and country, here and abroad for forty years and more, and should know a thing or two, and as I am a living man, I swear I think the girl loves you.'

'You are a fool, Ned,' said the younger.

'I may be a fool,' replied the first speaker, 'in matters where my own advantage is staked, but my eye is keen enough to see through the flimsy disguise of a country damsel at a glance; and I tell you, as surely as I hold this rod, the girl loves you.'

'Oh I this is downright headstrong folly,' replied the young fisherman. 'Why, Ned, you try to persuade me against my reason, that the event which is most to be deprecated has actually occurred. She is, no doubt, a pretty girl—a beautiful girl—but I have not lost my heart to her; and why should I wish her to be in love with me? Tush, man, the days of romance are gone, and a young gentleman may talk, and walk, and laugh with a pretty country maiden, and never breathe aspirations, or vows, or sighs about the matter; unequal matches are much oftener read of than made, and the man who could, even in thought, conceive a wish against the honour of an unsuspecting, artless girl, is a villain, for whom hanging is too good.'

This concluding sentence was uttered with an animation and excitement, which the mere announcement of an abstract moral sentiment could hardly account for.

'You are, then, indifferent, honestly and in sober earnest, indifferent to the girl?' inquired Dwyer.

'Altogether so,' was the reply.

'Then I have a request to make,' continued Dwyer, 'and I may as well urge it now as at any other time. I have been for nearly twenty years the faithful, and by no means useless, servant of your family; you know that I have rendered your father critical and important services—' he paused, and added hastily: 'you are not in the mood—I tire you, sir.'

'Nay,' cried O'Mara, 'I listen patiently—proceed.'

'For all these services, and they were not, as I have said, few or valueless, I have received little more reward than liberal promises; you have told me often that this should be mended—I'll make it easily done—I'm not unreasonable—I should be contented to hold Heathcote's ground, along with this small farm on which we stand, as full quittance of all obligations and promises between us.'

'But how the devil can I effect that for you; this farm, it is true, I, or my father, rather, may lease to you, but Heathcote's title we cannot impugn; and even if we could, you would not expect us to ruin an honest man, in order to make way for *you*, Ned.'

'What I am,' replied Dwyer, with the calmness of one who is so accustomed to contemptuous insinuations as to receive them with perfect indifference, 'is to be attributed to my devotedness to your honourable family—but that is neither here nor there. I do not ask you to displace Heath-cote, in order to made room for me. I know it is out of your power to do so. Now hearken to me for a moment; Heathcote's property, that which he has set out to tenants, is worth, say in rents, at most, one hundred pounds: half of this yearly amount is assigned to your father, until payment be made of a bond for a thousand pounds, with interest and soforth. Hear me patiently for a moment and I have done. Now go you to Heathcote, and tell him your father will burn the bond, and cancel the debt, upon one condition—that when I am in possession of this farm, which you can lease to me on what terms you think suitable, he will convey over his property to me, reserving what life-interest may appear fair, I engaging at the same time to marry his daughter, and make such settlements upon her as shall be thought fitting—he is not a fool—the man will close with the offer.'

O'Mara turned shortly upon Dwyer, and gazed upon him for a moment with an expression of almost unmixed resentment.

'How,' said he at length, '*you* contract to marry Ellen Heathcote? the poor, innocent, confiding, light-hearted girl. No, no, Edward Dwyer, I know you too well for that—your services, be they what they will, must not, shall not go unrewarded—your avarice shall be appeased—but not with a human sacrifice! Dwyer, I speak to you without disguise; you know me to be acquainted with your history, and what's more, with your character. Now tell me frankly, were I to do as you desire me, in cool blood, should I not prove myself a more uncompromising and unfeeling villain than humanity even in its most monstrous shapes has ever yet given birth to?'

Dwyer met this impetuous language with the unmoved and impenetrable calmness which always marked him when excitement would have appeared in others; he even smiled as he replied: (and Dwyer's smile, for I have seen it, was characteristically of that unfortunate kind which implies, as regards the emotions of others, not sympathy but derision).

'This eloquence goes to prove Ellen Heathcote something nearer to your heart than your great indifference would have led me to suppose.'

There was something in the tone, perhaps in the truth of the insinuation, which at once kindled the quick pride and the anger of O'Mara, and he instantly replied:

'Be silent, sir, this is insolent folly.'

Whether it was that Dwyer was more keenly interested in the success of his suit, or more deeply disappointed at its failure than he cared to express, or that he was in a less complacent mood than was his wont, it is certain that his countenance expressed more emotion at this direct insult than it had ever exhibited before under similar circumstances; for his eyes gleamed for an instant with savage and undisguised ferocity upon the young man, and a dark glow crossed his brow, and for the moment he looked about to spring at the throat of his insolent patron; but the impulse whatever it might be, was quickly suppressed, and before O'Mara had time to detect the scowl, it had vanished.

'Nay, sir,' said Dwyer, 'I meant no offence, and I will take none, at your hands at least. I will confess I care not, in love and soforth, a single bean for the girl; she was the mere channel through which her father's wealth, if such a pittance deserves the name, was to have flowed into my possession—'twas in respect of your family finances the most economical provision for myself which I could devise—a matter in which you, not I, are interested. As for women, they are all pretty much alike to me. I am too old myself to make nice distinctions, and too ugly to succeed by Cupid's arts; and when a man despairs of success, he soon ceases to care for it. So, if you know me, as you profess to do, rest satisfied "caeteris paribus;" the money part of the transaction being equally advantageous, I should regret the loss of Ellen Heathcote just as little as I should the escape of a minnow from my landing-net.'

They walked on for a few minutes in silence, which was not broken till Dwyer, who had climbed a stile in order to pass a low stone wall which lay in their way, exclaimed:

'By the rood, she's here—how like a philosopher you look."

The conscious blood mounted to O'Mara's cheek; he crossed the stile, and, separated from him only by a slight fence and a gate, stood the subject of their recent and somewhat angry discussion.

'God save you, Miss Heathcote,' cried Dwyer, approaching the gate.

The salutation was cheerfully returned, and before anything more could pass, O'Mara had joined the party.

My friend, that you may understand the strength and depth of those impetuous passions, that you may account for the fatal infatuation which led to the catastrophe which I have to relate, I must tell you, that though I have seen the beauties of cities and of courts, with all the splendour of studied ornament about them to enhance their graces, possessing charms which had made them known almost throughout the world, and worshipped with the incense of a thousand votaries, yet never, nowhere did I behold a being of such exquisite and touching beauty, as that possessed by the creature of whom I have just spoken. At the moment of which I write, she was standing near the gate, close to which several brown-armed, rosy-cheeked damsels were engaged in milking the peaceful cows, who stood picturesquely grouped together. She had just thrown back the hood which is the graceful characteristic of the Irish girl's attire, so that her small and classic head was quite uncovered, save only by the dark-brown hair, which with graceful simplicity was parted above her forehead. There was nothing to shade the clearness of her beautiful complexion; the delicately-formed features, so exquisite when taken singly, so indescribable when combined, so purely artless, yet so meet for all expression. She was a thing so very beautiful, you could not look on her without feeling your heart touched as by sweet music. Whose lightest action was a grace—whose lightest word a spell—no limner's art, though ne'er so perfect, could shadow forth her beauty; and do I dare with feeble words try to make you see it?[5] Providence is indeed no respecter of persons, its blessings and its inflictions are apportioned with an undistinguishing hand, and until the race is over, and life be done, none can know whether those perfections, which seemed its goodliest gifts, many not prove its most fatal; but enough of this.

Dwyer strolled carelessly onward by the banks of the stream, leaving his young companion leaning over the gate in close and interesting parlance with Ellen Heathcote; as he moved on, he half thought, half uttered words to this effect:

'Insolent young spawn of ingratitude and guilt, how long must I submit to be trod upon thus; and yet why should I murmur—his day is even now declining—and if I live a year, I shall see the darkness cover him and his for ever. Scarce half his broad estates shall save him—but I must wait—I am but a pauper now—a beggar's accusation is always a libel—they must reward me soon—and were I independent once, I'd make them feel my power, and feel it *so*, that I should die the richest or the best avenged servant of a great man that has ever been heard of—yes, I must wait—I must make sure of something at least—I must be able to stand by myself—and then—and then—' He clutched his fingers together, as if in the act of strangling the object of his hatred. 'But one thing shall save him—but one thing only—he shall pay me my own price—and if he acts liberally, as no doubt he will do, upon compulsion, why he saves his reputation—perhaps his neck—the insolent young whelp yonder would speak in an humbler key if he but knew his father's jeopardy—but all in good time.'

He now stood upon the long, steep, narrow bridge, which crossed the river close to Carrigvarah, the family mansion of the O'Maras; he looked back in the direction in which he had left his companion, and leaning upon the battlement, he ruminated long and moodily. At length he raised himself and said:

---

5   Father Purcell seems to have had an admiration for the beauties of nature, particularly as developed in the fair sex; a habit of mind which has been rather improved upon than discontinued by his successors from Maynooth.—ED,

'He loves the girl, and *will* love her more—I have an opportunity of winning favour, of doing service, which shall bind him to me; yes, he shall have the girl, if I have art to compass the matter. I must think upon it.'

He entered the avenue and was soon lost in the distance.

Days and weeks passed on, and young O'Mara daily took his rod and net, and rambled up the river; and scarce twelve hours elapsed in which some of those accidents, which invariably bring lovers together, did not secure him a meeting of longer or shorter duration, with the beautiful girl whom he so fatally loved.

One evening, after a long interview with her, in which he had been almost irresistibly prompted to declare his love, and had all but yielded himself up to the passionate impulse, upon his arrival at home he found a letter on the table awaiting his return; it was from his father to the following effect:

To Richard O'mara.
September, 17—, L—m, England.

MY DEAR SON,—

I have just had a severe attack of my old and almost forgotten enemy, the gout. This I regard as a good sign; the doctors telling me that it is the safest development of peccant humours; and I think my chest is less tormenting and oppressed than I have known it for some years. My chief reason for writing to you now, as I do it not without difficulty, is to let you know my pleasure in certain matters, in which I suspect some shameful, and, indeed, infatuated neglect on your part, "quem perdere vult deus prius dementat:" how comes it that you have neglected to write to Lady Emily or any of that family? the understood relation subsisting between you is one of extreme delicacy, and which calls for marked and courteous, nay, devoted attention upon your side. Lord—is already offended; beware what you do; for as you will find, if this match be lost by your fault or folly, by—I will cut you off with a shilling. I am not in the habit of using threats when I do not mean to fulfil them, and that you well know; however I do not think you have much real cause for alarm in this case. Lady Emily, who, by the way, looks if possible more charming than ever, is anything but hard-hearted, at least when *you* solicit; but do as I desire, and lose no time in making what excuse you may, and let me hear from you when you can fix a time to join me and your mother here.

Your sincere well-wisher and father,
RICHARD O'MARA.

In this letter was inclosed a smaller one, directed to Dwyer, and containing a cheque for twelve pounds, with the following words:

Make use of the enclosed, and let me hear if Richard is upon any wild scheme at present: I am uneasy about him, and not without reason; report to me speedily the result of your vigilance.

R. O'MARA.

Dwyer just glanced through this brief, but not unwelcome, epistle; and deposited it and its contents in the secret recesses of his breeches pocket, and then fixed his eyes upon the face of his companion, who sat opposite, utterly absorbed in the perusal of his father's letter, which he read again and again, pausing and muttering between whiles, and apparently lost in no very pleasing reflections. At length he very abruptly exclaimed:

'A delicate epistle, truly—and a politic—would that my tongue had been burned through before I assented to that doubly-cursed contract. Why, I am not pledged yet—I am not; there is neither writing, nor troth, nor word of honour, passed between us. My father has no right to pledge me, even though I told him I liked the girl, and would wish the match. 'Tis not enough that my father offers her my heart and hand; he has no right to do it; a delicate woman would not accept professions made by proxy. Lady Emily! Lady Emily! with all the tawdry frippery, and finery of dress and demeanour—compare *her* with—Pshaw! Ridiculous! How blind, how idiotic I have been.'

He relapsed into moody reflections, which Dwyer did not care to disturb, and some ten minutes might have passed before he spoke again. When he did, it was in the calm tone of one who has irrevocably resolved upon some decided and important act.

'Dwyer,' he said, rising and approaching that person, 'whatever god or demon told you, even before my own heart knew it, that I loved Ellen Heathcote, spoke truth. I love her madly—I never dreamed till now how fervently, how irrevocably, I am hers—how dead to me all other interests are. Dwyer, I know something of your disposition, and you no doubt think it strange that I should tell to you, of all persons, *such* a secret; but whatever be your faults, I think you are attached to our family. I am satisfied you will not betray me. I know—'

'Pardon me,' said Dwyer, 'if I say that great professions of confidence too frequently mark distrust. I have no possible motive to induce me to betray you; on the contrary, I would gladly assist and direct whatever plans you may have formed. Command me as you please; I have said enough.'

'I will not doubt you, Dwyer,' said O'Mara; ' I have taken my resolution—I have, I think, firmness to act up to it. To marry Ellen Heathcote, situated as I am, were madness; to propose anything else were worse, were villainy not to be named. I will leave the country to-morrow, cost what pain it may, for England. I will at once break off the proposed alliance with Lady Emily, and will wait until I am my own master, to open my heart to Ellen. My father may say and do what he likes; but his passion will not last. He will forgive me; and even were he to disinherit me, as he threatens, there is some property which must descend to me, which his will cannot affect. He cannot ruin my interests; he *shall not* ruin my happiness. Dwyer, give me pen and ink; I will write this moment.'

This bold plan of proceeding for many reasons appeared inexpedient to Dwyer, and he determined not to consent to its adoption without a struggle.

'I commend your prudence,' said he, 'in determining to remove yourself from the fascinating influence which has so long bound you here; but beware of offending your father. Colonel O'Mara is not a man to forgive an act of deliberate disobedience, and surely you are not mad enough to ruin yourself with him by offering an out-rageous insult to Lady Emily and to her family in her person; therefore you must not break off the understood contract which subsists between you by any formal act—hear me out patiently. You must let Lady Emily perceive, as you easily may, without rudeness or even coldness of manner, that she is perfectly indifferent to you; and when she understands this to be the case, if she possesses either delicacy or spirit, she will herself break off the engagement. Make what delay it is possible to effect; it is very possible that your father, who cannot, in all probability, live many months, may not live as many days if harassed and excited by such scenes as your breaking off your engagement must produce.'

'Dwyer,' said O'Mara, 'I will hear you out—proceed.'

'Besides, sir, remember,' he continued, 'the understanding which we have termed an engagement was entered into without any direct sanction upon your part; your father has committed *himself*, not *you*, to Lord—. Before a real contract can subsist, you must be an assenting party to it. I know of no casuistry subtle enough to involve you in any engagement whatever, without such an ingredient. Tush! you have an easy card to play.'

'Well,' said the young man, 'I will think on what you have said; in the meantime, I will write to my father to announce my immediate departure, in order to join him.'

'Excuse me,' said Dwyer, 'but I would suggest that by hastening your departure you but bring your dangers nearer. While you are in this country a letter now and then keeps everything quiet; but once across the Channel and with the colonel, you must either quarrel with him to your own destruction, or you must dance attendance upon Lady Emily with such assiduity as to commit yourself as completely as if you had been thrice called with her in the parish church. No, no; keep to this side of the Channel as long as you decently can. Besides, your sudden departure must appear suspicious, and will probably excite inquiry. Every good end likely to be accomplished by your absence will be effected as well by your departure for Dublin, where you may remain for three weeks or a month without giving rise to curiosity or doubt of an unpleasant kind; I would therefore advise you strongly to write immediately to the colonel, stating that business has occurred to defer your departure for a month, and you can then leave this place, if you think fit, immediately, that is, within a week or so.'

Young O'Mara was not hard to be persuaded. Perhaps it was that, un-acknowledged by himself, any argument which recommended his stay-ing, even for an hour longer than his first decision had announced, in the neighbourhood of Ellen Heathcote, appeared peculiarly cogent and convincing; however this may have been, it is certain that he followed the counsel of his cool-headed follower, who retired that night to bed with the pleasing conviction that he was likely soon to involve his young patron in all the intricacies of disguise and intrigue—a consummation which would leave him totally at the mercy of the favoured confidant who should pos-sess his secret.

Young O'Mara's reflections were more agitating and less satisfactory than those of his companion. He resolved upon leaving the country before two days had passed. He felt that he could not fairly seek to involve Ellen Heathcote in his fate by pledge or promise, until he had extricated himself from those trammels which constrained and embarrassed all his actions. His determination was so far prudent; but, alas! he also resolved that it was but right, but necessary, that he should see her before his departure. His leaving the country without a look or a word of parting kindness inter-changed, must to her appear an act of cold and heartless caprice; he could not bear the thought.

'No,' said he, 'I am not child enough to say more than prudence tells me ought to say; this cowardly distrust of my firmness I should and will contemn. Besides, why should I commit myself? It is possible the girl may not care for me. No, no; I need not shrink from this interview. I have no reason to doubt my firmness—none—none. I must cease to be governed by impulse. I am involved in rocks and quicksands; and a collected spirit, a quick eye, and a steady hand, alone can pilot me through. God grant me a safe voyage!'

The next day came, and young O'Mara did not take his fishing-rod as usual, but wrote two letters; the one to his father, announcing his inten-tion of departing speedily for England; the other to Lady Emily, contain-ing a cold but courteous apology for his apparent neglect. Both these were despatched to the post-office that evening, and upon the next morning he was to leave the country.

Upon the night of the momentous day of which we have just spoken, Ellen Heathcote glided silently and unperceived from among the busy crowds who were engaged in the gay dissipation furnished by what is in Ireland commonly called a dance (the expenses attendant upon which, music, etc., are defrayed by a subscription of one halfpenny each), and having drawn her mantle closely about her, was proceeding with quick steps to traverse the small field which separated her from her father's abode. She had not walked many yards when she became aware that a solitary figure, muffled in a cloak, stood in the pathway. It approached; a low voice whispered:

'Ellen.'

'Is it you, Master Richard?' she replied.

He threw back the cloak which had concealed his features.

'It is I, Ellen, he said; 'I have been watching for you. I will not delay you long.'

He took her hand, and she did not attempt to withdraw it; for she was too artless to think any evil, too confiding to dread it.

'Ellen,' he continued, even now unconsciously departing from the rigid course which prudence had marked out; 'Ellen, I am going to leave the country; going to-morrow. I have had letters from England. I must go; and the sea will soon be between us.'

He paused, and she was silent.

'There is one request, one entreaty I have to make,' he continued; 'I would, when I am far away, have something to look at which belonged to you. Will you give me—do not refuse it—one little lock of your beautiful hair?'

With artless alacrity, but with trembling hand, she took the scissors, which in simple fashion hung by her side, and detached one of the long and beautiful locks which parted over her forehead. She placed it in his hand.

Again he took her hand, and twice he attempted to speak in vain; at length he said:

'Ellen, when I am gone—when I am away—will you sometimes remember, sometimes think of me?'

Ellen Heathcote had as much, perhaps more, of what is noble in pride than the haughtiest beauty that ever trod a court; but the effort was useless; the honest struggle was in vain; and she burst into floods of tears, bitterer than she had ever shed before.

I cannot tell how passions rise and fall; I cannot describe the impetuous words of the young lover, as pressing again and again to his lips the cold, passive hand, which had been resigned to him, prudence, caution, doubts, resolutions, all vanished from his view, and melted into nothing. 'Tis for me to tell the simple fact, that from that brief interview they both departed promised and pledged to each other for ever.

Through the rest of this story events follow one another rapidly.

A few nights after that which I have just mentioned, Ellen Heathcote disappeared; but her father was not left long in suspense as to her fate, for Dwyer, accompanied by one of those mendicant friars who traversed the country then even more commonly than they now do, called upon Heathcote before he had had time to take any active measures for the recovery of his child, and put him in possession of a document which appeared to contain satisfactory evidence of the marriage of Ellen Heathcote with Richard O'Mara, executed upon the evening previous, as the date went to show; and signed by both parties, as well as by Dwyer and a servant of young O'Mara's, both these having acted as witnesses; and further supported by the signature of Peter Nicholls, a brother of the order of St. Francis, by whom the ceremony had been performed, and whom Heathcote had no difficulty in recognising in the person of his visitant.

This document, and the prompt personal visit of the two men, and above all, the known identity of the Franciscan, satisfied Heathcote as fully as anything short of complete publicity could have done. And his conviction was not a mistaken one.

Dwyer, before he took his leave, impressed upon Heathcote the necessity of keeping the affair so secret as to render it impossible that it should reach Colonel O'Mara's ears, an event which would have been attended with ruinous consequences to all parties. He refused, also, to permit Heathcote to see his daughter, and even to tell him where she was, until circumstances rendered it safe for him to visit her.

Heathcote was a harsh and sullen man; and though his temper was anything but tractable, there was so much to please, almost to dazzle him, in the event, that he accepted the terms which Dwyer imposed upon him without any further token of disapprobation than a shake of the head, and a gruff wish that 'it might prove all for the best.'

Nearly two months had passed, and young O'Mara had not yet departed for England. His letters had been strangely few and far between; and in short, his conduct was such as to induce Colonel O'Mara to hasten his return to Ireland, and at the same time to press an engagement, which Lord—, his son Captain N—, and Lady Emily had made to spend some weeks with him at his residence in Dublin.

A letter arrived for young O'Mara, stating the arrangement, and requiring his attendance in Dublin, which was accordingly immediately afforded.

He arrived, with Dwyer, in time to welcome his father and his distinguished guests. He resolved to break off his embarrassing connection with Lady Emily, without, however, stating the real motive, which he felt would exasperate the resentment which his father and Lord—would no doubt feel at his conduct.

He strongly felt how dishonourably he would act if, in obedience to Dwyer's advice, he seemed tacitly to acquiesce in an engagement which it was impossible for him to fulfil. He knew that Lady Emily was not capable of anything like strong attachment; and that even if she were, he had no reason whatever to suppose that she cared at all for him.

He had not at any time desired the alliance; nor had he any reason to suppose the young lady in any degree less indifferent. He regarded it now, and not without some appearance of justice, as nothing more than a kind of understood stipulation, entered into by their parents, and to be considered rather as a matter of business and calculation than as involving anything of mutual inclination on the part of the parties most nearly interested in the matter.

He anxiously, therefore, watched for an opportunity of making known his feelings to Lord—, as he could not with propriety do so to Lady Emily; but what at a distance appeared to be a matter of easy accomplishment, now, upon a nearer approach, and when the immediate impulse which had prompted the act had subsided, appeared so full of difficulty and almost inextricable embarrassments, that he involuntarily shrunk from the task day after day.

Though it was a source of indescribable anxiety to him, he did not venture to write to Ellen, for he could not disguise from himself the danger which the secrecy of his connection with her must incur by his communicating with her, even through a public office, where their letters might be permitted to lie longer than the gossiping inquisitiveness of a country town would warrant him in supposing safe.

It was about a fortnight after young O'Mara had arrived in Dublin, where all things, and places, and amusements; and persons seemed thoroughly stale, flat, and unprofitable, when one day, tempted by the unusual fineness of the weather, Lady Emily proposed a walk in the College Park, a favourite promenade at that time. She therefore with young O'Mara, accompanied by Dwyer (who, by-the-by, when he pleased, could act the gentleman sufficiently well), proceeded to the place proposed, where they continued to walk for some time.

'Why, Richard,' said Lady Emily, after a tedious and unbroken pause of some minutes, 'you are becoming worse and worse every day. You are growing absolutely intolerable; perfectly stupid! not one good thing have I heard since I left the house.'

O'Mara smiled, and was seeking for a suitable reply, when his design was interrupted, and his attention suddenly and painfully arrested, by the appearance of two figures, who were slowly passing the broad walk on which he and his party moved; the one was that of Captain N—, the other was the form of—Martin Heathcote!

O'Mara felt confounded, almost stunned; the anticipation of some impending mischief—of an immediate and violent collision with a young man whom he had ever regarded as his friend, were apprehensions which such a juxtaposition could not fail to produce.

'Is Heathcote mad?' thought he. 'What devil can have brought him here?'

Dwyer having exchanged a significant glance with O'Mara, said slightly to Lady Emily:

'Will your ladyship excuse me for a moment? I have a word to say to Captain N—, and will, with your permission, immediately rejoin you.'

He bowed, and walking rapidly on, was in a few moments beside the object of his and his patron's uneasiness.

Whatever Heathcote's object might be, he certainly had not yet declared the secret, whose safety O'Mara had so naturally desired, for Captain N—appeared in good spirits; and on coming up to his sister and her companion, he joined them for a moment, telling O'Mara, laughingly, that an old quiz had come from the country for the express purpose of telling tales, as it was to be supposed, of him (young O'Mara), in whose neighbourhood he lived.

During this speech it required all the effort which it was possible to exert to prevent O'Mara's betraying the extreme agitation to which his situation gave rise. Captain N—, however, suspected no-thing, and passed on without further delay.

Dinner was an early meal in those days, and Lady Emily was obliged to leave the Park in less than half an hour after the unpleasant meeting which we have just mentioned.

Young O'Mara and, at a sign from him, Dwyer having escorted the lady to the door of Colonel O'Mara's house, pretended an engagement, and departed together.

Richard O'Mara instantly questioned his comrade upon the subject of his anxiety; but Dwyer had nothing to communicate of a satisfactory nature. He had only time, while the captain had been engaged with Lady Emily and her companion, to say to Heathcote:

'Be secret, as you value your existence: everything will be right, if you be but secret.'

To this Heathcote had replied: 'Never fear me; I understand what I am about.'

This was said in such an ambiguous manner that it was impossible to conjecture whether he intended or not to act upon Dwyer's exhortation. The conclusion which appeared most natural, was by no means an agreeable one.

It was much to be feared that Heathcote having heard some vague report of O'Mara's engagement with Lady Emily, perhaps exaggerated, by the repetition, into a speedily approaching marriage, had become alarmed for his daughter's interest, and had taken this decisive step in order to prevent, by a disclosure of the circumstances of his clandestine union with Ellen, the possibility of his completing a guilty alliance with Captain N—'s sister. If he entertained the suspicions which they attributed to him, he had certainly taken the most effectual means to prevent their being re-alised. Whatever his object might be, his presence in Dublin, in company with Captain N—, boded nothing good to O'Mara.

They entered—'s tavern, in Dame Street, together; and there, over a hasty and by no means a comfortable meal, they talked over their plans and conjectures. Evening closed in, and found them still closeted together, with nothing to interrupt, and a large tankard of claret to sustain their desultory conversation.

Nothing had been determined upon, except that Dwyer and O'Mara should proceed under cover of the darkness to search the town for Heathcote, and by minute inquiries at the most frequented houses of entertainment, to ascertain his place of residence, in order to procuring a full and explanatory interview with him. They had each filled their last glass, and were sipping it slowly, seated with their feet stretched towards a bright cheerful fire; the small table which sustained the flagon of which we have spoken, together with two pair of wax candles, placed between them, so as to afford a convenient resting-place for the long glasses out of which they drank.

'One good result, at all events, will be effected by Heathcote's visit,' said O'Mara. 'Before twenty-four hours I shall do that which I should have done long ago. I shall, without reserve, state everything. I can no longer endure this suspense—this dishonourable secrecy—this apparent dissimulation. Every moment I have passed since my departure from the country has been one of embarrassment, of pain, of humiliation. To-morrow I will brave the storm, whether successfully or not is doubtful; but I had rather walk the high roads a beggar, than submit a day longer to be made the degraded sport of every accident—the miserable dependent upon a successful system of deception. Though *passive* deception, it is still unmanly, unworthy, unjustifiable deception. I cannot bear to think of it. I despise myself, but I will cease to be the despicable thing I have become. To-morrow sees me free, and this harassing subject for ever at rest.'

He was interrupted here by the sound of footsteps heavily but rapidly ascending the tavern staircase. The room door opened, and Captain N—, accompanied by a fashionably-attired young man, entered the room.

Young O'Mara had risen from his seat on the entrance of their unexpected visitants; and the moment Captain N—recognised his person, an evident and ominous change passed over his countenance. He turned hastily to withdraw, but, as it seemed, almost instantly changed his mind, for he turned again abruptly.

'This chamber is engaged, sir,' said the waiter.

'Leave the room, sir,' was his only reply.

'The room is engaged, sir,' repeated the waiter, probably believing that his first suggestion had been unheard.

'Leave the room, or go to hell!' shouted Captain N—; at the same time seizing the astounded waiter by the shoulder, he hurled him headlong into the passage, and flung the door to with a crash that shook the walls. 'Sir,' continued he, addressing himself to O'Mara, 'I did not hope to have met you until to-morrow. Fortune has been kind to me—draw, and defend yourself.'

At the same time he drew his sword, and placed himself in an attitude of attack.

'I will not draw upon *you*,' said O'Mara. 'I have, indeed, wronged you. I have given you just cause for resentment; but against your life I will never lift my hand.'

'You are a coward, sir,' replied Captain N—, with almost frightful vehemence, 'as every trickster and swindler *is*. You are a contemptible dastard—a despicable, damned villain! Draw your sword, sir, and defend your life, or every post and pillar in this town shall tell your infamy.'

'Perhaps,' said his friend, with a sneer, 'the gentleman can do better without his honour than without his wife.'

'Yes,' shouted the captain, 'his wife—a trull—a common—'

'Silence, sir!' cried O'Mara, all the fierceness of his nature roused by this last insult—'your object is gained; your blood be upon your own head.' At the same time he sprang across a bench which stood in his way, and pushing aside the table which supported the lights, in an instant their swords crossed, and they were engaged in close and deadly strife.

Captain N—was far the stronger of the two; but, on the other hand, O'Mara possessed far more skill in the use of the fatal weapon which they employed. But the narrowness of the room rendered this advantage hardly available.

Almost instantly O'Mara received a slight wound upon the forehead, which, though little more than a scratch, bled so fast as to obstruct his sight considerably.

Those who have used the foil can tell how slight a derangement of eye or of hand is sufficient to determine a contest of this kind; and this knowledge will prevent their being surprised when I say, that, spite of O'Mara's superior skill and practice, his adversary's sword passed twice through and through his body, and he fell heavily and helplessly upon the floor of the chamber.

Without saying a word, the successful combatant quitted the room along with his companion, leaving Dwyer to shift as best he might for his fallen comrade.

With the assistance of some of the wondering menials of the place, Dwyer succeeded in conveying the wounded man into an adjoining room, where he was laid upon a bed, in a state bordering upon insensibility—the blood flowing, I might say *welling*, from the wounds so fast as to show that unless the bleeding were speedily and effectually stopped, he could not live for half an hour.

Medical aid was, of course, instantly procured, and Colonel O'Mara, though at the time seriously indisposed, was urgently requested to attend without loss of time. He did so; but human succour and support were all too late. The wound had been truly dealt—the tide of life had ebbed; and his father had not arrived five minutes when young O'Mara was a corpse. His body rests in the vaults of Christ Church, in Dublin, without a stone to mark the spot.

The counsels of the wicked are always dark, and their motives often beyond fathoming; and strange, unaccountable, incredible as it may seem, I do believe, and that upon evidence so clear as to amount almost to demonstration, that Heathcote's visit to Dublin—his betrayal of the secret—and the final and terrible catastrophe which laid O'Mara in the grave, were brought about by no other agent than Dwyer himself.

I have myself seen the letter which induced that visit. The handwriting is exactly what I have seen in other alleged specimens of Dwyer's penmanship. It is written with an affectation of honest alarm at O'Mara's conduct, and expresses a conviction that if some of Lady Emily's family be not informed of O'Mara's real situation, nothing could prevent his concluding with her an advantageous alliance, then upon the tapis, and altogether throwing off his allegiance to Ellen—a step which, as the writer candidly asserted, would finally conduce as inevitably to his own disgrace as it immediately would to her ruin and misery.

The production was formally signed with Dwyer's name, and the post-script contained a strict injunction of secrecy, asserting that if it were as-certained that such an epistle had been despatched from such a quarter, it would be attended with the total ruin of the writer.

It is true that Dwyer, many years after, when this letter came to light, alleged it to be a forgery, an assertion whose truth, even to his dying hour, and long after he had apparently ceased to feel the lash of public scorn, he continued obstinately to maintain. Indeed this matter is full of mystery, for, revenge alone excepted, which I believe, in such minds as Dwyer's, seldom overcomes the sense of interest, the only intelligible motive which could have prompted him to such an act was the hope that since he had, through young O'Mara's interest, procured from the colonel a lease of a small farm upon the terms which he had originally stipulated, he might prosecute his plan touching the property of Martin Heathcote, rendering his daughter's hand free by the removal of young O'Mara. This appears to me too complicated a plan of villany to have entered the mind even of such a man as Dwyer. I must, therefore, suppose his motives to have originated out of circumstances connected with this story which may not have come to my ear, and perhaps never will.

Colonel O'Mara felt the death of his son more deeply than I should have thought possible; but that son had been the last being who had con-tinued to interest his cold heart. Perhaps the pride which he felt in his child had in it more of selfishness than of any generous feeling. But, be this as it may, the melancholy circumstances connected with Ellen Heath-cote had reached him, and his conduct towards her proved, more strongly than anything else could have done, that he felt keenly and justly, and, to a certain degree, with a softened heart, the fatal event of which she had been, in some manner, alike the cause and the victim.

He evinced not towards her, as might have been expected, any un-reasonable resentment. On the contrary, he exhibited great consideration, even tenderness, for her situation; and having ascertained where his son had placed her, he issued strict orders that she should not be disturbed, and that the fatal tidings, which had not yet reached her, should be with-held until they might be communicated in such a way as to soften as much as possible the inevitable shock.

These last directions were acted upon too scrupulously and too long; and, indeed, I am satisfied that had the event been communicated at once, however terrible and overwhelming the shock might have been, much of the bitterest anguish, of sickening doubts, of harassing suspense, would have been spared her, and the first tempestuous burst of sorrow having passed over, her chastened spirit might have recovered its tone, and her life have been spared. But the mistaken kindness which concealed from her the dreadful truth, instead of relieving her mind of a burden which it could not support, laid upon it a weight of horrible fears and doubts as to the affection of O'Mara, compared with which even the certainty of his death would have been tolerable.

One evening I had just seated myself beside a cheerful turf fire, with that true relish which a long cold ride through a bleak and shelterless country affords, stretching my chilled limbs to meet the genial influence, and imbibing the warmth at every pore, when my comfortable meditations were interrupted by a long and sonorous ringing at the door-bell evidently effected by no timid hand.

A messenger had arrived to request my attendance at the Lodge— such was the name which distinguished a small and somewhat antiquated building, occupying a peculiarly secluded position among the bleak and heathy hills which varied the surface of that not altogether uninteresting district, and which had, I believe, been employed by the keen and hardy ancestors of the O'Mara family as a convenient temporary residence during the sporting season.

Thither my attendance was required, in order to administer to a deeply distressed lady such comforts as an afflicted mind can gather from the sublime hopes and consolations of Christianity.

I had long suspected that the occupant of this sequestered, I might say desolate, dwelling-house was the poor girl whose brief story we are following; and feeling a keen interest in her fate—as who that had ever seen her *did not?*—I started from my comfortable seat with more eager alacrity than, I will confess it, I might have evinced had my duty called me in another direction.

In a few minutes I was trotting rapidly onward, preceded by my guide, who urged his horse with the remorseless rapidity of one who seeks by the speed of his progress to escape observation. Over roads and through bogs we splashed and clattered, until at length traversing the brow of a wild and rocky hill, whose aspect seemed so barren and forbidding that it might have been a lasting barrier alike to mortal sight and step, the lonely building became visible, lying in a kind of swampy flat, with a broad reedy pond or lake stretching away to its side, and backed by a farther range of monotonous sweeping hills, marked with irregular lines of grey rock, which, in the distance, bore a rude and colossal resemblance to the walls of a fortification.

Riding with undiminished speed along a kind of wild horse-track, we turned the corner of a high and somewhat ruinous wall of loose stones, and making a sudden wheel we found ourselves in a small quadrangle, surmounted on two sides by dilapidated stables and kennels, on another by a broken stone wall, and upon the fourth by the front of the lodge itself.

The whole character of the place was that of dreary desertion and decay, which would of itself have predisposed the mind for melancholy impressions. My guide dismounted, and with respectful attention held my horse's bridle while I got down; and knocking at the door with the handle of his whip, it was speedily opened by a neatly-dressed female domestic, and I was admitted to the interior of the house, and conducted into a small room, where a fire in some degree dispelled the cheerless air, which would otherwise have prevailed to a painful degree throughout the place.

I had been waiting but for a very few minutes when another female servant, somewhat older than the first, entered the room. She made some apology on the part of the person whom I had come to visit, for the slight delay which had already occurred, and requested me further to wait for a few minutes longer, intimating that the lady's grief was so violent, that without great effort she could not bring herself to speak calmly at all. As if to beguile the time, the good dame went on in a highly communicative strain to tell me, amongst much that could not interest me, a little of what I had desired to hear. I discovered that the grief of her whom I had come to visit was excited by the sudden death of a little boy, her only child, who was then lying dead in his mother's chamber.

'And the mother's name?' said I, inquiringly.

The woman looked at me for a moment, smiled, and shook her head with the air of mingled mystery and importance which seems to say, 'I am unfathomable.' I did not care to press the question, though I suspected that much of her apparent reluctance was affected, knowing that my doubts respecting the identity of the person whom I had come to visit must soon be set at rest, and after a little pause the worthy Abigail went on as fluently as ever. She told me that her young mistress had been, for the time she had been with her—that was, for about a year and a half—in declining health and spirits, and that she had loved her little child to a degree beyond expression—so devotedly that she could not, in all probability, survive it long.

While she was running on in this way the bell rang, and signing me to follow, she opened the room door, but stopped in the hall, and taking me a little aside, and speaking in a whisper, she told me, as I valued the life of the poor lady, not to say one word of the death of young O'Mara. I nodded acquiescence, and ascending a narrow and ill-constructed staircase, she stopped at a chamber door and knocked.

'Come in,' said a gentle voice from within, and, preceded by my conductress, I entered a moderately-sized, but rather gloomy chamber.

There was but one living form within it—it was the light and graceful figure of a young woman. She had risen as I entered the room; but owing to the obscurity of the apartment, and to the circumstance that her face, as she looked towards the door, was turned away from the light, which found its way in dimly through the narrow windows, I could not instantly recognise the features.

'You do not remember me, sir?' said the same low, mournful voice. 'I am—I *was*—Ellen Heathcote.'

'I do remember you, my poor child,' said I, taking her hand; 'I do remember you very well. Speak to me frankly—speak to me as a friend. Whatever I can do or say for you, is yours already; only speak.'

'You were always very kind, sir, to those—to those that *wanted* kindness.'

The tears were almost overflowing, but she checked them; and as if an accession of fortitude had followed the momentary weakness, she continued, in a subdued but firm tone, to tell me briefly the circumstances of her marriage with O'Mara. When she had concluded the recital, she paused for a moment; and I asked again:

'Can I aid you in any way—by advice or otherwise?'

'I wish, sir, to tell you all I have been thinking about,' she continued. 'I am sure, sir, that Master Richard loved me once—I am sure he did not think to deceive me; but there were bad, hard-hearted people about him, and his family were all rich and high, and I am sure he wishes *now* that he had never, never seen me. Well, sir, it is not in my heart to blame him. What was I that I should look at him?—an ignorant, poor, country girl—and he so high and great, and so beautiful. The blame was all mine—it was all my fault; I could not think or hope he would care for me more than a little time. Well, sir, I thought over and over again that since his love was gone from me for ever, I should not stand in his way, and hinder whatever great thing his family wished for him. So I thought often and often to write him a letter to get the marriage broken, and to send me home; but for one reason, I would have done it long ago: there was a little child, his and mine—the dearest, the loveliest.' She could not go on for a minute or two. 'The little child that is lying there, on that bed; but it is dead and gone, and there is no reason *now* why I should delay any more about it.'

She put her hand into her breast, and took out a letter, which she opened. She put it into my hands. It ran thus:

DEAR MASTER RICHARD,

My little child is dead, and your happiness is all I care about now. Your marriage with me is displeasing to your family, and I would be a burden to you, and in your way in the fine places, and among the great friends where you must be. You ought, therefore, to break the marriage, and I will sign whatever *you* wish, or your family. I will never try to blame you, Master Richard—do not think it—for I never deserved your love, and must not complain now that I have lost it; but I will always pray for you, and be thinking of you while I live.

While I read this letter, I was satisfied that so far from adding to the poor girl's grief, a full disclosure of what had happened would, on the contrary, mitigate her sorrow, and deprive it of its sharpest sting.

'Ellen,' said I solemnly, 'Richard O'Mara was never unfaithful to you; he is now where human reproach can reach him no more.'

As I said this, the hectic flush upon her cheek gave place to a paleness so deadly, that I almost thought she would drop lifeless upon the spot.

'Is he—is he dead, then?' said she, wildly.

I took her hand in mine, and told her the sad story as best I could. She listened with a calmness which appeared almost unnatural, until I had finished the mournful narration. She then arose, and going to the bedside, she drew the curtain and gazed silently and fixedly on the quiet face of the child: but the feelings which swelled at her heart could not be suppressed; the tears gushed forth, and sobbing as if her heart would break, she leant over the bed and took the dead child in her arms.

She wept and kissed it, and kissed it and wept again, in grief so passionate, so heartrending, as to draw bitter tears from my eyes. I said what little I could to calm her—to have sought to do more would have been a mockery; and observing that the darkness had closed in, I took my leave and departed, being favoured with the services of my former guide.

I expected to have been soon called upon again to visit the poor girl; but the Lodge lay beyond the boundary of my parish, and I felt a reluctance to trespass upon the precincts of my brother minister, and a certain degree of hesitation in intruding upon one whose situation was so very peculiar, and who would, I had no doubt, feel no scruple in requesting my attendance if she desired it.

A month, however, passed away, and I did not hear anything of Ellen. I called at the Lodge, and to my inquiries they answered that she was very much worse in health, and that since the death of the child she had been sinking fast, and so weak that she had been chiefly confined to her bed. I sent frequently to inquire, and often called myself, and all that I heard convinced me that she was rapidly sinking into the grave.

Late one night I was summoned from my rest, by a visit from the person who had upon the former occasion acted as my guide; he had come to summon me to the death-bed of her whom I had then attended.

With all celerity I made my preparations, and, not without considerable difficulty and some danger, we made a rapid night-ride to the Lodge, a distance of five miles at least. We arrived safely, and in a very short time—but too late.

I stood by the bed upon which lay the once beautiful form of Ellen Heathcote. The brief but sorrowful trial was past—the desolate mourner was gone to that land where the pangs of grief, the tumults of passion, regrets and cold neglect, are felt no more. I leant over the lifeless face, and scanned the beautiful features which, living, had wrought such magic on all that looked upon them. They were, indeed, much wasted; but it was impossible for the fingers of death or of decay altogether to obliterate the traces of that exquisite beauty which had so distinguished her. As I gazed on this most sad and striking spectacle, remembrances thronged fast upon my mind, and tear after tear fell upon the cold form that slept tranquilly and for ever.

A few days afterwards I was told that a funeral had left the Lodge at the dead of night, and had been conducted with the most scrupulous secrecy. It was, of course, to me no mystery.

Heathcote lived to a very advanced age, being of that hard mould which is not easily impressionable. The selfish and the hard-hearted survive where nobler, more generous, and, above all, more sympathising natures would have sunk for ever.

Dwyer certainly succeeded in extorting, I cannot say how, considerable and advantageous leases from Colonel O'Mara; but after his death he disposed of his interest in these, and having for a time launched into a sea of profligate extravagance, he became bankrupt, and for a long time I totally lost sight of him.

The rebellion of '98, and the events which immediately followed, called him forth from his lurking-places, in the character of an informer; and I myself have seen the hoary-headed, paralytic perjurer, with a scowl of derision and defiance, brave the hootings and the execrations of the indignant multitude.

Strange Event in the Life of Schalken the Painter

BEING A SEVENTH EXTRACT FROM THE LEGACY OF
THE LATE FRANCIS PURCELL, P. P. OF DRUMCOOLAGH.

YOU WILL no doubt be surprised, my dear friend, at the subject of the following narrative. What had I to do with Schalken, or Schalken with me? He had returned to his native land, and was probably dead and buried, before I was born; I never visited Holland nor spoke with a native of that country. So much I believe you already know. I must, then, give you my authority, and state to you frankly the ground upon which rests the credibility of the strange story which I am, about to lay before you.

I was acquainted, in my early days, with a Captain Vandael, whose father had served King William in the Low Countries, and also in my own unhappy land during the Irish campaigns. I know not how it happened that I liked this man's society, spite of his politics and religion: but so it was; and it was by means of the free intercourse to which our intimacy gave rise that I became possessed of the curious tale which you are about to hear.

I had often been struck, while visiting Vandael, by a remarkable picture, in which, though no connoisseur myself, I could not fail to discern some very strong peculiarities, particularly in the distribu-tion of light and shade, as also a certain oddity in the design itself, which interested my curiosity. It represented the interior of what might be a chamber in some antique religious building—the foreground was occupied by a female figure, arrayed in a species of white robe, part of which is arranged so as to form a veil. The dress, however, is not strictly that of any religious order. In its hand the figure bears a lamp, by whose light alone the form and face are illuminated; the features are marked by an arch smile, such as pretty women wear when engaged in successfully practising some roguish trick; in the background, and, excepting where the dim red light of an expiring fire serves to define the form, totally in the shade, stands the figure of a man equipped in the old fashion, with doublet and so forth, in an attitude of alarm, his hand being placed upon the hilt of his sword, which he appears to be in the act of drawing.

'There are some pictures,' said I to my friend, 'which impress one, I know not how, with a conviction that they represent not the mere ideal shapes and combinations which have floated through the imagination of the artist, but scenes, faces, and situations which have actually existed.

When I look upon that picture, something assures me that I behold the representation of a reality.'

Vandael smiled, and, fixing his eyes upon the painting musingly, he said:

'Your fancy has not deceived you, my good friend, for that picture is the record, and I believe a faithful one, of a remarkable and mysterious occurrence. It was painted by Schalken, and contains, in the face of the female figure, which occupies the most prominent place in the design, an accurate portrait of Rose Velderkaust, the niece of Gerard Douw, the first and, I believe, the only love of Godfrey Schalken. My father knew the painter well, and from Schalken himself he learned the story of the mysterious drama, one scene of which the picture has embodied. This painting, which is accounted a fine specimen of Schalken's style, was bequeathed to my father by the artist's will, and, as you have observed, is a very striking and interesting production.'

I had only to request Vandael to tell the story of the painting in order to be gratified; and thus it is that I am enabled to submit to you a faithful recital of what I heard myself, leaving you to reject or to allow the evidence upon which the truth of the tradition depends, with this one assurance, that Schalken was an honest, blunt Dutchman, and, I believe, wholly incapable of committing a flight of imagination; and further, that Vandael, from whom I heard the story, appeared firmly convinced of its truth.

There are few forms upon which the mantle of mystery and romance could seem to hang more ungracefully than upon that of the uncouth and clownish Schalken—the Dutch boor—the rude and dogged, but most cunning worker in oils, whose pieces delight the initiated of the present day almost as much as his manners disgusted the refined of his own; and yet this man, so rude, so dogged, so slovenly, I had almost said so savage, in mien and manner, during his after successes, had been selected by the capricious goddess, in his early life, to figure as the hero of a romance by no means devoid of interest or of mystery.

Who can tell how meet he may have been in his young days to play the part of the lover or of the hero—who can say that in early life he had been the same harsh, unlicked, and rugged boor that, in his maturer age, he proved—or how far the neglected rudeness which afterwards marked his air, and garb, and manners, may not have been the growth of that reckless apathy not unfrequently produced by bitter misfortunes and disappointments in early life?

These questions can never now be answered.

We must content ourselves, then, with a plain statement of facts, or what have been received and transmitted as such, leaving matters of speculation to those who like them.

When Schalken studied under the immortal Gerard Douw, he was a young man; and in spite of the phlegmatic constitution and unexcitable manner which he shared, we believe, with his countrymen, he was not incapable of deep and vivid impressions, for it is an established fact that the young painter looked with considerable interest upon the beautiful niece of his wealthy master.

Rose Velderkaust was very young, having, at the period of which we speak, not yet attained her seventeenth year, and, if tradition speaks truth, possessed all the soft dimpling charms of the fail; light-haired Flemish maidens. Schalken had not studied long in the school of Gerard Douw, when he felt this interest deepening into something of a keener and intenser feeling than was quite consistent with the tranquillity of his honest Dutch heart; and at the same time he perceived, or thought he perceived, flattering symptoms of a reciprocity of liking, and this was quite sufficient to determine whatever indecision he might have heretofore experienced, and to lead him to devote exclusively to her every hope and feeling of his heart. In short, he was as much in love as a Dutchman could be. He was not long in making his passion known to the pretty maiden herself, and his declaration was followed by a corresponding confession upon her part.

Schalken, however, was a poor man, and he possessed no counterbalancing advantages of birth or position to induce the old man to consent to a union which must involve his niece and ward in the strugglings and difficulties of a young and nearly friendless artist. He was, therefore, to wait until time had furnished him with opportunity, and accident with success; and then, if his labours were found sufficiently lucrative, it was to be hoped that his proposals might at least be listened to by her jealous guardian. Months passed away, and, cheered by the smiles of the little Rose, Schalken's labours were redoubled, and with such effect and improvement as reasonably to promise the realisation of his hopes, and no contemptible eminence in his art, before many years should have elapsed.

The even course of this cheering prosperity was, however, destined to experience a sudden and formidable interruption, and that, too, in a manner so strange and mysterious as to baffle all investigation, and throw upon the events themselves a shadow of almost supernatural horror.

Schalken had one evening remained in the master's studio considerably longer than his more volatile companions, who had gladly availed themselves of the excuse which the dusk of evening afforded, to withdraw from their several tasks, in order to finish a day of labour in the jollity and conviviality of the tavern.

But Schalken worked for improvement, or rather for love. Besides, he was now engaged merely in sketching a design, an operation which, unlike that of colouring, might be continued as long as there was light sufficient to distinguish between canvas and charcoal. He had not then, nor, indeed, until long after, discovered the peculiar powers of his pencil, and he was engaged in composing a group of extremely roguish-looking and grotesque imps and demons, who were inflicting various ingenious torments upon a perspiring and pot-bellied St. Anthony, who reclined in the midst of them, apparently in the last stage of drunkenness.

The young artist, however, though incapable of executing, or even of appreciating, anything of true sublimity, had nevertheless discernment enough to prevent his being by any means satisfied with his work; and many were the patient erasures and corrections which the limbs and features of saint and devil underwent, yet all without producing in their new arrangement anything of improvement or increased effect.

The large, old-fashioned room was silent, and, with the exception of himself, quite deserted by its usual inmates. An hour had passed—nearly two—without any improved result. Daylight had already declined, and twilight was fast giving way to the darkness of night. The patience of the young man was exhausted, and he stood before his unfinished production, absorbed in no very pleasing ruminations, one hand buried in the folds of his long dark hair, and the other holding the piece of charcoal which had so ill executed its office, and which he now rubbed, without much regard to the sable streaks which it produced, with irritable pressure upon his ample Flemish inexpressibles.

'Pshaw!' said the young man aloud, 'would that picture, devils, saint, and all, were where they should be—in hell!'

A short, sudden laugh, uttered start
lingly close to his ear, instantly responded to the ejaculation.

The artist turned sharply round, and now for the first time became aware that his labours had been overlooked by a stranger.

Within about a yard and a half, and rather behind him, there stood what was, or appeared to be, the figure of an elderly man: he wore a short cloak, and broad-brimmed hat with a conical crown, and in his hand, which was protected with a heavy, gauntlet-shaped glove, he carried a long ebony walking-stick, surmounted with what appeared, as it glittered dimly in the twilight, to be a massive head of gold, and upon his breast, through the folds of the cloak, there shone what appeared to be the links of a rich chain of the same metal.

The room was so obscure that nothing further of the appearance of the figure could be ascertained, and the face was altogether overshadowed by the heavy flap of the beaver which overhung it, so that not a feature could be discerned. A quantity of dark hair escaped from beneath this sombre hat, a circumstance which, connected with the firm, upright carriage of the intruder, proved that his years could not yet exceed threescore or thereabouts.

There was an air of gravity and importance about the garb of this person, and something indescribably odd, I might say awful, in the perfect, stone-like movelessness of the figure, that effectually checked the testy comment which had at once risen to the lips of the irritated artist. He therefore, as soon as he had suf-ficiently recovered the surprise, asked the stranger, civilly, to be seated, and desired to know if he had any message to leave for his master.

'Tell Gerard Douw,' said the unknown, without altering his attitude in the smallest degree, 'that Mynher Vanderhauseny of Rotterdam, desires to speak with him to-morrow evening at this hour, and, if he please, in this room, upon matters of weight—that is all. Good-night.'

The stranger, having finished this message, turned abruptly, and, with a quick but silent step, quitted the room, before Schalken had time to say a word in reply.

The young man felt a curiosity to see in what direction the burgher of Rotterdam would turn on quitting the studio, and for that purpose he went directly to the window which commanded the door.

A lobby of considerable extent intervened between the inner door of the painter's room and the street entrance, so that Schalken occupied the post of observation before the old man could possibly have reached the street.

He watched in vain, however. There was no other mode of exit.

Had the old man vanished, or was he lurking about the recesses of the lobby for some bad purpose? This last suggestion filled the mind of Schalken with a vague horror, which was so unaccountably intense as to make him alike afraid to remain in the room alone and reluctant to pass through the lobby.

However, with an effort which ap-peared very disproportioned to the occasion, he summoned resolution to leave the room, and, having double-locked the door and thrust the key in his pocket, without looking to the right or left, he traversed the passage which had so recently, perhaps still, contained the person of his mysterious visitant, scarcely venturing to breathe till he had arrived in the open street.

'Mynher Vanderhausen,' said Gerard Douw within himself, as the appointed hour approached, 'Mynher Vanderhausen of Rotterdam! I never heard of the man till yesterday. What can he want of me? A portrait, perhaps, to be painted; or a younger son or a poor relation to be apprenticed; or a collection to be valued; or—pshaw I there's no one in Rotterdam to leave me a legacy. Well, whatever the business may be, we shall soon know it all.'

It was now the close of day, and every easel, except that of Schalken, was deserted. Gerard Douw was pacing the apartment with the restless step of impatient expectation, every now and then humming a passage from a piece of music which he was himself composing; for, though no great proficient, he admired the art; sometimes pausing to glance over the work of one of his absent pupils, but more frequently placing himself at the window, from whence he might observe the passengers who threaded the obscure by-street in which his studio was placed.

'Said you not, Godfrey,' exclaimed Douw, after a long and fruitless gaze from his post of observation, and turning to Schalken—'said you not the hour of ap-pointment was at about seven by the clock of the Stadhouse?'

'It had just told seven when I first saw him, sir,' answered the student.

'The hour is close at hand, then,' said the master, consulting a horo-loge as large and as round as a full-grown orange. 'Mynher Vanderhausen, from Rotterdam—is it not so?'

'Such was the name.'

'And an elderly man, richly clad?' continued Douw.

'As well as I might see,' replied his pupil; 'he could not be young, nor yet very old neither, and his dress was rich and grave, as might become a citizen of wealth and consideration.'

At this moment the sonorous boom of the Stadhouse clock told, stroke after stroke, the hour of seven; the eyes of both master and student were directed to the door; and it was not until the last peal of the old bell had ceased to vibrate, that Douw exclaimed:

'So, so; we shall have his worship presently—that is, if he means to keep his hour; if not, thou mayst wait for him, Godfrey, if you court the acquaintance of a capricious burgomaster. As for me, I think our old Ley-den contains a sufficiency of such commodities, without an importation from Rotterdam.'

Schalken laughed, as in duty bound; and after a pause of some min-utes, Douw suddenly exclaimed:

'What if it should all prove a jest, a piece of mummery got up by Van-karp, or some such worthy! I wish you had run all risks, and cudgelled the old burgomaster, stadholder, or whatever else he may be, soundly. I would wager a dozen of Rhenish, his worship would have pleaded old acquain-tance before the third application.'

'Here he comes, sir,' said Schalken, in a low admonitory tone; and in-stantly, upon turning towards the door, Gerard Douw observed the same figure which had, on the day before, so unexpectedly greeted the vision of his pupil Schalken.

There was something in the air and mien of the figure which at once satisfied the painter that there was no mummery in the case, and that he really stood in the presence of a man of worship; and so, without hesitation, he doffed his cap, and courteously saluting the stranger, requested him to be seated.

The visitor waved his hand slightly, as, if in acknowledgment of the courtesy, but remained standing.

'I have the honour to see Mynher Vanderhausen, of Rotterdam?' said Gerard Douw.

'The same,' was the laconic reply of his visitant.

'I understand your worship desires to speak with me,' continued Douw, 'and I am here by appointment to wait your commands.'

'Is that a man of trust?' said Vanderhausen, turning towards Schalken, who stood at a little distance behind his master.

'Certainly,' replied Gerard.

'Then let him take this box and get the nearest jeweller or goldsmith to value its contents, and let him return hither with a certificate of the valuation.'

At the same time he placed a small case, about nine inches square, in the hands of Gerard Douw, who was as much amazed at its weight as at the strange abruptness with which it was handed to him.

In accordance with the wishes of the stranger, he delivered it into the hands of Schalken, and repeating *his* directions, despatched him upon the mission.

Schalken disposed his precious charge securely beneath the folds of his cloak, and rapidly traversing two or three narrow streets, he stopped at a corner house, the lower part of which was then occupied by the shop of a Jewish goldsmith.

Schalken entered the shop, and calling the little Hebrew into the obscurity of its back recesses, he proceeded to lay before him Vanderhausen's packet.

On being examined by the light of a lamp, it appeared entirely cased with lead, the outer surface of which was much scraped and soiled, and nearly white with age. This was with difficulty partially removed, and disclosed beneath a box of some dark and singularly hard wood; this, too, was forced, and after the removal of two or three folds of linen, its contents proved to be a mass of golden ingots, close packed, and, as the Jew declared, of the most perfect quality.

Every ingot underwent the scrutiny of the little Jew, who seemed to feel an epicurean delight in touching and testing these morsels of the glorious metal; and each one of them was replaced in the box with the exclamation:

'Mein Gott, how very perfect! not one grain of alloy—beautiful, beautiful!'

The task was at length finished, and the Jew certified under his hand the value of the ingots submitted to his examination to amount to many thousand rix-dollars.

With the desired document in his bosom, and the rich box of gold carefully pressed under his arm, and concealed by his cloak, he retraced his way, and entering the studio, found his master and the stranger in close conference.

Schalken had no sooner left the room, in order to execute the commission he had taken in charge, than Vanderhausen addressed Gerard Douw in the following terms:

'I may not tarry with you to-night more than a few minutes, and so I shall briefly tell you the matter upon which I come. You visited the town of Rotterdam some four months ago, and then I saw in the church of St. Lawrence your niece, Rose Velderkaust. I desire to marry her, and if I satisfy you as to the fact that I am very wealthy—more wealthy than any husband you could dream of for her—I expect that you will forward my views to the utmost of your authority. If you approve my proposal, you must close with it at once, for I cannot command time enough to wait for calculations and delays.'

Gerard Douw was, perhaps, as much astonished as anyone could be by the very unexpected nature of Mynher Vanderhausen's communication; but he did not give vent to any unseemly expression of surprise, for besides the motives supplied by prudence and politeness, the painter experienced a kind of chill and oppressive sensation, something like that which is supposed to affect a man who is placed unconsciously in immediate contact with something to which he has a natural anti-pathy—an undefined horror and dread while standing in the presence of the eccentric stranger, which made him very unwilling to say anything which might reasonably prove offensive.

'I have no doubt,' said Gerard, after two or three prefatory hems, 'that the connection which you propose would prove alike advantageous and honourable to my niece; but you must be aware that she has a will of her own, and may not acquiesce in what *we* may design for her advantage.'

'Do not seek to deceive me, Sir Painter,' said Vanderhausen; 'you are her guardian—she is your ward. She is mine if *you* like to make her so.'

The man of Rotterdam moved forward a little as he spoke, and Gerard Douw, he scarce knew why, inwardly prayed for the speedy return of Schalken.

'I desire,' said the mysterious gentleman, 'to place in your hands at once an evidence of my wealth, and a security for my liberal dealing with your niece. The lad will return in a minute or two with a sum in value five times the fortune which she has a right to expect from a husband. This shall lie in your hands, together with her dowry, and you may apply the united sum as suits her interest best; it shall be all exclusively hers while she lives. Is that liberal?'

Douw assented, and inwardly thought that fortune had been extraordinarily kind to his niece. The stranger, he thought, must be both wealthy and generous, and such an offer was not to be despised, though made by a humourist, and one of no very prepossessing presence.

Rose had no very high pretensions, for she was almost without dowry; indeed, altogether so, excepting so far as the deficiency had been supplied by the generosity of her uncle. Neither had she any right to raise any scruples against the match on the score of birth, for her own origin was by no means elevated; and as to other objections, Gerard resolved, and, indeed, by the usages of the time was warranted in resolving, not to listen to them for a moment.

'Sir,' said he, addressing the stranger, 'your offer is most liberal, and whatever hesitation I may feel in closing with it immediately, arises solely from my not having the honour of knowing anything of your family or station. Upon these points you can, of course, satisfy me without difficulty?'

'As to my respectability,' said the stranger, drily, 'you must take that for granted at present; pester me with no inquiries; you can discover nothing more about me than I choose to make known. You shall have sufficient security for my respectability—my word, if you are honourable: if you are sordid, my gold.'

'A testy old gentleman,' thought Douw; 'he must have his own way. But, all things considered, I am justified in giving my niece to him. Were she my own daughter, I would do the like by her. I will not pledge myself unnecessarily, however.'

'You will not pledge yourself unnecessarily,' said Vanderhausen, strangely uttering the very words which had just floated through the mind of his companion; 'but you will do so if it *is* necessary, I presume; and I will show you that I consider it in-dispensable. If the gold I mean to leave in your hands satisfy you, and if you desire that my proposal shall not be at once withdrawn, you must, before I leave this room, write your name to this engagement.'

Having thus spoken, he placed a paper in the hands of Gerard, the contents of which expressed an engagement entered into by Gerard Douw, to give to Wilken Vanderhausen, of Rotterdam, in marriage, Rose Velderkaust, and so forth, within one week of the date hereof.

While the painter was employed in reading this covenant, Schalken, as we have stated, entered the studio, and having delivered the box and the valuation of the Jew into the hands of the stranger, he was about to retire, when Vanderhausen called to him to wait; and, presenting the case and the certificate to Gerard Douw, he waited in silence until he had satisfied himself by an inspection of both as to the value of the pledge left in his hands. At length he said:

'Are you content?'

The painter said he would fain have an other day to consider.

'Not an hour,' said the suitor, coolly.

'Well, then,' said Douw, 'I am content; it is a bargain.'

'Then sign at once,' said Vanderhausen; 'I am weary.'

At the same time he produced a small case of writing materials, and Gerard signed the important document.

'Let this youth witness the covenant,' said the old man; and Godfrey Schalken unconsciously signed the instrument which bestowed upon another that hand which he had so long regarded as the object and reward of all his labours.

The compact being thus completed, the strange visitor folded up the paper, and stowed it safely in an inner pocket.

'I will visit you to-morrow night, at nine of the clock, at your house, Gerard Douw, and will see the subject of our contract. Farewell.' And so saying, Wilken Vanderhausen moved stiffly, but rapidly out of the room.

Schalken, eager to resolve his doubts, had placed himself by the window in order to watch the street entrance; but the experiment served only to support his suspicions, for the old man did not issue from the door. This was very strange, very odd, very fearful. He and his master returned together, and talked but little on the way, for each had his own sub-jects of reflection, of anxiety, and of hope.

Schalken, however, did not know the ruin which threatened his cherished schemes.

Gerard Douw knew nothing of the attachment which had sprung up between his pupil and his niece; and even if he had, it is doubtful whether he would have regarded its existence as any serious obstruction to the wishes of Mynher Vanderhausen.

Marriages were then and there matters of traffic and calculation; and it would have appeared as absurd in the eyes of the guardian to make a mutual attachment an essential element in a contract of marriage, as it would have been to draw up his bonds and receipts in the language of chivalrous romance.

The painter, however, did not communicate to his niece the important step which he had taken in her behalf, and his resolution arose not from any anticipation of opposition on her part, but solely from a ludicrous consciousness that if his ward were, as she very naturally might do, to ask him to describe the appearance of the bridegroom whom he destined for her, he would be forced to confess that he had not seen his face, and, if called upon, would find it impossible to identify him.

Upon the next day, Gerard Douw having dined, called his niece to him, and having scanned her person with an air of satisfaction, he took her hand, and looking upon her pretty, innocent face with a smile of kindness, he said:

'Rose, my girl, that face of yours will make your fortune.' Rose blushed and smiled. 'Such faces and such tempers seldom go together, and, when they do, the compound is a love-potion which few heads or hearts can resist. Trust me, thou wilt soon be a bride, girl. But this is trifling, and I am pressed for time, so make ready the large room by eight o'clock to-night, and give directions for supper at nine. I expect a friend to-night; and observe me, child, do thou trick thyself out handsomely. I would not have him think us poor or sluttish.'

With these words he left the chamber, and took his way to the room to which we have already had occasion to introduce our readers—that in which his pupils worked.

When the evening closed in, Gerard called Schalken, who was about to take his departure to his obscure and comfortless lodgings, and asked him to come home and sup with Rose and Vanderhausen.

The invitation was of course accepted, and Gerard Douw and his pupil soon found themselves in the handsome and somewhat antique-looking room which had been prepared for the reception of the stranger.

A cheerful wood-fire blazed in the capacious hearth; a little at one side an old-fashioned table, with richly-carved legs, was placed—destined, no doubt, to receive the supper, for which preparations were going forward; and ranged with exact regularity, stood the tall-backed chairs, whose ungracefulness was more than counterbalanced by their comfort.

The little party, consisting of Rose, her uncle, and the artist, awaited the arrival of the expected visitor with considerable impatience.

Nine o'clock at length came, and with it a summons at the street-door, which, being speedily answered, was followed by a slow and emphatic tread upon the staircase; the steps moved heavily across the lobby, the door of the room in which the party which we have described were assembled slowly opened, and there entered a figure which startled, almost appalled, the phlegmatic Dutchmen, and nearly made Rose scream with affright; it was the form, and arrayed in the garb, of Mynher Vanderhausen; the air, the gait, the height was the same, but the features had never been seen by any of the party before.

The stranger stopped at the door of the room, and displayed his form and face completely. He wore a dark-coloured cloth cloak, which was short and full, not falling quite to the knees; his legs were cased in dark purple silk stockings, and his shoes were adorned with roses of the same colour. The opening of the cloak in front showed the under-suit to consist of some very dark, perhaps sable material, and his hands were enclosed in a pair of heavy leather gloves which ran up considerably above the wrist, in the manner of a gauntlet. In one hand he carried his walking-stick and his hat, which he had removed, and the other hung heavily by his side. A quantity of grizzled hair descended in long tresses from his head, and its folds rested upon the plaits of a stiff ruff, which effectually concealed his neck.

So far all was well; but the face!—all the flesh of the face was coloured with the bluish leaden hue which is sometimes pro-duced by the operation of metallic medicines administered in excessive quantities; the eyes were enormous, and the white appeared both above and below the iris, which gave to them an expression of insanity, which was heightened by their glassy fixedness; the nose was well enough, but the mouth was writhed considerably to one side, where it opened in order to give egress to two long, discoloured fangs, which projected from the upper jaw, far below the lower lip; the hue of the lips themselves bore the usual relation to that of the face, and was consequently nearly black. The character of the face was malignant, even satanic, to the last degree; and, indeed, such a combination of horror could hardly be accounted for, except by supposing the corpse of some atrocious malefactor, which had long hung blackening upon the gibbet, to have at length become the habitation of a demon—the frightful sport of Satanic possession.

It was remarkable that the worshipful stranger suffered as little as possible of his flesh to appear, and that during his visit he did not once remove his gloves.

Having stood for some moments at the door, Gerard Douw at length found breath and collectedness to bid him welcome, and, with a mute inclination of the head, the stranger stepped forward into the room.

There was something indescribably odd, even horrible, about all his motions, something undefinable, that was unnatural, un-human—it was as if the limbs were guided and directed by a spirit unused to the management of bodily machinery.

The stranger said hardly anything during his visit, which did not exceed half an hour; and the host himself could scarcely muster courage enough to utter the few necessary salutations and courtesies: and, indeed, such was the nervous terror which the presence of Vanderhausen inspired, that very little would have made all his entertainers fly bellowing from the room.

They had not so far lost all self-possession, however, as to fail to observe two strange peculiarities of their visitor.

During his stay he did not once suffer his eyelids to close, nor even to move in the slightest degree; and further, there was a death-like stillness in his whole person, owing to the total absence of the heaving motion of the chest, caused by the process of respiration.

These two peculiarities, though when told they may appear trifling, produced a very striking and unpleasant effect when seen and observed. Vanderhausen at length relieved the painter of Leyden of his inauspicious presence; and with no small gratification the little party heard the street-door close after him.

'Dear uncle,' said Rose, 'what a frightful man! I would not see him again for the wealth of the States!'

'Tush, foolish girl!' said Douw, whose sensations were anything but comfortable. 'A man may be as ugly as the devil, and yet if his heart and actions are good, he is worth all the pretty-faced, perfumed puppies that walk the Mall. Rose, my girl, it is very true he has not thy pretty face, but I know him to be wealthy and liberal; and were he ten times more ugly—'

'Which is inconceivable,' observed Rose.

'These two virtues would be sufficient,' continued her uncle, 'to counterbalance all his deformity; and if not of power sufficient actually to alter the shape of the features, at least of efficacy enough to prevent one thinking them amiss.'

'Do you know, uncle,' said Rose, 'when I saw him standing at the door, I could not get it out of my head that I saw the old, painted, wooden figure that used to frighten me so much in the church of St. Laurence of Rotterdam.'

Gerard laughed, though he could not help inwardly acknowledging the justness of the comparison. He was resolved, however, as far as he could, to check his niece's inclination to ridicule the ugliness of her intended bridegroom, although he was not a little pleased to observe that she appeared totally exempt from that mysterious dread of the stranger which, he could not disguise it from himself, considerably affected him, as also his pupil Godfrey Schalken.

Early on the next day there arrived, from various quarters of the town, rich presents of silks, velvets, jewellery, and so forth, for Rose; and also a packet directed to Gerard Douw, which, on being opened, was found to contain a contract of marriage, formally drawn up, between Wilken

Vanderhausen of the Boom-quay, in Rotterdam, and Rose Velderkaust of Leyden, niece to Gerard Douw, master in the art of painting, also of the same city; and containing engagements on the part of Vanderhausen to make settlements upon his bride, far more splendid than he had before led her guardian to believe likely, and which were to be secured to her use in the most unexceptionable manner possible—the money being placed in the hands of Gerard Douw himself.

I have no sentimental scenes to describe, no cruelty of guardians, or magnanimity of wards, or agonies of lovers. The record I have to make is one of sordidness, levity, and interest. In less than a week after the first interview which we have just described, the contract of marriage was ful-filled, and Schalken saw the prize which he would have risked anything to secure, carried off triumphantly by his formidable rival.

For two or three days he absented himself from the school; he then returned and worked, if with less cheerfulness, with far more dogged resolution than before; the dream of love had given place to that of ambition.

Months passed away, and, contrary to his expectation, and, indeed, to the direct promise of the parties, Gerard Douw heard nothing of his niece, or her worshipful spouse. The interest of the money, which was to have been demanded in quarterly sums, lay unclaimed in his hands. He began to grow extremely uneasy.

Mynher Vanderhausen's direction in Rotterdam he was fully possessed of. After some irresolution he finally determined to journey thither—a tri-fling undertaking, and easily accomplished—and thus to satisfy himself of the safety and comfort of his ward, for whom he entertained an honest and strong affection.

His search was in vain, however. No one in Rotterdam had ever heard of Mynher Vanderhausen.

Gerard Douw left not a house in the Boom-quay untried; but all in vain. No one could give him any information whatever touching the object of his inquiry; and he was obliged to return to Leyden, nothing wiser than when he had left it.

On his arrival he hastened to the establishment from which Van-derhausen had hired the lumbering though, considering the times, most luxurious vehicle which the bridal party had employed to convey them to Rotterdam. From the driver of this machine he learned, that having proceeded by slow stages, they had late in the evening approached Rot-terdam; but that before they entered the city, and while yet nearly a mile from it, a small party of men, soberly clad, and after the old fashion, with peaked beards and moustaches, standing in the centre of the road, obstructed the further progress of the car-riage. The driver reined in his horses, much fearing, from the obscurity of the hour, and the loneliness of the road, that some mischief was intended.

His fears were, however, somewhat allayed by his observing that these strange men carried a large litter, of an antique shape, and which they immediately set down upon the pavement, whereupon the bridegroom, having opened the coach-door from within, descended, and having as-sisted his bride to do likewise, led her, weeping bitterly and wringing her hands, to the litter, which they both entered. It was then raised by the men who surrounded it, and speedily carried towards the city, and before it had proceeded many yards the darkness concealed it from the view of the Dutch charioteer.

In the inside of the vehicle he found a purse, whose contents more than thrice paid the hire of the carriage and man. He saw and could tell nothing more of Mynher Vanderhausen and his beautiful lady. This mys-tery was a source of deep anxiety and almost of grief to Gerard Douw.

There was evidently fraud in the dealing of Vanderhausen with him, though for what purpose committed he could not imagine. He greatly doubted how far it was possible for a man possessing in his countenance so strong an evidence of the presence of the most demoniac feelings, to be in reality anything but a villain; and every day that passed without his hearing from or of his niece, instead of inducing him to forget his fears, on the contrary tended more and more to exasperate them.

The loss of his niece's cheerful society tended also to depress his spirits; and in order to dispel this despondency, which often crept upon his mind after his daily employment was over, he was wont frequently to prevail upon Schalken to accompany him home, and by his presence to dispel, in some degree, the gloom of his otherwise solitary supper.

One evening, the painter and his pupil were sitting by the fire, having accomplished a comfortable supper, and had yielded to that silent pensive-ness sometimes induced by the process of digestion, when their reflec-tions were disturbed by a loud sound at the street-door, as if occasioned by some person rushing forcibly and repeatedly against it. A domestic had run without delay to ascertain the cause of the disturbance, and they heard him twice or thrice interrogate the applicant for admis-sion, but without producing an answer or any cessation of the sounds.

They heard him then open the hall-door, and immediately there fol-lowed a light and rapid tread upon the staircase. Schalken laid his hand on his sword, and advanced towards the door. It opened before he reached it, and Rose rushed into the room. She looked wild and haggard, and pale with exhaustion and terror; but her dress surprised them as much even as her unexpected appearance. It consisted of a kind of white woollen wrapper, made close about the neck, and descending to the very ground. It was much deranged and travel-soiled. The poor creature had hardly entered the chamber when she fell senseless on the floor. With some difficulty they succeeded in reviving her, and on recovering her senses she instantly ex-claimed, in a tone of eager, terrified impatience:

'Wine, wine, quickly, or I'm lost!'

Much alarmed at the strange agitation in which the call was made, they at once administered to her wishes, and she drank some wine with a haste and eagerness which surprised them. She had hardly swallowed it, when she exclaimed, with the same urgency:

'Food, food, at once, or I perish!'

A considerable fragment of a roast joint was upon the table, and Schalken immediately proceeded to cut some, but he was anticipated; for no sooner had she become aware of its presence than she darted at it with the rapacity of a vulture, and, seizing it in her hands she tore off the flesh with her teeth and swallowed it.

When the paroxysm of hunger had been a little appeased, she appeared suddenly to become aware how strange her conduct had been, or it may have been that other more agitating thoughts recurred to her mind, for she began to weep bitterly and to wring her hands.

'Oh! send for a minister of God,' said she; 'I am not safe till he comes; send for him speedily.'

Gerard Douw despatched a messenger instantly, and prevailed on his niece to allow him to surrender his bedchamber to her use; he also persuaded her to retire to it at once and to rest; her consent was extorted upon the condition that they would not leave her for a moment.

'Oh that the holy man were here!' she said; 'he can deliver me. The dead and the living can never be one—God has forbidden it.'

With these mysterious words she surrendered herself to their guidance, and they proceeded to the chamber which Gerard Douw had assigned to her use.

'Do not—do not leave me for a moment,' said she. 'I am lost for ever if you do.'

Gerard Douw's chamber was approached through a spacious apartment, which they were now about to enter. Gerard Douw and Schalken each carried a was candle, so that a sufficient degree of light was cast upon all surrounding objects. They were now entering the large chamber, which, as I have said, communicated with Douw's apartment, when Rose suddenly stopped, and, in a whisper which seemed to thrill with horror, she said:

'O God! he is here—he is here! See, see—there he goes!'

She pointed towards the door of the inner room, and Schalken thought he saw a shadowy and ill-defined form gliding into that apartment. He drew his sword, and raising the candle so as to throw its light with increased distinctness upon the objects in the room, he entered the chamber into which the shadow had glided. No figure was there—nothing but the furniture which belonged to the room, and yet he could not be deceived as to the fact that something had moved before them into the chamber.

A sickening dread came upon him, and the cold perspiration broke out in heavy drops upon his forehead; nor was he more composed when he heard the increased urgency, the agony of entreaty, with which Rose implored them not to leave her for a moment.

'I saw him,' said she. 'He's here! I cannot be deceived—I know him. He's by me—he's with me—he's in the room. Then, for God's sake, as you would save, do not stir from beside me!'

They at length prevailed upon her to lie down upon the bed, where she continued to urge them to stay by her. She frequently uttered incoherent sentences, repeating again and again, 'The dead and the living cannot be one—God has forbidden it!' and then again, 'Rest to the wakeful—sleep to the sleep-walkers.'

These and such mysterious and broken sentences she continued to utter until the clergyman arrived.

Gerard Douw began to fear, naturally enough, that the poor girl, owing to terror or ill-treatment, had become deranged; and he half suspected, by the suddenness of her appearance, and the unseasonableness of the hour, and, above all, from the wildness and terror of her manner, that she had made her escape from some place of confinement for lunatics, and was in immediate fear of pursuit. He resolved to summon medical advice as soon as the mind of his niece had been in some measure set at rest by the offices of the clergyman whose attendance she had so earnestly desired; and until this object had been attained, he did not venture to put any questions to her, which might possibly, by reviving painful or horrible recollections, increase her agitation.

The clergyman soon arrived—a man of ascetic countenance and venerable age—one whom Gerard Douw respected much, forasmuch as he was a veteran polemic, though one, perhaps, more dreaded as a combatant than beloved as a Christian—of pure morality, subtle brain, and frozen heart. He entered the chamber which communicated with that in which Rose reclined, and immediately on his arrival she requested him to pray for her, as for one who lay in the hands of Satan, and who could hope for deliverance—only from heaven.

That our readers may distinctly understand all the circumstances of the event which we are about imperfectly to describe, it is necessary to state the relative position of the parties who were engaged in it. The old clergyman and Schalken were in the anteroom of which we have already spoken; Rose lay in the inner chamber, the door of which was open; and by the side of the bed, at her urgent desire, stood her guardian; a candle burned in the bed-chamber, and three were lighted in the outer apartment

The old man now cleared his voice, as if about to commence; but before he had time to begin, a sudden gust of air blew out the candle which served to illuminate the room in which the poor girl lay, and she, with hurried alarm, exclaimed:

'Godfrey, bring in another candle; the darkness is unsafe.'

Gerard Douw, forgetting for the moment her repeated injunctions in the immediate impulse, stepped from the bedchamber into the other, in order to supply what she desired.

'O God I do not go, dear uncle!' shrieked the unhappy girl; and at the same time she sprang from the bed and darted after him, in order, by her grasp, to detain him.

But the warning came too late, for scarcely had he passed the threshold, and hardly had his niece had time to utter the startling exclamation, when the door which divided the two rooms closed violently after him, as if swung to by a strong blast of wind.

Schalken and he both rushed to the door, but their united and desperate efforts could not avail so much as to shake it.

Shriek after shriek burst from the inner chamber, with all the piercing loudness of despairing terror. Schalken and Douw applied every energy and strained every nerve to force open the door; but all in vain.

There was no sound of struggling from within, but the screams seemed to increase in loudness, and at the same time they heard the bolts of the latticed window withdrawn, and the window itself grated upon the sill as if thrown open.

One *last* shriek, so long and piercing and agonised as to be scarcely human, swelled from the room, and suddenly there followed a death-like silence.

A light step was heard crossing the floor, as if from the bed to the window; and almost at the same instant the door gave way, and, yielding to the pressure of the external applicants, they were nearly precipitated into the room. It was empty. The window was open, and Schalken sprang to a chair and gazed out upon the street and canal below. He saw no form, but he beheld, or thought he beheld, the waters of the broad canal beneath settling ring after ring in heavy circular ripples, as if a moment before disturbed by the immersion of some large and heavy mass.

No trace of Rose was ever after discovered, nor was anything certain respecting her mysterious wooer detected or even suspected; no clue whereby to trace the intricacies of the labyrinth and to arrive at a distinct conclusion was to be found. But an incident occurred, which, though it will not be received by our rational readers as at all approaching to evidence upon the matter, nevertheless produced a strong and a lasting impression upon the mind of Schalken.

Many years after the events which we have detailed, Schalken, then remotely situated, received an intimation of his father's death, and of his intended burial upon a fixed day in the church of Rotterdam. It was necessary that a very considerable journey should be performed by the funeral procession, which, as it will readily be believed, was not very numerously attended. Schalken with difficulty arrived in Rotterdam late in the day upon which the funeral was appointed to take place. The procession had not then arrived. Evening closed in, and still it did not appear.

Schalken strolled down to the church—be found it open—notice of the arrival of the funeral had been given, and the vault in which the body was to be laid had been opened. The official who corresponds to our sexton, on seeing a well-dressed gentleman, whose object was to attend the expected funeral, pacing the aisle of the church, hospitably invited him to share with him the comforts of a blazing wood fire, which, as was his custom in winter time upon such occasions, he had kindled on the hearth of a chamber which commu-nicated, by a flight of steps, with the vault below.

In this chamber Schalken and his entertainer seated themselves, and the sexton, after some fruitless attempts to engage his guest in conversation, was obliged to apply himself to his tobacco-pipe and can to solace his solitude.

In spite of his grief and cares, the fatigues of a rapid journey of nearly forty hours gradually overcame the mind and body of Godfrey Schalken, and he sank into a deep sleep, from which he was awakened by some one shaking him gently by the shoulder. He first thought that the old sexton had called him, but *he* was no longer in the room.

He roused himself, and as soon as he could clearly see what was around him, he perceived a female form, clothed in a kind of light robe of muslin, part of which was so disposed as to act as a veil, and in her hand she carried a lamp. She was moving rather away from him, and towards the flight of steps which conducted towards the vaults.

Schalken felt a vague alarm at the sight of this figure, and at the same time an irresistible impulse to follow its guidance. He followed it towards the vaults, but when it reached the head of the stairs, he paused; the figure paused also, and, turning gently round, displayed, by the light of the lamp it carried, the face and features of his first love, Rose Velderkaust. There was nothing horrible, or even sad, in the countenance. On the contrary, it wore the same arch smile which used to enchant the artist long before in his happy days.

A feeling of awe and of interest, too intense to be resisted, prompted him to follow the spectre, if spectre it were. She descended the stairs—he followed; and, turning to the left, through a narrow passage, she led him, to his infinite surprise, into what appeared to be an old-fashioned Dutch apartment, such as the pictures of Gerard Douw have served to immortalise.

Abundance of costly antique furniture was disposed about the room, and in one corner stood a four-post bed, with heavy black-cloth curtains around it; the figure frequently turned towards him with the same arch smile; and when she came to the side of the bed, she drew the curtains, and by the light of the lamp which she held towards its contents, she disclosed to the horror-stricken painter, sitting bolt upright in the bed, the livid and demoniac form of Vanderhausen. Schalken had hardly seen him when he fell senseless upon the floor, where he lay until discovered, on the next morning, by persons employed in closing the passages into the vaults. He was lying in a cell of considerable size, which had not been disturbed for a long time, and he had fallen beside a large coffin which was supported upon small stone pillars, a security against the attacks of vermin.

To his dying day Schalken was satisfied of the reality of the vision which he had witnessed, and he has left behind him a curious evidence of the impression which it wrought upon his fancy, in a painting executed shortly after the event we have narrated, and which is valuable as exhibiting not only the peculiarities which have made Schalken's pictures sought after, but even more so as presenting a portrait, as close and faithful as one taken from memory can be, of his early love, Rose Velderkaust, whose mysterious fate must ever remain matter of speculation.

The picture represents a chamber of antique masonry, such as might be found in most old cathedrals, and is lighted faintly by a lamp carried in the hand of a female figure, such as we have above attempted to describe; and in the background, and to the left of him who examines the painting, there stands the form of a man apparently aroused from sleep, and by his attitude, his hand being laid upon his sword, exhibiting considerable alarm: this last figure is illuminated only by the expiring glare of a wood or charcoal fire.

The whole production exhibits a beauti-ful specimen of that artful and singular distribution of light and shade which has rendered the name of Schalken immortal among the artists of his country. This tale is traditionary, and the reader will easily perceive, by our studiously omitting to heighten many points of the narrative, when a little additional colouring might have added effect to the recital, that we have desired to lay before him, not a figment of the brain, but a curious tradition connected with, and belonging to, the biography of a famous artist.

Scraps of Hibernian Ballads

BEING AN EIGHTH EXTRACT FROM THE LEGACY OF THE LATE FRANCIS PURCELL, P. P. OF DRUMCOOLAGH.

I HAVE observed, my dear friend, among other grievous misconceptions current among men otherwise well-informed, and which tend to degrade the pretensions of my native land, an impression that there exists no such thing as indigenous modern Irish composition deserving the name of poetry—a belief which has been thoughtlessly sustained and confirmed by the unconscion-able literary perverseness of Irishmen themselves, who have preferred the easy task of concocting humorous extravaganzas, which caricature with merciless exaggeration the pedantry, bombast, and blunders incident to the lowest order of Hibernian ballads, to the more pleasurable and patriotic duty of collecting together the many, many specimens of genuine poetic feeling, which have grown up, like its wild flowers, from the warm though neglected soil of Ireland.

In fact, the productions which have long been regarded as pure samples of Irish poetic composition, such as 'The Groves of Blarney,' and 'The Wedding of Ballyporeen,' 'Ally Croker,' etc., etc., are altogether spurious, and as much like the thing they call themselves 'as I to Hercules.'

There are to be sure in Ireland, as in all countries, poems which deserve to be laughed at. The native productions of which I speak, frequently abound in absurdities—absurdities which are often, too, provokingly mixed up with what is beautiful; but I strongly and absolutely deny that the prevailing or even the usual character of Irish poetry is that of comicality. No country, no time, is devoid of real poetry, or something approaching to it; and surely it were a strange thing if Ireland, abounding as she does from shore to shore with all that is beautiful, and grand, and savage in scenery, and filled with wild recollections, vivid passions, warm affections, and keen sorrow, could find no language to speak withal, but that of mummery and jest. No, her language is imperfect, but there is strength in its rudeness, and beauty in its wildness; and, above all, strong feeling flows through it, like fresh fountains in rugged caverns.

And yet I will not say that the language of genuine indigenous Irish composition is always vulgar and uncouth: on the contrary, I am in possession of some specimens, though by no means of the highest order as to poetic merit, which do not possess throughout a single peculiarity of diction. The lines which I now proceed to lay before you, by way of illustration, are from the pen of an unfortunate young man, of very humble birth, whose early hopes were crossed by the untimely death of her whom he loved. He was a self-educated man, and in after-life rose to high distinctions in the Church to which he devoted himself—an act which proves the sincerity of spirit with which these verses were written.

> 'When moonlight falls on wave and wimple,
> And silvers every circling dimple,
>   That onward, onward sails:
> When fragrant hawthorns wild and simple
>   Lend perfume to the gales,
> And the pale moon in heaven abiding,
> O'er midnight mists and mountains riding,
> Shines on the river, smoothly gliding
>   Through quiet dales,
>
> 'I wander there in solitude,
> Charmed by the chiming music rude
>   Of streams that fret and flow.
> For by that eddying stream SHE stood,
>   On such a night I trow:
> For HER the thorn its breath was lending,
> On this same tide HER eye was bending,
> And with its voice HER voice was blending
>   Long, long ago.
>
> Wild stream! I walk by thee once more,
> I see thy hawthorns dim and hoar,
>   I hear thy waters moan,
> And night-winds sigh from shore to shore,

With hushed and hollow tone;
But breezes on their light way winging,
And all thy waters heedless singing,
No more to me are gladness bringing—
  I am alone.

'Years after years, their swift way keeping,
Like sere leaves down thy current sweeping,
  Are lost for aye, and sped—
And Death the wintry soil is heaping
  As fast as flowers are shed.
And she who wandered by my side,
And breathed enchantment o'er thy tide,
That makes thee still my friend and guide—
  And she is dead.'

These lines I have transcribed in order to prove a point which I have heard denied, namely, that an Irish peasant—for their author was no more—may write at least correctly in the matter of measure, language, and rhyme; and I shall add several extracts in further illustration of the same fact, a fact whose assertion, it must be allowed, may appear somewhat paradoxical even to those who are acquainted, though superficially, with Hibernian composition. The rhymes are, it must be granted, in the generality of such productions, very latitudinarian indeed, and as a veteran votary of the muse once assured me, depend wholly upon the wowls (vowels), as may be seen in the following stanza of the famous 'Shanavan Voicth.'

  "'What'll we have for supper?"
    Says my Shanavan Voicth;
  "We'll have turkeys and roast **BEEF**,
  And we'll eat it very **SWEET**,
  And then we'll take a **SLEEP**,"
    Says my Shanavan Voicth.'

But I am desirous of showing you that, although barbarisms may and do exist in our native ballads, there are still to be found exceptions which furnish examples of strict correctness in rhyme and metre. Whether they be one whit the better for this I have my doubts. In order to establish my position, I subjoin a portion of a ballad by one Michael Finley, of whom more anon. The *Gentleman* spoken of in the song is Lord Edward Fitzgerald.

  'The day that traitors sould him and inimies bought him,
    The day that the red gold and red blood was paid—

Then the green turned pale and thrembled like the dead leaves in Autumn,
 And the heart an' hope iv Ireland in the could grave was laid.

'The day I saw you first, with the sunshine fallin' round ye,
 My heart fairly opened with the grandeur of the view:
For ten thousand Irish boys that day did surround ye,
 An' I swore to stand by them till death, an' fight for you.

'Ye wor the bravest gentleman, an' the best that ever stood,
 And your eyelid never thrembled for danger nor for dread,
An' nobleness was flowin' in each stream of your blood—
 My bleasing on you night au' day, an' Glory be your bed.

'My black an' bitter curse on the head, an' heart, an' hand,
 That plotted, wished, an' worked the fall of this Irish hero bold;
God's curse upon the Irishman that sould his native land,
 An' hell consume to dust the hand that held the thraitor's gold.'

Such were the politics and poetry of Michael Finley, in his day, perhaps, the most noted song-maker of his country; but as genius is never without its eccentricities, Finley had his peculiarities, and among these, perhaps the most amusing was his rooted aversion to pen, ink, and paper, in perfect independence of which, all his compositions were completed. It is impossible to describe the jealousy with which he regarded the presence of writing materials of any kind, and his ever wakeful fears lest some literary pirate should transfer his oral poetry to paper—fears which were not altogether without warrant, inasmuch as the recitation and singing of these original pieces were to him a source of wealth and importance. I recollect upon one occasion his detecting me in the very act of following his recitation with my pencil and I shall not soon forget his indignant scowl, as stopping abruptly in the midst of a line, he sharply exclaimed:

'Is my pome a pigsty, or what, that you want a surveyor's ground-plan of it?'

Owing to this absurd scruple, I have been obliged, with one exception, that of the ballad of 'Phaudhrig Crohoore,' to rest satisfied with such snatches and fragments of his poetry as my memory could bear away—a fact which must account for the mutilated state in which I have been obliged to present the foregoing specimen of his composition.

It was in vain for me to reason with this man of metres upon the unreasonableness of this despotic and exclusive assertion of copyright. I well remember his answer to me when, among other arguments, I urged the advisability of some care for the permanence of his reputation, as a motive to induce him to consent to have his poems written down, and thus reduced to a palpable and enduring form.

'I often noticed,' said he, 'when a mist id be spreadin', a little brier to look as big, you'd think, as an oak tree; an' same way, in the dimmness iv the nightfall, I often seen a man tremblin' and crassin' himself as if a sperit was before him, at the sight iv a small thorn bush, that he'd leap over with ase if the daylight and sunshine was in it. An' that's the rason why I think it id be better for the likes iv me to be remimbered in tradition than to be written in history.'

Finley has now been dead nearly eleven years, and his fame has not prospered by the tactics which he pursued, for his reputation, so far from being magnified, has been wholly obliterated by the mists of obscurity.

With no small difficulty, and no inconsiderable manoeuvring, I succeeded in procuring, at an expense of trouble and conscience which you will no doubt think but poorly rewarded, an accurate 'report' of one of his most popular recitations. It celebrates one of the many daring exploits of the once famous Phaudhrig Crohoore (in prosaic English, Patrick Connor). I have witnessed powerful effects produced upon large assemblies by Finley's recitation of this poem which he was wont, upon pressing invitation, to deliver at weddings, wakes, and the like; of course the power of the narrative was greatly enhanced by the fact that many of his auditors had seen and well knew the chief actors in the drama.

Phaudhrig Crohoore.

Oh, Phaudhrig Crohoore was the broth of a boy,
    And he stood six foot eight,
And his arm was as round as another man's thigh,
        'Tis Phaudhrig was great,—And his hair was as black as the shadows of night,
And hung over the scars left by many a fight;
And his voice, like the thunder, was deep, strong, and loud,
And his eye like the lightnin' from under the cloud.
And all the girls liked him, for he could spake civil,
And sweet when he chose it, for he was the divil.
An' there wasn't a girl from thirty-five undher,
    Divil a matter how crass, but he could come round her.
But of all the sweet girls that smiled on him, but one
Was the girl of his heart, an' he loved her alone.
An' warm as the sun, as the rock firm an' sure,
Was the love of the heart of Phaudhrig Crohoore;
An' he'd die for one smile from his Kathleen O'Brien,
For his love, like his hatred, was sthrong as the lion.

'But Michael O'Hanlon loved Kathleen as well
As he hated Crohoore—an' that same was like hell.
But O'Brien liked **HIM**, for they were the same parties,
The O'Briens, O'Hanlons, an' Murphys, and Cartys—
An' they all went together an' hated Crohoore,
For it's many the batin' he gave them before;
An' O'Hanlon made up to O'Brien, an' says he:
"I'll marry your daughter, if you'll give her to me."
And the match was made up, an' when Shrovetide came on,
The company assimbled three hundred if one:
There was all the O'Hanlons, an' Murphys, an' Cartys,
An' the young boys an' girls av all o' them parties;
An' the O'Briens, av coorse, gathered strong on day,
An' the pipers an' fiddlers were tearin' away;
There was roarin', an' jumpin', an' jiggin', an' flingin',
An' jokin', an' blessin', an' kissin', an' singin',
An' they wor all laughin'—why not, to be sure?—
How O'Hanlon came inside of Phaudhrig Crohoore.
An' they all talked an' laughed the length of the table,
Atin' an' dhrinkin' all while they wor able,
And with pipin' an' fiddlin' an' roarin' like tundher,
Your head you'd think fairly was splittin' asundher;
And the priest called out, "Silence, ye blackguards, agin!"
An' he took up his prayer-book, just goin' to begin,
An' they all held their tongues from their funnin' and bawlin',
So silent you'd notice the smallest pin fallin';

An' the priest was just beg'nin' to read, whin the door
Sprung back to the wall, and in walked Crohoore—
Oh! Phaudhrig Crohoore was the broth of a boy,
Ant he stood six foot eight,
An' his arm was as round as another man's thigh,
'Tis Phaudhrig was great—
An' he walked slowly up, watched by many a bright eye,
As a black cloud moves on through the stars of the sky,
An' none sthrove to stop him, for Phaudhrig was great,
Till he stood all alone, just apposit the sate
Where O'Hanlon and Kathleen, his beautiful bride,
Were sitting so illigant out side by side;
An' he gave her one look that her heart almost broke,
An' he turned to O'Brien, her father, and spoke,
An' his voice, like the thunder, was deep, sthrong, and loud,
An' his eye shone like lightnin' from under the cloud:

"I didn't come here like a tame, crawlin' mouse,
But I stand like a man in my inimy's house;
In the field, on the road, Phaudhrig never knew fear,
Of his foemen, an' God knows he scorns it here;

So lave me at aise, for three minutes or four,
To spake to the girl I'll never see more."
An' to Kathleen he turned, and his voice changed its tone,
For he thought of the days when he called her his own,
An' his eye blazed like lightnin' from under the cloud
On his false-hearted girl, reproachful and proud,
An' says he: "Kathleen bawn, is it thrue what I hear,
That you marry of your free choice, without threat or fear?
If so, spake the word, an' I'll turn and depart,
Chated once, and once only by woman's false heart."
Oh! sorrow and love made the poor girl dumb,
An' she thried hard to spake, but the words wouldn't come,
For the sound of his voice, as he stood there fornint her,
Wint could on her heart as the night wind in winther.
An' the tears in her blue eyes stood tremblin' to flow,
And pale was her cheek as the moonshine on snow;
Then the heart of bould Phaudhrig swelled high in its place,
For he knew, by one look in that beautiful face,

That though sthrangers an' foemen their pledged hands might sever,
Her true heart was his, and his only, for ever.
An' he lifted his voice, like the agle's hoarse call,
An' says Phaudhrig, "She's mine still, in spite of yez all!"
Then up jumped O'Hanlon, an' a tall boy was he,
An' he looked on bould Phaudhrig as fierce as could be,
An' says he, "By the hokey! before you go out,
Bould Phaudhrig Crohoore, you ,must fight for a bout."
Then Phaudhrig made answer: "I'll do my endeavour,"
An' with one blow he stretched bould O'Hanlon for ever.
In his arms he took Kathleen, an' stepped to the door;
And he leaped on his horse, and flung her before;
An' they all were so bother'd, that not a man stirred
Till the galloping hoofs on the pavement were heard.
Then up they all started, like bees in the swarm,
An' they riz a great shout, like the burst of a storm,
An' they roared, and they ran, and they shouted galore;
But Kathleen and Phaudhrig they never saw more.

'But them days are gone by, an' he is no more;
An' the green-grass is growin' o'er Phaudhrig Crohoore,
For he couldn't be aisy or quiet at all;
As he lived a brave boy, he resolved so to fall.
And he took a good pike—for Phaudhrig was great—
And he fought, and he died in the year ninety-eight.
An' the day that Crohoore in the green field was killed,
A sthrong boy was sthretched, and a sthrong heart was stilled.'

It is due to the memory of Finley to say that the foregoing ballad, though bearing throughout a strong resemblance to Sir Walter Scott's 'Lochinvar,' was nevertheless composed long before that spirited production had seen the light.

VOLUME THREE

Jim Sulivan's Adventures in the Great Snow

BEING A NINTH EXTRACT FROM THE LEGACY OF THE LATE FRANCIS PURCELL, P.P. OF DRUMCOOLAGH.

JIM SULIVAN was a dacent, honest boy as you'd find in the seven parishes, an' he was a beautiful singer, an' an illegant dancer intirely, an' a mighty plisant boy in himself; but he had the divil's bad luck, for he married for love, an 'av coorse he niver had an asy minute afther.

Nell Gorman was the girl he fancied, an' a beautiful slip of a girl she was, jist twenty to the minute when he married her. She was as round an' as complate in all her shapes as a firkin, you'd think, an' her two cheeks was as fat an' as red, it id open your heart to look at them.

But beauty is not the thing all through, an' as beautiful as she was she had the divil's tongue, an' the divil's timper, an' the divil's behaviour all out; an' it was impossible for him to be in the house with her for while you'd count tin without havin' an argymint, an' as sure as she riz an argymint with him she'd hit him a wipe iv a skillet or whatever lay next to her hand.

Well, this wasn't at all plasin' to Jim Sulivan you may be sure, an' there was scarce a week that his head wasn't plasthered up, or his back bint double, or his nose swelled as big as a pittaty, with the vilence iv her timper, an' his heart was scalded everlastin'ly with her tongue; so he had no pace or quietness in body or soul at all at all, with the way she was goin' an.

Well, your honour, one cowld snowin' evenin' he kim in afther his day's work regulatin' the men in the farm, an' he sat down very quite by the fire, for he had a scrimmidge with her in the mornin', an' all he wanted was an air iv the fire in pace; so divil a word he said but dhrew a stool an' sat down close to the fire. Well, as soon as the woman saw him,

'Move aff,' says she, 'an' don't be inthrudin' an the fire,' says she.

Well, he kept never mindin', an' didn't let an' to hear a word she was sayin', so she kim over an' she had a spoon in her hand, an' she took jist the smallest taste in life iv the boilin' wather out iv the pot, an' she dhropped it down an his shins, an' with that he let a roar you'd think the roof id fly aff iv the house.

'Hould your tongue, you barbarrian,' says she; 'you'll waken the child,' says she.

'An' if I done right,' says he, for the spoonful of boilin' wather riz him entirely, 'I'd take yourself,' says he, 'an' I'd stuff you into the pot an the fire, an' boil you.' says he, 'into castor oil,' says he.

'That's purty behavour,' says she; 'it's fine usage you're givin' me, isn't it?' says she, gettin' wickeder every minute; 'but before I'm boiled,' says she, 'thry how you like *that*,' says she; an', sure enough, before he had time to put up his guard, she hot him a rale terrible clink iv the iron spoon acrass the jaw.

'Hould me, some iv ye, or I'll murdher her,' says he.

'Will you?' says she, an' with that she hot him another tin times as good as the first.

'By jabers,' says he, slappin' himself behind, 'that's the last salute you'll ever give me,' says he; 'so take my last blessin',' says he, 'you ungovernable baste!' says he—an' with that he pulled an his hat an' walked out iv the door.

Well, she never minded a word he said, for he used to say the same thing all as one every time she dhrew blood; an' she had no expectation at all but he'd come back by the time supper id be ready; but faix the story didn't go quite so simple this time, for while he was walkin', lonesome enough, down the borheen, with his heart almost broke with the pain, for his shins an' his jaw was mighty troublesome, av course, with the thratement he got, who did he see but Mick Hanlon, his uncle's sarvint by, ridin' down, quite an asy, an the ould black horse, with a halter as long as himself.

'Is that Mr. Soolivan?' says the by. says he, as soon as he saw him a good bit aff.

'To be sure it is, ye spalpeen, you,' says Jim, roarin' out; 'what do you want wid me this time a-day?' says he.

'Don't you know me?' says the gossoon, 'it's Mick Hanlon that's in it,' says he.

'Oh, blur an agers, thin, it's welcome you are, Micky asthore,' says Jim; 'how is all wid the man an' the woman beyant?' says he.

'Oh!' says Micky, 'bad enough,' says he; 'the ould man's jist aff, an' if you don't hurry like shot,' says he, 'he'll be in glory before you get there,' says he.

'It's jokin' ye are,' says Jim, sorrowful enough, for he was mighty partial to his uncle intirely.

'Oh, not in the smallest taste,' says Micky; 'the breath was jist out iv him,' says he, 'when I left the farm. "An'," says he, "take the ould black horse," says he, "for he's shure-footed for the road," says he, "an' bring, Jim Soolivan here," says he, "for I think I'd die asy af I could see him onst,' says he.'

'Well,' says Jim, 'will I have time,' says he, 'to go back to the house, for it would be a consolation,' says he, 'to tell the bad news to the woman?' says he.

'It's too late you are already,' says Micky, 'so come up behind me, for God's sake,' says he, 'an' don't waste time;' an' with that he brought the horse up beside the ditch, an' Jim Soolivan mounted up behind Micky, an' they rode off; an' tin good miles it was iv a road, an' at the other side iv Keeper intirely; an' it was snowin' so fast that the ould baste could hardly go an at all at all, an' the two bys an his back was jist like a snowball all as one, an' almost fruz an' smothered at the same time, your honour; an' they wor both mighty sorrowful intirely, an' their toes almost dhroppin' aff wid the could.

And when Jim got to the farm his uncle was gettin' an illegantly, an' he was sittin' up sthrong an' warm in the bed, an' im-provin' every minute, an' no signs av dyin' an him at all at all; so he had all his throuble for nothin'.

But this wasn't all, for the snow kem so thick that it was impassible to get along the roads at all at all; an' faix, instead iv gettin' betther, next mornin' it was only tin times worse; so Jim had jist to take it asy, an' stay wid his uncle antil such times as the snow id melt.

Well, your honour, the evenin' Jim Soolivan wint away, whin the dark was closin' in, Nell Gorman, his wife, beginned to get mighty anasy in herself whin she didn't see him comin' back at all; an' she was gettin' more an' more frightful in herself every minute till the dark kem an, an' divil a taste iv her husband was coming at all at all.

'Oh!' says she, 'there's no use in pur-tendin', I know he's kilt himself; he has committed infantycide an himself,' says she, 'like a dissipated blig-gard as he always was,' says she, 'God rest his soul. Oh, thin, isn't it me an' not you, Jim Soolivan, that's the unforthunate woman,' says she, 'for ain't I cryin' here, an' isn't he in heaven, the bliggard,' says she. 'Oh, voh, voh, it's not at home comfortable with your wife an' family that you are, Jim Soolivan,' says she, 'but in the other world, you aumathaun, in glory wid the saints I hope,' says she. 'It's I that's the unforthunate famale,' says she, 'an' not yourself, Jim Soolivan,' says she.

An' this way she kep' an till mornin', cryin' and lamintin; an' wid the first light she called up all the sarvint bys, an' she tould them to go out an' to sarch every inch iv ground to find the corpse, 'for I'm sure,' says she, 'it's not to go hide himself he would,' says she.

Well, they went as well as they could, rummagin' through the snow, antil, at last, what should they come to, sure enough, but the corpse of a poor thravelling man, that fell over the quarry the night before by rason of the snow and some liquor he had, maybe; but, at any rate, he was as dead as a herrin', an' his face was knocked all to pieces jist like an over-boiled pitaty, glory be to God; an' divil a taste iv a nose or a chin, or a hill or a hollow from one end av his face to the other but was all as flat as a pancake. An' he was about Jim Soolivan's size, an' dhressed out exactly the same, wid a ridin' coat an' new corderhoys; so they carried him home, an' they were all as sure as daylight it was Jim Soolivan himself, an' they were wondhering he'd do sich a dirty turn as to go kill himself for spite.

Well, your honour, they waked him as well as they could, with what neighbours they could git togither, but by rason iv the snow, there wasn't enough gothered to make much divarsion; however it was a plisint wake enough, an' the churchyard an' the priest bein' convanient, as soon as the youngsthers had their bit iv fun and divarsion out iv the corpse, they burried it without a great dale iv throuble; an' about three days afther the berrin, ould Jim Mallowney, from th'other side iv the little hill, her own cousin by the mother's side—he had a snug bit iv a farm an' a house close by, by the same token—kem walkin' in to see how she was in her health, an' he dhrew a chair, an' he sot down an' beginned to converse her about one thing an' another, antil he got her quite an' asy into middlin' good humour, an' as soon as he seen it was time:

'I'm wondherin',' says he, 'Nell Gorman, sich a handsome, likely girl, id be thinkin' iv nothin' but lamintin' an' the likes,' says he, 'an' lingerin' away her days without any consolation, or gettin' a husband,' says he.

'Oh,' says she, 'isn't it only three days since I buried the poor man,' says she, 'an' isn't it rather soon to be talkin iv marryin' agin?'

'Divil a taste,' says he, 'three days is jist the time to a minute for cryin' afther a husband, an' there's no occasion in life to be keepin' it up,' says he; 'an' besides all that,' says he, 'Shrovetide is almost over, an' if you don't be sturrin' yourself an' lookin' about you, you'll be late,' says he, 'for this year at any rate, an' that's twelve months lost; an' who's to look afther the farm all that time,' says he, 'an' to keep the men to their work?' says he.

'It's thrue for you, Jim Mallowney,' says she, 'but I'm afeard the neighbours will be all talkin' about it,' says she.

'Divil's cure to the word,' says he.

'An' who would you advise?' says she.

'Young Andy Curtis is the boy,' says he.

'He's a likely boy in himself,' says she.

'An' as handy a gossoon as is out,' says he.

'Well, thin, Jim Mallowney,' says she, 'here's my hand, an' you may be talkin' to Andy Curtis, an' if he's willin' I'm agreeble—is that enough?' says she.

So with that he made off with himself straight to Andy Curtis; an' before three days more was past, the weddin' kem an, an' Nell Gorman an' Andy Curtis was married as complate as possible; an' if the wake was plisint the weddin' was tin times as agreeble, an' all the neighbours that could make their way to it was there, an' there was three fiddlers an' lots iv pipers, an' ould Connor Shamus[6] the piper himself was in it—by the same token it was the last weddin' he ever played music at, for the next mornin', whin he was goin' home, bein' mighty hearty an' plisint in himself, he was smothered in the snow, undher the ould castle; an' by my sowl he was a sore loss to the bys an' girls twenty miles round, for he was the illigantest piper, barrin' the liquor alone, that ever worked a bellas.

Well, a week passed over smart enough, an' Nell an' her new husband was mighty well continted with one another, for it was too soon for her to begin to regulate him the way she used with poor Jim Soolivan, so they wor comfortable enough; but this was too good to last, for the thaw kem an, an' you may be sure Jim Soolivan didn't lose a minute's time as soon as the heavy dhrift iv snow was melted enough between him and home to let him pass, for he didn't hear a word iv news from home sinst he lift it, by rason that no one, good nor bad, could thravel at all, with the way the snow was dhrifted.

So one night, when Nell Gorman an' her new husband, Andy Curtis, was snug an' warm in bed, an' fast asleep, an' everything quite, who should come to the door, sure enough, but Jim Soolivan himself, an' he beginned flakin' the door wid a big blackthorn stick he had, an' roarin' out like the divil to open the door, for he had a dhrop taken.

'What the divil's the matther?' says Andy Curtis, wakenin' out iv his sleep.

'Who's batin' the door?' says Nell; 'what's all the noise for?' says she.

'Who's in it?' says Andy.

'It's me,' says Jim.

'Who are you?' says Andy; 'what's your name?'

'Jim Soolivan,' says he.

'By jabers, you lie,' says Andy.

'Wait till I get at you,' says Jim, hittin' the door a lick iv the wattle you'd hear half a mile off.

'It's him, sure enough,' says Nell; 'I know his speech; it's his wandherin' sowl that can't get rest, the crass o' Christ betune us an' harm.'

'Let me in,' says Jim, 'or I'll dhrive the door in a top iv yis.'

---

6 Literally, Cornelius James—the last name employed as a patronymic. Connor is commonly used. Corney, pronounced Kurny, is just as much used in the South, as the short name for Cornelius.

'Jim Soolivan—Jim Soolivan,' says Nell, sittin' up in the bed, an' gropin' for a quart bottle iv holy wather she used to hang by the back iv the bed, 'don't come in, darlin'—there's holy wather here,' says she; 'but tell me from where you are is there anything that's throublin' your poor sinful sowl?' says she. 'An' tell me how many masses 'ill make you asy, an' by this crass, I'll buy you as many as you want,' says she.

'I don't know what the divil you mane,' says Jim.

'Go back,' says she, 'go back to glory, for God's sake,' says she.

'Divil's cure to the bit iv me 'ill go back to glory, or anywhere else,' says he, 'this blessed night; so open the door at onst' an' let me in,' says he.

'The Lord forbid,' says she.

'By jabers, you'd betther,' says he, 'or it 'ill be the worse for you,' says he; an' wid that he fell to wallopin' the door till he was fairly tired, an' Andy an' his wife crassin' themselves an' sayin' their prayers for the bare life all the time.

'Jim Soolivan,' says she, as soon as he was done, 'go back, for God's sake, an' don't be freakenin' me an' your poor fatherless childhren,' says she.

'Why, you bosthoon, you,' says Jim, 'won't you let your husband in,' says he, 'to his own house?' says he.

'You *wor* my husband, sure enough,' says she, 'but it's well you know, Jim Soolivan, you're not my husband *now*,' says she.

'You're as dhrunk as can be consaved, says Jim.

'Go back, in God's name, pacibly to your grave,' says Nell.

'By my sowl, it's to my grave you'll sind me, sure enough,' says he, 'you hard-hearted bain', for I'm jist aff wid the cowld,' says he.

'Jim Sulivan,' says she, 'it's in your dacent coffin you should be, you unforthunate sperit,' says she; 'what is it's annoyin' your sowl, in the wide world, at all?' says she; 'hadn't you everything complate?' says she, 'the oil, an' the wake, an' the berrin'?' says she.

'Och, by the hoky,' says Jim, 'it's too long I'm makin' a fool iv mysilf, gostherin' wid you outside iv my own door,' says he, 'for it's plain to be seen,' says he, 'you don't know what your're sayin', an' no one *Else* knows what you mane, you unforthunate fool,' says he; 'so, onst for all, open the door quietly,' says he, 'or, by my sowkins, I'll not lave a splinther together,' says he.

Well, whin Nell an' Andy seen he was getting vexed, they beginned to bawl out their prayers, with the fright, as if the life was lavin' them; an' the more he bate the door, the louder they prayed, until at last Jim was fairly tired out.

'Bad luck to you,' says he; 'for a rale divil av a woman,' says he. I 'can't get any advantage av you, any way; but wait till I get hould iv you, that's all,' says he. An' he turned aff from the door, an' wint round to the cow-house, an' settled himself as well as he could, in the sthraw; an' he was tired enough wid the thravellin' he had in the day-time, an' a good dale bothered with what liquor he had taken; so he was purty sure of slee-pin' wherever he thrun himself.

But, by my sowl, it wasn't the same way with the man an' the woman in the house—for divil a wink iv sleep, good or bad, could they get at all, wid the fright iv the sperit, as they supposed; an' with the first light they sint a little gossoon, as fast as he could wag, straight off, like a shot, to the priest, an' to desire him, for the love o' God, to come to them an the minute, an' to bring, if it was plasin' to his raverence, all the little things he had for sayin' mass, an' savin' sowls, an' banishin' sperits, an' freakenin' the divil, an' the likes iv that. An' it wasn't long till his raverence kem down, sure enough, on the ould grey mare, wid the little mass-boy behind him, an' the prayer-books an' Bibles, an' all the other mystarious articles that was wantin', along wid him; an' as soon as he kem in, 'God save all here,' says he.

'God save ye, kindly, your raverence,' says they.

'An' what's gone wrong wid ye?' says he; 'ye must be very bad,' says he,' entirely, to disturb my devotions,' says he, 'this way, jist at breakfast-time,' says he.

'By my sowkins,' says Nell, 'it's bad enough we are, your raverence,' says she, 'for it's poor Jim's sperit,' says she; 'God rest his sowl, wherever it is,' says she, 'that was wandherin' up an' down, oppossite the door all night,' says she, 'in the way it was no use at all, thryin' to get a wink iv sleep,' says she.

'It's to lay it, you want me, I suppose,' says the priest.

'If your raverence 'id do that same, it 'id be plasin' to us,' says Andy.

'It'll be rather expinsive,' says the priest.

'We'll not differ about the price, your raverence,' says Andy.

'Did the sperit stop long?' says the priest.

'Most part iv the night,' says Nell, 'the Lord be merciful to us all!' says she.

'That'll make it more costly than I thought,' says he. 'An' did it make much noise?' says he.

'By my sowl, it's it that did,' says Andy; 'leatherin' the door wid sticks and stones,' says he, 'antil I fairly thought every minute,' says he, 'the ould boords id smash, an' the sperit id be in an top iv us—God bless us,' says he.

'Phiew!' says the priest; 'it'll cost a power iv money.'

'Well, your raverence,' says Andy, 'take whatever you like,' says he; 'only make sure it won't annoy us any more,' says he.

'Oh! by my sowkins,' says the priest, 'it'll be the quarest ghost in the siven parishes,' says he, 'if it has the courage to come back,' says he, 'afther what I'll do this mornin', plase God,' says he; 'so we'll say twelve pounds;

an' God knows it's chape enough,' says he, 'considherin' all the sarcum-stances,' says he.

Well, there wasn't a second word to the bargain; so they paid him the money down, an' he sot the table doun like an althar, before the door, an' he settled it out vid all the things he had wid him; an' he lit a bit iv a holy candle, an' he scathered his holy wather right an' left; an' he took up a big book, an' he wint an readin' for half an hour, good; an' whin he kem to the end, he tuck hould iv his little bell, and he beginned to ring it for the bare life; an', by my sowl, he rung it so well, that he wakened Jim Sulivan in the cow-house, where he was sleepin', an' up he jumped, widout a minute's delay, an' med right for the house, where all the family, an' the priest, an' the little mass-boy was assimbled, layin' the ghost; an' as soon as his raver-ence seen him comin' in at the door, wid the fair fright, he flung the bell at his head, an' hot him sich a lick iv it in the forehead, that he sthretched him on the floor; but fain; he didn't wait to ax any questions, but he cut round the table as if the divil was afther him, an' out at the door, an' didn't stop even as much as to mount an his mare, but leathered away down the borheen as fast as his legs could carry him, though the mud was up to his knees, savin' your presence.

Well, by the time Jim kem to himself, the family persaved the mistake, an' Andy wint home, lavin' Nell to make the explanation. An' as soon as Jim heerd it all, he said he was quite contint to lave her to Andy, entirely; but the priest would not hear iv it; an' he jist med him marry his wife over again, an' a merry weddin' it was, an' a fine collection for his raverence. An' Andy was there along wid the rest, an' the priest put a small pinnance upon him, for bein' in too great a hurry to marry a widdy.'

An' bad luck to the word he'd allow anyone to say an the business, ever after, at all, at all; so, av coorse, no one offinded his raverence, by spakin' iv the twelve pounds he got for layin' the sperit.

An' the neighbours wor all mighty well plased, to be sure, for gettin' all the diversion of a wake, an' two weddin's for nothin'

A Chapter in the History of a Tyrone Family

BEING A TENTH EXTRACT FROM THE LEGACY OF THE LATE FRANCIS PURCELL, P.P. OF DRUMCOOLAGH.

Introduction.

IN THE following narrative, I have endeavoured to give as nearly as possible the ipsissima verba of the valued friend from whom I received it, conscious that any aberration from *her* mode of telling the tale of her own life would at once impair its accuracy and its effect.

Would that, with her words, I could also bring before you her animated gesture, her expressive countenance, the solemn and thrilling air and accent with which she related the dark passages in her strange story; and, above all, that I could communicate the impressive consciousness that the narrator had seen with her own eyes, and personally acted in the scenes which she described; these accompaniments, taken with the additional circumstance that she who told the tale was one far too deeply and sadly impressed with religious principle to misrepresent or fabricate what she repeated as fact, gave to the tale a depth of interest which the events recorded could hardly, themselves, have produced.

I became acquainted with the lady from whose lips I heard this narrative nearly twenty years since, and the story struck my fancy so much that I committed it to paper while it was still fresh in my mind; and should its perusal afford you entertainment for a listless half hour, my labour shall not have been bestowed in vain.

I find that I have taken the story down as she told it, in the first person, and perhaps this is as it should be.

She began as follows:

My maiden name was Richardson,[7] the designation of a family of some distinction in the county of Tyrone. I was the younger of two daughters, and we were the only children. There was a difference in our ages of nearly six years, so that I did not, in my childhood, enjoy that close companion-

---

7   I have carefully altered the names as they appear in the original MSS., for the reader will see that some of the circumstances recorded are not of a kind to reflect honour upon those involved in them; and as many are still living, in every way honoured and honourable, who stand in close relation to the principal actors in this drama, the reader will see the necessity of the course which we have adopted.

ship which sisterhood, in other circumstances, necessarily involves; and while I was still a child, my sister was married.

The person upon whom she bestowed her hand was a Mr. Carew, a gentleman of property and consideration in the north of England.

I remember well the eventful day of the wedding; the thronging carriages, the noisy menials, the loud laughter, the merry faces, and the gay dresses. Such sights were then new to me, and harmonised ill with the sorrowful feelings with which I regarded the event which was to separate me, as it turned out, for ever from a sister whose tenderness alone had hitherto more than supplied all that I wanted in my mother's affection.

The day soon arrived which was to remove the happy couple from Ashtown House. The carriage stood at the hall-door, and my poor sister kissed me again and again, telling me that I should see her soon.

The carriage drove away, and I gazed after it until my eyes filled with tears, and, returning slowly to my chamber, I wept more bitterly and, so to speak, more desolately, than ever I had done before.

My father had never seemed to love or to take an interest in me. He had desired a son, and I think he never thoroughly forgave me my unfortunate sex.

My having come into the world at all as his child he regarded as a kind of fraudulent intrusion, and as his antipathy to me had its origin in an imperfection of mine, too radical for removal, I never even hoped to stand high in his good graces.

My mother was, I dare say, as fond of me as she was of anyone; but she was a woman of a masculine and a worldly cast of mind. She had no tenderness or sympathy for the weaknesses, or even for the affections, of woman's nature and her demeanour towards me was peremptory, and often even harsh.

It is not to be supposed, then, that I found in the society of my parents much to supply the loss of my sister. About a year after her marriage, we received letters from Mr. Carew, containing accounts of my sister's health, which, though not actually alarming, were calculated to make us seriously uneasy. The symptoms most dwelt upon were loss of appetite and cough.

The letters concluded by intimating that he would avail himself of my father and mother's repeated invitation to spend some time at Ashtown, particularly as the physician who had been consulted as to my sister's health had strongly advised a removal to her native air.

There were added repeated assurances that nothing serious was apprehended, as it was supposed that a deranged state of the liver was the only source of the symptoms which at first had seemed to intimate consumption.

In accordance with this announcement, my sister and Mr. Carew arrived in Dublin, where one of my father's carriages awaited them, in readiness to start upon whatever day or hour they might choose for their departure

It was arranged that Mr. Carew was, as soon as the day upon which they were to leave Dublin was definitely fixed, to write to my father, who intended that the two last stages should be performed by his own horses, upon whose speed and safety far more reliance might be placed than upon those of the ordinary post-horses, which were at that time, almost without exception, of the very worst order. The journey, one of about ninety miles, was to be divided; the larger portion being reserved for the second day.

On Sunday a letter reached us, stating that the party would leave Dublin on Monday, and, in due course, reach Ashtown upon Tuesday evening.

Tuesday came the evening closed in, and yet no carriage; darkness came on, and still no sign of our expected visitors.

Hour after hour passed away, and it was now past twelve; the night was remarkably calm, scarce a breath stirring, so that any sound, such as that produced by the rapid movement of a vehicle, would have been audible at a considerable distance. For some such sound I was feverishly listening.

It was, however, my father's rule to close the house at nightfall, and the window-shutters being fastened, I was unable to reconnoitre the avenue as I would have wished. It was nearly one o'clock, and we began almost to despair of seeing them upon that night, when I thought I distinguished the sound of wheels, but so remote and faint as to make me at first very uncertain. The noise approached; it became louder and clearer; it stopped for a moment.

I now heard the shrill screaming of the rusty iron, as the avenue-gate revolved on its hinges; again came the sound of wheels in rapid motion.

'It is they,' said I, starting up; 'the carriage is in the avenue.'

We all stood for a few moments breathlessly listening. On thundered the vehicle with the speed of a whirlwind; crack went the whip, and clatter went the wheels, as it rattled over the uneven pavement of the court. A general and furious barking from all the dogs about the house, hailed its arrival.

We hurried to the hall in time to hear the steps let down with the sharp clanging noise peculiar to the operation, and the hum of voices exerted in the bustle of arrival. The hall-door was now thrown open, and we all stepped forth to greet our visitors.

The court was perfectly empty; the moon was shining broadly and brightly upon all around; nothing was to be seen but the tall trees with their long spectral shadows, now wet with the dews of midnight.

We stood gazing from right to left, as if suddenly awakened from a dream; the dogs walked suspiciously, growling and snuffing about the court, and by totally and suddenly ceasing their former loud barking, expressing the predominance of fear.

We stared one upon another in perplexity and dismay, and I think I never beheld more pale faces assembled. By my father's direction, we looked about to find anything which might indicate or account for the noise which we had heard; but no such thing was to be seen—even the mire which lay upon the avenue was undisturbed. We returned to the house, more panic-struck than I can describe.

On the next day, we learned by a messenger, who had ridden hard the greater part of the night, that my sister was dead. On Sunday evening, she had retired to bed rather unwell, and, on Monday, her indisposition declared itself unequivocally to be malignant fever. She became hourly worse and, on Tuesday night, a little after midnight, she expired.[8]

I mention this circumstance, because it was one upon which a thousand wild and fantastical reports were founded, though one would have thought that the truth scarcely required to be improved upon; and again, because it produced a strong and lasting effect upon my spirits, and indeed, I am inclined to think, upon my character.

---

8 The residuary legatee of the late Frances Purcell, who has the honour of selecting such of his lamented old friend's manuscripts as may appear fit for publication, in order that the lore which they contain may reach the world before scepticism and utility have robbed our species of the precious gift of credulity, and scornfully kicked before them, or trampled into annihilation those harmless fragments of picturesque superstition which it is our object to preserve, has been subjected to the charge of dealing too largely in the marvellous; and it has been half insinuated that such is his love for diablerie, that he is content to wander a mile out of his way, in order to meet a fiend or a goblin, and thus to sacrifice all regard for truth and accuracy to the idle hope of affrighting the imagination, and thus pandering to the bad taste of his reader. He begs leave, then, to take this opportunity of asserting his perfect innocence of all the crimes laid to his charge, and to assure his reader that he never *pandered to his bad taste*, nor went one inch out of his way to introduce witch, fairy, devil, ghost, or any other of the grim fraternity of the redoubted Raw-head-and-bloody-bones. His province, touching these tales, has been attended with no difficulty and little responsibility; indeed, he is accountable for nothing more than an alteration in the names of persons mentioned therein, when such a step seemed necessary, and for an occasional note, whenever he conceived it possible, innocently, to edge in a word. These tales have been *written down*, as the heading of each announces, by the Rev. Francis Purcell, P.P., of Drumcoolagh; and in all the instances, which are many, in which the present writer has had an opportunity of comparing the manuscript of his departed friend with the actual traditions which are current amongst the families whose fortunes they pretend to illustrate, he has uniformly found that whatever of supernatural occurred in the story, so far from having been exaggerated by him, had been rather softened down, and, wherever it could be attempted, accounted for.

I was, for several years after this occurrence, long after the violence of my grief subsided, so wretchedly low-spirited and nervous, that I could scarcely be said to live; and during this time, habits of indecision, arising out of a listless acquiescence in the will of others, a fear of encountering even the slightest opposition, and a disposition to shrink from what are commonly called amusements, grew upon me so strongly, that I have scarcely even yet altogether overcome them.

We saw nothing more of Mr. Carew. He returned to England as soon as the melancholy rites attendant upon the event which I have just mentioned were performed; and not being altogether inconsolable, he married again within two years; after which, owing to the remoteness of our relative situations, and other circumstances, we gradually lost sight of him.

I was now an only child; and, as my elder sister had died without issue, it was evident that, in the ordinary course of things, my father's property, which was altogether in his power, would go to me; and the consequence was, that before I was fourteen, Ashtown House was besieged by a host of suitors. However, whether it was that I was too young, or that none of the aspirants to my hand stood sufficiently high in rank or wealth, I was suffered by both parents to do exactly as I pleased; and well was it for me, as I afterwards found, that fortune, or rather Providence, had so ordained it, that I had not suffered my affections to become in any degree engaged, for my mother would never have suffered any *silly fancy* of mine, as she was in the habit of styling an attachment, to stand in the way of her ambitious views—views which she was determined to carry into effect, in defiance of every obstacle, and in order to accomplish which she would not have hesitated to sacrifice anything so unreasonable and contemptible as a girlish passion.

When I reached the age of sixteen, my mother's plans began to develop them-selves; and, at her suggestion, we moved to Dublin to sojourn for the winter, in order that no time might be lost in disposing of me to the best advantage.

I had been too long accustomed to consider myself as of no importance whatever, to believe for a moment that I was in reality the cause of all the bustle and preparation which surrounded me, and being thus relieved from the pain which a consciousness of my real situation would have inflicted, I journeyed towards the capital with a feeling of total indifference.

My father's wealth and connection had established him in the best society, and, consequently, upon our arrival in the metropolis we commanded whatever enjoyment or advantages its gaieties afforded.

The tumult and novelty of the scenes in which I was involved did not fail con-siderably to amuse me, and my mind gradually recovered its tone, which was naturally cheerful.

It was almost immediately known and reported that I was an heiress, and of course my attractions were pretty generally acknowledged.

Among the many gentlemen whom it was my fortune to please, one, ere long, established himself in my mother's good graces, to the exclusion of all less important aspirants. However, I had not understood or even remarked his attentions, nor in the slightest degree suspected his or my mother's plans respecting me, when I was made aware of them rather abruptly by my mother herself.

We had attended a splendid ball, given by Lord M—, at his residence in Stephen's Green, and I was, with the assist-ance of my waiting-maid, employed in rapidly divesting myself of the rich ornaments which, in profuseness and value, could scarcely have found their equals in any private family in Ireland.

I had thrown myself into a lounging-chair beside the fire, listless and exhausted, after the fatigues of the evening, when I was aroused from the reverie into which I had fallen by the sound of footsteps approaching my chamber, and my mother entered.

'Fanny, my dear,' said she, in her softest tone, 'I wish to say a word or two with you before I go to rest. You are not fatigued, love, I hope?'

'No, no, madam, I thank you,' said I, rising at the same time from my seat, with the formal respect so little practised now.

'Sit down, my dear,' said she, placing herself upon a chair beside me; 'I must chat with you for a quarter of an hour or so. Saunders' (to the maid) 'you may leave the room; do not close the room-door, but shut that of the lobby.'

This precaution against curious ears having been taken as directed, my mother proceeded.

'You have observed, I should suppose, my dearest Fanny—indeed, you *must* have observed Lord Glenfallen's marked attentions to you?'

'I assure you, madam—' I began.

'Well, well, that is all right,' interrupted my mother; 'of course you must be modest upon the matter; but listen to me for a few moments, my love, and I will prove to your satisfaction that your modesty is quite unnecessary in this case. You have done better than we could have hoped, at least so very soon. Lord Glenfallen is in love with you. I give you joy of your conquest;' and saying this, my mother kissed my forehead.

'In love with me!' I exclaimed, in unfeigned astonishment.

'Yes, in love with you,' repeated my mother; 'devotedly, distractedly in love with you. Why, my dear, what is there wonderful in it? Look in the glass, and look at these,' she continued, pointing with a smile to the jewels which I had just removed from my person, and which now lay a glittering heap upon the table.

'May there not,' said I, hesitating between confusion and real alarm—
'is it not possible that some mistake may be at the bottom of all this?'

'Mistake, dearest! none,' said my mother. 'None; none in the world.
Judge for yourself; read this, my love.' And she placed in my hand a letter,
addressed to herself, the seal of which was broken. I read it through with
no small surprise. After some very fine complimentary flourishes upon my
beauty and perfections, as also upon the antiquity and high reputation of our
family, it went on to make a formal proposal of marriage, to be communicated or not to me at present, as my mother should deem expedient; and the
letter wound up by a request that the writer might be permitted, upon our return to Ashtown House, which was soon to take place, as the spring was now
tolerably advanced, to visit us for a few days, in case his suit was approved.

'Well, well, my dear,' said my mother, impatiently; 'do you know who
Lord Glenfallen is?'

'I do, madam,' said I rather timidly, for I dreaded an altercation with
my mother.

'Well, dear, and what frightens you?' continued she. 'Are you afraid of
a title? What has he done to alarm you? he is neither old nor ugly.'

I was silent, though I might have said, 'He is neither young
nor handsome.'

'My dear Fanny,' continued my mother, 'in sober seriousness you have
been most fortunate in engaging the affections of a nobleman such as
Lord Glenfallen, young and wealthy, with first-rate—yes, acknowledged
first-rate abilities, and of a family whose influence is not exceeded by that
of any in Ireland. Of course you see the offer in the same light that I do—
indeed I think you *must*.'

This was uttered in no very dubious tone. I was so much astonished by
the suddenness of the whole communication that I literally did not know
what to say.

'You are not in love?' said my mother, turning sharply, and fixing her
dark eyes upon me with severe scrutiny.

'No, madam,' said I, promptly; horrified, as what young lady would
not have been, at such a query.

'I'm glad to hear it,' said my mother, drily. 'Once, nearly twenty years
ago, a friend of mine consulted me as to how he should deal with a
daughter who had made what they call a love-match—beggared herself, and disgraced her family; and I said, without hesitation, take no
care for her, but cast her off. Such punishment I awarded for an offence
committed against the reputation of a family not my own; and what I
advised respecting the child of another, with full as small compunction
I would *do* with mine. I cannot conceive anything more unreasonable or

intolerable than that the fortune and the character of a family should be marred by the idle caprices of a girl.'

She spoke this with great severity, and paused as if she expected some observation from me.

I, however, said nothing.

'But I need not explain to you, my dear Fanny,' she continued, 'my views upon this subject; you have always known them well, and I have never yet had reason to believe you likely, voluntarily, to offend me, or to abuse or neglect any of those advantages which reason and duty tell you should be improved. Come hither, my dear; kiss me, and do not look so frightened. Well, now, about this letter, you need not answer it yet; of course you must be allowed time to make up your mind. In the meantime I will write to his lordship to give him my permission to visit us at Ashtown. Good-night, my love.'

And thus ended one of the most disagreeable, not to say astounding, conversations I had ever had. It would not be easy to describe exactly what were my feelings towards Lord Glenfallen;—whatever might have been my mother's suspicions, my heart was perfectly disengaged—and hitherto, although I had not been made in the slightest degree acquainted with his real views, I had liked him very much, as an agreeable, well-informed man, whom I was always glad to meet in society. He had served in the navy in early life, and the polish which his manners received in his after inter-course with courts and cities had not served to obliterate that frankness of manner which belongs proverbially to the sailor.

Whether this apparent candour went deeper than the outward bear-ing, I was yet to learn. However, there was no doubt that, as far as I had seen of Lord Glenfallen, he was, though perhaps not so young as might have been desired in a lover, a singularly pleasing man; and whatever feel-ing unfavourable to him had found its way into my mind, arose altogether from the dread, not an unreasonable one, that constraint might be prac-tised upon my inclinations. I reflected, however, that Lord Glenfallen was a wealthy man, and one highly thought of; and although I could never expect to love him in the romantic sense of the term, yet I had no doubt but that, all things considered, I might be more happy with him than I could hope to be at home.

When next I met him it was with no small embarrassment, his tact and good breeding, however, soon reassured me, and effectually prevented my awkwardness being remarked upon. And I had the satisfaction of leav-ing Dublin for the country with the full conviction that nobody, not even those most intimate with me, even suspected the fact of Lord Glenfallen's having made me a formal proposal.

This was to me a very serious subject of self-gratulation, for, besides my instinctive dread of becoming the topic of the speculations of gossip, I felt that if the situation which I occupied in relation to him were made publicly known, I should stand committed in a manner which would scarcely leave me the power of retraction.

The period at which Lord Glenfallen had arranged to visit Ashtown House was now fast approaching, and it became my mother's wish to form me thoroughly to her will, and to obtain my consent to the proposed marriage before his arrival, so that all things might proceed smoothly, without apparent opposition or objection upon my part. Whatever objections, therefore, I had entertained were to be subdued; whatever disposition to resistance I had exhibited or had been supposed to feel, were to be completely eradicated before he made his appearance; and my mother addressed herself to the task with a decision and energy against which even the barriers, which her imagination had created, could hardly have stood.

If she had, however, expected any determined opposition from me, she was agreeably disappointed. My heart was perfectly free, and all my feelings of liking and preference were in favour of Lord Glenfallen; and I well knew that in case I refused to dispose of myself as I was desired, my mother had alike the power and the will to render my existence as utterly miserable as even the most ill-assorted marriage could possibly have done.

You will remember, my good friend, that I was very young and very completely under the control of my parents, both of whom, my mother particularly, were unscrupulously determined in matters of this kind, and willing, when voluntary obedience on the part of those within their power was withheld, to compel a forced acquiescence by an unsparing use of all the engines of the most stern and rigorous domestic discipline.

All these combined, not unnaturally, induced me to resolve upon yielding at once, and without useless opposition, to what appeared almost to be my fate.

The appointed time was come, and my now accepted suitor arrived; he was in high spirits, and, if possible, more entertaining than ever.

I was not, however, quite in the mood to enjoy his sprightliness; but whatever I wanted in gaiety was amply made up in the triumphant and gracious good-humour of my mother, whose smiles of benevolence and exultation were showered around as bountifully as the summer sunshine.

I will not weary you with unnecessary prolixity. Let it suffice to say, that I was married to Lord Glenfallen with all the attendant pomp and circumstance of wealth, rank, and grandeur. According to the usage of the times, now humanely reformed, the ceremony was made, until long past midnight, the season of wild, uproarious, and promiscuous feasting and revelry.

Of all this I have a painfully vivid recollection, and particularly of the little annoyances inflicted upon me by the dull and coarse jokes of the wits and wags who abound in all such places, and upon all such occasions.

I was not sorry when, after a few days, Lord Glenfallen's carriage appeared at the door to convey us both from Ashtown; for any change would have been a relief from the irksomeness of ceremonial and formality which the visits received in honour of my newly-acquired titles hourly entailed upon me.

It was arranged that we were to proceed to Cahergillagh, one of the Glenfallen estates, lying, however, in a southern county, so that, owing to the difficulty of the roads at the time, a tedious journey of three days intervened.

I set forth with my noble companion, followed by the regrets of some, and by the envy of many; though God knows I little deserved the latter. The three days of travel were now almost spent, when, passing the brow of a wild heathy hill, the domain of Cahergillagh opened suddenly upon our view.

It formed a striking and a beautiful scene. A lake of considerable extent stretching away towards the west, and reflecting from its broad, smooth waters, the rich glow of the setting sun, was overhung by steep hills, covered by a rich mantle of velvet sward, broken here and there by the grey front of some old rock, and exhibiting on their shelving sides, their slopes and hollows, every variety of light and shade; a thick wood of dwarf oak, birch, and hazel skirted these hills, and clothed the shores of the lake, running out in rich luxuriance upon every promontory, and spreading upward considerably upon the side of the hills.

'There lies the enchanted castle,' said Lord Glenfallen, pointing towards a considerable level space intervening between two of the picturesque hills, which rose dimly around the lake.

This little plain was chiefly occupied by the same low, wild wood which covered the other parts of the domain; but towards the centre a mass of taller and statelier forest trees stood darkly grouped together, and among them stood an ancient square tower, with many buildings of a humbler character, forming together the manor-house, or, as it was more usually called, the Court of Cahergillagh.

As we approached the level upon which the mansion stood, the winding road gave us many glimpses of the time-worn castle and its surrounding buildings; and seen as it was through the long vistas of the fine old trees, and with the rich glow of evening upon it, I have seldom beheld an object more picturesquely striking.

I was glad to perceive, too, that here and there the blue curling smoke ascended from stacks of chimneys now hidden by the rich, dark ivy which, in a great measure, covered the building. Other indications of comfort made themselves manifest as we approached; and indeed, though the place was evidently one of considerable antiquity, it had nothing whatever of the gloom of decay about it.

'You must not, my love,' said Lord Glenfallen, 'imagine this place worse than it is. I have no taste for antiquity—at least I should not choose a house to reside in because it is old. Indeed I do not recollect that I was even so romantic as to overcome my aversion to rats and rheumatism, those faithful attendants upon your noble relics of feudalism; and I much prefer a snug, modern, unmysterious bedroom, with well-aired sheets, to the waving tapestry, mildewed cushions, and all the other interesting appliances of romance. However, though I cannot promise you all the discomfort generally belonging to an old castle, you will find legends and ghostly lore enough to claim your respect; and if old Martha be still to the fore, as I trust she is, you will soon have a supernatural and appropriate anecdote for every closet and corner of the mansion; but here we are—so, without more ado, welcome to Cahergillagh!'

We now entered the hall of the castle, and while the domestics were employed in conveying our trunks and other luggage which we had brought with us for immediate use to the apartments which Lord Glenfallen had selected for himself and me, I went with him into a spacious sitting-room, wainscoted with finely polished black oak, and hung round with the portraits of various worthies of the Glenfallen family.

This room looked out upon an extensive level covered with the softest green sward, and irregularly bounded by the wild wood I have before mentioned, through the leafy arcade formed by whose boughs and trunks the level beams of the setting sun were pouring. In the distance a group of dairy-maids were plying their task, which they accompanied throughout with snatches of Irish songs which, mellowed by the distance, floated not unpleasingly to the ear; and beside them sat or lay, with all the grave importance of conscious protection, six or seven large dogs of various kinds. Farther in the distance, and through the cloisters of the arching wood, two or three ragged urchins were employed in driving such stray kine as had wandered farther than the rest to join their fellows.

As I looked upon this scene which I have described, a feeling of tranquillity and happiness came upon me, which I have never experienced in so strong a degree; and so strange to me was the sensation that my eyes filled with tears.

Lord Glenfallen mistook the cause of my emotion, and taking me kindly and tenderly by the hand, he said:

'Do not suppose, my love, that it is my intention to *settle* here. Whenever you desire to leave this, you have only to let me know your wish, and it shall be complied with; so I must entreat of you not to suffer any circumstances which I can control to give you one moment's uneasiness. But here is old Martha; you must be introduced to her, one of the heirlooms of our family.'

A hale, good-humoured, erect old woman was Martha, and an agreeable contrast to the grim, decrepid hag which my fancy had conjured up, as the depository of all the horrible tales in which I doubted not this old place was most fruitful.

She welcomed me and her master with a profusion of gratulations, alternately kissing our hands and apologising for the liberty, until at length Lord Glenfallen put an end to this somewhat fatiguing ceremonial by requesting her to conduct me to my chamber if it were prepared for my reception.

I followed Martha up an old-fashioned oak staircase into a long, dim passage, at the end of which lay the door which communicated with the apartments which had been selected for our use; here the old woman stopped, and respectfully requested me to proceed.

I accordingly opened the door, and was about to enter, when something like a mass of black tapestry, as it appeared, disturbed by my sudden approach, fell from above the door, so as completely to screen the aperture; the startling unexpectedness of the occurrence, and the rustling noise which the drapery made in its descent, caused me involuntarily to step two or three paces backwards. I turned, smiling and half-ashamed, to the old servant, and said:

'You see what a coward I am.'

The woman looked puzzled, and, without saying any more, I was about to draw aside the curtain and enter the room, when, upon turning to do so, I was surprised to find that nothing whatever interposed to obstruct the passage.

I went into the room, followed by the servant-woman, and was amazed to find that it, like the one below, was wainscoted, and that nothing like drapery was to be found near the door.

'Where is it?' said I; 'what has become of it?'

'What does your ladyship wish to know?' said the old woman.

'Where is the black curtain that fell across the door, when I attempted first to come to my chamber?' answered I.

'The cross of Christ about us!' said the old woman, turning suddenly pale.

'What is the matter, my good friend?' said I; 'you seem frightened.'

'Oh no, no, your ladyship,' said the old woman, endeavouring to conceal her agitation; but in vain, for tottering towards a chair, she sank into it, looking so deadly pale and horror-struck that I thought every moment she would faint.

'Merciful God, keep us from harm and danger!' muttered she at length.

'What can have terrified you so?' said I, beginning to fear that she had seen something more than had met my eye. 'You appear ill, my poor woman!'

'Nothing, nothing, my lady,' said she, rising. 'I beg your ladyship's pardon for making so bold. May the great God defend us from misfortune!'

'Martha,' said I, 'something *has* frightened you very much, and I insist on knowing what it is; your keeping me in the dark upon the subject will make me much more uneasy than anything you could tell me. I desire you, therefore, to let me know what agitates you; I command you to tell me.'

'Your ladyship said you saw a black curtain falling across the door when you were coming into the room,' said the old woman.

'I did,' said I; 'but though the whole thing appears somewhat strange, I cannot see anything in the matter to agitate you so excessively.'

'It's for no good you saw that, my lady,' said the crone; 'something terrible is coming. It's a sign, my lady—a sign that never fails.'

'Explain, explain what you mean, my good woman,' said I, in spite of myself, catching more than I could account for, of her superstitious terror.

'Whenever something—something *bad* is going to happen to the Glenfallen family, some one that belongs to them sees a black handkerchief or curtain just waved or falling before their faces. I saw it myself,' continued she, lowering her voice, 'when I was only a little girl, and I'll never forget it. I often heard of it before, though I never saw it till then, nor since, praised be God. But I was going into Lady Jane's room to waken her in the morning; and sure enough when I got first to the bed and began to draw the curtain, something dark was waved across the division, but only for a moment; and when I saw rightly into the bed, there was she lying cold and dead, God be merciful to me! So, my lady, there is small blame to me to be daunted when any one of the family sees it; for it's many's the story I heard of it, though I saw it but once.'

I was not of a superstitious turn of mind, yet I could not resist a feeling of awe very nearly allied to the fear which my companion had so unreservedly expressed; and when you consider my situation, the loneliness, antiquity, and gloom of the place, you will allow that the weakness was not without excuse.

In spite of old Martha's boding predictions, however, time flowed on in an unruffled course. One little incident however, though trifling in itself, I must relate, as it serves to make what follows more intelligible.

Upon the day after my arrival, Lord Glenfallen of course desired to make me acquainted with the house and domain; and accordingly we set forth upon our ramble. When returning, he became for some time silent and moody, a state so unusual with him as considerably to excite my surprise.

I endeavoured by observations and questions to arouse him—but in vain. At length, as we approached the house, he said, as if speaking to himself:

' 'Twere madness—madness—madness,' repeating the words bitterly—'sure and speedy ruin.'

There was here a long pause; and at length, turning sharply towards me, in a tone very unlike that in which he had hitherto addressed me, he said:

'Do you think it possible that a woman can keep a secret?'

'I am sure,' said I, 'that women are very much belied upon the score of talkativeness, and that I may answer your question with the same directness with which you put it—I reply that *I do* think a woman can keep a secret.'

'But I do not,' said he, drily.

We walked on in silence for a time. I was much astonished at his unwonted abruptness—I had almost said rudeness.

After a considerable pause he seemed to recollect himself, and with an effort resuming his sprightly manner, he said:

'Well, well, the next thing to keeping a secret well is, not to desire to possess one—talkativeness and curiosity generally go together. Now I shall make test of you, in the first place, respecting the latter of these qualities. I shall be your *bluebeard*—tush, why do I trifle thus? Listen to me, my dear Fanny; I speak now in solemn earnest. What I desire is intimately, inseparably, connected with your happiness and honour as well as my own; and your compliance with my request will not be difficult. It will impose upon you a very trifling restraint during your sojourn here, which certain events which have occurred since our arrival have determined me shall not be a long one. You must promise me, upon your sacred honour, that you will visit *only* that part of the castle which can be reached from the front entrance, leaving the back entrance and the part of the building commanded immediately by it to the menials, as also the small garden whose high wall you see yonder; and never at any time seek to pry or peep into them, nor to open the door which communicates from the front part of the house through the corridor with the back. I do not urge this in jest or in caprice, but from a solemn conviction that danger and misery will be the certain consequences of your not observing what I prescribe. I cannot explain myself further at present. Promise me, then, these things, as you hope for peace here, and for mercy hereafter.'

I did make the promise as desired, and he appeared relieved; his manner recovered all its gaiety and elasticity: but the recollection of the strange scene which I have just described dwelt painfully upon my mind.

More than a month passed away without any occurrence worth recording; but I was not destined to leave Cahergillagh without further adventure. One day, intending to enjoy the pleasant sunshine in a ramble through the woods, I ran up to my room to procure my bonnet and shawl. Upon entering the chamber, I was surprised and somewhat startled to find it occupied. Beside the fireplace, and nearly opposite the door, seated in a large, old-fashioned elbow-chair, was placed the figure of a lady. She appeared to be nearer fifty than forty, and was dressed suitably to her age, in a handsome suit of flowered silk; she had a profusion of trinkets and jewellery about her person, and many rings upon her fingers. But although very rich, her dress was not gaudy or in ill taste. But what was remarkable in the lady was, that although her features were handsome, and upon the whole pleasing, the pupil of each eye was dimmed with the whiteness of cataract, and she was evidently stone-blind. I was for some seconds so surprised at this unaccountable apparition, that I could not find words to address her.

'Madam,' said I, 'there must be some mistake here—this is my bed-chamber.'

'Marry come up,' said the lady, sharply; '*your* chamber! Where is Lord Glenfallen?'

'He is below, madam,' replied I; 'and I am convinced he will be not a little surprised to find you here.'

'I do not think he will,' said she; 'with your good leave, talk of what you know something about. Tell him I want him. Why does the minx dilly-dally so?'

In spite of the awe which this grim lady inspired, there was something in her air of confident superiority which, when I considered our relative situations, was not a little irritating.

'Do you know, madam, to whom you speak?' said I.

'I neither know nor care,' said she; 'but I presume that you are some one about the house, so again I desire you, if you wish to continue here, to bring your master hither forthwith.'

'I must tell you, madam,' said I, 'that I am Lady Glenfallen.'

'What's that?' said the stranger, rapidly.

'I say, madam,' I repeated, approaching her that I might be more distinctly heard, 'that I am Lady Glenfallen.'

'It's a lie, you trull!' cried she, in an accent which made me start, and at the same time, springing forward, she seized me in her grasp, and shook me violently, repeating, 'It's a lie—it's a lie!' with a rapidity and vehemence which swelled every vein of her face. The violence of her action, and the fury which convulsed her face, effectually terrified me, and dis-engaging myself from her grasp, I screamed as loud as I could for help. The blind woman continued to pour out a torrent of abuse upon me, foaming at the mouth with rage, and impotently shaking her clenched fists towards me.

I heard Lord Glenfallen's step upon the stairs, and I instantly ran out; as I passed him I perceived that he was deadly pale, and just caught the words: 'I hope that demon has not hurt you?'

I made some answer, I forget what, and he entered the chamber, the door of which he locked upon the inside. What passed within I know not; but I heard the voices of the two speakers raised in loud and angry altercation.

I thought I heard the shrill accents of the woman repeat the words, 'Let her look to herself,' but I could not be quite sure. This short sentence, however, was, to my alarmed imagination, pregnant with fearful meaning.

The storm at length subsided, though not until after a conference of more than two long hours. Lord Glenfallen then returned, pale and agitated.

'That unfortunate woman,' said he, 'is out of her mind. I daresay she treated you to some of her ravings; but you need not dread any further in-terruption from her: I have brought her so far to reason. She did not hurt you, I trust.'

'No, no,' said I; 'but she terrified me beyond measure.'

'Well,' said he, 'she is likely to behave better for the future; and I dare swear that neither you nor she would desire, after what has passed, to meet again.'

This occurrence, so startling and un-pleasant, so involved in mystery, and giving rise to so many painful surmises, afforded me no very agreeable food for rumination.

All attempts on my part to arrive at the truth were baffled; Lord Glen-fallen evaded all my inquiries, and at length peremptorily forbid any fur-ther allusion to the matter. I was thus obliged to rest satisfied with what I had actually seen, and to trust to time to resolve the perplexities in which the whole transaction had involved me.

Lord Glenfallen's temper and spirits gradually underwent a complete and most painful change; he became silent and abstracted, his manner to me was abrupt and often harsh, some grievous anxiety seemed ever pres-ent to his mind; and under its influence his spirits sunk and his temper became soured.

I soon perceived that his gaiety was rather that which the stir and excitement of society produce, than the result of a healthy habit of mind; every day confirmed me in the opinion, that the considerate good-nature which I had so much admired in him was little more than a mere manner; and to my infinite grief and surprise, the gay, kind, open-hearted nobleman who had for months followed and flattered me, was rapidly assuming the form of a gloomy, morose, and singularly selfish man. This was a bitter discovery, and I strove to conceal it from myself as long as I could; but the truth was not to be denied, and I was forced to believe that Lord Glenfallen no longer loved me, and that he was at little pains to conceal the alteration in his sentiments.

One morning after breakfast, Lord Glen-fallen had been for some time walking silently up and down the room, buried in his moody reflections, when pausing suddenly, and turning towards me, he exclaimed:

'I have it—I have it! We must go abroad, and stay there too; and if that does not answer, why—why, we must try some more effectual expedient. Lady Glenfallen, I have become involved in heavy embarrassments. A wife, you know, must share the fortunes of her husband, for better for worse; but I will waive my right if you prefer remaining here—here at Cahergillagh. For I would not have you seen elsewhere without the state to which your rank entitles you; besides, it would break your poor mother's heart,' he added, with sneering gravity. 'So make up your mind—Cahergillagh or France. I will start if possible in a week, so determine between this and then.'

He left the room, and in a few moments I saw him ride past the window, followed by a mounted servant. He had directed a domestic to inform me that he should not be back until the next day.

I was in very great doubt as to what course of conduct I should pursue, as to accompanying him in the continental tour so suddenly determined upon. I felt that it would be a hazard too great to encounter; for at Cahergillagh I had always the consciousness to sustain me, that if his temper at any time led him into violent or unwarrantable treatment of me, I had a remedy within reach, in the protection and support of my own family, from all useful and effective communication with whom, if once in France, I should be entirely debarred.

As to remaining at Cahergillagh in solitude, and, for aught I knew, exposed to hidden dangers, it appeared to me scarcely less objectionable than the former proposition; and yet I feared that with one or other I must comply, unless I was prepared to come to an actual breach with Lord Glenfallen. Full of these unpleasing doubts and perplexities, I retired to rest.

I was wakened, after having slept uneasily for some hours, by some person shaking me rudely by the shoulder; a small lamp burned in my room, and by its light, to my horror and amazement, I discovered that my visitant was the self-same blind old lady who had so terrified me a few weeks before.

I started up in the bed, with a view to ring the bell, and alarm the domestics; but she instantly anticipated me by saying:

'Do not be frightened, silly girl! If I had wished to harm you I could have done it while you were sleeping; I need not have wakened you. Listen to me, now, attentively and fearlessly, for what I have to say interests you to the full as much as it does me. Tell me here, in the presence of God, did Lord Glenfallen marry you—*actually marry* you? Speak the truth, woman.'

'As surely as I live and speak,' I replied, 'did Lord Glenfallen marry me, in presence of more than a hundred witnesses.'

'Well,' continued she, 'he should have told you *then*, before you married him, that he had a wife living, which wife I am. I feel you tremble—tush! do not be frightened. I do not mean to harm you. Mark me now—you are *not* his wife. When I make my story known you will be so neither in the eye of God nor of man. You must leave this house upon to-morrow. Let the world know that your husband has another wife living; go you into retirement, and leave him to justice, which will surely overtake him. If you remain in this house after to-morrow you will reap the bitter fruits of your sin.'

So saying, she quitted the room, leaving me very little disposed to sleep.

Here was food for my very worst and most terrible suspicions; still there was not enough to remove all doubt. I had no proof of the truth of this woman's statement.

Taken by itself, there was nothing to induce me to attach weight to it; but when I viewed it in connection with the extraordinary mystery of some of Lord Glen-fallen's proceedings, his strange anxiety to exclude me from certain portions of the mansion, doubtless lest I should encounter this person—the strong influence, nay, command which she possessed over him, a circumstance clearly established by the very fact of her residing in the very place where, of all others, he should least have desired to find her—her thus acting, and continuing to act in direct contradiction to his wishes; when, I say, I viewed her disclosure in connection with all these circumstances, I could not help feeling that there was at least a fearful verisimilitude in the allegations which she had made.

Still I was not satisfied, nor nearly so. Young minds have a reluctance almost insurmountable to believing, upon anything short of unquestionable proof, the existence of premeditated guilt in anyone whom they have ever trusted; and in support of this feeling I was assured that if the assertion of Lord Glenfallen, which nothing in this woman's manner had led me to disbelieve, were true, namely that her mind was unsound, the whole fabric of my doubts and fears must fall to the ground.

I determined to state to Lord Glenfallen freely and accurately the substance of the communication which I had just heard, and in his words and looks to seek for its proof or refutation. Full of these thoughts, I remained wakeful and excited all night, every moment fancying that I heard the step or saw the figure of my recent visitor, towards whom I felt a species of horror and dread which I can hardly describe.

There was something in her face, though her features had evidently been handsome, and were not, at first sight, unpleasing, which, upon a nearer inspection, seemed to indicate the habitual prevalence and indulgence of evil passions, and a power of expressing mere animal anger, with an intenseness that I have seldom seen equalled, and to which an almost unearthly effect was given by the convulsive quivering of the sightless eyes.

You may easily suppose that it was no very pleasing reflection to me to consider that, whenever caprice might induce her to return, I was within the reach of this violent and, for aught I knew, insane woman, who had, upon that very night, spoken to me in a tone of menace, of which her mere words, divested of the manner and look with which she uttered them, can convey but a faint idea.

Will you believe me when I tell you that I was actually afraid to leave my bed in order to secure the door, lest I should again encounter the dreadful object lurking in some corner or peeping from behind the window-curtains, so very a child was I in my fears.

The morning came, and with it Lord Glenfallen. I knew not, and indeed I cared not, where he might have been; my thoughts were wholly engrossed by the terrible fears and suspicions which my last night's conference had suggested to me. He was, as usual, gloomy and abstracted, and I feared in no very fitting mood to hear what I had to say with patience, whether the charges were true or false.

I was, however, determined not to suffer the opportunity to pass, or Lord Glenfallen to leave the room, until, at all hazards, I had unburdened my mind.

'My lord,' said I, after a long silence, summoning up all my firmness— 'my lord, I wish to say a few words to you upon a matter of very great importance, of very deep concernment to you and to me.'

I fixed my eyes upon him to discern, if possible, whether the announcement caused him any uneasiness; but no symptom of any such feeling was perceptible.

'Well, my dear,' said he, 'this is no doubt a very grave preface, and portends, I have no doubt, something extraordinary. Pray let us have it without more ado.'

He took a chair, and seated himself nearly opposite to me.

'My lord,' said I, 'I have seen the person who alarmed me so much a short time since, the blind lady, again, upon last night.' His face, upon which my eyes were fixed, turned pale; he hesitated for a moment, and then said:

'And did you, pray, madam, so totally forget or spurn my express command, as to enter that portion of the house from which your promise, I might say your oath, excluded you?—answer me that!' he added fiercely.

'My lord,' said I, 'I have neither forgotten your *commands*, since such they were, nor disobeyed them. I was, last night, wakened from my sleep, as I lay in my own chamber, and accosted by the person whom I have mentioned. How she found access to the room I cannot pretend to say.'

'Ha! this must be looked to,' said he, half reflectively; 'and pray,' added he, quickly, while in turn he fixed his eyes upon me, 'what did this person say? since some comment upon her communication forms, no doubt, the sequel to your preface.'

'Your lordship is not mistaken,' said I; 'her statement was so extraordinary that I could not think of withholding it from you. She told me, my lord, that you had a wife living at the time you married me, and that she was that wife.'

Lord Glenfallen became ashy pale, almost livid; he made two or three efforts to clear his voice to speak, but in vain, and turning suddenly from me, he walked to the window. The horror and dismay which, in the olden time, overwhelmed the woman of Endor when her spells unexpectedly conjured the dead into her presence, were but types of what I felt when thus presented with what appeared to be almost unequivocal evidence of the guilt whose existence I had before so strongly doubted.

There was a silence of some moments, during which it were hard to conjecture whether I or my companion suffered most.

Lord Glenfallen soon recovered his self-command; he returned to the table, again sat down and said:

'What you have told me has so astonished me, has unfolded such a tissue of motiveless guilt, and in a quarter from which I had so little reason to look for ingratitude or treachery, that your announcement almost deprived me of speech; the person in question, however, has one excuse, her mind is, as I told you before, unsettled. You should have remembered that, and hesitated to receive as unexceptionable evidence against the honour of your husband, the ravings of a lunatic. I now tell you that this is the last time I shall speak to you upon this subject, and, in the presence of the God who is to judge me, and as I hope for mercy in the day of judgment, I swear that the charge thus brought against me is utterly false, unfounded, and ridiculous; I defy the world in any point to taint my honour; and, as I have never taken the opinion of madmen touching your character or morals, I think it but fair to require that you will evince a like tenderness for me; and now, once for all, never again dare to repeat to me your insulting suspicions, or the clumsy and infamous calumnies of fools. I shall instantly let the worthy lady who contrived this somewhat original device, understand fully my opinion upon the matter. Good morning;' and with these words he left me again in doubt, and involved in all horrors of the most agonising suspense.

I had reason to think that Lord Glenfallen wreaked his vengeance upon the author of the strange story which I had heard, with a violence which was not satisfied with mere words, for old Martha, with whom I was a great favourite, while attending me in my room, told me that she feared her master had ill-used the poor blind Dutch woman, for that she had heard her scream as if the very life were leaving her, but added a request that I should not speak of what she had told me to any one, particularly to the master.

'How do you know that she is a Dutch woman?' inquired I, anxious to learn anything whatever that might throw a light upon the history of this person, who seemed to have resolved to mix herself up in my fortunes.

'Why, my lady,' answered Martha, 'the master often calls her the Dutch hag, and other names you would not like to hear, and I am sure she is neither English nor Irish; for, whenever they talk together, they speak some queer foreign lingo, and fast enough, I'll be bound. But I ought not to talk about her at all; it might be as much as my place is worth to mention her—only you saw her first yourself, so there can be no great harm in speaking of her now.'

'How long has this lady been here?' continued I.

'She came early on the morning after your ladyship's arrival,' answered she; 'but do not ask me any more, for the master would think nothing of turning me out of doors for daring to speak of her at all, much less to you, my lady.'

I did not like to press the poor woman further, for her reluctance to speak on this topic was evident and strong.

You will readily believe that upon the very slight grounds which my information afforded, contradicted as it was by the solemn oath of my husband, and derived from what was, at best, a very questionable source, I could not take any very decisive measure whatever; and as to the menace of the strange woman who had thus unaccountably twice intruded herself into my chamber, although, at the moment, it occasioned me some uneasiness, it was not, even in my eyes, sufficiently formidable to induce my departure from Cahergillagh.

A few nights after the scene which I have just mentioned, Lord Glenfallen having, as usual, early retired to his study, I was left alone in the parlour to amuse myself as best I might.

It was not strange that my thoughts should often recur to the agitating scenes in which I had recently taken a part.

The subject of my reflections, the solitude, the silence, and the lateness of the hour, as also the depression of spirits to which I had of late been a constant prey, tended to produce that nervous excitement which places us wholly at the mercy of the imagination.

In order to calm my spirits I was endeavouring to direct my thoughts into some more pleasing channel, when I heard, or thought I heard, uttered, within a few yards of me, in an odd, half-sneering tone, the words,

'There is blood upon your ladyship's throat.'

So vivid was the impression that I started to my feet, and involuntarily placed my hand upon my neck.

I looked around the room for the speaker, but in vain.

I went then to the room-door, which I opened, and peered into the passage, nearly faint with horror lest some leering, shapeless thing should greet me upon the threshold.

When I had gazed long enough to assure myself that no strange object was within sight, 'I have been too much of a rake lately; I am racking out my nerves,' said I, speaking aloud, with a view to reassure myself.

I rang the bell, and, attended by old Martha, I retired to settle for the night.

While the servant was—as was her custom—arranging the lamp which I have already stated always burned during the night in my chamber, I was employed in undressing, and, in doing so, I had recourse to a large looking-glass which occupied a considerable portion of the wall in which it was fixed, rising from the ground to a height of about six feet—this mirror filled the space of a large panel in the wainscoting opposite the foot of the bed.

I had hardly been before it for the lapse of a minute when something like a black pall was slowly waved between me and it.

'Oh, God! there it is,' I exclaimed, wildly. 'I have seen it again, Martha—the black cloth.'

'God be merciful to us, then!' answered she, tremulously crossing herself. 'Some misfortune is over us.'

'No, no, Martha,' said I, almost instantly recovering my collectedness; for, although of a nervous temperament, I had never been superstitious. 'I do not believe in omens. You know I saw, or fancied I saw, this thing before, and nothing followed.'

'The Dutch lady came the next morning,' replied she.

'But surely her coming scarcely deserved such a dreadful warning,' I replied.

'She is a strange woman, my lady,' said Martha; 'and she is not *gone* yet—mark my words.'

'Well, well, Martha,' said I, 'I have not wit enough to change your opinions, nor inclination to alter mine; so I will talk no more of the matter. Good-night,' and so I was left to my reflections.

After lying for about an hour awake, I at length fell into a kind of doze; but my imagination was still busy, for I was startled from this unrefreshing sleep by fancying that I heard a voice close to my face exclaim as before:

'There is blood upon your ladyship's throat.'

The words were instantly followed by a loud burst of laughter.

Quaking with horror, I awakened, and heard my husband enter the room. Even this was it relief.

Scared as I was, however, by the tricks which my imagination had played me, I preferred remaining silent, and pretending to sleep, to attempting to engage my husband in conversation, for I well knew that his mood was such, that his words would not, in all probability, convey anything that had not better be unsaid and unheard.

Lord Glenfallen went into his dressing-room, which lay upon the right-hand side of the bed. The door lying open, I could see him by himself, at full length upon a sofa, and, in about half an hour, I became aware, by his deep and regularly drawn respiration, that he was fast asleep.

When slumber refuses to visit one, there is something peculiarly irritating, not to the temper, but to the nerves, in the consciousness that some one is in your immediate presence, actually enjoying the boon which you are seeking in vain; at least, I have always found it so, and never more than upon the present occasion.

A thousand annoying imaginations harassed and excited me; every object which I looked upon, though ever so familiar, seemed to have acquired a strange phantom-like character, the varying shadows thrown by the flickering of the lamplight, seemed shaping themselves into grotesque and unearthly forms, and whenever my eyes wandered to the sleeping figure of my husband, his features appeared to undergo the strangest and most demoniacal contortions.

Hour after hour was told by the old clock, and each succeeding one found me, if possible, less inclined to sleep than its predecessor.

It was now considerably past three; my eyes, in their involuntary wanderings, happened to alight upon the large mirror which was, as I have said, fixed in the wall opposite the foot of the bed. A view of it was commanded from where I lay, through the curtains. As I gazed fixedly upon it, I thought I perceived the broad sheet of glass shifting its position in relation to the bed; I riveted my eyes upon it with intense scrutiny; it was no deception, the mirror, as if acting of its own impulse, moved slowly aside, and disclosed a dark aperture in the wall, nearly as large as an ordinary door; a figure evidently stood in this, but the light was too dim to define it accurately.

It stepped cautiously into the chamber, and with so little noise, that had I not actually seen it, I do not think I should have been aware of its presence. It was arrayed in a kind of woollen night-dress, and a white handkerchief or cloth was bound tightly about the head; I had no difficulty, spite of the strangeness of the attire, in recognising the blind woman whom I so much dreaded.

She stooped down, bringing her head nearly to the ground, and in that attitude she remained motionless for some moments, no doubt in order to ascertain if any suspicious sound were stirring.

She was apparently satisfied by her observations, for she immediately recommenced her silent progress towards a ponderous mahogany dressing-table of my husband's. When she had reached it, she paused again, and appeared to listen attentively for some minutes; she then noiselessly opened one of the drawers, from which, having groped for some time, she took something, which I soon perceived to be a case of razors. She opened it, and tried the edge of each of the two instruments upon the skin of her hand; she quickly selected one, which she fixed firmly in her grasp. She now stooped down as before, and having listened for a time, she, with the hand that was disengaged, groped her way into the dressing-room where Lord Glenfallen lay fast asleep.

I was fixed as if in the tremendous spell of a nightmare. I could not stir even a finger; I could not lift my voice; I could not even breathe; and though I expected every moment to see the sleeping man murdered, I could not even close my eyes to shut out the horrible spectacle, which I had not the power to avert.

I saw the woman approach the sleeping figure, she laid the unoccupied hand lightly along his clothes, and having thus ascertained his identity, she, after a brief interval, turned back and again entered my chamber; here she bent down again to listen.

I had now not a doubt but that the razor was intended for my throat; yet the terrific fascination which had locked all my powers so long, still continued to bind me fast.

I felt that my life depended upon the slightest ordinary exertion, and yet I could not stir one joint from the position in which I lay, nor even make noise enough to waken Lord Glenfallen.

The murderous woman now, with long, silent steps, approached the bed; my very heart seemed turning to ice; her left hand, that which was disengaged, was upon the pillow; she gradually slid it forward towards my head, and in an instant, with the speed of lightning, it was clutched in my hair, while, with the other hand, she dashed the razor at my throat.

A slight inaccuracy saved me from instant death; the blow fell short, the point of the razor grazing my throat. In a moment, I know not how, I found myself at the other side of the bed, uttering shriek after shriek; the wretch was, however, determined if possible to murder me.

Scrambling along by the curtains, she rushed round the bed towards me; I seized the handle of the door to make my escape. It was, however, fastened. At all events, I could not open it. From the mere instinct of recoiling terror, I shrunk back into a corner. She was now within a yard of me. Her hand was upon my face.

I closed my eyes fast, expecting never to open them again, when a blow, inflicted from behind by a strong arm, stretched the monster senseless at my feet. At the same moment the door opened, and several domestics, alarmed by my cries, entered the apartment.

I do not recollect what followed, for I fainted. One swoon succeeded another, so long and death-like, that my life was considered very doubtful.

At about ten o'clock, however, I sunk into a deep and refreshing sleep, from which I was awakened at about two, that I might swear my deposition before a magistrate, who attended for that purpose.

I accordingly did so, as did also Lord Glenfallen, and the woman was fully committed to stand her trial at the ensuing assizes.

I shall never forget the scene which the examination of the blind woman and of the other parties afforded.

She was brought into the room in the custody of two servants. She wore a kind of flannel wrapper which had not been changed since the night before. It was torn and soiled, and here and there smeared with blood, which had flowed in large quantities from a wound in her head. The white handkerchief had fallen off in the scuffle, and her grizzled hair fell in masses about her wild and deadly pale countenance.

She appeared perfectly composed, however, and the only regret she expressed throughout, was at not having succeeded in her attempt, the object of which she did not pretend to conceal.

On being asked her name, she called herself the Countess Glenfallen, and refused to give any other title.

'The woman's name is Flora Van-Kemp,' said Lord Glenfallen.

'It *was*, it *was*, you perjured traitor and cheat!' screamed the woman; and then there followed a volley of words in some foreign language. 'Is there a magistrate here?' she resumed; 'I am Lord Glenfallen's wife—I'll prove it—write down my words. I am willing to be hanged or burned, so *he* meets his deserts. I did try to kill that doll of his; but it was he who put it into my head to do it—two wives were too many; I was to murder her, or she was to hang me; listen to all I have to say.'

Here Lord Glenfallen interrupted.

'I think, sir,' said he, addressing the magistrate, 'that we had better proceed to business; this unhappy woman's furious recriminations but waste our time. If she refuses to answer your questions, you had better, I presume, take my depositions.'

'And are you going to swear away my life, you black-perjured murderer?' shrieked the woman. 'Sir, sir, sir, you must hear me,' she continued, addressing the magistrate; 'I can convict him—he bid me murder that girl, and then, when I failed, he came behind me, and struck me down, and now he wants to swear away my life. Take down all I say.'

'If it is your intention,' said the magistrate, 'to confess the crime with which you stand charged, you may, upon producing sufficient evidence, criminate whom you please.'

'Evidence!—I have no evidence but myself,' said the woman. 'I will swear it all—write down my testimony—write it down, I say—we shall hang side by side, my brave lord—all your own handy-work, my gentle husband.'

This was followed by a low, insolent, and sneering laugh, which, from one in her situation, was sufficiently horrible.

'I will not at present hear anything,' replied he, 'but distinct answers to the questions which I shall put to you upon this matter.'

'Then you shall hear nothing,' replied she sullenly, and no inducement or intimidation could bring her to speak again.

Lord Glenfallen's deposition and mine were then given, as also those of the servants who had entered the room at the moment of my rescue.

The magistrate then intimated that she was committed, and must proceed directly to gaol, whither she was brought in a carriage; of Lord Glenfallen's, for his lordship was naturally by no means in-different to the effect which her vehement accusations against himself might produce, if uttered before every chance hearer whom she might meet with between Cahergillagh and the place of confinement whither she was despatched.

During the time which intervened between the committal and the trial of the prisoner, Lord Glenfallen seemed to suffer agonies of mind which baffle all description; he hardly ever slept, and when he did, his slumbers seemed but the instruments of new tortures, and his waking hours were, if possible, exceeded in intensity of terrors by the dreams which disturbed his sleep.

Lord Glenfallen rested, if to lie in the mere attitude of repose were to do so, in his dressing-room, and thus I had an opportunity of witnessing, far oftener than I wished it, the fearful workings of his mind. His agony often broke out into such fearful paroxysms that delirium and total loss of reason appeared to be impending. He frequently spoke of flying from the country, and bringing with him all the witnesses of the appalling scene upon which the prosecution was founded; then, again, he would fiercely lament that the blow which he had inflicted had not ended all.

The assizes arrived, however, and upon the day appointed Lord Glenfallen and I attended in order to give our evidence.

The cause was called on, and the prisoner appeared at the bar.

Great curiosity and interest were felt respecting the trial, so that the court was crowded to excess.

The prisoner, however, without appearing to take the trouble of listening to the indictment, pleaded guilty, and no repre-sentations on the part of the court availed to induce her to retract her plea.

After much time had been wasted in a fruitless attempt to prevail upon her to reconsider her words, the court proceeded, according to the usual form, to pass sentence.

This having been done, the prisoner was about to be removed, when she said, in a low, distinct voice:

'A word—a word, my lord!—Is Lord Glenfallen here in the court?'

On being told that he was, she raised her voice to a tone of loud menace, and continued:

'Hardress, Earl of Glenfallen, I accuse you here in this court of justice of two crimes,—first, that you married a second wife, while the first was living; and again, that you prompted me to the murder, for attempting which I am to die. Secure him—chain him—bring him here.'

There was a laugh through the court at these words, which were naturally treated by the judge as a violent extemporary recrimination, and the woman was desired to be silent.

'You won't take him, then?' she said; 'you won't try him? You'll let him go free?'

It was intimated by the court that he would certainly be allowed 'to go free,' and she was ordered again to be removed.

Before, however, the mandate was executed, she threw her arms wildly into the air, and uttered one piercing shriek so full of preternatural rage and despair, that it might fitly have ushered a soul into those realms where hope can come no more.

The sound still rang in my ears, months after the voice that had uttered it was for ever silent.

The wretched woman was executed in accordance with the sentence which had been pronounced.

For some time after this event, Lord Glenfallen appeared, if possible, to suffer more than he had done before, and altogether his language, which often amounted to half confessions of the guilt imputed to him, and all the circumstances connected with the late occurrences, formed a mass of evidence so convincing that I wrote to my father, detailing the grounds of my fears, and imploring him to come to Cahergillagh without delay, in order to remove me from my husband's control, previously to taking legal steps for a final separation.

Circumstanced as I was, my existence was little short of intolerable, for, besides the fearful suspicions which attached to my husband, I plainly perceived that if Lord Glenfallen were not relieved, and that speedily, insanity must supervene. I therefore expected my father's arrival, or at least a letter to announce it, with indescribable impatience.

About a week after the execution had taken place, Lord Glenfallen one morning met me with an unusually sprightly air.

'Fanny,' said he, 'I have it now for the first time in my power to explain to your satisfaction everything which has hitherto appeared suspicious or mysterious in my conduct. After breakfast come with me to my study, and I shall, I hope, make all things clear.'

This invitation afforded me more real pleasure than I had experienced for months. Something had certainly occurred to tranquillize my husband's mind in no ordinary degree, and I thought it by no means impossible that he would, in the proposed interview, prove himself the most injured and innocent of men.

Full of this hope, I repaired to his study at the appointed hour. He was writing busily when I entered the room, and just raising his eyes, he requested me to be seated.

I took a chair as he desired, and remained silently awaiting his leisure, while he finished, folded, directed, and sealed his letter. Laying it then upon the table with the address downward, he said,

'My dearest Fanny, I know I must have appeared very strange to you and very unkind—often even cruel. Before the end of this week I will show you the necessity of my conduct—how impossible it was that I should have seemed otherwise. I am conscious that many acts of mine must have inevitably given rise to painful suspicions—suspicions which, indeed, upon one occasion, you very properly communicated to me. I have got two letters from a quarter which commands respect, containing information as to the course by which I may be enabled to prove the negative of all the crimes which even the most credulous suspicion could lay to my charge. I expected a third by this morning's post, containing documents which will set the matter for ever at rest, but owing, no doubt, to some neglect, or, perhaps, to some difficulty in collecting the papers, some inevitable delay, it has not come to hand this morning, according to my expectation. I was finishing one to the very same quarter when you came in, and if a sound rousing be worth anything, I think I shall have a special messenger before two days have passed. I have been anxiously considering with myself, as to whether I had better imperfectly clear up your doubts by submitting to your inspection the two letters which I have already received, or wait till I can triumphantly vindicate myself by the production of the documents which I have already mentioned, and I have, I think, not unnaturally decided upon the latter course. However, there is a person in the next room whose testimony is not without its value excuse me for one moment.'

So saying, he arose and went to the door of a closet which opened from the study; this he unlocked, and half opening the door, he said, 'It is only I,' and then slipped into the room and carefully closed and locked the door behind him.

I immediately heard his voice in animated conversation. My curiosity upon the subject of the letter was naturally great, so, smothering any little scruples which I might have felt, I resolved to look at the address of the letter which lay, as my husband had left it, with its face upon the table. I accordingly drew it over to me and turned up the direction.

For two or three moments I could scarce believe my eyes, but there could be no mistake—in large characters were traced the words, 'To the Archangel Gabriel in Heaven.'

I had scarcely returned the letter to its original position, and in some degree recovered the shock which this unequivocal proof of insanity produced, when the closet door was unlocked, and Lord Glenfallen re-entered the study, carefully closing and locking the door again upon the outside.

'Whom have you there?' inquired I, making a strong effort to appear calm.

'Perhaps,' said he, musingly, 'you might have some objection to seeing her, at least for a time.'

'Who is it?' repeated I.

'Why,' said he, 'I see no use in hiding it—the blind Dutchwoman. I have been with her the whole morning. She is very anxious to get out of that closet; but you know she is odd, she is scarcely to be trusted.'

A heavy gust of wind shook the door at this moment with a sound as if something more substantial were pushing against it.

'Ha, ha, ha!—do you hear her?' said he, with an obstreperous burst of laughter.

The wind died away in a long howl, and Lord Glenfallen, suddenly checking his merriment, shrugged his shoulders, and muttered:

'Poor devil, she has been hardly used.'

'We had better not tease her at present with questions,' said I, in as unconcerned a tone as I could assume, although I felt every moment as if I should faint.

'Humph! may be so,' said he. 'Well, come back in an hour or two, or when you please, and you will find us here.'

He again unlocked the door, and entered with the same precautions which he had adopted before, locking the door upon the inside; and as I hurried from the room, I heard his voice again exerted as if in eager parley.

I can hardly describe my emotions; my hopes had been raised to the highest, and now, in an instant, all was gone—the dreadful consummation was accomplished—the fearful retribution had fallen upon the guilty man—the mind was destroyed—the power to repent was gone.

The agony of the hours which followed what I would still call my *awful* interview with Lord Glenfallen, I cannot describe; my solitude was, however, broken in upon by Martha, who came to inform me of the arrival of a gentleman, who expected me in the parlour.

I accordingly descended, and, to my great joy, found my father seated by the fire.

This expedition upon his part was easily accounted for: my communications had touched the honour of the family. I speedily informed him of the dreadful malady which had fallen upon the wretched man.

My father suggested the necessity of placing some person to watch him, to prevent his injuring himself or others.

I rang the bell, and desired that one Edward Cooke, an attached servant of the family, should be sent to me.

I told him distinctly and briefly the nature of the service required of him, and, attended by him, my father and I proceeded at once to the study.

The door of the inner room was still closed, and everything in the outer chamber remained in the same order in which I had left it.

We then advanced to the closet-door, at which we knocked, but without receiving any answer.

We next tried to open the door, but in vain—it was locked upon the inside. We knocked more loudly, but in vain.

Seriously alarmed, I desired the servant to force the door, which was, after several violent efforts, accomplished, and we entered the closet.

Lord Glenfallen was lying on his face upon a sofa.

'Hush!' said I, 'he is asleep.' We paused for a moment.

'He is too still for that,' said my father.

We all of us felt a strong reluctance to approach the figure.

'Edward,' said I, 'try whether your master sleeps.'

The servant approached the sofa where Lord Glenfallen lay. He leant his ear towards the head of the recumbent figure, to ascertain whether the sound of breathing was audible. He turned towards us, and said:

'My lady, you had better not wait here; I am sure he is dead!'

'Let me see the face,' said I, terribly agitated; 'you *may* be mistaken.'

The man then, in obedience to my command, turned the body round, and, gracious God! what a sight met my view. He was, indeed, perfectly dead.

The whole breast of the shirt, with its lace frill, was drenched with gore, as was the couch underneath the spot where he lay.

The head hung back, as it seemed, almost severed from the body by a frightful gash, which yawned across the throat. The instrument which had inflicted it was found under his body.

All, then, was over; I was never to learn the history in whose termination I had been so deeply and so tragically involved.

The severe discipline which my mind had undergone was not bestowed in vain. I directed my thoughts and my hopes to that place where there is no more sin, nor danger, nor sorrow.

Thus ends a brief tale whose prominent incidents many will recognise as having marked the history of a distinguished family; and though it refers to a somewhat distant date, we shall be found not to have taken, upon that account, any liberties with the facts, but in our statement of all the incidents to have rigorously and faithfully adhered to the truth.

An Adventure of Hardress Fitzgerald, A Royalist Captain

BEING AN ELEVENTH EXTRACT FROM THE LEGACY OF THE LATE FRANCIS PURCELL, P.P. OF DRUMCOOLAGH.

THE FOLLOWING brief narrative contains a faithful account of one of the many strange incidents which chequered the life of Hardress Fitzgerald—one of the now-forgotten heroes who flourished during the most stirring and, though the most disastrous, by no means the least glorious period of our eventful history.

He was a captain of horse in the army of James, and shared the fortunes of his master, enduring privations, encountering dangers, and submitting to vicissitudes the most galling and ruinous, with a fortitude and a heroism which would, if coupled with his other virtues have rendered the unhappy monarch whom he served, the most illustrious among unfortunate princes.

I have always preferred, where I could do so with any approach to accuracy, to give such relations as the one which I am about to submit to you, in the first person, and in the words of the original narrator, believing that such a form of recitation not only gives freshness to the tale, but in this particular instance, by bringing before me and steadily fixing in my mind's eye the veteran royalist who himself related the occurrence which I am about to record, furnishes an additional stimulant to my memory, and a proportionate check upon my imagination.

As nearly as I can recollect then, his statement was as follows:

After the fatal battle of the Boyne, I came up in disguise to Dublin, as did many in a like situation, regarding the capital as furnishing at once a good central position of observation, and as secure a lurking-place as I cared to find.

I would not suffer myself to believe that the cause of my royal master was so desperate as it really was; and while I lay in my lodgings, which consisted of the garret of a small dark house, standing in the lane which runs close by Audoen's Arch, I busied myself with continual projects for the raising of the country, and the re-collecting of the fragments of the defeated army—plans, you will allow, sufficiently magnificent for a poor devil who dared scarce show his face abroad in the daylight.

I believe, however, that I had not much reason to fear for my personal safety, for men's minds in the city were greatly occupied with public events, and private amusements and debaucheries, which were, about that time, carried to an excess which our country never knew before, by reason of the raking together from all quarters of the empire, and indeed from most parts of Holland, the most dissolute and des-perate adventurers who cared to play at hazard for their lives; and thus there seemed to be but little scrutiny into the characters of those who sought concealment.

I heard much at different times of the intentions of King James and his party, but nothing with certainty.

Some said that the king still lay in Ireland; others, that he had crossed over to Scotland, to encourage the Highlanders, who, with Dundee at their head, had been stirring in his behoof; others, again, said that he had taken ship for France, leaving his followers to shift for themselves, and regarding his kingdom as wholly lost, which last was the true version, as I afterwards learned.

Although I had been very active in the wars in Ireland, and had done many deeds of necessary but dire severity, which have often since troubled me much to think upon, yet I doubted not but that I might easily obtain protection for my person and property from the Prince of Orange, if I sought it by the ordinary submissions; but besides that my conscience and my affections resisted such time-serving concessions, I was resolved in my own mind that the cause of the royalist party was by no means desperate, and I looked to keep myself unimpeded by any pledge or promise given to the usurping Dutchman, that I might freely and honourably take a share in any struggle which might yet remain to be made for the right.

I therefore lay quiet, going forth from my lodgings but little, and that chiefly under cover of the dusk, and conversing hardly at all, except with those whom I well knew.

I had like once to have paid dearly for relaxing this caution; for going into a tavern one evening near the Tholsel, I had the confidence to throw off my hat, and sit there with my face quite exposed, when a fellow coming in with some troopers, they fell a-boozing, and being somewhat warmed, they began to drink 'Confusion to popery,' and the like, and to compel the peaceable persons who happened to sit there, to join them in so doing.

Though I was rather hot-blooded, I was resolved to say nothing to attract notice; but, at the same time, if urged to pledge the toasts which they were compelling others to drink, to resist doing so.

With the intent to withdraw myself quietly from the place, I paid my reckoning, and putting on my hat, was going into the street, when the countryman who had come in with the soldiers called out:

'Stop that popish tom-cat!'

And running across the room, he got to the door before me, and, shutting it, placed his back against it, to prevent my going out.

Though with much difficulty, I kept an appearance of quietness, and turning to the fellow, who, from his accent, I judged to be northern, and whose face I knew—though, to this day, I cannot say where I had seen him before—I observed very calmly:

*'Sir, I came in here with no other design than to refresh myself, without offending any man. I have paid my reckoning, and now desire to go forth. If there is anything within reason that I can do to satisfy you, and to prevent trouble and delay to myself, name your terms, and if they be but fair, I will frankly comply with them.'

He quickly replied:

'You are Hardress Fitzgerald, the bloody popish captain, that hanged the twelve men at Derry.'

I felt that I was in some danger, but being a strong man, and used to perils of all kinds, it was not easy to disconcert me.

I looked then steadily at the fellow, and, in a voice of much confidence, I said:

'I am neither a Papist, a Royalist, nor a Fitzgerald, but an honester Protestant, mayhap, than many who make louder professions.'

'Then drink the honest man's toast,' said he. 'Damnation to the pope, and confusion to skulking Jimmy and his runaway crew.'

'Yourself shall hear me,' said I, taking the largest pewter pot that lay within my reach. 'Tapster, fill this with ale; I grieve to say I can afford nothing better.'

I took the vessel of liquor in my hand, and walking up to him, I first made a bow to the troopers who sat laughing at the sprightliness of their facetious friend, and then another to himself, when saying, 'G—damn yourself and your cause!' I flung the ale straight into his face; and before he had time to recover himself, I struck him with my whole force and weight with the pewter pot upon the head, so strong a blow, that he fell, for aught I know, dead upon the floor, and nothing but the handle of the vessel remained in my hand.

I opened the door, but one of the dragoons drew his sabre, and ran at me to avenge his companion. With my hand I put aside the blade of the sword, narrowly escaping what he had intended for me, the point actually tearing open my vest. Without allowing him time to repeat his thrust, I struck him in the face with my clenched fist so sound a blow that he rolled back into the room with the force of a tennis ball.

It was well for me that the rest were half drunk, and the evening dark; for otherwise my folly would infallibly have cost me my life. As it was, I reached my garret in safety, with a resolution to frequent taverns no more until better times.

My little patience and money were well-nigh exhausted, when, after much doubt and uncertainty, and many conflicting reports, I was assured that the flower of the Royalist army, under the Duke of Berwick and General Boisleau, occupied the city of Limerick, with a determination to hold that fortress against the prince's forces; and that a French fleet of great power, and well freighted with arms, ammunition, and men, was riding in the Shannon, under the walls of the town. But this last report was, like many others then circulated, untrue; there being, indeed, a promise and expectation of such assistance, but no arrival of it till too late.

The army of the Prince of Orange was said to be rapidly approaching the town, in order to commence the siege.

On hearing this, and being made as certain as the vagueness and unsatisfactory nature of my information, which came not from any authentic source, would permit; at least, being sure of the main point, which all allowed—namely, that Limerick was held for the king—and being also naturally fond of enterprise, and impatient of idleness, I took the resolution to travel thither, and, if possible, to throw myself into the city, in order to lend what assistance I might to my former companions in arms, well knowing that any man of strong constitution and of some experience might easily make himself useful to a garrison in their straitened situation.

When I had taken this resolution, I was not long in putting it into execution; and, as the first step in the matter, I turned half of the money which remained with me, in all about seventeen pounds, into small wares and merchandise such as travelling traders used to deal in; and the rest, excepting some shillings which I carried home for my immediate expenses, I sewed carefully in the lining of my breeches waistband, hoping that the sale of my commodities might easily supply me with subsistence upon the road.

I left Dublin upon a Friday morning in the month of September, with a tolerably heavy pack upon my back.

I was a strong man and a good walker, and one day with another travelled easily at the rate of twenty miles in each day, much time being lost in the towns of any note on the way, where, to avoid suspicion, I was obliged to make some stay, as if to sell my wares.

I did not travel directly to Limerick, but turned far into Tipperary, going near to the borders of Cork.

Upon the sixth day after my departure from Dublin I learned, *certainly*, from some fellows who were returning from trafficking with the soldiers, that the army of the prince was actually encamped before Limerick, upon the south side of the Shannon.

In order, then, to enter the city without interruption, I must needs cross the river, and I was much in doubt whether to do so by boat from Kerry, which I might have easily done, into the Earl of Clare's land, and thus into the beleaguered city, or to take what seemed the easier way, one, however, about which I had certain misgivings—which, by the way, afterwards turned out to be just enough. This way was to cross the Shannon at O'Brien's Bridge, or at Killaloe, into the county of Clare.

I feared, however, that both these passes were guarded by the prince's forces, and resolved, if such were the case, not to essay to cross, for I was not fitted to sustain a scrutiny, having about me, though pretty safely secured, my commission from King James—which, though a dangerous companion, I would not have parted from but with my life.

I settled, then, in my own mind, that if the bridges were guarded I would walk as far as Portumna, where I might cross, though at a considerable sacrifice of time; and, having determined upon this course, I turned directly towards Killaloe.

I reached the foot of the mountain, or rather high hill, called Keeper—which had been pointed out to me as a landmark—lying directly between me and Killaloe, in the evening, and, having ascended some way, the darkness and fog overtook me.

The evening was very chilly, and myself weary, hungry, and much in need of sleep, so that I preferred seeking to cross the hill, though at some risk, to remaining upon it throughout the night. Stumbling over rocks and sinking into bog-mire, as the nature of the ground varied, I slowly and laboriously plodded on, making very little way in proportion to the toil it cost me.

After half an hour's slow walking, or rather rambling, for, owing to the dark, I very soon lost my direction, I at last heard the sound of running water, and with some little trouble reached the edge of a brook, which ran in the bottom of a deep gully. This I knew would furnish a sure guide to the low grounds, where I might promise myself that I should speedily meet with some house or cabin where I might find shelter for the night.

The stream which I followed flowed at the bottom of a rough and swampy glen, very steep and making many abrupt turns, and so dark, owing more to the fog than to the want of the moon (for, though not high, I believe it had risen at the time), that I continually fell over fragments of rock and stumbled up to my middle into the rivulet, which I sought to follow.

In this way, drenched, weary, and with my patience almost exhausted, I was toiling onward, when, turning a sharp angle in the winding glen, I found myself within some twenty yards of a group of wild-looking men, gathered in various attitudes round a glowing turf fire.

I was so surprised at this rencontre that I stopped short, and for a time was in doubt whether to turn back or to accost them.

A minute's thought satisfied me that I ought to make up to the fellows, and trust to their good faith for whatever assistance they could give me.

I determined, then, to do this, having great faith in the impulses of my mind, which, whenever I have been in jeopardy, as in my life I often have, always prompted me aright.

The strong red light of the fire showed me plainly enough that the group consisted, not of soldiers, but of Irish kernes, or countrymen, most of them wrapped in heavy mantles, and with no other covering for their heads than that afforded by their long, rough hair.

There was nothing about them which I could see to intimate whether their object were peaceful or warlike; but I afterwards found that they had weapons enough, though of their own rude fashion.

There were in all about twenty persons assembled around the fire, some sitting upon such blocks of stone as happened to lie in the way; others stretched at their length upon the ground.

'God save you, boys!' said I, advancing towards the party.

The men who had been talking and laughing together instantly paused, and two of them—tall and powerful fellows—snatched up each a weapon, something like a short halberd with a massive iron head, an instrument which they called among themselves a rapp, and with two or three long strides they came up with me, and laying hold upon my arms, drew me, not, you may easily believe, making much resistance, towards the fire.

When I reached the place where the figures were seated, the two men still held me firmly, and some others threw some handfuls of dry fuel upon the red embers, which, blazing up, cast a strong light upon me.

When they had satisfied themselves as to my appearance, they began to question me very closely as to my purpose in being upon the hill at such an unseasonable hour, asking me what was my occupation, where I had been, and whither I was going.

These questions were put to me in English by an old half-military looking man, who translated into that language the suggestions which his companions for the most part threw out in Irish.

I did not choose to commit myself to these fellows by telling them my real character and purpose, and therefore I represented myself as a poor travelling chapman who had been at Cork, and was seeking his way to Killaloe, in order to cross over into Clare and thence to the city of Galway.

My account did not seem fully to satisfy the men.

I heard one fellow say in Irish, which language I understood, 'Maybe he is a spy.'

They then whispered together for a time, and the little man who was their spokesman came over to me and said:

'Do you know what we do with spies? we knock their brains out my friend.'

He then turned back to them with whom he had been whispering, and talked in a low tone again with them for a considerable time.

I now felt very uncomfortable, not knowing what these savages—for they appeared nothing better—might design against me.

Twice or thrice I had serious thoughts of breaking from them, but the two guards who were placed upon me held me fast by the arms; and even had I succeeded in shaking them off, I should soon have been overtaken, encumbered as I was with a heavy pack, and wholly ignorant of the lie of the ground; or else, if I were so exceedingly lucky as to escape out of their hands, I still had the chance of falling into those of some other party of the same kind.

I therefore patiently awaited the issue of their deliberations, which I made no doubt affected me nearly.

I turned to the men who held me, and one after the other asked them, in their own language, 'Why they held me?' adding, 'I am but a poor pedlar, as you see. I have neither money nor money's worth, for the sake of which you should do me hurt. You may have my pack and all that it contains, if you desire it—but do not injure me.'

To all this they gave no answer, but savagely desired me to hold my tongue.

I accordingly remained silent, determined, if the worst came, to declare to the whole party, who, I doubted not, were friendly, as were all the Irish peasantry in the south, to the Royal cause, my real character and design; and if this avowal failed me, I was resolved to make a desperate effort to escape, or at least to give my life at the dearest price I could.

I was not kept long in suspense, for the little veteran who had spoken to me at first came over, and desiring the two men to bring me after him, led the way along a broken path, which wound by the side of the steep glen.

I was obliged willy nilly to go with them, and, half-dragging and half-carrying me, they brought me by the path, which now became very steep, for some hundred yards without stopping, when suddenly coming to a stand, I found myself close before the door of some house or hut, I could not see which, through the planks of which a strong light was streaming.

At this door my conductor stopped, and tapping gently at it, it was opened by a stout fellow, with buff-coat and jack-boots, and pistols stuck in his belt, as also a long cavalry sword by his side.

He spoke with my guide, and to my no small satisfaction, in French, which convinced me that he was one of the soldiers whom Louis had sent to support our king, and who were said to have arrived in Limerick, though, as I observed above, not with truth.

I was much assured by this circumstance, and made no doubt but that I had fallen in with one of those marauding parties of native Irish, who, placing themselves under the guidance of men of courage and experience, had done much brave and essential service to the cause of the king.

The soldier entered an inner door in the apartment, which opening disclosed a rude, dreary, and dilapidated room, with a low plank ceiling, much discoloured by the smoke which hung suspended in heavy masses, descending within a few feet of the ground, and completely obscuring the upper regions of the chamber.

A large fire of turf and heath was burning under a kind of rude chimney, shaped like a large funnel, but by no means discharging the functions for which it was intended. Into this inauspicious apartment was I conducted by my strange companions. In the next room I heard voices employed, as it seemed, in brief questioning and answer; and in a minute the soldier re-entered the room, and having said, 'Votre prisonnier—le general veut le voir,' he led the way into the inner room, which in point of comfort and cleanliness was not a whit better than the first.

Seated at a clumsy plank table, placed about the middle of the floor, was a powerfully built man, of almost colossal stature—his military accoutrements, cuirass and rich regimental clothes, soiled, deranged, and spattered with recent hard travel; the flowing wig, surmounted by the cocked hat and plume, still rested upon his head. On the table lay his sword-belt with its appendage, and a pair of long holster pistols, some papers, and pen and ink; also a stone jug, and the fragments of a hasty meal. His attitude betokened the languor of fatigue. His left hand was buried beyond the lace ruffle in the breast of his cassock, and the elbow of his right rested upon the table, so as to support his head. From his mouth protruded a tobacco-pipe, which as I entered he slowly withdrew.

A single glance at the honest, good-humoured, comely face of the soldier satisfied me of his identity, and removing my hat from my head I said, 'God save General Sarsfield!'

The general nodded

'I am a prisoner here under strange circumstances,' I continued 'I appear before you in a strange disguise. You do not recognise Captain Hardress Fitzgerald!'

'Eh, how's this?' said he, approaching me with the light.

'I am that Hardress Fitzgerald,' I repeated, 'who served under you at the Boyne, and upon the day of the action had the honour to protect your person at the expense of his own.' At the same time I turned aside the hair which covered the scar which you well know upon my forehead, and which was then much more remarkable than it is now.

The general on seeing this at once recognised me, and embracing me cordially, made me sit down, and while I unstrapped my pack, a tedious job, my fingers being nearly numbed with cold, sent the men forth to procure me some provision.

The general's horse was stabled in a corner of the chamber where we sat, and his war-saddle lay upon the floor. At the far end of the room was a second door, which stood half open; a bogwood fire burned on a hearth somewhat less rude than the one which I had first seen, but still very little better appointed with a chimney, for thick wreaths of smoke were eddying, with every fitful gust, about the room. Close by the fire was strewed a bed of heath, intended, I supposed, for the stalwart limbs of the general.

'Hardress Fitzgerald,' said he, fixing his eyes gravely upon me, while he slowly removed the tobacco-pipe from his mouth, 'I remember you, strong, bold and cunning in your warlike trade; the more desperate an enterprise, the more ready for it, you. I would gladly engage you, for I know you trustworthy, to perform a piece of duty requiring, it may be, no extraordinary quality to fulfil; and yet perhaps, as accidents may happen, demanding every attribute of daring and dexterity which belongs to you.'

Here he paused for some moments.

I own I felt somewhat flattered by the terms in which he spoke of me, knowing him to be but little given to compliments; and not having any plan in my head, farther than the rendering what service I might to the cause of the king, caring very little as to the road in which my duty might lie, I frankly replied:

'Sir, I hope, if opportunity offers, I shall prove to deserve the honourable terms in which you are pleased to speak of me. In a righteous cause I fear not wounds or death; and in discharging my duty to my God and my king, I am ready for any hazard or any fate. Name the service you require, and if it lies within the compass of my wit or power, I will fully and faithfully perform it. Have I said enough?'

'That is well, very well, my friend; you speak well, and manfully,' replied the general. 'I want you to convey to the hands of General Boisleau, now in the city of Limerick, a small written packet; there is some danger, mark me, of your falling in with some outpost or straggling party of the prince's army. If you are taken unawares by any of the enemy you must dispose of the packet inside your person, rather than let it fall into their hands—that is, you must eat it. And if they go to question you with thumb-screws, or the like, answer nothing; let them knock your brains out first.' In illustration, I suppose, of the latter alternative, he knocked the ashes out of his pipe upon the table as he uttered it.

'The packet,' he continued, 'you shall have to-morrow morning. Meantime comfort yourself with food, and afterwards with sleep; you will want, mayhap, all your strength and wits on the morrow.'

I applied myself forthwith to the homely fare which they had provided, and I confess that I never made a meal so heartily to my satisfaction.

It was a beautiful, clear, autumn morning, and the bright beams of the early sun were slanting over the brown heath which clothed the sides of the mountain, and glittering in the thousand bright drops which the melting hoar-frost had left behind it, and the white mists were lying like broad lakes in the valleys, when, with my pedlar's pack upon my back, and General Sarsfield's precious despatch in my bosom, I set forth, refreshed and courageous.

As I descended the hill, my heart expanded and my spirits rose under the influences which surrounded me. The keen, clear, bracing air of the morning, the bright, slanting sunshine, the merry songs of the small birds, and the distant sounds of awakening labour that floated up from the plains, all conspired to stir my heart within me, and more like a mad-cap boy, broken loose from school, than a man of sober years upon a mission of doubt and danger, I trod lightly on, whistling and singing alternately for very joy.

As I approached the object of my early march, I fell in with a countryman, eager, as are most of his kind, for news.

I gave him what little I had collected, and professing great zeal for the king, which, indeed, I always cherished, I won upon his confidence so far, that he became much more communicative than the peasantry in those quarters are generally wont to be to strangers.

From him I learned that there was a company of dragoons in William's service, quartered at Willaloe; but he could not tell whether the passage of the bridge was stopped by them or not. With a resolution, at all events, to make the attempt to cross, I approached the town. When I came within sight of the river, I quickly perceived that it was so swollen with the recent rains, as, indeed, the countryman had told me, that the fords were wholly impassable.

I stopped then, upon a slight eminence overlooking the village, with a view to reconnoitre and to arrange my plans in case of interruption. While thus engaged, the wind blowing gently from the west, in which quarter Limerick lay, I distinctly heard the explosion of the cannon, which played from and against the city, though at a distance of eleven miles at the least.

I never yet heard the music that had for me half the attractions of that sullen sound, and as I noted again and again the distant thunder that proclaimed the perils, and the valour, and the faithfulness of my brethren, my heart swelled with pride, and the tears rose to my eyes; and lifting up my hands to heaven, I prayed to God that I might be spared to take a part in the righteous quarrel that was there so bravely maintained.

I felt, indeed, at this moment a longing, more intense than I have the power to describe, to be at once with my brave companions in arms, and so inwardly excited and stirred up as if I had been actually within five minutes' march of the field of battle.

It was now almost noon, and I had walked hard since morning across a difficult and broken country, so that I was a little fatigued, and in no small degree hungry. As I approached the hamlet, I was glad to see in the window of a poor hovel several large cakes of meal displayed, as if to induce purchasers to enter.

I was right in regarding this exhi-bition as an intimation that entertainment might be procured within, for upon entering and inquiring, I was speedily invited by the poor woman, who, it appeared, kept this humble house of refreshment, to lay down my pack and seat myself by a ponderous table, upon which she promised to serve me with a dinner fit for a king; and indeed, to my mind, she amply fulfilled her engagement, supplying me abundantly with eggs, bacon, and wheaten cakes, which I discussed with a zeal which almost surprised myself.

Having disposed of the solid part of my entertainment, I was proceeding to regale myself with a brimming measure of strong waters, when my attention was arrested by the sound of horses' hoofs in brisk motion upon the broken road, and evidently approaching the hovel in which I was at that moment seated.

The ominous clank of sword scabbards and the jingle of brass accoutrements announced, unequivocally, that the horsemen were of the military profession.

'The red-coats will stop here undoubtedly,' said the old woman, observing, I suppose, the anxiety of my countenance; 'they never pass us without coming in for half an hour to drink or smoke. If you desire to avoid them, I can hide you safely; but don't lose a moment. They will be here before you can count a hundred.'

I thanked the good woman for her hospitable zeal; but I felt a repugnance to concealing myself as she suggested, which was enhanced by the consciousness that if by any accident I were de-tected while lurking in the room, my situation would of itself inevitably lead to suspicions, and probably to discovery.

I therefore declined her offer, and awaited in suspense the entrance of the soldiers.

I had time before they made their appearance to move my seat hurriedly from the table to the hearth, where, under the shade of the large chimney, I might observe the coming visitors with less chance of being myself remarked upon.

As my hostess had anticipated, the horsemen drew up at the door of the hut, and five dragoons entered the dark chamber where I awaited them.

Leaving their horses at the entrance, with much noise and clatter they proceeded to seat themselves and call for liquor.

Three of these fellows were Dutchmen, and, indeed, all belonged, as I afterwards found, to a Dutch regiment, which had been recruited with Irish and English, as also partly officered from the same nations.

Being supplied with pipes and drink they soon became merry; and not suffering their smoking to interfere with their conversation, they talked loud and quickly, for the most part in a sort of barbarous language, neither Dutch nor English, but compounded of both.

They were so occupied with their own jocularity that I had very great hopes of escaping observation altogether, and remained quietly seated in a corner of the chimney, leaning back upon my seat as if asleep.

My taciturnity and quiescence, however, did not avail me, for one of these fellows coming over to the hearth to light his pipe, perceived me, and looking me very hard in the face, he said:

'What countryman are you, brother, that you sit with a covered head in the room with the prince's soldiers?'

At the same time he tossed my hat off my head into the fire. I was not fool enough, though somewhat hot-blooded, to suffer the insolence of this fellow to involve me in a broil so dangerous to my person and ruinous to my schemes as a riot with these soldiers must prove. I therefore, quietly taking up my hat and shaking the ashes out of it, observed:

'Sir, I crave your pardon if I have offended you. I am a stranger in these quarters, and a poor, ignorant, humble man, desiring only to drive my little trade in peace, so far as that may be done in these troublous times.'

'And what may your trade be?' said the same fellow.

'I am a travelling merchant,' I replied; 'and sell my wares as cheap as any trader in the country.'

'Let us see them forthwith,' said he; 'mayhap I or my comrades may want something which you can supply. Where is thy chest, friend? Thou shalt have ready money' (winking at his companions), 'ready money, and good weight, and sound metal; none of your rascally pinchbeck. Eh, my lads? Bring forth the goods, and let us see.'

Thus urged, I should have betrayed myself had I hesitated to do as required; and anxious, upon any terms, to quiet these turbulent men of war, I unbuckled my pack and exhibited its contents upon the table before them.

'A pair of lace ruffles, by the Lord!' said one, unceremoniously seizing upon the articles he named.

'A phial of perfume,' continued another, tumbling over the farrago which I had submitted to them, 'wash-balls, combs, stationery, slippers, small knives, tobacco; by—, this merchant is a prize! Mark me, honest fellow, the man who wrongs thee shall suffer—'fore Gad he shall; thou shalt be fairly dealt with' (this he said while in the act of pocketing a small silver tobacco-box, the most valuable article in the lot). 'You shall come with me to head-quarters; the captain will deal with you, and never haggle about the price. I promise thee his good will, and thou wilt consider me accordingly. You'll find him a profitable customer—he has money without end, and throws it about like a gentleman. If so be as I tell thee, I shall expect, and my comrades here, a piece or two in the way of a compliment—but of this anon. Come, then, with us; buckle on thy pack quickly, friend.'

There was no use in my declaring my willingness to deal with themselves in preference to their master; it was clear that they had resolved that I should, in the most expeditious and advantageous way, turn my goods into money, that they might excise upon me to the amount of their wishes.

The worthy who had taken a lead in these arrangements, and who by his stripes I perceived to be a corporal, having insisted on my taking a dram with him to cement our newly-formed friendship, for which, however, he requested me to pay, made me mount behind one of his comrades; and the party, of which I thus formed an unwilling member, moved at a slow trot towards the quarters of the troop.

They reined up their horses at the head of the long bridge, which at this village spans the broad waters of the Shannon connecting the opposite counties of Tipperary and Clare.

A small tower, built originally, no doubt, to protect and to defend this pass, occupied the near extremity of the bridge, and in its rear, but connected with it, stood several straggling buildings rather dilapidated.

A dismounted trooper kept guard at the door, and my conductor having, dismounted, as also the corporal, the latter inquired:

'Is the captain in his quarters?'

'He is,' replied the sentinel.

And without more ado my companion shoved me into the entrance of the small dark tower, and opening a door at the extremity of the narrow chamber into which we had passed from the street, we entered a second room in which were seated some half-dozen officers of various ranks and ages, engaged in drinking, and smoking, and play.

I glanced rapidly from man to man, and was nearly satisfied by my inspection, when one of the gentlemen whose back had been turned towards the place where I stood, suddenly changed his position and looked towards me.

As soon as I saw his face my heart sank within me, and I knew that my life or death was balanced, as it were, upon a razor's edge.

The name of this man whose unexpected appearance thus affected me was Hugh Oliver, and good and strong reason had I to dread him, for so bitterly did he hate me, that to this moment I do verily believe he would have compassed my death if it lay in his power to do so, even at the hazard of his own life and soul, for I had been—though God knows with many sore strugglings and at the stern call of public duty—the judge and condemner of his brother; and though the military law, which I was called upon to administer, would permit no other course or sentence than the bloody one which I was compelled to pursue, yet even to this hour the recollection of that deed is heavy at my breast.

As soon as I saw this man I felt that my safety depended upon the accident of his not recognising me through the disguise which I had assumed, an accident against which were many chances, for he well knew my person and appearance.

It was too late now to destroy General Sarsfield's instructions; any attempt to do so would ensure detection. All then depended upon a cast of the die.

When the first moment of dismay and heart-sickening agitation had passed, it seemed to me as if my mind acquired a collectedness and clearness more complete and intense than I had ever experienced before.

I instantly perceived that he did not know me, for turning from me to the soldier with all air of indifference, he said,

'Is this a prisoner or a deserter? What have you brought him here for, sirra?'

'Your wisdom will regard him as you see fit, may it please you,' said the corporal. 'The man is a travelling merchant, and, overtaking him upon the road, close by old Dame MacDonagh's cot, I thought I might as well make a sort of prisoner of him that your honour might use him as it might appear most convenient; he has many commododies which are not unworthy of price in this wilderness, and some which you may condescend to make use of yourself. May he exhibit the goods he has for sale, an't please you?'

'Ay, let us see them,' said he.

'Unbuckle your pack,' exclaimed the corporal, with the same tone of command with which, at the head of his guard, he would have said 'Recover your arms.' 'Unbuckle your pack, fellow, and show your goods to the captain—here, where you are.'

The conclusion of his directions was suggested by my endeavouring to move round in order to get my back towards the windows, hoping, by keeping my face in the shade, to escape detection.

In this manoeuvre, however, I was foiled by the imperiousness of the soldier; and inwardly cursing his ill-timed interference, I proceeded to present my merchandise to the loving contemplation of the officers who thronged around me, with a strong light from an opposite window full upon my face.

As I continued to traffic with these gentlemen, I observed with no small anxiety the eyes of Captain Oliver frequently fixed upon me with a kind of dubious inquiring gaze.

'I think, my honest fellow,' he said at last, 'that I have seen you somewhere before this. Have you often dealt with the military?'

'I have traded, sir,' said I, 'with the soldiery many a time, and always been honourably treated. Will your worship please to buy a pair of lace ruffles?—very cheap, your worship.'

'Why do you wear your hair so much over your face, sir?' said Oliver, without noticing my suggestion. 'I promise you, I think no good of thee; throw back your hair, and let me see thee plainly. Hold up your face, and look straight at me; throw back your hair, sir.'

I felt that all chance of escape was at an end; and stepping forward as near as the table would allow me to him, I raised my head, threw back my hair, and fixed my eyes sternly and boldly upon his face.

I saw that he knew me instantly, for his countenance turned as pale as ashes with surprise and hatred. He started up, placing his hand instinctively upon his sword-hilt, and glaring at me with a look so deadly, that I thought every moment he would strike his sword into my heart. He said in a kind of whisper: 'Hardress Fitzgerald?'

'Yes;' said I, boldly, for the excitement of the scene had effectually stirred my blood, 'Hardress Fitzgerald is before you. I know you well,

Captain Oliver. I know how you hate me. I know how you thirst for my blood; but in a good cause, and in the hands of God, I defy you.'

'You are a desperate villain, sir,' said Captain Oliver; 'a rebel and a murderer! Holloa, there! guard, seize him!'

As the soldiers entered, I threw my eyes hastily round the room, and observing a glowing fire upon the hearth, I suddenly drew General Sarsfield's packet from my bosom, and casting it upon the embers, planted my foot upon it.

'Secure the papers!' shouted the captain; and almost instantly I was laid prostrate and senseless upon the floor, by a blow from the butt of a carbine.

I cannot say how long I continued in a state of torpor; but at length, having slowly recovered my senses, I found myself lying firmly handcuffed upon the floor of a small chamber, through a narrow loop-hole in one of whose walls the evening sun was shining. I was chilled with cold and damp, and drenched in blood, which had flowed in large quantities from the wound on my head. By a strong effort I shook off the sick drowsiness which still hung upon me, and, weak and giddy, I rose with pain and difficulty to my feet.

The chamber, or rather cell, in which I stood was about eight feet square, and of a height very disproportioned to its other dimensions; its altitude from the floor to the ceiling being not less than twelve or fourteen feet. A narrow slit placed high in the wall admitted a scanty light, but sufficient to assure me that my prison contained nothing to render the sojourn of its tenant a whit less comfortless than my worst enemy could have wished.

My first impulse was naturally to examine the security of the door, the loop-hole which I have mentioned being too high and too narrow to afford a chance of escape. I listened attentively to ascer-tain if possible whether or not a guard had been placed upon the outside.

Not a sound was to be heard. I now placed my shoulder to the door, and sought with all my combined strength and weight to force it open. It, however, resisted all my efforts, and thus baffled in my appeal to mere animal power, exhausted and disheartened, I threw myself on the ground.

It was not in my nature, however, long to submit to the apathy of despair, and in a few minutes I was on my feet again.

With patient scrutiny I endeavoured to ascertain the nature of the fastenings which secured the door.

The planks, fortunately, having been nailed together fresh, had shrunk considerably, so as to leave wide chinks between each and its neighbour.

By means of these apertures I saw that my dungeon was secured, not by a lock, as I had feared, but by a strong wooden bar, running horizontally across the door, about midway upon the outside.

'Now,' thought I, 'if I can but slip my fingers through the opening of the planks, I can easily remove the bar, and then—'

My attempts, however, were all frustrated by the manner in which my hands were fastened together, each embarrassing the other, and rendering my efforts so hopelessly clumsy, that I was obliged to give them over in despair.

I turned with a sigh from my last hope, and began to pace my narrow prison floor, when my eye suddenly encountered an old rusty nail or hold-fast sticking in the wall.

All the gold of Plutus would not have been so welcome as that rusty piece of iron.

I instantly wrung it from the wall, and inserting the point between the planks of the door into the bolt, and working it backwards and forwards, I had at length the unspeakable satisfaction to perceive that the beam was actually yielding to my efforts, and gradually sliding into its berth in the wall.

I have often been engaged in struggles where great bodily strength was required, and every thew and sinew in the system taxed to the uttermost; but, strange as it may appear, I never was so completely exhausted and overcome by any labour as by this comparatively trifling task.

Again and again was I obliged to desist, until my cramped finger-joints recovered their power; but at length my perseverance was rewarded, for, little by little, I succeeded in removing the bolt so far as to allow the door to open sufficiently to permit me to pass.

With some squeezing I succeeded in forcing my way into a small passage, upon which my prison-door opened.

This led into a chamber somewhat more spacious than my cell, but still containing no furniture, and affording no means of escape to one so crippled with bonds as I was.

At the far extremity of this room was a door which stood ajar, and, stealthily passing through it, I found myself in a room containing nothing but a few raw hides, which rendered the atmosphere nearly intolerable.

Here I checked myself, for I heard voices in busy conversation in the next room.

I stole softly to the door which separated the chamber in which I stood from that from which the voices proceeded.

A moment served to convince me that any attempt upon it would be worse than fruitless, for it was secured upon the outside by a strong lock, besides two bars, all which I was enabled to ascertain by means of the same defect in the joining of the planks which I have mentioned as belonging to the inner door.

I had approached this door very softly, so that, my proximity being wholly unsuspected by the speakers within, the conversation continued without interruption.

Planting myself close to the door, I applied my eye to one of the chinks which separated the boards, and thus obtained a full view of the chamber and its occupants.

It was the very apartment into which I had been first conducted. The outer door, which faced the one at which I stood, was closed, and at a small table were seated the only tenants of the room—two officers, one of whom was Captain Oliver. The latter was reading a paper, which I made no doubt was the document with which I had been entrusted.

'The fellow deserves it, no doubt' said the junior officer. 'But, me-thinks, considering our orders from head-quarters, you deal somewhat too hastily.'

'Nephew, nephew,' said Captain Oliver, 'you mistake the tenor of our orders. We were directed to conciliate the peasantry by fair and gentle treatment, but not to suffer spies and traitors to escape. This packet is of some value, though not, in all its parts, intelligible to me. The bearer has made his way hither under a disguise, which, along with the other circum-stances of his appearance here, is sufficient to convict him as a spy.'

There was a pause here, and after a few minutes the younger officer said:

'Spy is a hard term, no doubt, uncle; but it is possible—nay, likely, that this poor devil sought merely to carry the parcel with which he was charged in safety to its destination. Pshaw! he is sufficiently punished if you duck him, for ten minutes or so, between the bridge and the mill-dam.'

'Young man,' said Oliver, somewhat sternly, 'do not obtrude your ad-vice where it is not called for; this man, for whom you plead, murdered your own father!'

I could not see how this announcement affected the person to whom it was addressed, for his back was towards me; but I conjectured, easily, that my last poor chance was gone, for a long silence ensued. Captain Oliver at length resumed:

'I know the villain well. I know him capable of any crime; but, by—, his last card is played, and the game is up. He shall not see the moon rise to-night.'

There was here another pause.

Oliver rose, and going to the outer door, called:

'Hewson! Hewson!'

A grim-looking corporal entered.

'Hewson, have your guard ready at eight o'clock, with their carbines clean, and a round of ball-cartridge each. Keep them sober; and, further, plant two upright posts at the near end of the bridge, with a cross one at top, in the manner of a gibbet. See to these matters, Hewson: I shall be with you speedily.'

The corporal made his salutations, and retired.

Oliver deliberately folded up the papers with which I had been commissioned, and placing them in the pocket of his vest, he said:

'Cunning, cunning Master Hardress Fitzgerald hath made a false step; the old fox is in the toils. Hardress Fitzgerald, Hardress Fitzgerald, I will blot you out.'

He repeated these words several times, at the same time rubbing his finger strongly upon the table, as if he sought to erase a stain:

'I will blot you out!'

There was a kind of glee in his manner and expression which chilled my very heart.

'You shall be first shot like a dog, and then hanged like a dog: shot to-night, and hung to-morrow; hung at the bridge-head—hung, until your bones drop asunder!'

It is impossible to describe the exultation with which he seemed to dwell upon, and to particularise the fate which he intended for me.

I observed, however, that his face was deadly pale, and felt assured that his conscience and inward convictions were struggling against his cruel resolve. Without further comment the two officers left the room, I suppose to oversee the preparations which were being made for the deed of which I was to be the victim.

A chill, sick horror crept over me as they retired, and I felt, for the moment, upon the brink of swooning. This feeling, however, speedily gave place to a sensation still more terrible. A state of excitement so intense and tremendous as to border upon literal madness, supervened; my brain reeled and throbbed as if it would burst; thoughts the wildest and the most hideous flashed through my mind with a spontaneous rapidity that scared my very soul; while, all the time, I felt a strange and frightful impulse to burst into uncontrolled laughter.

Gradually this fearful paroxysm passed away. I kneeled and prayed fervently, and felt comforted and assured; but still I could not view the slow approaches of certain death without an agitation little short of agony.

I have stood in battle many a time when the chances of escape were fearfully small. I have confronted foemen in the deadly breach. I have marched, with a constant heart, against the cannon's mouth. Again and again has the beast which I bestrode been shot under me; again and again have I seen the comrades who walked beside me in an instant laid for ever in the dust; again and again have I been in the thick of battle, and of its mortal dangers, and never felt my heart shake, or a single nerve tremble: but now, helpless, manacled, imprisoned, doomed, forced to watch the approaches of an inevitable fate—to wait, silent and moveless, while death as it were crept towards me, human nature was taxed to the uttermost to bear the horrible situation.

I returned again to the closet in which I had found myself upon recovering from the swoon.

The evening sunshine and twilight was fast melting into darkness, when I heard the outer door, that which communicated with the guard-room in which the officers had been amusing themselves, opened and locked again upon the inside.

A measured step then approached, and the door of the wretched cell in which I lay being rudely pushed open, a soldier entered, who carried something in his hand; but, owing to the obscurity of the place, I could not see what.

'Art thou awake, fellow?' said he, in a gruff voice. 'Stir thyself; get upon thy legs.'

His orders were enforced by no very gentle application of his military boot.

'Friend,' said I, rising with difficulty, 'you need not insult a dying man. You have been sent hither to conduct me to death. Lead on! My trust is in God, that He will forgive me my sins, and receive my soul, redeemed by the blood of His Son.'

There here intervened a pause of some length, at the end of which the soldier said, in the same gruff voice, but in a lower key:

'Look ye, comrade, it will be your own fault if you die this night. On one condition I promise to get you out of this hobble with a whole skin; but if you go to any of your d—d gammon, by G—, before two hours are passed, you will have as many holes in your carcase as a target.'

'Name your conditions,' said I, 'and if they consist with honour, I will never balk at the offer.'

'Here they are: you are to be shot to-night, by Captain Oliver's orders. The carbines are cleaned for the job, and the cartridges served out to the men. By G—, I tell you the truth!'

Of this I needed not much persuasion, and intimated to the man my conviction that he spoke the truth.

'Well, then,' he continued, 'now for the means of avoiding this ugly business. Captain Oliver rides this night to head-quarters, with the papers which you carried. Before he starts he will pay you a visit, to fish what he can out of you with all the fine promises he can make. Humour him a little, and when you find an opportunity, stab him in the throat above the cuirass.'

'A feasible plan, surely,' said I, raising my shackled hands, 'for a man thus completely crippled and without a weapon.'

'I will manage all that presently for you,' said the soldier. 'When you have thus dealt with him, take his cloak and hat, and so forth, and put them on; the papers you will find in the pocket of his vest, in a red leather case. Walk boldly out. I am appointed to ride with Captain Oliver, and you will find me holding his horse and my own by the door. Mount quickly, and I will do the same, and then we will ride for our lives across the bridge. You will find the holster-pistols loaded in case of pursuit; and, with the devil's help, we shall reach Limerick without a hair hurt. My only condition is, that when you strike Oliver, you strike home, and again and again, until he is *finished*; and I trust to your honour to remember me when we reach the town.'

I cannot say whether I resolved right or wrong, but I thought my situation, and the conduct of Captain Oliver, warranted me in acceding to the conditions propounded by my visitant, and with alacrity I told him so, and desired him to give me the power, as he had promised to do, of executing them.

With speed and promptitude he drew a small key from his pocket, and in an instant the manacles were removed from my hands.

How my heart bounded within me as my wrists were released from the iron gripe of the shackles! The first step toward freedom was made—my self-reliance returned, and I felt assured of success.

'Now for the weapon,' said I.

'I fear me, you will find it rather clumsy,' said he; 'but if well handled, it will do as well as the best Toledo. It is the only thing I could get, but I sharpened it myself; it has an edge like a skean.'

He placed in my hand the steel head of a halberd. Grasping it firmly, I found that it made by no means a bad weapon in point of convenience; for it felt in the hand like a heavy dagger, the portion which formed the blade or point being crossed nearly at the lower extremity by a small bar of metal, at one side shaped into the form of an axe, and at the other into that of a hook. These two transverse appendages being muffled by the folds of my cravat, which I removed for the purpose, formed a perfect guard or hilt, and the lower extremity formed like a tube, in which the pike-handle had been inserted, afforded ample space for the grasp of my hand; the point had been made as sharp as a needle, and the metal he assured me was good.

Thus equipped he left me, having observed, 'The captain sent me to bring you to your senses, and give you some water that he might find you proper for his visit. Here is the pitcher; I think I have revived you sufficiently for the captain's purpose.'

With a low savage laugh he left me to my reflections.

Having examined and adjusted the weapon, I carefully bound the ends of the cravat, with which I had secured the cross part of the spear-head, firmly round my wrist, so that in case of a struggle it might not easily be forced from my hand; and having made these precautionary dispositions, I sat down upon the ground with my back against the wall, and my hands together under my coat, awaiting my visitor.

The time wore slowly on; the dusk became dimmer and dimmer, until it nearly bordered on total darkness.

'How's this?' said I, inwardly; 'Captain Oliver, you said I should not see the moon rise to-night. Methinks you are somewhat tardy in fulfilling your prophecy.'

As I made this reflection, a noise at the outer door announced the entrance of a visitant. I knew that the decisive moment was come, and letting my head sink upon my breast, and assuring myself that my hands were concealed, I waited, in the at-titude of deep dejection, the approach of my foe and betrayer.

As I had expected, Captain Oliver entered the room where I lay. He was equipped for instant duty, as far as the imperfect twilight would al-low me to see; the long sword clanked upon the floor as he made his way through the lobbies which led to my place of confinement; his ample military cloak hung upon his arm; his cocked hat was upon his head, and in all points he was prepared for the road.

This tallied exactly with what my strange informant had told me.

I felt my heart swell and my breath come thick as the awful moment which was to witness the death-struggle of one or other of us approached.

Captain Oliver stood within a yard or two of the place where I sat, or rather lay; and folding his arms, he remained silent for a minute or two, as if arranging in his mind how he should address me.

'Hardress Fitzgerald,' he began at length, 'are you awake? Stand up, if you desire to hear of matters nearly touching your life or death. Get up, I say.'

I arose doggedly, and affecting the awkward movements of one whose hands were bound,

'Well,' said I, 'what would you of me? Is it not enough that I am thus imprisoned without a cause, and about, as I suspect, to suffer a most unjust and violent sentence, but must I also be disturbed during the few moments left me for reflection and repentance by the presence of my persecutor? What do you want of me?'

'As to your punishment, sir,' said he, 'your own deserts have no doubt sug-gested the likelihood of it to your mind; but I now am with you to let you know that whatever mitigation of your sentence you may look for, must be earned by your compliance with my orders. You must frankly and fully explain the contents of the packet which you endeavoured this day to destroy; and further, you must tell all that you know of the designs of the popish rebels.'

'And if I do this I am to expect a mitigation of my punishment—is it not so?'

Oliver bowed.

'And what *is* this mitigation to be? On the honour of a soldier, what is it to be?' inquired I.

'When you have made the disclosure required,' he replied, 'you shall hear. 'Tis then time to talk of indulgences.'

'Methinks it would then be too late,' answered I. 'But a chance is a chance, and a drowning man will catch at a straw. You are an honourable man, Captain Oliver. I must depend, I suppose, on your good faith. Well, sir, before I make the desired communication I have one question more to put. What is to befall me in case that I, remembering the honour of a soldier and a gentleman, reject your infamous terms, scorn your mitigations, and defy your utmost power?'

'In that case,' replied he, coolly, 'before half an hour you shall be a corpse.'

'Then God have mercy on your soul!' said I; and springing forward, I dashed the weapon which I held at his throat.

I missed my aim, but struck him full in the mouth with such force that most of his front teeth were dislodged, and the point of the spear-head passed out under his jaw, at the ear.

My onset was so sudden and unexpected that he reeled back to the wall, and did not recover his equilibrium in time to prevent my dealing a second blow, which I did with my whole force. The point unfortunately struck the cuirass, near the neck, and glancing aside it inflicted but a flesh wound, tearing the skin and tendons along the throat.

He now grappled with me, strange to say, without uttering any cry of alarm; being a very powerful man, and if anything rather heavier and more strongly built than I, he succeeded in drawing me with him to the ground. We fell together with a heavy crash, tugging and straining in what we were both conscious was a mortal struggle. At length I succeeded in getting over him, and struck him twice more in the face; still he struggled with an energy which nothing but the tremendous stake at issue could have sustained.

I succeeded again in inflicting several more wounds upon him, any one of which might have been mortal. While thus contending he clutched his hands about my throat, so firmly that I felt the blood swelling the veins of my temples and face almost to bursting. Again and again I struck the weapon deep into his face and throat, but life seemed to adhere in him with an almost *insect* tenacity.

My sight now nearly failed, my senses almost forsook me; I felt upon the point of suffocation when, with one desperate effort, I struck him another and a last blow in the face. The weapon which I wielded had lighted upon the eye, and the point penetrated the brain; the body quivered under me, the deadly grasp relaxed, and Oliver lay upon the ground a corpse!

As I arose and shook the weapon and the bloody cloth from my hand, the moon which he had foretold I should never see rise, shone bright and broad into the room, and disclosed, with ghastly distinctness, the mangled features of the dead soldier; the mouth, full of clotting blood and broken teeth, lay open; the eye, close by whose lid the fatal wound had been inflicted, was not, as might have been expected, bathed in blood, but had started forth nearly from the socket, and gave to the face, by its fearful unlikeness to the other glazing orb, a leer more hideous and unearthly than fancy ever saw. The wig, with all its rich curls, had fallen with the hat to the floor, leaving the shorn head exposed, and in many places marked by the recent struggle; the rich lace cravat was drenched in blood, and the gay uniform in many places soiled with the same.

It is hard to say, with what feelings I looked upon the unsightly and revolting mass which had so lately been a living and a comely man. I had not any time, however, to spare for reflection; the deed was done—the responsibility was upon me, and all was registered in the book of that God who judges rightly.

With eager haste I removed from the body such of the military accoutrements as were necessary for the purpose of my disguise. I buckled on the sword, drew off the military boots, and donned them myself, placed the brigadier wig and cocked hat upon my head, threw on the cloak, drew it up about my face, and proceeded, with the papers which I found as the soldier had foretold me, and the key of the outer lobby, to the door of the guard-room; this I opened, and with a firm and rapid tread walked through the officers, who rose as I entered, and passed without question or interruption to the street-door. Here I was met by the grim-looking corporal, Hewson, who, saluting me, said:

'How soon, captain, shall the file be drawn out and the prisoner despatched?'

'In half an hour,' I replied, without raising my voice.

The man again saluted, and in two steps I reached the soldier who held the two horses, as he had intimated.

'Is all right?' said he, eagerly.

'Ay,' said I, 'which horse am I to mount?'

He satisfied me upon this point, and I threw myself into the saddle; the soldier mounted his horse, and dashing the spurs into the flanks of the animal which I bestrode, we thundered along the narrow bridge. At the far extremity a sentinel, as we approached, called out, 'Who goes there? stand, and give the word!' Heedless of the interruption, with my heart bounding with excitement, I dashed on, as did also the soldier who accompanied me.

'Stand, or I fire! give the word!' cried the sentry.

'God save the king, and to hell with the prince!' shouted I, flinging the cocked hat in his face as I galloped by.

The response was the sharp report of a carbine, accompanied by the whiz of a bullet, which passed directly between me and my comrade, now riding beside me.

'Hurrah!' I shouted; 'try it again, my boy.'

And away we went at a gallop, which bid fair to distance anything like pursuit.

Never was spur more needed, however, for soon the clatter of horses' hoofs, in full speed, crossing the bridge, came sharp and clear through the stillness of the night.

Away we went, with our pursuers close behind; one mile was passed, another nearly completed. The moon now shone forth, and, turning in the saddle, I looked back upon the road we had passed.

One trooper had headed the rest, and was within a hundred yards of us.

I saw the fellow throw himself from his horse upon the ground.

I knew his object, and said to my comrade:

'Lower your body—lie flat over the saddle; the fellow is going to fire.'

I had hardly spoken when the report of a carbine startled the echoes, and the ball, striking the hind leg of my companion's horse, the poor animal fell headlong upon the road, throwing his rider head-foremost over the saddle.

My first impulse was to stop and share whatever fate might await my comrade; but my second and wiser one was to spur on, and save myself and my despatch.

I rode on at a gallop, turning to observe my comrade's fate. I saw his pursuer, having remounted, ride rapidly up to him, and, on reaching the spot where the man and horse lay, rein in and dismount.

He was hardly upon the ground, when my companion shot him dead with one of the holster-pistols which he had drawn from the pipe; and, leaping nimbly over a ditch at the side of the road, he was soon lost among the ditches and thorn-bushes which covered that part of the country.

Another mile being passed, I had the satisfaction to perceive that the pursuit was given over, and in an hour more I crossed Thomond Bridge, and slept that night in the fortress of Limerick, having delivered the packet, the result of whose safe arrival was the destruction of William's great train of artillery, then upon its way to the besiegers.

Years after this adventure, I met in France a young officer, who I found had served in Captain Oliver's regiment; and he explained what I had never before understood—the motives of the man who had wrought my deliverance. Strange to say, he was the foster-brother of Oliver, whom he thus devoted to death, but in revenge for the most grievous wrong which one man can inflict upon another!

'The Quare Gander.'

BEING A TWELFTH EXTRACT FROM THE LEGACY OF THE LATE FRANCIS PURCELL, P.P. OF DRUMCOOLAGH.

AS I rode at a slow walk, one soft autumn evening, from the once noted and noticeable town of Emly, now a squalid village, towards the no less remarkable town of Tipperary, I fell into a meditative mood.

My eye wandered over a glorious landscape; a broad sea of corn-fields, that might have gladdened even a golden age, was waving before me; groups of little cabins, with their poplars, osiers, and light mountain ashes, clustered shelteringly around them, were scattered over the plain; the thin blue smoke arose floating through their boughs in the still evening air. And far away with all their broad lights and shades, softened with the haze of approaching twilight, stood the bold wild Galties.

As I gazed on this scene, whose richness was deepened by the melancholy glow of the setting sun, the tears rose to my eyes, and I said:

'Alas, my country! what a mournful beauty is thine. Dressed in loveliness and laughter, there is mortal decay at thy heart: sorrow, sin, and shame have mingled thy cup of misery. Strange rulers have bruised thee, and laughed thee to scorn, and they have made all thy sweetness bitter.

Thy shames and sins are the austere fruits of thy miseries, and thy miseries have been poured out upon thee by foreign hands. Alas, my stricken country! clothed with this most pity-moving smile, with this most unutterably mournful loveliness, thou sore-grieved, thou desperately-beloved! Is there for thee, my country, a resurrection?'

I know not how long I might have continued to rhapsodize in this strain, had not my wandering thoughts been suddenly recalled to my own immediate neighbourhood by the monotonous clatter of a horse's hoofs upon the road, evidently moving, at that peculiar pace which is neither a walk nor a trot, and yet partakes of both, so much in vogue among the southern farmers.

In a moment my pursuer was up with me, and checking his steed into a walk he saluted me with much respect. The cavalier was a light-built fellow, with good-humoured sun-burnt features, a shrewd and lively black eye, and a head covered with a crop of close curly black hair, and surmounted with a turf-coloured caubeen, in the pack-thread band of which was stuck a short pipe, which had evidently seen much service.

My companion was a dealer in all kinds of local lore, and soon took occasion to let me see that he was so.

After two or three short stories, in which the scandalous and supernatural were happily blended, we happened to arrive at a narrow road or bohreen leading to a snug-looking farm-house.

'That's a comfortable bit iv a farm,' observed my comrade, pointing towards the dwelling with his thumb; 'a shnug spot, and belongs to the Mooneys this long time. 'Tis a noted place for what happened wid the famous gandher there in former times.'

'And what was that?' inquired I.

'What was it happened wid the gandher!' ejaculated my companion in a tone of indignant surprise; 'the gandher iv Ballymacrucker, the gandher! Your raverance must be a stranger in these parts. Sure every fool knows all about the gandher, and Terence Mooney, that was, rest his sowl. Begorra, 'tis surprisin' to me how in the world you didn't hear iv the gandher; and may be it's funnin me ye are, your raverance.'

I assured him to the contrary, and conjured him to narrate to me the facts, an unacquaintance with which was sufficient it appeared to stamp me as an ignoramus of the first magnitude.

It did not require much entreaty to induce my communicative friend to relate the circumstance, in nearly the following words:

'Terence Mooney was an honest boy and well to do; an' he rinted the biggest farm on this side iv the Galties; an' bein' mighty cute an' a sevare worker, it was small wonder he turned a good penny every harvest. But unluckily he was blessed with an ilegant large family iv daughters, an' iv coorse his heart was allamost bruck, striving to make up fortunes for the whole of them. An' there wasn't a conthrivance iv any soart or description for makin' money out iv the farm, but he was up to.

'Well, among the other ways he had iv gettin' up in the world, he always kep a power iv turkeys, and all soarts iv poul-trey; an' he was out iv all rason partial to geese—an' small blame to him for that same—for twice't a year you can pluck them as bare as my hand—an' get a fine price for the feathers, an' plenty of rale sizable eggs—an' when they are too ould to lay any more, you can kill them, an' sell them to the gintlemen for goslings, d'ye see, let alone that a goose is the most manly bird that is out.

'Well, it happened in the coorse iv time that one ould gandher tuck a wondherful likin' to Terence, an' divil a place he could go serenadin' about the farm, or lookin' afther the men, but the gandher id be at his heels, an' rubbin' himself agin his legs, an' lookin' up in his face jist like any other Christian id do; an' begorra, the likes iv it was never seen—Terence Mooney an' the gandher wor so great.

'An' at last the bird was so engagin' that Terence would not allow it to be plucked any more, an' kep it from that time out for love an' affection— just all as one like one iv his childer.

'But happiness in perfection never lasts long, an' the neighbours begin'd to suspect the nathur an' intentions iv the gandher, an' some iv them said it was the divil, an' more iv them that it was a fairy.

'Well, Terence could not but hear something of what was sayin', an' you may be sure he was not altogether asy in his mind about it, an' from one day to another he was gettin' more ancomfortable in himself, until he determined to sind for Jer Garvan, the fairy docthor in Garryowen, an' it's he was the ilegant hand at the business, an' divil a sperit id say a crass word to him, no more nor a priest. An' moreover he was very great wid ould Terence Mooney—this man's father that' was.

'So without more about it he was sint for, an' sure enough the divil a long he was about it, for he kem back that very evenin' along wid the boy that was sint for him, an' as soon as he was there, an' tuck his supper, an' was done talkin' for a while, he begined of coorse to look into the gandher.

'Well, he turned it this away an' that away, to the right an' to the left, an' straight-ways an' upside-down, an' when he was tired handlin' it, says he to Terence Mooney:

'"Terence," says he, "you must remove the bird into the next room," says he, "an' put a petticoat," says he, "or anny other convaynience round his head," says he.

'"An' why so?" says Terence.

235

"'Becase,' says Jer, says he.

"'Becase what?' says Terence.

"'Becase,' says Jer, "if it isn't done you'll never be asy again," says he, "or pusilanimous in your mind," says he; "so ax no more questions, but do my biddin'," says he.

"'Well,' says Terence, "have your own way," says he.

'An' wid that he tuck the ould gandher, an' giv' it to one iv the gossoons.

"'An' take care," says he, "don't smother the crathur," says he.

'Well, as soon as the bird was gone, says Jer Garvan says he:

"'Do you know what that ould gandher *is*, Terence Mooney?"

"'Divil a taste,' says Terence.

"'Well then,' says Jer, "the gandher is your own father," says he.

"'It's jokin' you are,' says Terence, turnin' mighty pale; "how can an ould gandher be my father?" says he.

"'I'm not funnin' you at all,' says Jer; "it's thrue what I tell you, it's your father's wandhrin' sowl," says he, "that's naturally tuck pissession iv the ould gandher's body," says he. "I know him many ways, and I wondher," says he, "you do not know the cock iv his eye yourself," says he.

"'Oh blur an' ages!' says Terence, "what the divil will I ever do at all at all," says he; "it's all over wid me, for I plucked him twelve times at the laste," says he.

"'That can't be helped now,' says Jer; "it was a sevare act surely," says he, "but it's too late to lamint for it now," says he; "the only way to privint what's past," says he, "is to put a stop to it before it happens," says he.

"'Thrue for you,' says Terence, "but how the divil did you come to the knowledge iv my father's sowl," says he, "bein' in the owld gandher," says he.

"'If I tould you,' says Jer, "you would not undherstand me," says he, "without book-larnin' an' gasthronomy," says he; "so ax me no questions," says he, "an' I'll tell you no lies. But blieve me in this much," says he, "it's your father that's in it," says he; "an' if I don't make him spake to-morrow mornin'," says he, "I'll give you lave to call me a fool," says he.

"'Say no more,' says Terence, "that settles the business," says he; "an' oh! blur and ages is it not a quare thing," says he, "for a dacent respictable man," says he, "to be walkin' about the coun-thry in the shape iv an ould gandher," says he; "and oh, murdher, murdher! is not it often I plucked him," says he, "an' tundher and ouns might not I have ate him," says he; and wid that he fell into a could parspiration, savin' your prisince, an was on the pint iv faintin' wid the bare notions iv it.

'Well, whin he was come to himself agin, says Jerry to him quite an' asy:

"'Terence,' says he, "don't be aggravatin' yourself," says he; "for I have a plan composed that 'ill make him spake out," says he, "an' tell what it is in the world he's wantin'," says he; "an' mind an' don't be comin' in wid your gosther, an' to say agin anything I tell you," says he, "but jist purtind, as soon as the bird is brought back," says he, "how that we're goin' to sind him to-morrow mornin' to market," says he. "An' if he don't spake to-night," says he, "or gother himself out iv the place," says he, "put him into the hamper airly, and sind him in the cart," says he, "straight to Tipperary, to be sould for ating," says he, "along wid the two gossoons," says he, "an' my name isn't Jer Garvan," says he, "if he doesn't spake out before he's half-way," says he. "An' mind," says he, "as soon as iver he says the first word," says he, "that very minute bring him aff to Father Crotty," says he; "an' if his raverince doesn't make him ratire," says he, "like the rest iv his parishioners, glory be to God," says he, "into the siclusion iv the flames iv purgathory," says he, "there's no vartue in my charums," says he.

'Well, wid that the ould gandher was let into the room agin, an' they all bigined to talk iv sindin' him the nixt mornin' to be sould for roastin' in Tipperary, jist as if it was a thing andoubtingly settled. But divil a notice the gandher tuck, no more nor if they wor spaking iv the Lord-Liftinant; an' Terence desired the boys to get ready the kish for the poulthry, an' to "settle it out wid hay soft an' shnug," says he, "for it's the last jauntin' the poor ould gandher 'ill get in this world," says he.

'Well, as the night was gettin' late, Terence was growin' mighty sorrowful an' down-hearted in himself entirely wid the notions iv what was goin' to happen. An' as soon as the wife an' the crathurs war fairly in bed, he brought out some illigint potteen, an' himself an' Jer Garvan sot down to it; an' begorra, the more anasy Terence got, the more he dhrank, and himself and Jer Garvan finished a quart betune them. It wasn't an imparial though, an' more's the pity, for them wasn't anvinted antil short since; but divil a much matther it signifies any longer if a pint could hould two quarts, let alone what it does, sinst Father Mathew—the Lord purloin his raverence—begin'd to give the pledge, an' wid the blessin' iv timperance to deginerate Ireland.

'An' begorra, I have the medle myself; an' it's proud I am iv that same, for abstamiousness is a fine thing, although it's mighty dhry.

'Well, whin Terence finished his pint, he thought he might as well stop; "for enough is as good as a faste," says he; "an' I pity the vagabond," says he, "that is not able to conthroul his licquor," says he, "an' to keep constantly inside iv a pint measure," said he; an' wid that he wished Jer Garvan a good-night, an' walked out iv the room.

'But he wint out the wrong door, bein' a thrifle hearty in himself, an' not rightly knowin' whether he was standin' on his head or his heels, or both iv them at the same time, an' in place iv gettin' into bed, where did he thrun himself but into the poulthry hamper, that the boys had settled out ready for the gandher in the mornin'. An' sure enough he sunk down soft an' complate through the hay to the bottom; an' wid the turnin' and roulin' about in the night, the divil a bit iv him but was covered up as shnug as a lumper in a pittaty furrow before mornin'.

'So wid the first light, up gets the two boys, that war to take the sperit, as they consaved, to Tipperary; an' they cotched the ould gandher, an' put him in the hamper, and clapped a good wisp iv hay an' the top iv him, and tied it down sthrong wid a bit iv a coard, and med the sign iv the crass over him, in dhread iv any harum, an' put the hamper up an the car, wontherin' all the while what in the world was makin' the ould burd so surprisin' heavy.

'Well, they wint along quite anasy towards Tipperary, wishin' every minute that some iv the neighbours bound the same way id happen to fall in with them, for they didn't half like the notions iv havin' no company but the bewitched gandher, an' small blame to them for that same.

'But although they wor shaking in their skhins in dhread iv the ould bird beginnin' to convarse them every minute, they did not let an' to one another, bud kep singin' an' whistlin' like mad, to keep the dread out iv their hearts.

'Well, afther they war on the road betther nor half an hour, they kem to the bad bit close by Father Crotty's, an' there was one divil of a rut three feet deep at the laste; an' the car got sich a wondherful chuck goin' through it, that it wakened Terence widin in the basket.

' "Bad luck to ye," says he, "my bones is bruck wid yer thricks; what the divil are ye doin' wid me?"

'"Did ye hear anything quare, Thady?" says the boy that was next to the car, turnin' as white as the top iv a musharoon; "did ye hear anything quare soundin' out iv the hamper?" says he.

'"No, nor you,' says Thady, turnin' as pale as himself, "it's the ould gandher that's gruntin' wid the shakin' he's gettin'," says he.

'"Where the divil have ye put me into," says Terence inside, "bad luck to your sowls," says he, "let me out, or I'll be smothered this minute," says he.

'"There's no use in purtending," says the boy, "the gandher's spakin', glory be to God," says he.

'"Let me out, you murdherers," says Terence.

'"In the name iv the blessed Vargin," says Thady, "an' iv all the holy saints, hould yer tongue, you unnatheral gandher," says he.

'"Who's that, that dar to call me nick-names?" says Terence inside, roaring wid the fair passion, "let me out, you blasphamious infiddles," says he, "or by this crass I'll stretch ye," says he.

"'In the name iv all the blessed saints in heaven," says Thady, "who the divil are ye?"

"'Who the divil would I be, but Terence Mooney," says he. "It's myself that's in it, you unmerciful bliggards," says he, "let me out, or by the holy, I'll get out in spite iv yes," says he, "an' by jaburs, I'll wallop yes in arnest," says he.

"'It's ould Terence, sure enough," says Thady, "isn't it cute the fairy docthor found him out," says he.

"'I'm an the pint iv snuffication," says Terence, "let me out, I tell you, an' wait till I get at ye," says he, "for begorra, the divil a bone in your body but I'll powdher,' says he.

'An' wid that, he biginned kickin' and flingin' inside in the hamper, and dhrivin his legs agin the sides iv it, that it was a wonder he did not knock it to pieces.

'Well, as soon as the boys seen that, they skelped the ould horse into a gallop as hard as he could peg towards the priest's house, through the ruts, an' over the stones; an' you'd see the hamper fairly flyin' three feet up in the air with the joultin'; glory be to God.

'So it was small wondher, by the time they got to his Raverince's door, the breath was fairly knocked out of poor Terence, so that he was lyin' speechless in the bottom iv the hamper.

'Well, whin his Raverince kem down, they up an' they tould him all that happened, an' how they put the gandher into the hamper, an' how he beginned to spake, an' how he confissed that he was ould Terence Mooney; an' they axed his honour to advise them how to get rid iv the spirit for good an' all.

'So says his Raverince, says he:

"'I'll take my booke," says he, "an' I'll read some rale sthrong holy bits out iv it," says he, "an' do you get a rope and put it round the hamper," says he, "an' let it swing over the runnin' wather at the bridge," says he, "an' it's no matther if I don't make the spirit come out iv it," says he.

'Well, wid that, the priest got his horse, and tuck his booke in undher his arum, an' the boys follied his Raverince, ladin' the horse down to the bridge, an' divil a word out iv Terence all the way, for he seen it was no use spakin', an' he was afeard if he med any noise they might thrait him to another gallop an finish him intirely.

'Well, as soon as they war all come to the bridge, the boys tuck the rope they had with them, an' med it fast to the top iv the hamper an' swung it fairly over the bridge, lettin' it hang in the air about twelve feet out iv the wather.

'An' his Raverince rode down to the bank of the river, close by, an' beginned to read mighty loud and bould intirely.

'An' when he was goin' on about five minutes, all at onst the bottom iv the hamper kem out, an' down wint Terence, falling splash dash into the water, an' the ould gandher a-top iv him. Down they both went to the bottom, wid a souse you'd hear half a mile off.

'An' before they had time to rise agin, his Raverince, wid the fair astonishment, giv his horse one dig iv the spurs, an' before he knew where he was, in he went, horse an' all, a-top iv them, an' down to the bottom.

'Up they all kem agin together, gaspin' and puffin', an' off down wid the current wid them, like shot in under the arch iv the bridge till they kem to the shallow wather.

'The ould gandher was the first out, and the priest and Terence kem next, pantin' an' blowin' an' more than half dhrounded, an' his Raverince was so freckened wid the droundin' he got, and wid the sight iv the sperit, as he consaved, that he wasn't the better of it for a month.

'An' as soon as Terence could spake, he swore he'd have the life of the two gossoons; but Father Crotty would not give him his will. An' as soon as he was got quiter, they all endivoured to explain it; but Terence consaved he went raly to bed the night before, and his wife said the same to shilter him from the suspicion for havin' th' dthrop taken. An' his Raverince said it was a mysthery, an' swore if he cotched anyone laughin' at the accident, he'd lay the horsewhip across their shouldhers.

'An' Terence grew fonder an' fonder iv the gandher every day, until at last he died in a wondherful old age, lavin' the gandher afther him an' a large family iv childher.

'An' to this day the farm is rinted by one iv Terence Mooney's lenial and legitimate postariors.'

Billy Malowney's Taste of Love and Glory

LET THE reader fancy a soft summer evening, the fresh dews falling on bush and flower. The sun has just gone down, and the thrilling vespers of thrushes and blackbirds ring with a wild joy through the saddened air; the west is piled with fantastic clouds, and clothed in tints of crimson and amber, melting away into a wan green, and so eastward into the deepest blue, through which soon the stars will begin to peep.

Let him fancy himself seated upon the low mossy wall of an ancient churchyard, where hundreds of grey stones rise above the sward, under the fantastic branches of two or three half-withered ash-trees, spreading their arms in everlasting love and sorrow over the dead.

The narrow road upon which I and my companion await the tax-cart that is to carry me and my basket, with its rich fruitage of speckled trout, away, lies at his feet, and far below spreads an undulating plain, rising westward again into soft hills, and traversed (every here and there visibly) by a winding stream which, even through the mists of evening, catches and returns the funereal glories of the skies.

As the eye traces its wayward wanderings, it loses them for a moment in the heaving verdure of white-thorns and ash, from among which floats from some dozen rude chimneys, mostly unseen, the transparent blue film of turf smoke. There we know, although we cannot see it, the steep old bridge of Carrickadrum spans the river; and stretching away far to the right the valley of Lisnamoe: its steeps and hollows, its straggling hedges, its fair-green, its tall scattered trees, and old grey tower, are disappearing fast among the discoloured tints and haze of evening.

Those landmarks, as we sit listlessly expecting the arrival of our modest conveyance, suggest to our companion—a bare-legged Celtic brother of the gentle craft, somewhat at the wrong side of forty, with a turf-coloured caubeen, patched frieze, a clear brown complexion, dark-grey eyes, and a right pleasant dash of roguery in his features—the tale, which, if the reader pleases, he is welcome to hear along with me just as it falls from the lips of our humble comrade.

His words I can give, but your own fancy must supply the advantages of an intelligent, expressive countenance, and, what is perhaps harder still, the harmony of his glorious brogue, that, like the melodies of our own dear country, will leave a burden of mirth or of sorrow with nearly equal propriety, tickling the diaphragm as easily as it plays with the heart-strings, and is in itself a national music that, I trust, may never, never—scouted and despised though it be—never cease, like the lost tones of our harp, to be heard in the fields of my country, in welcome or endearment, in fun or in sorrow, stirring the hearts of Irish men and Irish women.

My friend of the caubeen and naked shanks, then, commenced, and continued his relation, as nearly as possible, in the following words:

Av coorse ye often heerd talk of Billy Malowney, that lived by the bridge of Carrickadrum. 'Leum-a-rinka' was the name they put on him, he was sich a beautiful dancer. An' faix, it's he was the rale sportin' boy, every way—killing the hares, and gaffing the salmons, an' fightin' the men, an' funnin' the women, and coortin' the girls; an' be the same token, there was not a colleen inside iv his jurisdiction but was breakin' her heart wid the fair love iv him.

Well, this was all pleasant enough, to be sure, while it lasted; but in-human beings is born to misfortune, an' Bill's divarshin was not to last always. A young boy can't be continially coortin' and kissin' the girls (an' more's the pity) without exposin' himself to the most eminent parril; an' so signs all' what should happen Billy Malowney himself, but to fall in love at last wid little Molly Donovan, in Coolnamoe.

I never could ondherstand why in the world it was Bill fell in love wid *her*, above all the girls in the country. She was not within four stone weight iv being as fat as Peg Brallaghan; and as for redness in the face, she could not hould a candle to Judy Flaherty. (Poor Judy! she was my sweet-heart, the darlin', an' coorted me constant, ever antil she married a boy of the Butlers; an' it's twenty years now since she was buried under the ould white-thorn in Garbally. But that's no matther!)

Well, at any rate, Molly Donovan tuck his fancy, an' that's everything! She had smooth brown hair—as smooth as silk-an' a pair iv soft coaxin' eyes—an' the whitest little teeth you ever seen; an', bedad, she was every taste as much in love wid himself as he was.

Well, now, he was raly stupid wid love: there was not a bit of fun left in him. He was good for nothin' an airth bud sittin' under bushes, smokin' tobacky, and sighin' till you'd wonder how in the world he got wind for it all.

An', bedad, he was an illigant scholar, moreover; an', so signs, it's many's the song he made about her; an' if you'd be walkin' in the evening, a mile away from Carrickadrum, begorra you'd hear him singing out like a bull, all across the country, in her praises.

Well, ye may be sure, ould Tim Donovan and the wife was not a bit too well plased to see Bill Malowney coortin' their daughter Molly; for, do ye mind, she was the only child they had, and her fortune was thirty-five pounds, two cows, and five illigant pigs, three iron pots and a skillet, an' a trifle iv poultry in hand; and no one knew how much besides, whenever the Lord id be plased to call the ould people out of the way into glory!

So, it was not likely ould Tim Donovan id be fallin' in love wid poor Bill Malowney as aisy as the girls did; for, barrin' his beauty, an' his gun, an' his dhudheen, an' his janius, the divil a taste of property iv any sort or description he had in the wide world!

Well, as bad as that was, Billy would not give in that her father and mother had the smallest taste iv a right to intherfare, good or bad.

'An' you're welcome to rayfuse me,' says he, 'whin I ax your lave,' says he; 'an' I'll ax your lave,' says he, 'whenever I want to coort yourselves,' says he;

'but it's your daughter I'm coortin' at the present,' says he, 'an that's all I'll say,' says he; 'for I'd as soon take a doase of salts as be discoursin' ye,' says he.

So it was a rale blazin' battle betune himself and the ould people; an', begorra, there was no soart iv blaguardin' that did not pass betune them; an' they put a solemn injection on Molly again seein' him or meetin' him for the future.

But it was all iv no use. You might as well be pursuadin' the birds agin flying, or sthrivin' to coax the stars out iv the sky into your hat, as be talking common sinse to them that's fairly bothered and burstin' wid love. There's nothin' like it. The toothache an' cholic together id compose you betther for an argyment than itself. It leaves you fit for nothin' bud nansinse.

It's stronger than whisky, for one good drop iv it will make you drunk for one year, and sick, begorra, for a dozen.

It's stronger than the say, for it'll carry you round the world an' never let you sink, in sunshine or storm; an,' begorra, it's stronger than Death himself, for it is not afeard iv him, bedad, but dares him in every shape.

But lovers has quarrels sometimes, and, begorra, when they do, you'd a'most imagine they hated one another like man and wife. An' so, signs an, Billy Malowney and Molly Donovan fell out one evening at ould Tom Dundon's wake; an' whatever came betune them, she made no more about it but just draws her cloak round her, and away wid herself and the sarvant-girl home again, as if there was not a corpse, or a fiddle, or a taste of divarsion in it.

Well, Bill Malowney follied her down the boreen, to try could he deludher her back again; but, if she was bitther before, she gave it to him in airnest when she got him alone to herself, and to that degree that he wished her safe home, short and sulky enough, an' walked back again, as mad as the devil himself, to the wake, to pay a respect to poor Tom Dundon.

Well, my dear, it was aisy seen there was something wrong avid Billy Malowney, for he paid no attintion the rest of the evening to any soart of divarsion but the whisky alone; an' every glass he'd drink it's what he'd be wishing the divil had the women, an' the worst iv bad luck to all soarts iv courting, until, at last, wid the goodness iv the sperits, an' the badness iv his temper, an' the constant flusthration iv cursin', he grew all as one as you might say almost, saving your presince, bastely drunk!

Well, who should he fall in wid, in that childish condition, as he was deploying along the road almost as straight as the letter S, an' cursin' the girls, an' roarin' for more whisky, but the recruiting-sargent iv the Welsh Confusileers.

So, cute enough, the sargent begins to converse him, an' it was not long until he had him sitting in Murphy's public-house, wid an elegant dandy iv punch before him, an' the king's money safe an' snug in the lowest wrinkle of his breeches-pocket.

So away wid him, and the dhrums and fifes playing, an' a dozen more unforthunate bliggards just listed along with him, an' he shakin' hands wid the sargent, and swearin' agin the women every minute, until, be the time he kem to himself, begorra, he was a good ten miles on the road to Dublin, an' Molly and all behind him.

It id be no good tellin' you iv the letters he wrote to her from the barracks there, nor how she was breaking her heart to go and see him just wanst before he'd go; but the father an' mother would not allow iv it be no manes.

An' so in less time than you'd be thinkin' about it, the colonel had him polished off into it rale elegant soger, wid his gun exercise, and his bagnet exercise, and his small sword, and broad sword, and pistol and dagger, an' all the rest, an' then away wid him on boord a man-a-war to furrin parts, to fight for King George agin Bonyparty, that was great in them times.

Well, it was very soon in everyone's mouth how Billy Malowney was batin' all before him, astonishin' the ginerals, an frightenin' the inimy to that degree, there was not a Frinchman dare say parley voo outside of the rounds iv his camp.

You may be sure Molly was proud iv that same, though she never spoke a word about it; until at last the news kem home that Billy Malowney was surrounded an' murdered by the Frinch army, under Napoleon Bonyparty himself. The news was brought by Jack Brynn Dhas, the peddlar, that said he met the corporal iv the regiment on the quay iv Limerick, an' how he brought him into a public-house and thrated him to a naggin, and got all the news about poor Billy Malowney out iv him while they war dhrinkin' it; an' a sorrowful story it was.

The way it happened, accordin' as the corporal tould him, was jist how the Jook iv Wellington detarmined to fight a rale tarin' battle wid the Frinch, and Bonyparty at the same time was aiqually detarmined to fight the divil's own scrimmidge wid the British foorces.

Well, as soon as the business was pretty near ready at both sides, Bonyparty and the general next undher himself gets up behind a bush, to look at their inimies through spy-glasses, and thry would they know any iv them at the distance.

'Bedadad!' says the gineral, afther a divil iv a long spy, 'I'd bet half a pint,' says he, 'that's Bill Malowney himself,' says he, 'down there,' says he.

'Och!' says Bonypart, 'do you tell me so?' says he—'I'm fairly heart-scalded with that same Billy Malowney,' says he; 'an' I think if I was wanst shut iv him I'd bate the rest iv them aisy,' says he.

'I'm thinking so myself,' says the gineral, says he; 'but he's a tough bye,' says he.

'Tough!' says Bonypart, 'he's the divil,' says he.

'Begorra, I'd be better plased.' says the gineral, says he, 'to take himself than the Duke iv Willinton,' says he, 'an' Sir Edward Blakeney into the bargain,' says he.

'The Duke of Wellinton and Gineral Blakeney,' says Bonypart, 'is great for planning, no doubt,' says he; 'but Billy Malowney's the boy for *action*,' says he—'an' action's everything, just now,' says he.

So wid that Bonypart pushes up his cocked hat, and begins scratching his head, and thinning and considherin' for the bare life, and at last says he to the gineral:

'Gineral Commandher iv all the Foorces,' says he, 'I've hot it,' says he: 'ordher out the forlorn hope,' says he, 'an' give them as much powdher, both glazed and blasting,' says he, 'an' as much bullets do ye mind, an' swan-dhrops an' chain-shot,' says he, 'an' all soorts iv waipons an' combustables as they can carry; an' let them surround Bill Malowney,' says he, 'an' if they can get any soort iv an advantage,' says he, 'let them knock him to smithereens,' says he, 'an' then take him presner,' says he; 'an' tell all the bandmen iv the Frinch army,' says he, 'to play up "Garryowen," to keep up their sperits,' says he, 'all the time they're advancin'. An' you may promise them anything you like in my name,' says he; for, by my sowl, I don't think its many iv them 'ill come back to throuble us,' says he, winkin' at him.

So away with the gineral, an' he ordhers out the forlorn hope, all' tells the band to play, an' everything else, just as Bonypart desired him. An' sure enough, whin Billy Malowney heerd the music where he was standin' taking a blast of the dhudheen to compose his mind for murdherin' the Frinchmen as usual, being mighty partial to that tune intirely, he cocks his ear a one side, an' down he stoops to listen to the music; but, begorra, who should be in his rare all the time but a Frinch grannideer behind a bush, and seeing him stooped in a convanient forum, bedad he let flies at him sthraight, and fired him right forward between the legs an' the small iv the back, glory be to God! with what they call (saving your presence) a bum-shell.

Well, Bill Malowney let one roar out iv him, an' away he rowled over the field iv battle like a slitther (as Bonypart and the Duke iv Wellington, that was watching the manoeuvres from a distance, both consayved) into glory.

An' sure enough the Frinch was overjoyed beyant all bounds, an' small blame to them—an' the Duke of Wellington, I'm toult, was never all out the same man sinst.

At any rate, the news kem home how Billy Malowney was murdhered by the Frinch in furrin parts.

Well, all this time, you may be sure, there was no want iv boys comin' to coort purty Molly Donovan; but one way ar another, she always kept puttin' them off constant. An' though her father and mother was nathurally anxious to get rid of her respickably, they did not like to marry her off in spite iv her teeth.

An' this way, promising one while and puttin' it off another, she conthrived to get on from one Shrove to another, until near seven years was over and gone from the time when Billy Malowney listed for furrin sarvice.

It was nigh hand a year from the time whin the news iv Leum-a-rinka bein' killed by the Frinch came home, an' in place iv forgettin' him, as the saisins wint over, it's what Molly was growin' paler and more lonesome every day, antil the neighbours thought she was fallin' into a decline; and this is the way it was with her whin the fair of Lisnamoe kem round.

It was a beautiful evenin', just at the time iv the reapin' iv the oats, and the sun was shinin' through the red clouds far away over the hills iv Cahirmore.

Her father an' mother, an' the boys an' girls, was all away down in the fair, and Molly Sittin' all alone on the step of the stile, listening to the foolish little birds whistlin' among the leaves—and the sound of the mountain-river flowin' through the stones an' bushes—an' the crows flyin' home high overhead to the woods iv Glinvarlogh—an' down in the glen, far away, she could see the fair-green iv Lisnamoe in the mist, an' sunshine among the grey rocks and threes—an' the cows an' the horses, an' the blue frieze, an' the red cloaks, an' the tents, an' the smoke, an' the ould round tower—all as soft an' as sorrowful as a dhrame iv ould times.

An' while she was looking this way, an' thinking iv Leum-a-rinka— poor Bill iv the dance, that was sleepin' in his lonesome glory in the fields iv Spain—she began to sing the song he used to like so well in the ould times—

'*Shule, shule, shale a-roon;*'

an' when she ended the verse, what do you think but she heard a manly voice just at the other side iv the hedge, singing the last words over again!

Well she knew it; her heart flutthered up like a little bird that id be wounded, and then dhropped still in her breast. It was himself. In a minute he was through the hedge and standing before her.

'Leum!' says she.

'Mavourneen cuishla machree!' says he; and without another word they were locked in one another's arms.

Well, it id only be nansinse for me thryin' an' tell ye all the foolish things they said, and how they looked in one another's faces, an' laughed, an' cried, an' laughed again; and how, when they came to themselves, and she was able at last to believe it was raly Billy himself that was there, actially holdin' her hand, and lookin' in her eyes the same way as ever, barrin' he was browner and boulder, an' did not, maybe, look quite as merry in himself as he used to do in former times—an' fondher for all, an' more lovin' than ever—how he tould her all about the wars wid the Frinchmen—an' how he was wounded, and left for dead in the field iv battle, bein' shot through the breast, and how he was discharged, an' got a pinsion iv a full shillin' a day—and how he was come back to liv the rest iv his days in the sweet glen iv Lisnamoe, an' (if only *she'd* consint) to marry herself in spite iv them all.

Well, ye may aisily think they had plinty to talk about, afther seven years without once seein' one another; and so signs on, the time flew by as swift an' as pleasant as a bird on the wing, an' the sun wint down, an' the moon shone sweet an' soft instead, an' they two never knew a ha'porth about it, but kept talkin' an' whisperin', an' whisperin' an' talkin'; for it's wondherful how often a tinder-hearted girl will bear to hear a purty boy tellin' her the same story constant over an' over; ontil at last, sure enough, they heerd the ould man himself comin' up the boreen, singin' the 'Colleen Rue'—a thing he never done barrin' whin he had a dhrop in; an' the misthress walkin' in front iv him, an' two illigant Kerry cows he just bought in the fair, an' the sarvint boys dhriving them behind.

'Oh, blessed hour!' says Molly, 'here's my father.'

'I'll spake to him this minute,' says Bill.

'Oh, not for the world,' says she; 'he's singin' the "Colleen Rue," ' says she, 'and no one dar raison with him,' says she.

'An' where 'll I go, thin?' says he, 'for they're into the haggard an top iv us,' says he, 'an' they'll see me iv I lep through the hedge,' says he.

'Thry the pig-sty,' says she, 'mavourneen,' says she, 'in the name iv God,' says she.

'Well, darlint,' says he, 'for your sake,' says he, 'I'll condescend to them animals,' says he.

An' wid that he makes a dart to get in; bud, begorra, it was too late— the pigs was all gone home, and the pig-sty was as full as the Burr coach wid six inside.

'Och! blur-an'-agers,' says he, 'there is not room for a suckin'-pig,' says he, 'let alone a Christian,' says he.

'Well, run into the house, Billy,' says she, 'this minute,' says she, 'an' hide yourself antil they're quiet,' says she, 'an' thin you can steal out,' says she, 'anknownst to them all,' says she.

247

'I'll do your biddin', says he, 'Molly asthore,' says he.

'Run in thin,' says she, 'an' I'll go an' meet them,' says she.

So wid that away wid her, and in wint Billy, an' where 'id he hide himself bud in a little closet that was off iv the room where the ould man and woman slep'. So he closed the doore, and sot down in an ould chair he found there convanient.

Well, he was not well in it when all the rest iv them comes into the kitchen, an' ould Tim Donovan singin' the 'Colleen Rue' for the bare life, an' the rest iv them sthrivin' to humour him, and doin' exactly everything he bid them, because they seen he was foolish be the manes iv the liquor.

Well, to be sure all this kep' them long enough, you may be sure, from goin' to bed, so that Billy could get no manner iv an advantage to get out iv the house, and so he sted sittin' in the dark closet in state, cursin' the 'Colleen Rue,' and wondherin' to the divil whin they'd get the ould man into his bed. An', as if that was not delay enough, who should come in to stop for the night but Father O'Flaherty, of Cahirmore, that was buyin' a horse at the fair! An' av course, there was a bed to be med down for his raverence, an' some other attintions; an' a long discoorse himself an' ould Mrs. Donovan had about the slaughter iv Billy Malowney, an' how he was buried on the field iv battle; an' his raverence hoped he got a dacent funeral, an' all the other convaniences iv religion. An' so you may suppose it was pretty late in the night before all iv them got to their beds.

Well, Tim Donovan could not settle to sleep at all at all, an' so he kep' discoorsin' the wife about the new cows he bought, an' the strippers he sould, an' so an for better than an hour, ontil from one thing to another he kem to talk about the pigs, an' the poulthry; and at last, having nothing betther to discoorse about, he begun at his daughter Molly, an' all the heartscald she was to him be raison iv refusin' the men. An' at last says he:

'I onderstand,' says he, 'very well how it is,' says he. 'It's how she was in love,' says he, 'wid that bliggard, Billy Malowney,' says he, 'bad luck to him!' says he; for by this time he was coming to his raison.

'Ah!' says the wife, says she, 'Tim darlint, don't be cursin' them that's dead an' buried,' says she.

'An' why would not I,' says he, 'if they desarve it?' says he.

'Whisht,' says she, 'an' listen to that,' says she. 'In the name of the Blessed Vargin,' says she, 'what *is* it?' says she.

An' sure enough what was it but Bill Malowney that was dhroppin' asleep in the closet, an' snorin' like a church organ.

'Is it a pig,' says he, 'or is it a Christian?'

'Arra! listen to the tune iv it,' says she; 'sure a pig never done the like is that,' says she.

'Whatever it is,' says he, 'it's in the room wid us,' says he. 'The Lord be marciful to us!' says he.

'I tould you not to be cursin',' says she; 'bad luck to you,' says she, 'for an ommadhaun!' for she was a very religious woman in herself.

'Sure, he's buried in Spain,' says he; 'an' it is not for one little innocent expression,' says he, 'he'd be comin' all that a way to annoy the house,' says he.

Well, while they war talkin', Bill turns in the way he was sleepin' into an aisier imposture; and as soon as he stopped snorin' ould Tim Donovan's courage riz agin, and says he:

'I'll go to the kitchen,' says he, 'an' light a rish,' says he.

An' with that away wid him, an' the wife kep' workin' the beads all the time, an' before he kem back Bill was snorin' as loud as ever.

'Oh! bloody wars—I mane the blessed saints about us!—that deadly sound,' says he; 'it's going on as lively as ever,' says he.

'I'm as wake as a rag,' says his wife, says she, 'wid the fair anasiness,' says she. 'It's out iv the little closet it's comin',' says she.

'Say your prayers,' says he, 'an' hould your tongue,' says he, 'while I discoorse it,' says he. 'An' who are ye,' says he, 'in the name iv of all the holy saints?' says he, givin' the door a dab iv a crusheen that wakened Bill inside. 'I ax,' says he, 'who are you?' says he.

Well, Bill did not rightly remember where in the world he was, but he pushed open the door, an' says he:

'Billy Malowney's my name,' says he, 'an' I'll thank ye to tell me a better,' says he.

Well, whin Tim Donovan heard that, an' actially seen that it was Bill himself that was in it, he had not strength enough to let a bawl out iv him, but he dhropt the candle out iv his hand, an' down wid himself on his back in the dark.

Well, the wife let a screech you'd hear at the mill iv Killraghlin, an'—

'Oh,' says she, 'the spirit has him, body an' bones!' says she. 'Oh, holy St. Bridget—oh, Mother iv Marcy—oh, Father O'Flaherty!' says she, screechin' murdher from out iv her bed.

Well, Bill Malowney was not a minute remimberin' himself, an' so out wid him quite an' aisy, an' through the kitchen; bud in place iv the door iv the house, it's what he kem to the door iv Father O'Flaherty's little room, where he was jist wakenin' wid the noise iv the screechin' an' battherin'; an' bedad, Bill makes no more about it, but he jumps, wid one boult, clever an' clane into his raverance's bed.

'What do ye mane, you uncivilised bliggard?' says his raverance. 'Is that a venerable way,' says he, 'to approach your clargy?' says he.

'Hould your tongue,' says Bill, 'an' I'll do ye no harum,' says he.

'Who are you, ye scoundhrel iv the world?' says his raverance.

'Whisht!' says he? 'I'm Billy Malowney,' says he.

'You lie!' says his raverance for he was frightened beyont all bearin'—an' he makes but one jump out iv the bed at the wrong side, where there was only jist a little place in the wall for a press, an' his raverance could not as much as turn in it for the wealth iv kingdoms. 'You lie,' says he; 'but for feared it's the truth you're tellin',' says he, 'here's at ye in the name iv all the blessed saints together!' says he.

An' wid that, my dear, he blazes away at him wid a Latin prayer iv the strongest description, an', as he said himself afterwards, that was iv a nature that id dhrive the divil himself up the chimley like a puff iv tobacky smoke, wid his tail betune his legs.

'Arra, what are ye sthrivin' to say,' says Bill; says he, 'if ye don't hould your tongue,' says he, 'wid your parly voo;' says he, 'it's what I'll put my thumb on your windpipe,' says he, 'an' Billy Malowney never wint back iv his word yet,' says he.

'Thundher-an-owns,' says his raverance, says he—seein' the Latin took no infect on him, at all at all an' screechin' that you'd think he'd rise the thatch up iv the house wid the fair fright—'and thundher and blazes, boys, will none iv yes come here wid a candle, but lave your clargy to be choked by a spirit in the dark?' says he.

Well, be this time the sarvint boys and the rest iv them wor up an' half dressed, an' in they all run, one on top iv another, wid pitchforks and spades, thinkin' it was only what his raverence slep' a dhrame iv the like, by means of the punch he was afther takin' just before he rowl'd himself into the bed. But, begorra, whin they seen it was raly Bill Malowney himself that was in it, it was only who'd be foremost out agin, tumblin' backways, one over another, and his raverence roarin' an' cursin' them like mad for not waitin' for him.

Well, my dear, it was betther than half an hour before Billy Malowney could explain to them all how it raly was himself, for begorra they were all iv them persuadin' him that he was a spirit to that degree it's a wondher he did not give in to it, if it was only to put a stop to the argiment.

Well, his raverence tould the ould people then, there was no use in sthrivin' agin the will iv Providence an' the vagaries iv love united; an' whin they kem to undherstand to a sartinty how Billy had a shillin' a day for the rest iv his days, begorra they took rather a likin' to him, and considhered at wanst how he must have riz out of all his nansinse entirely, or his gracious Majesty id never have condescinded to show him his countenance that way every day of his life, on a silver shillin'.

An' so, begorra, they never stopt till it was all settled—an' there was not sich a weddin' as that in the counthry sinst. It's more than forty years ago, an' though I was no more nor a gossoon myself, I remimber it like yestherday. Molly never looked so purty before, an' Billy Malowney was plisant beyont all hearin,' to that degree that half the girls in it was fairly tarin' mad—only they would not let on—they had not him to themselves in place iv her. An' begorra I'd be afeared to tell ye, because you would not believe me, since that blessid man Father Mathew put an end to all soorts of sociality, the Lord reward him, how many gallons iv pottieen whisky was dhrank upon that most solemn and tindher occasion.

Pat Hanlon, the piper, had a faver out iv it; an' Neddy Shawn Heigue, mountin' his horse the wrong way, broke his collar-bone, by the manes iv fallin' over his tail while he was feelin' for his head; an' Payther Brian, the horse-docther, I am tould, was never quite right in the head ever afther; an' ould Tim Donovan was singin' the 'Colleen Rue' night and day for a full week; an' begorra the weddin' was only the foundation iv fun, and the beginning iv divarsion, for there was not a year for ten years afther, an' more, but brought round a christenin' as regular as the sasins revarted.

www.ingramcontent.com/pod-product-compliance
Lightning Source LLC
Chambersburg PA
CBHW060735180626
46819CB00001B/30